LUNCHING AT LAURA'S

And then she came to the last of the Extras and stopped at the door, suddenly filled again with nostalgia. The whole family coming to lunch, every one of them except the small children who had to be at school; it would be like Christmas used to be in the old days when Ma and Poppa had been alive; when they had eaten roast carp and drunk too much Tokay and laughed so much that she had made herself sick and had first been disgraced and then petted till she felt better—and her eyes prickled and angrily she rubbed her nose with the back of her hand and pushed open the door. This was really getting ridiculous. Quite ridiculous. Why get into such a state because the family was coming? They had a right to be here, didn't they? Of course they did . . .

Also in Arrow by Claire Rayner

The Burning Summer
The Running Years
Family Chorus
The Virus Man

LUNCHING AT LAURA'S

Claire Rayner

ARROW BOOKS

For Adam
who cares about good cooking
With love

Arrow Books Limited
62-65 Chandos Place, London WC2N 4NW

An imprint of Century Hutchinson Limited

London Melbourne Sydney Auckland
Johannesburg and agencies throughout
the world

First published in Great Britain by Hutchinson 1986
Arrow edition 1987

Printed and bound in Great Britain by
Anchor Brendon Limited, Tiptree, Essex

ISBN 0 09 952580 1

1

'Lunching? At Laura's,' said the heavy voice at the other end of the phone. It was almost possible to smell the cigar smoke that had thickened it. 'Where else should I be? I'll see you there, if you like. I got a man coming in from LA, but I can see you there, five minutes, ten minutes, around half past one. Maybe we can come to an arrangement, who knows?' And the phone clicked in the young man's ear, and he put it back on the desk with a thump and sat and scowled at it.

Bloody Braham, bloody, bloody Braham; he knew perfectly well that someone in shoes as new as his wasn't up to getting a table at Laura's; he'd only been in the business a year or so, only made one decent commercial that got a mention in 'Campaign'. Who was he to have the clout to get a table at Laura's for lunch? But not to be there today would be professional suicide; to make a series of commercials for 'Setalight' would be the biggest thing that had happened to him since leaving the Film School. Get that under his belt, and he could start hawking his script around, maybe get some development money – and with visions of feature films dancing in his head the young man pulled the phone towards him again and checked the number of Laura's; maybe he'd be lucky?

Just let me get through, please, he prayed, as he keyed the phone and the sounds clicked softly in his ear; just let me get through. But the line was engaged, of course, and went on being engaged. And on and on –

Because everyone in London, it seemed, was trying to get a table at Laura's this morning. Secretaries in editors' offices and film and television studios and publishing houses failed again and again to get anything but the engaged tone, and for everyone who eventually managed to get through, a dozen failed. And even those who to their amazement did get a ringing tone and then the familiar light husky voice that said only 'Hmm?', which everyone knew was Laura herself, for no one else at the restaurant was allowed to take bookings, had to swallow their disappointment as best they might for Laura's was fully booked and had been since eleven that morning. Even Braham of 'Setalight' was turned away, a fact which would have much warmed the eager young man's heart, if only he'd known. But he didn't, and like everyone else who wanted a table at Laura's and couldn't have one, he finally slammed down the phone and rang Langan's instead. Getting a table there was much easier –

'Here,' Maritza said firmly. 'Here you'll never make a living.' And she hitched Kati more comfortably on to her right hip and with her other hand rubbed her aching back beneath the thick cloth of her heavy over-coat, and her stays creaked with the movement. Her belly pushed against the whalebone, and she breathed as deeply as she could and then set her hand on her front. She was so round and full with this pregnancy that it seemed to tip her backwards; maybe this was a good sign? Maybe this baby would live, please God, and be a little brother at last for Kati?

'Listen,' Viktor said, trying to sound authoritative and knowing he sounded pleading as he always did; how a man his size could be put in his place so often and so thoroughly by so ridiculous a little thing as his Maritza never ceased to amaze him. 'Listen, dolly, old Ari, he made a living here, didn't he? Three years I been working for him, ever since we got off the boat from the old country, and hasn't he paid me my wages regular enough? So why – '

'Paid your wages!' Maritza exploded. 'That mumser, that Greek gunif, paid your wages? You've worked yourself to a shadow for him and all for peanuts, peanuts, you hear me? And now because he says jump you want to jump and give him what little I managed we should save out of the peanuts and what we brought with us? You got peanuts for a brain, Viktor Halascz, that's what you've got. Peanuts for a brain!'

'But dolly, the opportunity – '

'It's an opportunity like you're the Prince of Wales, you schlemiel! Opportunity – look at the place! It sits here like a bug under a bed so no one should ever see it – '

'But like a bug under a bed, it makes itself felt. It makes itself felt!' And Viktor began to laugh, fatly, pleased with himself and his joke. But not for long.

'Oh, sure, sure it does!' Kati began to wriggle in Maritza's arms and she set her down on the cobbles and let her run off and then turned and stood in front of her husband with her head tilted so that she could look up at his face, fully a foot above her. Her curly hair was escaping from her bun as usual under the ostrich-feathered hat and was springing around her head like a ridiculous crown and her chubby face was flushed with rage as she chattered at him. 'Sure it does! Six or seven schlemiels, fools and gamblers like the pair of you, they come and they eat and they never pay, they only play cards, win their dinners, lose their dinners, and this you call making itself felt? This you want to spend our money on, to buy such a place as no one except a meshuggeneh would ever think of buying – '

'Who said buy?' Viktor said mildly. 'Did I say buy? Did I ever use such a word? Did anyone hear me say buy?' And he stared piously at the heavy grey January sky that peered down between the buildings into Little Vinegar Yard as though he confidently expected an answer.

She blinked at him and then rubbed her face with one small hand, brushing away the drizzle that was beginning to seep everywhere. 'You said – ' she began uncertainly.

'I said, we should use our money to run the place. This is what I said. We got some money, you're always telling me we got so much – twenty-three pounds you've saved, a lot of money, and I said we should use it, make it grow for us. Use it here – make it a better restaurant. Greek food – such garbage you couldn't sell to anyone but ignorant spielers like Ari and his crew – but good Hungarian food, the way I cook it? Now, there's a different piece of fish!'

She said nothing, staring at him with her eyes glittering a little and he laughed again, and began to relax. 'You see what I mean, dolly? Good Hungarian food, a bissel goulash, a few galuska, jellied carp come the holidays – we could make money here.'

'So what happens to Ari? The Greek mumser, what happens to him? He sits there and smiles and nods at you, you should cook Hungarian instead of his rubbish? What happens to Ari?'

Viktor shrugged and seemed to expand with self satisfaction as he relaxed. He had her where he wanted her now; at last, it was time for a husband to assert himself. 'Ari? I should worry about Ari! Let Aristotle worry about Ari! A bit of philosophy – it's what he'll need. He's going back to Athens, that's what he's doing – '

'Back to – ' She whirled then and stared at the little shop behind them, at its grimy windows and the battered board over them on which was painted in uncertain lettering *Aristotle Popodopolous. Good Food. Good Drink*. 'He's just walked out and left this place? Just like that?'

'You could say that.' This was getting better and better, Viktor decided, grinning so widely that his beard seemed about to fall off his face. 'You could say that. Anyway, it's mine now.'

'This place is – ' She turned back to him, her eyes sharp as she narrowed her lids a little. 'It's not so easy. I may not be a great genius, but this I know, you got to have papers, proper papers – '

He reached into his pocket and held out to her the big envelope full of paper. 'Here it is,' he said simply. 'The papers. I tell you, it's ours, dolly. See? Look at this one – ' He pulled out one of the documents. 'See? Dated and signed, all proper. Aristotle Popodopolous, January 1st 1893, to Viktor Halascz. All signed proper. We just got to spend a little, fixing the place up. Buy the food to cook, get the rooms upstairs fit for us – you and me and Kati and, please God, the new one – and we've got our own business and a new flat into the bargain. Better than that hole in Flower Street – at last, Viktor Halascz is a mensch, a real person, a man of affairs, no more a stinking waiter in a Greek bit of rubbish, but his own man – '

There were tears slithering down her round cheeks now

as she stared at him and she opened her mouth and shook her head and tried to smile and could only hiccup and he leaned over and hugged her close, and Kati, across the yard, catching the emotion in the air, came running across on her chubby six year old legs, her gaiters half-unbuttoned as usual, and tried to push herself between them.

'He just gave it to you? That lovely man, that Ari, he gave you such a present as his lovely restaurant, this beautiful place?'

He was still hugging her close and he spoke softly into her hair which was just beneath his chin as her head fitted so neatly into the circle of his throat as it always did, but she heard him.

'No presents, dolly. It's mine by right, believe me. I won it all above board.'

There was a sharp little silence that almost creaked with tension and then she pulled back and stared up at him, and even in the fading light he could see the way her eyes glittered. 'You did what?'

'A bissel poker, dolly. A bissel cards. I got me a straight flush and he got only – '

'You gambled – ' she said softly. 'You gambled? Tell me, what was the bets you was making? What was you using you should play this game for such winnings?'

'Me?' he said uneasily. 'What does it matter, dolly? I won, didn't I?'

'I want I should know all about our new business, the business that makes such a man of you, from the beginning. I want I should know everything. What was it you played with?'

'I told him we had twenty-three pounds and – '

But he couldn't say another word. She was hitting him, beating his chest with her small fists and with all the strength there was in her body and shrieking so loudly it made his head ring. He never would understand women, he told himself, as he tried to dodge her blows without hurting her – not easy with that great belly on her – never, if he lived to be the oldest man in Soho. Hadn't he got them their very own restaurant? What was she so mad about? He'd never understand her, not ever.

Quite when Laura's had first achieved its special place in the pantheon of London restaurants none of its regulars could quite remember. It was rather like Eros or Selfridges or the Tower of London; something that had always been there, and run in the same sort of way, and certainly always would be. It was the only London restaurant of any standing which refused to take lunch bookings from anyone until the morning of the day the table was wanted; the only London restaurant which was so hidden away in the tangle of Soho streets that you couldn't possibly find it without first being taken there by one of the cognoscenti; the only London restaurant which had Laura herself. Laura with her round face with its pointed chin and the curly hair which stood up all over her head like a child's, and her neat compact little body. Laura who said little but saw much, and who knew everyone of her regular customers not only by name but by the sort of private details that would have startled and worried them had they realised the depth of her knowledge. Laura, who was the most discreet and most sensible and most successful restaurateur there had ever been.

She had always been there and always would be, people would tell each other, except for the few very old customers who had been eating there for so many years that they had known her father, old Tibor, when he had been active in the place, and a few of whom had known her grandfather Zolly Horvath too, but no one listened to them; they were too old to be interesting to the sort of people for whom Laura's had become the most important place to be seen. Old people had no place in the glittering ranks of the film business or the television world or Fleet Street or publishing; these were young men's businesses, even sometimes young women's, people for whom to be in the right place, in the right clothes, at the right time, was what mattered most of all. And Laura's was indisputably the rightest place of all.

Getting to be one of her lunchers took a special technique.

First you started by booking for dinner; it was quite different in the evenings at Laura's, because she accepted bookings then. You might have to wait three or even four weeks for a table to be available, but at least you could get in. And very agreeable it was to do so, for dining at Laura's was quite different from lunching there. The midday wheelers and dealers vanished to be replaced by people of quieter elegance, though just as much style. There were Shakespearian actors, and authors who were so distinguished their titles never appeared in the best selling lists, and certainly were well above being picked for the Booker, and well known conductors between concerts, and politicians of such eminence that they hardly ever had to visit their constituencies. There were Americans of so much sophistication that they had heard of Laura's even in their remote fastnesses and booked tables by phone from California and New York, and academics from Oxbridge for whom dinner at Laura's was as essential a part of a London visit as an afternoon spent at the London Library.

And once you got your table, then you were in for delight as well as fashion. Even the most knowledgeable of feeders had to admit that the food at Laura's was something special. Classic Hungarian, but so refined and so well cooked and presented that it had lost the peasant roughness that so often characterises such food, and had become something that was so subtle and yet so startling and interesting that it made classic French cookery seem positively dull, and Nouvelle Cuisine even more pretentious than it looked. The cold wild cherry soup was of so superb a quality that there were diners who swore they would kill for it, while the jellied pikes served with Laura's famous pink horseradish sauce and cucumber salad was so valued by one American regular that he had portions of it flown over to Washington via Concorde when he gave dinner parties for White House people. The chef's way with duck livers was one of the most copied by hopeful foodies – none of whom ever managed to replicate its remarkable delicate spiciness; while there were those who said that the galuska – tiny thimble shaped egg dumplings – would float to the ceiling if they weren't so attached to the divine sauces which accompanied the meat and fish dishes.

No one could serve pörkölt – goulash – like Laura's. No one could roast carp like Laura's. No one understood paprika dishes like Laura's. The wine list was intelligent, the Tokays superb, the coffee perfect and the puddings so splendid that their sinfulness could be ignored. Nothing that tasted like them could be regarded as mere conveyors of calories from mouth to belly and hips; these were works of art, the diners would tell each other blissfully and send for second helpings. Altogether, Laura's was a gourmet's delight and a glutton's heaven.

It was that which attached its regulars to it. Once you had discovered Laura's and eaten there, there was no way you would not return, unless you were one of those very rare people who take no interest in their food at all. For the average person with any pretensions to late twentieth century culture, Laura's was a find; indeed, *the* find. And, they would tell each other joyfully, so reasonable! It was possible for two of you to dine and drink well at one of the blue and white clothed tables, your heels hooked comfortably over the stretchers of your high-backed rush-seated chair, surrounded by the vaguely mittel-European ambience of white panelled walls decorated with pieces of hand woven cloth in sludgy colours fashioned into wallets and pouches and simple hangings, smelling the faint fresh earthiness of the plant plots which trailed lines of green creepers over the floor to ceiling windows and their glittering square panes, and sit there for two or three hours, talking and murmuring and drinking Tokay and coffee, yet spending no more than fifteen pounds a head; considering that generally in London restaurants you'd be lucky if you got any change out of sixty quid these days, that was value, real hard value.

Once you started dining at Laura's, she got to know your face. She would sit there at her rather shabby old corner desk with its big red-covered register and spikes for bills and the battered Victorian japanned tin box which was her till, the light shining on her bent head and lifting the curly dark hair to a reddish glow, and seemed not to watch at all; but she always knew who was there, and who with, and what they ordered and how they behaved.

If any newcomer was anything but polite to her waiters – who were old and deliberate in their movements, but in their own way as efficient as any snake-hipped out-of-work actor of the sort employed by so many London restaurants these days – then there would never again be a table available for him. But anyone who showed the right sort of appreciation of her establishment, ordering food judiciously and showing a decent respect for the advice of old Maxie, the wine waiter who knew more about Hungarian and French wines than anyone in the world (he despised all German wines on principle; his family's experience during the last two wars had given him a profound disgust for anything Teutonic) were welcomed readily when next they tried to book a table. What was more, they would be greeted by name when they arrived and welcomed by Laura's famous little smile, that lifted the corners of her lips so sharply that her mouth looked as triangular as a kitten's, in a way that would make them feel remarkably warm. And if by any chance they had recently achieved some success in their chosen fields, she would congratulate them, showing an awareness of what books were being published, what plays were being premiered, what TV programmes were being launched, that was encyclopaedic.

It was no wonder, diners would tell each other, that so many famous authors gave her copies of their books, and no wonder she displayed them so well, for they marched round the shelves that were set almost at ceiling level in serried rows, the titles and pictures of the authors all clearly lit by the discreet floodlights set into the ceiling. Each book was lovingly inscribed to Laura, some with long messages extolling her food sprawling all over the jacket, and diners waiting for dilatory guests would wander round and stare at them and marvel at how many people knew and seemed to love Laura.

And would be grateful, too, that the books were there to beguile them, for there was no bar at the restaurant; this was not a place where one sloshed spirits or drank fashionable over-coloured cocktails, and ruined one's palate with nuts and olives and potato crisps. This was a place for serious eating and gentle pleasure, in the evenings.

But not at lunchtimes. Oh, never at lunchtimes. There is still no bar and no spirit-sloshing – one can order scotch or gin before lunch but Maxie makes it clear he is not impressed if you do – and there is still the serious eating, but the ambience is quite different.

The soft dinnertime lighting gives way to a greenish glow that comes from the daylight that pours through the creepers decorating the huge window, lifting the red tiles on the floor to an even richer crimson and flattering quite outrageously the faces of the girls who sit at the window tables. (It flatters the men too, of course, a fact which many a young actor has found useful.) The sounds change, with the buzz of conversation becoming sharper and more urgent, and though the eighteen tables are cleverly scattered around the big, irregularly shaped room so that a degree of privacy can be enjoyed at each, it is still possible, if you use your ears intelligently, to pick up a good deal of what your neighbours are saying.

That of course, is one of the most valuable things about Laura's at lunchtime. It isn't only important that you be seen there; it is also important that you hear there. And sometimes, talk there; many are the useful deals that have been swung as the result of a judicious leak neatly dropped between the shredded marrow with baked veal and a bowl of fresh raspberries.

'You didn't hear what he said?' Zolly said, and wiped the table between Viktor's elbows with so much vigour that he almost knocked the pot of toothpicks flying. 'He said it twice, real loud. You didn't hear?'

'No I did not,' Viktor grunted and stared at the boy from beneath his heavy brows. It was all very well to be interested in your job, but there was a point at which it got to be suspicious. This one, working all the hours he was asked and still hanging around afterwards, and always arriving first thing in the morning before any of the others; very suspicious. And now, all this confidential chat.

Not that it wasn't useful. The last time Zolly had come to tell him tales of things he'd overheard, Viktor had been able to get hold of a box of butter and several pounds of sugar; real prizes in 1918, the fourth year of this lousy war. If only he liked the feller; he ought to, a nice Hungarian boy like him; hadn't his father been one of Viktor's cronies in the good old days before the war? But this Zolly, with his pale face and drooping apology for a moustache, he wasn't attractive like his wicked old father had been. None of the swashbuckling splendour of the old country about this child of London's gutters.

Viktor sighed as he stared at the boy's fragile body and pale somewhat tubercular face and told himself sternly not to be so narrow minded. 'So what did he say? There's a tin of best Budapest paprika, real *erös nemes* coming in on the next troop train, especially for me, hmm?'

Zolly shook his head, unsmiling. No sense of humour either, poor Zolly, thought Viktor.

'No. He said as how the building on the corner was being taken over by a new firm as soon as the war's over. And everyone knows that won't be too long now. They'll be employing a lot of people, he said, at least thirty workers on the upper floors. Thirty people, eating lunch every day, supper at night. Could be good for us – '

'Thirty? All of them eating with us every day? I should cocoa! You know what they say in the old country? *Ne igyas elöre a meduc borëve* – don't go counting no chickens.'

'Even if only half of them come, it could still be good business. If we had room for them.'

'Hey? Room for them?'

'Seven tables you got here, seven tables. It's nice. Brings in customers, room for forty two every day, but it ain't enough. You pull down that wall there, and the one between the big store room and the kitchen, and you got a bigger kitchen, because you use up the dead space, and you get in a few more tables – fours is better than sixes, you can move 'em around more easy, get more people in, and then – '

Viktor's face had gone a deep, brick red and he stared at the thin, white-faced boy with his eyes so wide the whites could be seen all round them. He knew he looked more than a little alarming, but Zolly seemed unperturbed and stood there turning his rag between his hands, his long apron flapping against his thin knees in the breeze from the open door, and stared coolly back at him.

'So listen, already, whose restaurant is this? Yours or mine? *Ez mindehen fútesz* – this beats everything! Whose place *is* this, I want to know?'

'Oh, your family's, Mr. Halascz, no question of that,' Zolly said calmly. 'But I like to take an interest. Seeing as I'm going to be family – '

'You're going to be *what*?' Viktor shouted. 'You're going to be no such bloody thing, you jumped up little piece of – '

'Anya Maritza says,' Zolly said and still stood there quietly turning his rag between his hands, the only sign he showed of nervousness, 'yesterday she said, Magda and me. It's all settled. As soon as the war's over, she said. So tell me, Mr. Halascz, what do you say to my idea, hmm? We pull down the wall there, and in the kitchen, make it bigger, get in more tables, offer a discount to the new firm on the corner – we could make some money here, a lot of money – '

'I'll be dead and in my grave first!' Viktor roared. 'And so will you be before you marry my little Magda, you piece of horse shit! Go and play with yourself – go on, out of my sight!'

Which was how by the time Viktor stood beside his Magda the year after the war ended, in the summer of 1919, and gave her away to her skinny husband, Zoltan Horvath, Halascz's restaurant had grown from forty-two covers to sixty, and all of them always occupied by the office workers from the tobacco importers firm on the corner. Viktor never stopped complaining about the way Zolly meddled till the day he died, but there wasn't much he could do about it. Not with the way Zolly always managed to overhear such useful things and the way Maritza listened to him.

'Women,' Viktor would say to anyone who would listen to him, 'women! They make a madness out of a business, the things they do, a madness. Never let 'em anywhere near business, they'll ruin it.' And he'd deal another hand of cards and shake his head at his cronies while Zolly got on in the kitchen. What else could a poor put-upon business man do?

2

'Bloody woman!' the man in the calico apron muttered and picked up the tray of wrinkled yellow peppers and shoved it furiously onto the trolley, ready to push it out to his van, doubled parked in Old Compton Street. 'You can't do business with bloody women – '

'Not if you try to give 'em rubbish when they've ordered and paid for quality,' Angie said tartly. 'You do that to anyone with any sense and you'll get a flea in your ear whether they wear skirts or pants. Next time you try your tricks on some of the blokes down Frith Street – them you can cheat as much as you like – they'll never notice, fools like them. But when you've been in this business a bit longer you'll know you don't try any of your nonsense here with Miss Horvath. She's forgotten more than you'll ever know about what's what. Sooner you learn that the better for you. Or she won't buy no more from your firm, and if she stops, then your boss'll want to know why, and believe you me, you'll be right in it.'

'Oh, go and piss in your beer and get off my ear'ole,' the man said and shoved his trolley out of Little Vinegar Yard into Old Compton Street and got to his van just as the traffic warden shoved the ticket under his windscreen wiper. He wasn't having a good day at all.

'Next time he tries that, I'll have his bleedin' guts for garters,' Angie said with great satisfaction and slammed the door shut and went padding back towards the kitchens, collecting the big punnets of mushrooms from the serving table as he went. 'Sorry I hadn't noticed, Mizz Horvy – '

Finding a suitable mode of address for his employer had given Angie a good deal of anxiety in the early days, when she'd first taken over from her father. He had worked at the place for over forty years, ever since he'd been taken on as a scruffy fifteen year old kitchen boy. He had known the Old Man, her grandfather Zolly, had grieved with the family when he had died the year after his son, young Zoltan, was killed in North Africa, had worked with the only surviving son, Tibor, to keep the restaurant going through the bad years of the war and the even worse years of austerity that followed with peace, had been there when Tibor married Louisa and when Laura was born, and had seen her grow up. But now all the old ones had gone and it was her restaurant, he couldn't call her what he had when she had been a baby; to address his boss as Lollipop would hardly have been proper. Even 'Laura' would, he felt, have been disgraceful. But Miss Horvath would have been too formal. He had worried a good deal before he had come up with the diminutive he now used, but it pleased him, and he regarded it as his own personal property. Heaven help any other employee who dared to let it pass his lips.

'Not your fault, Angie. And he won't try it again,' Laura said. 'He won't get the chance. I'll tell old Barnett to send a different delivery man in future. Will you be able to manage with the peppers you've got?'

'I'll send Freddy down Berwick Street,' Angie said. 'He's the only one with any sairchel – the rest are senseless. But he'll get me good stuff. And I need 'em for the lecso – I got enough for the restaurant but not for both the Extras as want it.'

'Well, if you can't get good peppers, then give the City TV lot more rizi-bizi instead – you've got enough mushrooms there for an extra pot – and do some more red cabbage for the Trust. We'd better keep the lecso for Anya's party – '

'I should think so!' Angie said, scandalised, and went padding on his way to shout and nag at the boys in the kitchen until they were all fit to throw knives at his head. Not that they would. All chefs were temperamental – it was as essential a part of them as their white toques – and the staff at Laura's took a deep pride in Angie's temper when they compared notes with other kitchen boys over a drink at the Crown and Two Chairmen or the Dog and Duck on the corners of Bateman Street. It was good to be able to tell them how much worse their lot was than anyone else's in Soho.

Laura watched him go and then turned back to her ledger, to finish entering the morning's market bills. No need to worry, even today with all three of the Extras in use, and one of them for so special a party. Angie would manage. He always did, and she suddenly heard her father's voice deep in her mind.

'Angelo Alzano? He's the best bloody Hungarian chef that ever came out of Italy. He wouldn't know a zabaglione if it bit him on the neck like Vlad the Vampire, but when it comes to paprika – phttt!'

And the memory of that odd little sound he used to make was so vivid, even though he had been dead now for over two years, it was almost as though he was still here with her, sitting in his corner the way he had for so many years while she had run the restaurant around him.

Poor old Poppa, she thought, he'd have loved to be here today, Anya's party and all – and then she shook herself mentally and applied her mind to her job. The ledger had to be kept up every day, otherwise she would lose track of things. She had done the morning's buying at Billingsgate, leaving Angie to Nine Elms and the fruit and vegetables, and Leno to Smithfield, so that she wouldn't be too tired; usually she managed two out of the three markets on her own (and unlike many of her competitors in Soho, she insisted still on doing as her father and grandfather had, buying always from the market, never from a trade supplier), but today was to be a special day, and she needed that little extra rest, so she hadn't got up till half past five. A rare pleasure that, on a working day.

But it was oddly difficult to concentrate this morning and after she had filled in another column in the neat round writing that looked so very like her, she lifted her chin and looked around her.

The tables were all ready, set early this morning by Dan and Janos, Miklos and Jon, with Maxie fussing round them like an old hen, and she looked at them with pleasure. Quite why she had chosen to dress her tables as she did she was never to know, but there it was; she had selected old fashioned bone handled cutlery, even though it meant it all had to be hand washed and couldn't be done in the great dishwasher that stood at the back of the kitchen, and the thick, white, fluted china even though that too looked old fashioned, just because she liked it, and she had been right. It looked so exactly as it should, with the heavy crystal – it had gone a little against the grain to buy Czechoslovakian rather than Hungarian, but the fact was they made better glass – and the blue and white patterned tablecloths. The high backed chairs with the pretty rush seats stood neatly four square at each table and she counted the covers with her eyes; every one of them booked since eleven o'clock this morning – and even as she thought it the phone rang again and she picked it up and said, 'Hmm?' and then, 'So sorry – we're full today. Call me tomorrow,' and cradled the phone and smiled; Poppa would have sat there so proudly today, to see his restaurant so busy and so successful.

Outside in Little Vinegar Yard there was a clatter of heels and she looked through the lattice of the creepers to see Mucky go by, and smiled again. He too was a part of the restaurant, even though he hardly ever came in – only on his birthday, and every Christmas Eve – but he had always been there in the Yard, and always would be, just like herself. She could see his shop clearly with its windows full of dumpy cigarette packages that had been there for over thirty years to her own certain knowledge, and the fascia board, with its indecipherable legend on its shabby blistered paint, and shook her head, amused.

That anyone as dapper and neat as Mucky always was should keep premises as dilapidated and dusty as his shop looked was an absurdity, but there it was; it amused him to leave the exterior looking as it did. Inside it was quite different, of course; she went in sometimes for the sheer pleasure of seeing the way the wood of the vast fitting that occupied the wall behind the high mahogany counter glowed with polish, and to enjoy the satiny gleam of the brass fittings on the myriad drawers that embellished it. Mucky stocked every kind of pipe tobacco and cigarette and cigar that had ever been invented, as well as a range of beautiful pipes that brought customers from miles around, and, though Laura didn't smoke, her father had, and the scent of Mucky's lovely little shop always reminded her of the way he used to take her with him whenever he went to buy his own special Dutch cigars, small and dark and singularly fragrant – and again she shook herself.

She really was being absurdly sentimental today, wallowing in memories. Stupid; there was too much to do to indulge herself like this, and she watched Mucky disappear into his shop and then bent her head again to her ledgers and set briskly to work. The Extras had to be checked and the kitchens visited yet, and it was already almost twelve. Wasting time like this was a luxury she could never afford, and certainly not today.

She closed the ledgers at last, and with one more look round, and a tweak at a dead leaf in the pot of primroses which stood on her desk, went briskly to the door that led to the kitchens. She'd start there and then go upstairs to the Extras, making sure Angie was happy, for unless he was, nothing would go right.

Angie was indeed happy. The meat his assistant Leno had brought him back from Smithfield was exactly what he would have bought himself – though he would have died rather than admit as much – and already the beef for the goulash of the day was simmering in its fragrant stock and the pork cutlets were marinading in wine and garlic on their big white platters. The most junior of the kitchen boys was pushing veal through the mincer while Leno kept an eye on him at the same time as trimming the small steak medallions for the *Sistergös Lecsos Ermek*, one of Angie's specialities; the whole place was richly fragrant with the redolence of roasting food and the scent of onions and garlic, peppers and cucumbers, while the heat from the great ovens shimmered around the busy white figures. Angie himself was slicing duck's liver into strips with dazzling speed while shouting instructions at everyone else at the top of his voice in an apparent fury. But no one was fooled. Angie was happy and it showed.

'I forgot to tell you – I got the first of the fresh marrows, Mizz Horvy!' Angie roared as he saw her. 'I'll do an extra pot for you. Just for you. First of the season always had to be yours, ever since you was little.'

Angie would never tire of making sure all his staff knew how long he had been part of the place. 'Doing it now, we are – Henry, you great lump of tripe, what the hell are you doing? Get on with those potatoes – Leno, look at that bloody fool – he'll mince his fingers as well as the veal if you don't watch him. I don't want my meat polluted, for God's sake – watch what he's doing – Dan, get out of here – I got enough with my own people, without you bleedin' waiters under my feet – '

The kitchen clattered and roared and hissed and Laura looked round at the great steaming chrome pans and the flaring gas jets on the ovens and hobs – Angie wouldn't be caught dead cooking on electricity, and only grudgingly had allowed one electric oven into his domain – and the sweating red faced occupants and smiled at those who had the temerity to risk Angie's wrath and look up and catch her eye, and left them to it. She knew better than ever to interfere where she had no right to be; the restaurant might bear her name, and be her total responsibility, but in the kitchens Angie was king and she was too much of the queen of her own part of her establishment to meddle with him. At a pinch, she could run the kitchen; once she had had to, when Angie had developed pneumonia as a result of insisting on going on working all through a flu epidemic, and had been taken, protesting hoarsely, to hospital. But that had been an emergency. If she had ever tried to do it under any other circumstances, Angie would have been deeply wounded; and rightly so. Even his beloved Mizz Horvy had no right to be in his kitchen without his consent.

She went back through the main restaurant to the doorway on the far side that led to the stairs, and then hesitated as she looked upwards. On each side of the narrow staircase just below the cornices of the warmly panelled walls were pictures of simpering black ringletted gypsy girls in improbable dresses with tight bodices, or distant views of plains fringed by mountains, but she wasn't looking at those. They had been put there by her great-grandfather so many years ago that no one ever looked at them any more. They had been part of her life for ever and she would no more have removed them than she would have taken off the roof. It was what lay above the staircase that made her pause, and for a moment she stood there on the bottom step, remembering.

There had been the flat above there, when she had been small. She and Ma and Poppa had lived there in those three big rooms for so long that it didn't seem possible that they wouldn't be there waiting when she went up. She knew that it was all different now; that the flat had been gutted and made into the three Extras for private parties. She knew that where their small bathroom, the pride of her grandmother's heart, had once been there was now a servery, knew that outside the door that had led to her bedroom and where there had been the set of shelves on which she had kept all her school texts and her precious collection of story books there was now a pine coat rack for guests to use; knew that all traces of the family had vanished. There was nothing left of the place that had been home for so long, yet for all that, as she stood there at the bottom looking up into the brightness at the top, she felt the weight of the years sitting on her. It was as though she were seven years old again, and coming home from school at St. Martin's, calling 'Ma!' and hoping there was shredded new season's marrow today, because it was her favourite in all the world – and again she shook her head and told herself firmly to stop being so stupidly sentimental. There was too much to do to allow such nonsense to waste her energies like this –

The brightness at the top dimmed as someone appeared and began to run down and then stopped as he caught sight of her.

'Oh, sorry, Miss Horvath!' It was one of the kitchen boys, and he stood there so pink with shyness that he looked rather like a freshly made fondant ice set in cream, with his whites wrapped round him so tidily. The towel at his neck was damp with anxiety and she smiled at him and stood back so that he could pass her.

'Mr. Angie, Miss, he sent me to fetch the big platter from the far Extra, he said he needed it for Anya Z- er – ZZ – er – your special party, Miss.'

'Then you'd better take it to him,' Laura said equably. 'And the name is Zsuzske – I know it looks odd when it's written down but it's easy to say. Say treasure.'

'Eh?'

'Say treasure – go on. I'll tell you how to say her name and then you can go back and impress Angie. Treasure.'

'Treasure,' he said obediently.

'Now say just the end of the word – leave off the "tre" bit – just say "jer". Keep the "j" soft.'

He obeyed, almost squirming with embarrassment, but she ignored that, feeling oddly that it was important he managed the pronunciation correctly.

'Right. Now say it twice – "Jer Jer". Like that. With a soft "j", remember – '

He tried it, reddening even more if that were possible and she laughed.

'Well done! Now say cat without the "t" at the end. After you've said "Jer Jer" twice – so it comes out right – Zsuzske. Actually it's the same as Susie, believe it or not. She's my great aunt Susie. She was ninety-one yesterday and this party is to celebrate that. The whole of my family will be here. Well, almost – so it's an important day, and an important party.'

'Yes, Miss Horvath.' He hesitated, emboldened by her friendliness. 'I thought her first name was Anya, like my gran'ma. She's called Annie. I thought Z – er ZZ – er Zsuzske was her last name, like.'

'Anya means Momma in Hungarian,' Laura said and then, suddenly in a hurry to get rid of him, jerked her chin and said crisply, 'On your way now. Tell Angie I'll bring the big blue and white bowl for the lecso. Cut along now – he'll be waiting for you – '

He cut and she ran lightly up the stairs and went from room to room, checking the tables, counting the number of covers set against the lists of names pinned to each door and making sure the flowers were all fresh and the wine ready in their coolers, if white, or sitting uncorked and gently breathing, if red. No more time for sentimental nostalgia now.

'The Trust,' she murmured as she checked the first of the Extras. Nine of them. Mrs. Capitelli and her son Giaccomo, Leo Levy and Edward Malplackett – hmm, that was interesting. Leo Levy was to be the new Chairman of the Trust, but Malplackett was to take over the secretaryship. Which meant he would in effect be running the Vinegar Trust. That could make a lot of difference; she'd have to keep an eye and ear on his activities. A nice enough chap on the surface but a shade too ambitious for other people's good and rather keener on their cash than their comfort; and Miss Foster and Mrs. Garcia and her Friend – no one had ever found out what her name was – and Mr. Bassett the wine merchant and Mr. Olaffson from the fish shop. They were all having the spiced sausage to start with, and then the pisztra – poached pink trout and cucumber salad and new potatoes – and Angie had made them a special dobosch. She had seen it waiting on the desserts table in the kitchen, a great wheel of a cake with its scored amber toffee surface and its nut encrusted sides. She had tapped the crisp top with one finger nail for the pleasure of hearing the faint plangent sound that came back at her; drum cake – it was well named.

Then the second biggest room; seventeen of them, from City TV in Frith Street. The Documentary Department, whatever that meant. It had always amused her that a TV company had come to that part of the street. She used to stand there sometimes on her way home from school and stare up at the blue plaque on the wall of Number 22. 'John Logie Baird – first demonstrated television here, 1926.' A pity they hadn't come to the same building; it would have been so elegant a thing to have done – well, what were they having?

Clearly someone who knew her menu well had chosen this lunch; a range of her best starters – the spiced mixed salad with sausages and the *Hazi Disznosaft*, the pressed boar's head which Angie, she knew, had made with loving care yesterday evening, and the veal pancakes with paprika sauce, and then – she grinned then as she saw the next course. No wonder Angie was in such high good humour. He liked nothing better than the chance to roast a goose; he must be feeling marvellous. All the vegetables on their list were to be served too, and she grimaced as she saw that lecso was underlined. Everyone loved the spicy mixture of peppers and tomatoes and onions; well, they might have to go without in here. It was Anya Zsuzske's favourite, too, and a shortage of peppers meant a shortage of lecso. Damn the man from Barnetts who had tried to palm off inferior goods on her. As if she wouldn't have spotted the substitution, she who was famous in all the markets for her buying and her bargaining skills; the man was a fool! But there it was – not enough lecso unless Angie's boy had been lucky in Berwick Street market, round the corner.

She checked the rest of the menu and lifted her brows. Good luck to them if they could manage it all; sweet cheese pancakes with chocolate sauce, and mignons, the little chocolate truffles that were so richly indigestible, and the delicate pastry shells full of chopped nuts called love letters, and then a bowl of liptauer cheese rich with paprika. They'd get no work done this afternoon after that lot, especially if they got through all the wine that Maxie had left standing ready for them. Seventeen people and two dozen bottles? How they ever got their programmes made would never cease to amaze her. They drank more like full-blooded Hungarians than Englishmen.

And then she came to the last of the Extras and stopped at the door, suddenly filled again with nostalgia. The whole family coming to lunch, every one of them except the small children who had to be at school; it would be like Christmas used to be in the old days when Ma and Poppa had been alive; when they had eaten roast carp and drunk too much Tokay and laughed so much that she had made herself sick and had first been disgraced and then petted till she felt better – and her eyes prickled and angrily she rubbed her nose with the back of her hand and pushed open the door. This was really getting ridiculous. Quite ridiculous. Why get into such a state because the family was coming? They had a right to be here, didn't they? Of course they did –

3

'They've got a right to be considered. It's always sons who ought to be considered. Sons and grandsons,' Viktor said and scowled, trying not to look at her. But it was difficult because she was sitting very upright in the tall chair she had found in Caledonian market for just five shillings and of which she was so proud, because it was higher than average and when she sat in it she looked almost as big as other people.

'But you have three daughters,' she said. 'Don't forget, Viktor. What you have is three daughters.'

'So? And don't they have three husbands between 'em? What for should I beat my head for the three of them? I should worry about Ferenc Kiss, that one so clever he'll cut himself one of these days? Why should I make it easier for him to swank about and tell other people all the time he knows better than what they do? Hey? And – Laszlo Balog – it's high time Laszlo Layabout Balog got up off his toochus and started to work a bit harder for our Zsuzske and her with three babies! I make it too easy for him, and he won't never consider his responsibilities, won't never count up the mouths he ought to be feeding and won't never get his nose out of his stinking books and then – '

'Viktor, how often do you have to be told? It's got nothing to do with the boys, what they do, what they don't do. You're wrong anyway – Ferenc is a good man, he'll do well enough. He needs a little more time, is all – he's been unlucky – '

'Unlucky? That one? He needs time, that one? Listen Maritza, wake up already! The man's only five years younger than I am! How much more time does he need, for God's sake? Isn't it bad enough our Kati marries a man so old, he's more my age than hers, without you keep on making excuses for him?'

'All the more reason we treat the girls right,' Maritza said. 'All the more reason. I was just glad he married her. You were too – and he's good to her, loves her, treats her good, never throws nothing up in her face. All the more reason we treat her right. Her and the others, too.'

There was a little silence and Viktor stared at her and then got to his feet and went lumbering over to the window to look down into the Yard. It was getting dark now, and the gaslight in the tobacconist across the way had been lit so that bars of yellow were thrown across the greasy black cobbles. A child in dirty, stained trousers appeared from beneath the archway that led out to Dean Street and went hopping through to the shop and Viktor stared down at him and remembered Istvan at that age. So short a time ago, it seemed, and now he was a married man with a pregnant wife and –

He turned back from the window and tried glaring at Maritza again. 'I tell you, sons and grandsons, that's what it ought to be. That's the way it always was in the Old Country. Property stays in the family – the ones with the family name. There's only one Halascz – Istvan. Whoever gives money to sons-in-law? Hmm? I should give my money to that Ferenc, to Laszlo who says how he's going to be the biggest diamond merchant in the world but spends all his time his nose in books? There's Istvan I got to think of and his Eva – pregnant and – '

'And there's our three girls. Our Kati and our Zsuzske and our Magda. Three good girls, hard working girls every one of them. She's down there now, Magda, with Zolly and working, working – '

'Zolly! That stinking lousy Zolly!' roared Viktor. 'Now we have it – the truth. It's all for that stinking heap of offal you force on me to be a son-in-law, that diseased streak of crap you found in a gutter and brought here to be the devil on my back – ' He warmed to his theme and his voice rose to fill the dim room as he let his tongue roll round every Hungarian and Yiddish curse he could think of and Maritza sat unmoved, letting him rant on; and downstairs, Zolly, chopping fish on a great wooden board in the kitchen with sharp twists of his bird-boned hands and with his pale tired face sweating in the glow of the light from the big ovens, grinned sourly. The old man was off again. If he spent even a quarter of the energy he used on cursing me in doing some of the work around here, he thought, I'd be able to get to bed before midnight sometimes –

'Anya told me she was going to talk to him about money and wills,' Magda said equably from the other side of the kitchen where she was rolling hazelnuts to a floury mass, ready to make a dobosch. 'She's got it in her head she's going to die. She got a pain in her belly last week – I told her, it's too much thinking does it to her, she'll live longer than any of us, Poppa included. But she don't listen.'

She lifted her head and stopped thumping her hazelnuts for a moment and then shook her head admiringly. 'You have to hand it to him. He can go on like that for hours, and still find a new way to badmouth you.'

'Don't I know it,' grunted Zolly and went on chopping his fish. Whatever happened in the row upstairs, whoever won, it would make no difference to him. Without him and his efforts there would be no Halascz's restaurant, no money to talk about, no need to discuss wills. His parents-in-law knew it as well as he did, but there, the old man had to pretend he didn't.

'I'm going to change the fascia next month,' he said suddenly and Magda lifted her head and stared at him, puzzled, her face red in the stove light and gleaming with sweat. 'It's time my name was on it, Horvath's not Halascz's.'

She shook her head. 'Do me a favour, Zolly. The way Poppa is, it'd drive him out of his mind. You got some cash in hand? Spend it on electric light in here. Gaslight's all right for the restaurant, maybe, but in here we need electricity. It's time – '

And he made a face and returned to his fish. She was right of course; she always was. Ten years they'd been married now, ten years and two small boys and still she was part of the business and still she was always right about everything, just as the old man upstairs was always wrong. One of these days, he promised himself, and thumped the fish even harder to underline the promise, one of these days I'll get the recognition I'm entitled to. One of these days this place'll be called Horvath's, not Halascz's. The old devil will have to give in and do it right.

'I tell you, Maritza, it just ain't right.' Viktor had begun to quieten down. 'Sons and grandsons and – '

'Zolly's and Magda's two boys too? Little Zolly and Tibor, you'd give them the same as Istvan and his boy? If that Eva has a boy.' Maritza sniffed then. 'She don't look no great shakes to me, that one. No better made than I was at her age – worse. She'll have girls, just like I did. Just you wait and see.'

Viktor stared at her, furious, robbed of words by his own anger and then threw both his hands up in the air in an exaggerated gesture of renunciation. 'I wash my hands of the whole affair. My hands are washed, you hear me? *You* talk to this bloody lawyer you're so fond of, *you* make the arrangements. Me, I don't care. I try to do the right thing, keep the property where it belongs – in the hands of the man, the one who understands, the man who is entitled because he has the name, the family name. *Istvan.* I try to do it right, and all I get from you is mouth, mouth, mouth. I'm sick of it. I'm going over to Rupert Street. I'm going to play a bit of klobiosh with Ruby Perlman and his brother, get a bit of intelligent company. I need it, on account you're driving me *meshuggah*. I'll be a crazy man fit for Colney Hatch, I stay here another minute with you. Do as you like – only don't expect me to sign nothing.' And he went clattering down the stairs and across the dark restaurant to stamp out of Little Vinegar Yard, well pleased with himself.

He'd stood up to her. He'd made a point. He'd won an argument by the simple method of not staying to hear her have the last word. What was more, he'd got out of working this evening and actually told her he was going gambling. And if he chose to play poker instead of klobiosh tonight she couldn't say a word, not a word. Let her idiot of a Zolly do the work. He, Viktor, had better things to do.

And Maritza, sitting in her high backed chair in the dark room above the restaurant, smiled at the window and nodded her head. She'd arrange it tomorrow with that fancy new solicitor who'd come to the restaurant last week and told her what a good service he could give with such things as wills and family affairs and money in general. A nice young man, who understood when he'd met a business woman. She'd go and see him, and make the arrangements. And Viktor would do as she told him and sign papers, and she could die easy, knowing she'd done the right thing by her girls. They had a right, didn't they? Of course they did.

By the time Laura had finished checking the last of the Extras, and had set the presents for Anya Zsuzske ready by her place at the head of the table, there were sounds from below that told her that lunchtime had begun. The first rattle of the door, the soft buzz of voices, Maxie's dull rumble as he greeted a familiar face, the higher tones of a convivial customer looking forward to a couple of hours of happy greed, and she stopped by the long mirror on the wall besides the customers' coat stand to look at herself, needing to be sure, as an actress would have to be sure, that she was fit to step onto her stage.

Because it was Zsuzske's party she had dressed more than usually carefully this morning, going through her wardrobe in the five o'clock lamplight, yawning and trying to imagine how she would look by daylight, and not sure she had chosen well, but now she could see she had. The deep heather colour of her well-fitted dress and the old, cream lace collar that set it off looked both neat and becoming, and for once her hair was behaving itself. It had a great tendency to curl ever more wildly when she was busy, and that took years off her, making her look like a schoolgirl. She regarded this as her major handicap; at thirty-five, with a successful business well and truly under her hands, she should be elegant and soignée and should look her age; instead she looked rather like a more than usually sensible head girl in a well run school, and that always annoyed her. But since there was nothing much she could do about that she had to live with it, and she took her comb and lipstick from the pocket in the seam of her dress (no restaurateur could ever manage without pockets, she had long ago told the woman who made her clothes) and made swift repairs and then, pulling her dress more neatly round her firm hips, went quietly downstairs to start on the second phase of her day's work.

The labour of the morning, the dawn marketing, the book-keeping, the organising and supervision were now over. She had to be hostess, unruffled soother of anxieties both behind the scenes in the kitchen and in her main arena, the restaurant, and also later, a guest at her family's party. All that before an afternoon of clearing up and more book-keeping and preparing for the evening's repeat performance. It was a formidable day's labour, yet no one looking at her as she emerged into the cool green light of her restaurant would have guessed she had anything at all on her mind apart from the pleasure of the moment, which was greeting the first arrivals from City Television who were coming in from Frith Street.

Alistair Balfour smiled as he saw her and held out both hands expansively. 'My dear Laura! Now I feel I am alive! To see you – it was what I needed most of all. *How* are you? Have you been supervising my dumplings for me as they should be supervised?'

'How could I have had any thought in my mind today other than your dumplings, Mr. Balfour?' He had long ago begged her to call him by his first name – as did many others – but it was one of her rules never so to address customers; and she was not being merely proper in being so firm about it. She knew that her careful way of speech amused people and gave her a style that many admired; it was a sort of gimmick, but none the worse for that. 'And the rizi bizi and goose – '

'And the lecso – ' Alistair said greedily but she ignored that, looking at the man standing beside him. He was a good deal younger than Balfour, who was lean and elegant and grey all over – hair, clothes, everything – and clearly past fifty; this man was wearing a suit and a neat tie but still managed somehow to look unkempt as a boy would. He had dark hair that curled very tightly and yet wildly on his big head, and a heavy face with a full mobile mouth and wide dark eyes. About thirty, Laura thought, and then was irritated with herself; she was doing this too often lately, looking at people and trying to assess their age in relation to her own. It seemed so short a time ago that she had been just a girl; sometimes it felt as though she had gone to bed one night as a nineteen year old and woken up next day to discover someone had stolen fifteen years in the night. To be thirty-five – only five years off forty; ridiculous –

Now she stifled the thought as Balfour, recognising his social responsibility, said, 'Laura, this is a newcomer to City. Used to make commercials – you know, those shampoo ones where everyone runs barefoot through long grass in slow motion. He's just joined us to do some real work – the sort that doesn't make money – '

The young man reddened and held out one hand. 'How do you do, Miss – er – Miss – '

'Horvath – but everyone calls me Laura,' she said and shook his hand. 'And you are – '

'Sorry, Laura,' Balfour said. 'Joel – ah – what is it – Coplin. Ah, here are Buzzy and Jeffrey at last – come along, chaps. I've no doubt the wine waits above, winking at the glass's brim – '

There was a little flurry of excitement as more people arrived and then a positive traffic jam as still more came into the Yard and towards the door of the restaurant. The day, which had started dull, had lightened considerably and there was now a thin sunshine splattering the cobbles and people seemed happy enough to linger outside in the faint warmth and wait as Maxie and Janos took coats from those who could get in and stowed them and Dan and Miklos showed people to tables, and Jon ushered those from City in towards the staircase.

Laura moved through the hubbub, welcoming people by

name, never seeming at a loss for an identity and Joel Coplin watched her, lingering at the foot of the stairs as his guide and mentor, Balfour, greeted other people. Was she Soho born and bred, he wondered? Had she been a child in these streets, and had her parents before her grown up here too? This was a mental game he found himself playing more and more, wondering about the people he saw around him in the streets, and he made a small grimace at himself and tried to fix his attention on the people to whom Balfour was now introducing him. It was quite absurd to have been as affected as this by finding himself working in Frith Street.

'Buzzy Lethbridge, this is Joel Coplin, our newest director. Just joined us. Jeffrey, of course, you know Joel – must do. You interviewed him, I imagine, when he joined us – '

Jeffrey Charlton, a tall thin and very lugubrious man, shook Joel's hand limply. 'No – actually – good to see you, Coplin. Know about you, of course. It was Brian Crowner I think who took you on? Yes – I was in LA doing a bit of selling, you know, so it was Brian – yes. Good to have you with us – now, Alistair, is everything organised, pens and paper and so forth? We *are* supposed to be having a think tank, after all. It's not just food, I hope.'

'It's mostly food,' Alistair said blithely and grinned. 'Oh, it's all right, I've got the folders ready. Sally's bringing 'em. Now, Buzzy, you take Joel up, and I'll sort out the others – here they come – ' And he went busily to greet the newest arrivals now pushing through the door as the room buzzed with talk and laughter and the first corks began to pop as Maxie set to work in real earnest.

'You picked a good time to join City,' Buzzy said as he led the way up the stairs. 'This think tank Alistair organises every spring – it's the best thing we do all year. He's a greedy bastard, thank God. You're in for a treat.'

'I'm sure,' Joel said politely and stood looking around at the big room into which Buzzy had shown him. It was cool and clean and the table that was set in the middle for seventeen people looked inviting, but he was looking at the walls.

'That panelling, sir – it looks to be very old. How old is it, do you suppose?'

'You're an American,' Buzzy discovered, tilting his smooth dark head to one side and looking directly at Joel for the first time. 'Yes, of course you are. You look like an American. Like that chap who married that actress – the one with the nose, you know who I mean?'

Joel, trying not to let his irritation show, said, 'Canadian, sir. Not American. Canadian.'

'Same thing,' Buzzy said cheerfully. 'No damn difference so far as I can tell. You all talk the same – now, where's the menu? Let's see what Alistair's organised for us this year. Goose, no less! Jesus, that'll make everyone fart tomorrow. Good day to be out on a shoot, if you ask me. Share these good things with the open air – you like Hungarian food, Collins?'

'Coplin, sir,' Joel said, still polite. Stupid bastard, he was thinking; got to keep well out of your way, and he began to edge down the table so that he could sit as far away as possible from Buzzy who had clearly earmarked a chair for himself. 'Yes, I think I do. Not sure I know a great deal about it.'

'Don't suppose you get much more than hamburgers in America, hey? Well, you've come to the right place here. You'll get good food here – '

'You've been to the States, sir?' Joel said, his voice silky. 'Know it well?'

'Hmm?' Lethbridge was still staring down at the menu he was holding. 'Hell, no. I'm the financial manager, remember, not one of the poor sods who have to go wandering around, selling the stuff we make. I just deal in the money once it's in. Never been further West than the Algarve, thank God. You won't get me going to America – not my style at all. See enough of what they get up to there on the screen. No offence, old boy, of course.'

'Oh, none in the world,' Joel said savagely and went to stand by the window to stare out into the Yard as at last other people came tramping up the stairs to fill the room with noise and chatter. How long had this building been here? And what sort of people had been in it when it had been, as it must once have been, a house where people lived rather than worked? Everything about the shape of this elegant room showed that it had been a private dwelling once, no matter what some philistines had done to it since and he turned his head to look again at the handsome pale amber panelling that marched round the walls. A beautiful place; he'd have to find out more about it, if he could.

And then, as Jeffrey Charlton took his place at the head of the table and Alistair Balfour jerked his chin at Joel to show him where he should sit, he pushed the thought away. Damn it, he was here to make a living in television, not to indulge his new found passion for history. He'd get over it eventually, no doubt. He'd only been in the country a few weeks after all, and at City TV in Frith Street only four days. He'd get used to being here eventually, he hoped. And he smoothed his napkin on his lap and looked with interest at the plate of sausage and pepper salad that was being set before him. It certainly looked attractive and it smelled fascinating. He was, he discovered, hungry.

4

By half past one, the system was running at full blast, and doing it as smoothly as butter melting on a hot plate. In the kitchen Angie was roaring steadily at the top of his not inconsiderable voice as dish after dish emerged from his flashing hands to be snatched from the serving table by Dan and Janos, Miklos and Jon, and delivered to the tables in the restaurant. Leno and the rest of the kitchen staff circled and bustled, dodging and dancing to the tune of his shouting and Maxie shot in and out of his cubby hole with its wine racks, beside the cold room, his corkscrew so busy that it should have been red hot.

Upstairs all of the Extras were full and happy, with Zsuzske at last settled in her place (it had taken over ten minutes to get her large bulk up the stairs, pulled in front by her son Paul and propelled from behind by her grandsons Charles and Richard) and the casual waiters who had been brought in for the day to look after them were coping well. The serving of the main dishes had been so carefully planned by Angie that all they had to do was collect food from the dumb waiter that trundled its rickety way up from the kitchens below to the little servery at the top of the stairs and set it on the tables; each serving was clearly marked, and each side dish was provided in sufficient quantity for all the lunchers to be able to help themselves without risk of supplies running out. There was even enough lesco, for Freddy had wrought well at Berwick Street market and brought back enough plump glossy yellow peppers to make gallons of it.

Laura, sitting at her high desk, looked around her domain, cocked an ear for sounds of discontent from above and hearing none, relaxed. Soon, she would be able to hand over to Maxie, who would in his turn allow Dan to deal with any late requests for more wine, and be able to join the family upstairs. She had been able to greet her great aunt, kissing her papery old cheeks affectionately, but she wanted to spend a little time sitting beside her. She was profoundly deaf now, old Anya Zsuzske, but for all that, it was possible to talk to her a little, and Laura wanted to do that, if she could. There couldn't be much time left for conversation with a woman of ninety one.

She caught sight of the three men with their heads together on the other side of the restaurant, at the table in the corner near the door, and her brows creased a little. That was an odd collection; she hadn't noticed before quite how odd but now she could relax and she watched them from under her brows, puzzled.

Joe Davriosh; she knew him, of course. Everyone knew him. The estate agency he ran in a small alley that ran off Bourchier Street was a shabby place, but everyone knew that there were few sales or lettings of premises in and around Soho that did not somehow touch the little office, whoever was selling what and to whom and that some of the money that changed hands always managed to stick to Joe Davriosh's eager fat fingers even if he had nothing to do with the deal. To see him in the restaurant was not unusual; she accepted his bookings because he was so much a part of the Soho scene that it was impossible not to, though she didn't really like him. She had no reason to feel so about him; he had never done her or any friends of hers any harm for all his meddling greed. All she knew was the gossip that went round about him, and the way brows went up and lip corners went down when his name was mentioned, but still she didn't like him much, and she certainly didn't like the man he had brought with him.

Him she had often seen, and had as often refused when he had tried to book her tables. She had no control over the guests her customers brought of course, so she could do nothing about it, but she was unhappy in the extreme to see Donald Preston sitting at one of her pretty tables, even if it wasn't one of the best.

She bent her head to her cash box as the man looked up,

not wanting to catch his eye. He looked harmless enough; no one could pick any quarrel with his neat dark suit complete with double breasted waistcoat and sober tie. There was nothing in the least flamboyant about him; he looked more like a respectable middle aged Harley Street doctor who was balding a little, running to fat perhaps, tiring a little, than what he was, which was the owner of at least three of the strip shows within a stone's throw of Little Vinegar Yard, and it was whispered, of one or two even more unsavoury businesses.

Laura had often wondered whether her dislike of the man and his doings was based on a distaste for sex itself rather than his exploitation of it; was she being as prissy and absurd as her mother had been, she who had reddened with shame if anyone so much as mentioned underwear in her hearing, and who had regarded any comment, let alone discussion, of the relationship between the sexes as disgusting? Her mother had come from so respectable and ordinary an English family that marrying anyone as exotic as a Hungarian – even one who was a second generation immigrant and therefore as English to listen to and look at as she was herself – had been shocking enough; she had learned to change many of her attitudes during the twenty three years of her marriage to Tibor, but she had never lost her dislike of public displays or talk of sex, and inevitably much of her thinking had been passed on to her only daughter. Is that why I hate the man so? Laura asked herself now, pushing away from the surface of her mind the deeper doubt that sometimes assailed her. That she was in fact as narrow as her mother in every way; after all, wasn't she still unmarried at thirty five? Hadn't she avoided men all her life so far?

But that was not to be thought of, so she didn't, and looked instead at the other man sitting with Davriosh and Preston, wondering who he was; but she couldn't recognise him, and commonsensibly she pushed the question away too. If he were to have any business with the other two that might affect this, her own corner of Soho, she'd find out soon enough. She always did, after all – and she lifted her brows at Maxie who looked swiftly round, checking his tables, and then nodded, and as though they had discussed it she knew it was now all right to go upstairs. Maxie would cope from now on; and she slipped quietly out of her seat and went as unobtrusively as she could to the staircase. No need for anyone to be aware that she wasn't there, as she usually was, watching over their comfort all through their lunches.

'Who owns the place?' the third man at the Davriosh table asked, as he watched her go. 'Whoever it is, he's got a good one there. Not much she doesn't see, is there? I've noticed – '

'She does,' Davriosh said, and reached for a piece of bread with which to mop up the last of the paprika sauce which had adorned his chicken. 'And she doesn't miss a goddammed thing; not a goddammed bloody thing. If she fancies you, you can get a table here. If she doesn't, forget it. She'll never take your bookings, will she, Don, hey?' And he grinned wickedly at the man facing him.

'I don't blame her. She's a lady of principle,' Donald Preston said lugubriously. 'I wouldn't take my bookings if I owned a place like this. Full of class, full of it. Never mind. She'll take them in future. Once we get this business sorted out.'

'If she's still here,' the other man said quietly. He was a small man, quiet and nondescript, with the sort of vaguely ordinary face and vaguely ordinary manner that made him quite unmemorable. The person who saw him in the morning and recognised him when he met him again in the afternoon was rare; generally he went about his business as unremarked and as anonymous as one of the sparrows that chattered in the gutters outside in Little Vinegar Yard. It was an appearance he had long cultivated, and of which he was very proud; it was a considerable business asset to look so dull and ordinary, he would tell his colleagues on the rare occasions when he was in an expansive and talkative mood. 'The man they hate but never remember,' he would say and laugh softly and contentedly.

'What do you mean, if she's still here? No reason why she shouldn't get a lease, is there?'

'No, not if she can afford it. And is willing to wait for it of course. Building – it takes time. She may lose so much of her goodwill while the building goes up there's nothing left to take a lease for.'

Davriosh laughed at that, and pushed his now almost clean plate away, regretfully. 'Forget it, Reggie. This one, lose her goodwill? Not as long as you've got an arse to sit on.'

The small man looked directly at him for the first time, and for a moment Davriosh looked nonplussed. There was an air of offence about him and he remembered with a sudden uneasiness that he was an important client and said placatingly, 'You should forgive the expression. But you know what I mean. She's popular, is Laura. Very. No way would her customers leave her. They love her too much.' And he began to whistle softly between his teeth, 'Laura – footsteps that you hear down the hall at night – Laura, but she's only a dream – ' and then grinned again. 'It doesn't exactly fit, but you see what I mean. She's furniture around here.'

'So she'll get a lease,' Preston said impatiently. 'What worries me more now is getting her out in the first place.'

'It won't be easy,' Davriosh said. 'I don't want you to think it will be. But I think I can do it. Given time.' He stopped then and waved at Dan and, catching his eye, made coffee pouring gestures. 'It'll take time and it might take money.' He looked quickly at the man he had called Reggie and then away, but he was sitting staring down at his hands which were folded neatly on the table cloth, and seemed not to have heard him.

'More money?' Preston said. 'Why?'

Davriosh shrugged. 'There'll be palms to grease, people to sweeten. You know how it is. These things take effort. Nothing comes from nothing.'

'I understood you to say you could arrange this for us,' the man Reggie said, and now he did look at Davriosh, very directly. His eyes were an odd pale green, with faint lines around the irises. Joe found them unpleasant to look at and his gaze shifted away.

'I can, of course I can. I've done it before, I can do it again. There ain't no one nowhere who won't sell eventually.

Like the man says, everyone's got his price, her price. You just got to work out what it is. But it takes money is all I'm saying.'

'Well, you can have it. Within reason. As long as you deliver as per our contract.'

'I've got no contract.' Davriosh sounded alarmed. 'I signed nothing at all – '

Reggie smiled again, the same creasing of his face that left the pale gooseberry eyes quite unlit. 'I know, Mr. Davriosh. But an arrangement is for me an *arrangement*. I need no signatures. I make promises, and I keep them. I am given promises, and I expect them fulfilled. It's a very simple way to do business.'

'Yes,' Davriosh said uneasily and leaned back gratefully as Dan arrived with coffee and the offer of puddings. 'Got good mignon today, gentlemen,' he murmured. 'Or the liptauer? Very nice, very sharp and spicy – the best Angie did this week– I recommend.'

'No more,' Preston said brusquely. 'Only coffee and brandies. No more food.' And then as soon as Dan had gone, said sharply to the small man sitting once again contemplating his own folded hands, 'Listen, Statler, let me be clear about all this. All we've agreed to do is try to get these properties cleared so that they can be bought up. No rough stuff, nothing nasty – '

'Of course.' He still looked at his hands. 'What else could we agree?'

'I just want it clear, that's all. I'm no softer than the next man and I like to do good business but I know where to draw the line. None of this pushing people around, you understand? A little quiet talking is one thing. Being rough is another.'

Now the other man did look up. 'Do I look rough, Mr. Preston?'

Preston looked at him and then swept one hand over his balding head, for a fine sweat had broken out on its gleaming expanse, but said nothing.

'There'll be a few problems, apart from Laura, you know,' Davriosh said after a long pause, one that he seemed to find threatening suddenly. 'I mean, there's the old boy across the Yard, and there's the adjoining properties – ' He giggled then, a little shrilly. 'Glad it doesn't involve the jazz club. I can tell you, that could get very complicated, Ronnie Scott's and all – '

'Of course not,' Statler said. 'Publicity.'

They both nodded, absurdly in time with each other, and then aware of the effect laughed, though Statler's eyes still seemed uninvolved in what the rest of his face was doing. 'Look,' he said, and leaned forwards, suddenly confidential and friendly. 'Look, I must reassure you. I'm no villain out to rape the city or the good people who live in it. None of this dramatic stuff, believe me. You mustn't think all property developers are villains, you know. Men like you, with your experience – you should know better! All I want to do is take this block of ramshackle old places and put something beautiful and lasting in their place. I'm the first to understand the importance of environment, of people's lives and homes and jobs – ' He smiled at them and they looked back at him, doubtfully, puzzled by the change in him. The remote chilly figure of the first part of lunch had vanished behind the friendly reasonable man who sat and smiled at them now and Preston said carefully, 'Yes – yes, I'm sure.'

'So, there it is, you see. Nothing at all alarming, hmm? Just an arrangement made between us, and which we'll carry out sensibly, hmm? No need for contracts on paper. We have binding contracts on our words as businessmen – '

'As businessmen,' Davriosh said and laughed. He had swallowed all his double brandy quickly, and since he had inflicted the most punishment on the two bottles of wine that had accompanied their food he was looking flushed and glittering now. 'Such businessmen! Tarts and tricks, hey? Tarts and tricks – ' and he looked at Preston and winked, but Preston ignored him and looked instead at Statler.

'It's not only the owners of the properties who'll need to be considered,' he said. 'There's the Trust.'

'The Trust?' Statler said. 'Who or what do they trust?'

'Nobody,' Preston said promptly and Joe Davriosh laughed. 'They're the Vinegar Trust. Those people I pointed out to you when we got here. They went upstairs to one of the private rooms as we got here. An old Italian woman – her husband started a business forty, fifty years ago selling theatre costumes, ballet shoes, you know the sort of thing. She and her son, they've been busy in it since Adam was a nipper. She's been the boss since the old man died but now she's retiring. Going to the country to live with her daughter and her kids, so someone else has to take over.'

'You know a lot,' Davriosh said, staring at him. 'You sound like an old girl in a launderette, the way you gossip – '

'It's relevant information. The Trust can be – well, a nuisance or an asset. It depends. They meddle a lot, that's for sure. I've had 'em on my back for years. Years,' he added feelingly and then grimaced. 'Not that I blame 'em. I hate my business as much as they do. The girls are enough to make you sick, the way they carry on, and the punters are worse. It's a lousy stinking business however you look at it and I hate it.'

Davriosh blinked owlishly at him. 'So why stay in it?'

'Because it's a bloody good living. Bloody good. But as soon as I can get a better one, I'll be out, believe me. Sex is dead, anyway. The way everyone's going on it'll be back to net curtains on the piano legs this time next year. There'll be no market any more – '

'If you believe that you'll believe anything,' Statler said. 'What do you mean, the Trust have been on your back?'

'They want the sex shops out, the strip shows closed, all the girls got rid of. You know what these people are. Keep it the way it always was, they say, as though there weren't always girls on the game round here, and spielers and robbers and Christ knows who else. But there it is, they make a nuisance of themselves. And they could make a nuisance of themselves to you too.' And he shot a malicious little glance at Statler and then grinned at Davriosh. 'You'd better be warned.'

'I'm warned,' Statler said and looked at Davriosh. 'Do you know these people?'

'I told you, I know everyone. Everyone.' And he looked round the restaurant. 'I could tell you who everyone was at each of these tables and a lot more about 'em than they'd like you to know. Take over there – the feller with the tie pin? You see the one? If that diamond was any bigger he'd get a crick in his neck. He's the biggest – '

'I'm not sure I want to know,' Statler said, and looked prim. 'I'm interested only in my own affairs. If this Trust could be a nuisance then I need to know it can be dealt with.'

'Who else is there in it?' Davriosh said to Preston, apparently completely forgetting his claim to know everything about everybody.

'I'm not sure at present. They haven't been after me so much this past few months. Not since I sorted out the licences for the shops – used to be Leo Levy, the tailor chap, you know? His dad's been in Dean Street a long time. Oh, yes, and Olaffson from the fish shop and a chap called Malplackett and – '

'Malplackett?' Davriosh sat up straighter and slowly smiled. 'Then that's all right. O.K. Reggie. No need to worry. I can deal with the Trust if I have to.'

'Good.' Statler once again produced that sudden brilliant smile. 'No more business! At least, no more about mine. Tell me, Preston, about these girls of yours. Now, there's a business that really fascinates me! How do you first get into it? How do you organise it? And how – ' And his voice dropped as the three of them leaned closer and began to talk and laugh so loudly that Laura, coming down for a swift check that all was well before returning to her family party reassured herself that there was nothing to worry about after all. They were just the usual three men swopping dirty jokes after a fine lunch and good wine had mellowed them. It was nothing more than that.

And she went back upstairs after sorting out the first of the bills that were ready for payment, contented and comfortable. All was well at her restaurant today, just as it was every day and always would be. It was a comfortable feeling to have.

5

There were twenty seven people in the third Extra, so even though it was the largest of the rooms, it was crowded. People were sitting more closely together than was ideal and had to jockey to get room to work their elbows as they ate, but it didn't seem to matter. They all appeared to be so content to be together that they were good tempered about their discomfort; which was a remarkable way for so large and so very Hungarian a family to be, Laura thought as she came back into the room and looked round at them all. She had such vivid memories of so many family parties when parents had bawled and wept at children, and adult children had spoken witheringly to parents, and brothers and cousins had almost come to blows and sisters-in-law had attacked each other with such barbed tongues that you could almost see the sparks fly between them, that this peaceful scene was really unusual.

Her lips quirked then as she saw how carefully Dolly and Evelyn had distanced themselves from each other. Those two couldn't help but argue when they were within hearing distance of each other, so it was surprisingly kind of them to try to keep the peace for Anya Zsuzske's party in this way. She must tell them both, separately of course, how much she appreciated that.

She slipped into her place between the old lady and her own youngest brother, Alex and neither paid her any attention. Anya Zsuzske was too busily engaged in gobbling duck's liver and lecso (she had an incredible appetite for one of her age, and there were some of the irreverent younger members of the family who maintained that the only reason the old girl had lived so long was that she couldn't bear to die before her next meal was due) and Alex was busily talking to his young cousin Sammy Hallash, Steven and Dolly's son.

Laura frowned a little at that; the boy was so very young, so very good looking and so clearly dazzled by his handsome actor cousin. She'd have to speak to Alex about that; his private life was his own affair, of course, and as merely a sister she had no right to make judgements about his choice of partners, but there was no way she was going to let him start any sort of episode with young Sammy. The boy was really very naive under his veneer of knowingness, and much too vulnerable. And anyway, the thought of what his mother would do and say if she discovered that Alex was getting too friendly with her precious boy didn't bear thinking of. Everyone knew Alex was gay – he had always been at some pains to make sure they all knew it, announcing his sexual preferences so publicly and so often that his cousin Richard Balog had said dryly that he had come out like a shell from a repeater anti-aircraft gun and still was, and they were reasonably tolerant of them. But that tolerance would be sorely stretched if he involved Sammy in his affairs.

It was nice they had all come again this year, she thought, as she let her gaze move along the animated chewing faces. It would have pleased her father to see them all here at his table. And then her brows creased a little, and it was almost as though Dolly had heard her thought and had cried at her down the long room, 'Our table, Laura, ours – '

Because of course, there were other shareholders in the restaurant, even though it bore her name and she did all the work. The matter of the ownership and the rates due to the others from the place had always been one of deep interest to all of them, even those who had sold or given away their inherited portions of it, and she drew a sharp little breath in through her nose as she saw Dolly lean back to speak imperiously to the waiter who had been serving extra vegetables to her husband Steven beside her. Damn the woman, always behaving as though she were in charge of the place; damn her, damn her, damn her, and Laura caught the waiter's eye and lifted her brows at him and he, for all he was a casual, knew where his duty lay and immediately abandoned Dolly to come to her, and Laura allowed a shaft of pleasure to shoot through her as she saw the scowl that Dolly immediately produced.

She sent the waiter for more liver for Anya Zsuzske, who had cleaned her plate and was now sitting looking at its emptiness with obvious disappointment on her vast and sagging old face, and smiled at Dolly who pointedly looked away and Laura sighed, annoyed with herself for giving in to her moment of spleen. So silly, really –

And yet it wasn't. Didn't she work all the hours God gave and a great many more besides to make the place what it was? Wasn't it her efforts, her expertise, her total dedication that gave the others so much money? And she let the numbers run through her head as they so often did.

On her average takings of £2,000 a day, that brought in £600,000 a year, and with a profitability of over 25% that left net profits after tax and all her overheads of between £150,000 and £160,000 a year for the rest of them. Which meant that Ilona Cord got up to £40,000 and Paul Balog got the same, and Dolly and Evelyn Hallash shared the quarter due to their branch of the family, while she herself, of course, took the last £40,000, for she had bought the whole of the Horvath share from her brothers Alex and Timothy, when their father had died. It had cost her all she had and an overdraft besides, but she had felt the need to own as much as she could of the restaurant, and it had been worth the financial effect. It was starting to pay off, too, for her overdraft had been shrinking steadily, though all the repairs and renovations she had had to do last year had made it rather large again.

Never mind, she thought now, never mind. It was worth getting all the work done, and in a few years she'd repay all the debts if they went on being as financially effective as they were now, and she looked at the richly glowing panelling and smiled with pleasure at the sight of it.

Taking it all round, they do well, Paul and Ilona and Evelyn and Dolly, she thought, since they do nothing to earn what they get each year, and also own their shares of this beautiful place, and she looked again at Dolly and tried to stifle her deep and almost instinctive dislike of her. It wasn't just her bony face with the sharp black eyes, and careful makeup, or the expensively dressed lean frame that she was clearly so proud of, for she always looked at Laura's neat roundness with an obvious sneer on her face. It ran more deeply than that. Perhaps if her husband hadn't indulged her so much she wouldn't be so unpleasant? Perhaps if he had bought his sister Evelyn's share of the inheritance that had come to the three of them, as well as Daniel's, when Daniel had gone through that bad patch with his dress factory and had needed cash in a hurry, Dolly wouldn't be so obviously jealous of her sister-in-law?

Not that Evelyn was all that much easier to get on with; that a woman should become so sour and so touchy just because she was unmarried seemed to Laura to be arrant nonsense, but there it was. Hungarian all the way through to her middle, in spite of having been born and reared in London, Evelyn saw herself through the eyes of the old country and the old people, and so regarded herself as a total and humiliated failure because she was a spinster – and now she was well into her fifties that seemed an irremediable state – and behaved appallingly to everyone as a result. The rivalry between her and her sister-in-law was as much her fault as Dolly's –

Laura pulled her attention away from them. Her great uncle Istvan's family had always been the least likeable of them all, which was odd, remembering what a nice old man he'd been. She could recall him so clearly, sitting night after night at her father's corner table downstairs, talking interminably about horses and dogs – for he had been an inveterate gambler – and laughing up at her when she had come to bring them another bottle of Tokay, and she was sad, suddenly at the loss of him. He had died some three or four years before her father, and yet still she missed them both.

On the far side of Anya Zsuzske Paul leaned forward solicitously as the waiter arrived and brought her another big plateful of food and he said anxiously, 'Laura, are you sure she should? I mean, she's already had the stuffed pancakes, you know. Surely we shouldn't let her have any more – '

'Oh, stop fussing, Paul.' His brother Freddy, sitting on his other side, nudged him sharply. 'Let the old duck have what she wants. If she keels over as a result she'll die happy and you can't say it'd be premature, can you?' And he grinned down the table at their other brother, Leonard, and shouted, 'You agree, Lenny? Let Anya have all she wants, greedy old darling – you agree?'

Leonard who hated above all things being called Lenny, regarding it as an infra dig label for so eminent a dentist as himself, frowned.

'It's up to Paul,' he said frostily. 'He looks after her, which is more than you ever do – '

'Or you,' snapped Freddy, and was clearly about to say more, but his wife Ruth very obviously kicked him under the table and he subsided, and Laura again felt her lips quirk.

It was quite absurd that these three were brothers; both Freddy and Leonard were so prosperous, so round, so obviously earthy and practical and so very clearly old men. Leonard, the oldest, must be, she worked it out – sixty five or so, and was bald as well as plump, and quite ridiculously pleased with himself, while Freddy, a couple of years younger, looked what he was, a successful businessman (and it amused the family greatly that he dealt in garden novelties, and particularly gnomes) who had let himself run to seed.

Paul, on the other hand, looked wonderful. He too, must be sixty now, she thought, but he didn't look it; possibly fifty, he could easily be taken for younger with his thick mane of glossy silver hair and his lean body and well kept face. As clearly a man of intellect and spirit and sensitivity as his brothers were men of hard cash and practicality, he had nothing in common with them, and indeed seemed to have little in common with any of his relations. A quiet person, sensitive, hiding himself and his feelings behind that well made face and the watchful dark eyes, it seemed as natural as breathing that he should be an actor. Not as successful as he should have been perhaps, with his looks and presence, but still, he made a living and had a lifestyle that left him free to look after his mother to whom he was clearly very attached. A *nice* man, my cousin Paul, Laura thought, and once again wondered briefly about what sort of person was hiding behind that elegant surface.

She had from time to time wondered about him; was he, like her brother, gay? It was easy to think so, for he had never married; yet he was always to be seen out and about with women. He often brought them to dine with her downstairs, clearly proud of the family connection and she had always been amused to see how dazzled by him the most beautiful women could be. She had seen them turn to stare at him, ignoring their own escorts quite blatantly, and surely, she asked herself now, that wouldn't happen if he were – and she shook herself mentally and smiled at Paul, leaning forwards to touch his hand across old Anya Zsuzske's bulk.

'I wouldn't worry, Paul,' she said. 'I've seen your Anya eat more than this and still come up smiling,' and she bent her head and spoke loudly directly into the old woman's ear. 'Are you all right, Anya Zsuzske? Can you eat some more?'

The old lady looked at her with her deep eyes, still dark and lively for all her great age and said in a surprisingly melodious voice, 'Of course I can. It's the only thing I get any fun out of any more. The liver – it's good – tell Angie – ' And she began to eat again.

Paul made a little moué and looked at his mother doubtfully, and then, catching Laura's eye, managed a smile and she smiled back as reassuringly as she could and he returned to his own meal.

'Laura!' She looked up and across the table, further down, and saw Philip Cord grinning at her. 'Laura!' he said again. 'I have to say it. This is marvellous. I've made a pig of myself and loved every moment. It's all right for everyone else – they're used to it, but to me it's a revelation!' And he lifted his glass at her and she bent her head in acknowledgement, furious with herself as she felt the redness rise in her cheeks.

Ever since the party had begun she had been trying not

to notice him. Not to ignore him, precisely, but just to be unaware of his presence, as though that were possible, and she began to eat, pushing her galuskas around her plate in a way that would have scandalised Angie, who prided himself on the delicacy of his dumplings. It was, she told herself yet again, quite absurd to let this man upset her so. She ought to be used to him by now, for heaven's sake. He and Ilona had been back in England almost a year now, and they had come to eat downstairs several times; they had moved from seeming like little more than recently introduced acquaintances to being members of the family again – yet still she found it uncomfortable to be with him.

She had wondered at first whether her unease stemmed entirely from Ilona. She knew Ilona's history of course; in this family everyone talked so much it was impossible not to know far more about everyone else than she sometimes wanted to know – and that she was tense and possessive about her good looking young husband was understandable.

It wasn't just that he was fifteen years her junior; it was the fact that he had been so very impecunious when they had married – she a few days before her fortieth birthday and he a glowing twenty five year old – and she had been so very well off. It had caused a considerable fuss in the family when Ilona's father Gyorgy had died and his will had been made public; no one had ever done what he had done; to leave all his money to one child, and she a girl, ignoring the claims of not only her sister but her brother – that had been much more than a nine days wonder. They had all talked about it interminably for months, and looked sideways at Ilona; to have been so publicly branded by her own father as a hopeless spinster – that had been dreadful, but she had gone her way through it all holding her head as high as she could. Her father had meant kindly; the fact that his will had been worded in an unfortunately tactless manner could not be helped.

For he had left her his whole fortune on the grounds that her sister was married to a comfortably off man (Susan, much to her father's admiration, had married a very successful owner of three jeweller's shops) and her brother was as well provided for as a busy G.P. should be. It had been Ilona who needed the major share of the family property to keep her in her lonely old age, Gyorgy had told the world in his will, and so there it was. She had it.

And then she had met and married Philip Cord in a story book affair that had left them all gasping and darkly prognosticating big trouble in the future. He would rob her blind, the sisters-in-law, Dolly and Evelyn, had announced, united for once in the face of a common enemy, and then go and leave her, mark their words –

He hadn't. They had been married now – Laura worked it out as she always did work out all sums; being accurate with numbers was one of her minor obsessions – for almost sixteen years. Not bad for a man they all swore was a fortune hunter. Whether he was a faithful husband no one could know; Laura suspected he was not, not only because of the way Ilona always looked so very watchful when she was with him but also, she had to admit, because of the way he made her feel.

There was something so practised and glossy about Philip; she had seen other women not only stare at him with unashamed interest, but had seen even some she would have regarded as cool and sophisticated in the extreme reduced to blushing and stammering by his attention. It wasn't that he was so spectacularly good looking; he wasn't, though he had a great deal of dark gold hair that was very attractive; or that he was so witty; his conversation was largely commonplace. It was something else. A warmth that seemed to emanate from him to wrap his listener in comfort, a look in his eyes that made you feel he was really interested in you and only you, a sort of sideways grin that was conspiratorial and which drew you into his special world of delicious private jokes and fun – and she looked up and again caught his eye and there that look was again, and once more she blushed and tried to return her attention to her galuskas.

With luck he and Ilona would go back to live in Florida again, where Ilona had bought a flat and where they spent long periods of time. Philip was said to be something in the art dealer line; no one had ever actually seen any exhibition with which he had to do, nor did he seem to be attached to any particular gallery, but it didn't seem to matter anyway. They lived quietly and comfortably, he and Ilona, either in Florida or in their small house on Harrow Hill. And I should have more sense, Laura told herself stoutly than to let myself become so silly and fussed when he turns on his charm. I don't envy Ilona with that one. I'm not surprised she's so anxious; and deliberately she caught Ilona's eye and said loudly, 'Ilona – I adore that suit. You look wonderful in it. It has to be American – I wish we could get clothes like that here – '

Ilona looked first startled and then, oddly, relieved, and smiled and her whole face lifted, so that she looked much younger and much more attractive. She had always had a good face, with the high cheekbones and broad forehead that had been so vivid a feature of old Viktor's face, going by the family photographs, and when she smiled she looked stunning. Most of the time, though, she sat with her face closed and still with the pair of lines that were etched between her brows whenever she looked at her husband scarring her face with fear. Someone ought to tell her to be more relaxed, to smile more and then she wouldn't have to be so fearful about him, Laura thought. I'll tell her. One of these days I'll tell her. But she knew she never would.

The waiters had cleared the dishes from the main courses now and were getting ready to serve the vast birthday cake which Angie had made and decorated in the shape of a ninety one and there was a little stir at the end of the table as her cousin Richard Balog got to his feet. Laura took a deep breath and steeled herself; she always hated this part of the proceedings.

'Everyone – everyone!' Richard was tapping on his glass with a knife over and over again, until at last they had all stopped chattering and had turned expectantly towards him. 'Everyone! Relatives and friends – and to my own amazement it's possible to be both in this family!' There was the usual titter of laughter at this hoary old joke, which someone made every year. 'I want to make one toast before we make the special one of the day, to dear Anya Zsuzske who, though she isn't actually Mummy to every one of us, certainly feels as though she is. We're very proud of her and thrilled to be here yet again at her birthday party – and just as thrilled with what has been provided here for us all today. As ever, it's been a sumptuous feast – I'm off to Champneys tomorrow. I have to go every year to get rid of several extra inches after Anya Zsuzske's birthday party – but I wouldn't have missed a single glorious mouthful. And as ever, I want to say for all of us a heartfelt thank you to the person who made it possible – our own dear Laura, the queen of Soho. Whoops. Erase that, run it again – the queen of Soho restaurants!'

And as the second time-honoured joke of the day came trotting out Laura raised her glass to him and the table and managed to smile without, she hoped, looking as embarrassed and irritated as she felt.

'It's my pleasure – mine and Angie's,' she said. 'All I ask is that you remember to pop into the kitchen before you go and tell him you enjoyed your lunch. He cares more for this family than we do ourselves, as well as you all know. Well, here's to next year – and here's to our own Anya Zsuzske.'

And then they were all on their feet with glasses held high, looking at the old lady who sat vast and Buddha-like in her place at the head of the table staring at the great cake that had been set ceremoniously in front of her by the waiter and clearly much more interested in that than in the toast they were drinking to her.

Nothing, Laura thought as she leaned over to help the old lady make the first cut in the iced confection, nothing is ever any different. Every year it's like this – and that's the way it ought to be, really. I'm glad it is – I think. And she set to work to cut the cake and distribute it as quickly as she could, so that she could go downstairs and finish off the normal lunchtime work. There was still half the day to get through yet –

She had managed to forget her discomfiture about Philip Cord completely, until he stopped her as they all milled about downstairs, ready to leave, and murmured in her ear, 'Laura – I'll be in to see you later this week. Just me on my own. There's something I really must talk to you about,' and then went before she could say anything, either in agreement or protest. She tried to tell herself she didn't want to see him and that really he was being a wretched nuisance, pushing himself on her like this. But she wasn't convinced in the slightest.

6

'The thing is, getting the information in on time, and making sure it's accurate,' Leo said. 'I know how it is with these things – I used to do the newsletter for an old people's charity I worked for when I was single, and it was the biggest headache. 'Still – ' He brightened. 'If you're really willing to help that'll make a big difference. I mean, the old people's thing, I was on my own. *Completely*. Same with the Balls and theatre trips and things like that I used to organise. Always there ready to share the fun, oh, yes, but when it came to the work, they didn't want to know – '

'It's always the same,' Edward Malplackett said. 'If there's someone willing and able then everyone thinks he's a work-horse and leave it all to him. But I'll gladly help. Any way you like. Just say the word, and I'll be there.'

'Mind you, I'm not complaining about the Trust.' Leo sounded suspicious suddenly. 'It's a privilege and a pleasure to be the Chairman, believe me. I wouldn't have taken on the job if I didn't reckon I could bring something useful to it.'

'Oh, I'm sure,' Malplackett said and smiled. 'It's not something I'd ever take on I can assure you. Far more involved than I could cope with. But I'm always glad to be useful as Secretary because that's in the background. Can't be doing with all the public bits, you see. All the chairing of meetings and being spokesman at public affairs – no, that I could never handle. Not my style. But a bit of background work to help things along – that suits me nicely.'

Leo relaxed; the glory that was to come to him as Chairman of the Trust was clearly safe, and he beamed on the older man. 'Splendid. Good to have you aboard. We should be able to get a good deal done now. Mrs. Capitelli – good old soul in many ways, did a sound job, but no fire in her, know what I mean? A Trust like ours should have had much more effect this past fifteen years – but look how it's been. The number of real businesses in the area cut by over half, nothing but strippers and peep shows these days. Got to put a stop to it – and got to try and get rid of some of those that are already here. It won't be easy – it's always better to keep 'em out than to have to get rid of 'em once they get in, like mice, eh? But we can spice things up a bit.' He laughed, pleased with himself. 'The Vinegar Trust'll spice things up a bit, no question.' And he tied his camel hair coat belt into a modish knot, pulled the collar round his ears to give himself a rakish air, and sleeked his hair back with both hands.

'The newsletter,' Malplackett said putting on his own much less elegant raincoat. 'It's a great idea, I really like it. I thought – I can collect information about which businesses are coming, which are going – that sort of thing? Not just local gossip, but real facts, eh?'

'Absolutely,' Leo said. 'Absolutely. Real facts – ' He looked at his watch and pursed his lips importantly. 'Look at that. Half past three! Lunch here eats your day the way we eat the food, eh? I've got a lot to get out this afternoon – time I was back – '

'I'll walk along with you,' Malplackett said easily. 'My next appointment's at half past four, so I'm not in too much of a rush. I was thinking – a column about property values – would that be useful?'

'Property values? How do you mean?' Leo was suddenly guarded and he went out through the now almost empty restaurant, nodding at Laura and Maxie as he went, leaving the other man to follow him. Out in Little Vinegar Yard he lifted his chin and took a deep breath of the chill spring air, and then looked sideways and with some suspicion again at Malplackett who had fallen into step beside him as they made their way to the archway that led to Frith Street. 'We want a newsletter people'll read. Don't want to make it too dry, do we?'

'Nothing too revealing, of course,' Malplackett murmured. 'I don't want everyone knowing what rent I'm paying for my little office or what my rates are, any more than you do for your shop. I just thought – when a property changes hands, it could be useful for all of us to know the sort of money involved. Helps us keep an eye on our own investments.'

Again Leo relaxed. 'Oh, I see what you mean. Not any sort of table of comparative values, nothing like that – '

'Good God, no!' Malplackett looked scandalised. 'No one'd co-operate on a thing like that. But everyone'd want to know what a place fetched, wouldn't they? *Really* fetched I mean. You can't trust the estate agents – least of all people like Davriosh. They lie the way they breathe – naturally. But the real figures – that would be interesting. Take Laura's now – that little place – suppose that went on the market. Wouldn't it be useful to know what she got for it?'

Leo laughed. 'Laura's? She wouldn't sell that till the day the sky falls in. And even then she'd wait till the day after – '

'Still and all, it'd be really interesting to know what value the place has. I mean, take yours. Good street frontage, building in good heart, ample workshops, I imagine – compare that with a little place in Little Vinegar Yard, like Laura's!'

Leo was feeling more expansive by the minute and he put his hand companionably on the other's shoulder as they halted on the kerb to let a string of traffic pass them. 'My place? Well, yes, I've no complaints. My grandfather took just the one shop, you know, when he came here to Soho. That was in 1923. It was my father added the next door premises and knocked through, in '55, and it was me who overhauled the flats upstairs and turned 'em into the workshops. Not bad, now, eh? I've got fifteen people working up there. Fifteen – '

'Ought to be more businessmen like you, these hard times. We need people who create jobs, hmm? I wish I could – '

'Well, come on now, Malplackett, it's different for you! Commission agent – not the same at all. You don't manufacture, you see, that's the thing. Business needs you, of course – you keep the wheels turning and so forth – but it's not the same as making something. The rag trade, you see – it's different.'

'Don't I know it,' Malplackett said feelingly and smiled again as they reached Levy's shop. 'I think, you know, I might pop in. I could do with a new suit. Been thinking about it for a few months, but you know how it is. It's a matter of getting round to it. A nice medium weight worsted? In a fine stripe, perhaps? Navy – now that'd make a change for me. I've been wearing grey for too long – '

'I've got a fantastic piece of cloth, fantastic – a fourteen ounce West of England – it makes up like a dream – ' At once Leo was all tailor, and he urged his companion towards his shop door. 'You'll love it – '

'And I was thinking,' Malplackett murmured. 'I can put some business your way, perhaps. I get to so many of the big offices, possibly I can arrange for your chap to come in some time, with a few swatches, a style book, even take some measures? Get a busy chap in his office and you can do very good business – it's just an idea.'

'And it's one I like,' Leo said delightedly. 'I've been thinking vaguely along those lines anyway. Great minds, hey? Great minds – '

'And we'll see what I can do about stuff for the newsletter, hmm? I'll just need a letter of authorisation from you and then I can get all the information I want. I dare say you can arrange that?'

'Of course,' Leo said as they disappeared into the shop. 'Of course! Now, the cloth I want to show you is just over there. Mary? Hey, Mary! Get me that bolt of eleven seventeen, will you, from the back shelves?' and the door closed behind them with a little snap.

Joel Coplin came out into Frith Street and stood for a moment with his hands in his pocket and his chin up, breathing deeply. It had been an excellent lunch; rather too excellent, for he couldn't remember when he'd last eaten quite so much at one sitting, and he made a little grimace as he remembered the way the others had out-gobbled him with enormous gusto and shown no ill effects whatsoever. He felt stuffed and it wasn't the most agreeable of sensations. Buzzy Lethbridge had been highly amused when he'd been unwary enough to say so, laughing at him loudly, so that the rest of the table could share in his discomfiture.

'Told you Americans weren't used to good food, old boy, didn't I? If you've been feeding on hamburgers and ice cream all your life Laura's has to be a revelation – you'll get used to the right sort of living, don't you fret. Now you're with City, old man, you've no notion how your ways'll change!'

'Buzzy, you're an ignorant slob,' Alistair had said amiably and grinned at Joel. 'Ignore him, Coplin. It's all a pose, you know. He likes to pretend he's your bluff Britisher, that everyone in the world is bloody except Englishmen, and that anything Americans do they have to do worser. It doesn't mean a thing. He's trying to rile you. Don't be riled.'

'I'm not. Not in the least,' Joel said as easily as he could, hating Lethbridge more cordially by the second. 'Just a shade overfed, was the point I was trying to make. An excellent lunch, sir.'

'Don't sir me, for Christ's sake,' Balfour said, and grinned even more widely. 'Or you'll confuse Lethbridge so much he'll blow up. And then who'll pay out our expenses? Glad you enjoyed it. Have you got a folder, by the way? Sally, give Mr. Coplin a folder. Time we pretended to get some work done here, I suppose, dammit – '

Standing now in Frith Street Joel looked back over the past hour with gloom adding to his existing discomfort. He'd joined City because they'd seemed a lively and forward looking company who'd given him the chance to do some interesting work. He'd been happy enough making his commercials in Toronto, and would have been there still if he hadn't had a letter from Jeffrey Charlton offering him the chance to work in England; the award he'd got at the last Cannes affair had clearly been of some value after all, he'd thought, when the letter had come. He knew now that it was a routine thing with City. Anyone who won an award was immediately offered a short term contract; then the company could boast legitimately of the quality of its creative team. It was a shabby ploy, he now felt, and he'd been a fool to be hooked by it, but there it was; the combination of the flattery of being headhunted across the Atlantic and the company's address in Frith Street had been enough to uproot him. And now, he told himself, remembering the way they had talked, now his roots were bleeding damned painfully.

The floweriness of that thought made him grin then; stupid bugger I am, he told himself. They're not that much worse than any of the companies I worked with in Canada, after all. This is a lousy competitive business, the worst there is, so there's always this sort of bullshitting; what am I complaining about? And didn't I get what I wanted? And again he took a deep breath and his stomach began to settle and he felt a little better.

Getting what he'd wanted had been a surprise, seeing that he hadn't realised he'd wanted it. They had talked in a desultory sort of fashion about the work of the previous year; the company had actually made a good deal of money, he heard – a comforting discovery that – and had a fair quantity of bread and butter work lined up; training films for Government funded bodies and one or two big commercial companies, a contract to make a children's series for France and some very lucrative language teaching films for Saudi Arabia as well as some equally valuable contracts for schools' television in Nigeria. But they wanted more than just moneymaking projects, he discovered, listening to Jeffrey Charlton as he prodded at them all.

'It's not enough just to know we're secure at present,' he had said, his voice crackling dryly, and his face set in its lugubrious lines. 'What we need is to make more impact on Channel Four. I want to be a class company, not just a bunch of drears turning over the same old money. *Real* money comes from creative force – and we aren't using enough. I'm sick of seeing other people's logos littering my bloody screen at home. There should be more City stuff – and there won't be till we get some sound documentary ideas. And drama too, of course. That's the new departure for this year, if I get the chance. But it's Docs that matter most at the moment. We're prepared to invest in good ones, right, Buzzy? Yes, right. We're prepared to invest. But we need some better ideas than the rubbish here – ' And he'd flicked disdainfully at his copy of the folder they'd all been given.

Joel had agreed with him. He'd gone through the folder which listed, as well as the previous year's efforts and the still outstanding work for the year, a list of documentary ideas that had been put up by various members of the department, and a drearier lot of turgid rubbish, he told himself, he hadn't seen for a long time. No wonder they'd headhunted him if this was the best work they could field. Anything would be better than what they had; it reflected little credit on him that they'd come after him, even as a routine. They'd have taken anyone new without as well as with Cannes awards, he suspected, who could come up with better ideas than this. There wasn't one that hadn't been done umpteen times before.

'There isn't one idea here that hasn't been done umpteen times already,' Brian Crowner said loudly, and Joel felt even more depressed. Christ, was it so infectious being here that he was thinking the same thoughts as this dreary lot already? Would his own ideas be as useless as this list?

'I mean, look at it!' Crowner went on. 'Surrogate mothers, test tube babies, abortion, teenagers on the Pill – not one the Beeb hasn't done in the last season and – '

'If I'm offered any more gynaecological television I shall throw up,' Charlton said. 'I've seen enough festering fannies on the screen to send me into a bloody monastery. Oh, all *right*, Sally – ' as the girl sitting at the end of the table glowered at him. 'No offence meant, but dammit, even you have to agree we've had enough of that sort of thing – '

'Women don't get all that much air time,' Sally said loudly. 'And if you really want to get to Channel Four it's women you should be thinking about. And there are plenty of viewers who'd rather have fannies than all your macho ballswinging, I can tell you – '

'If we get into another of these pro and anti feminist arguments I'm leaving right now,' Alistair said. 'Sally is right, Jeffrey is right, everyone's bloody right and I don't want to hear another word on it. Sorry, Jeffrey, but there it is. I'm bored out of my skull with hearing the same old business trotted out – '

'Northern Ireland,' Crowner said quickly. 'There are three subjects out of Ireland here. I suppose that's a possibility if it's Channel Four you're after – '

'I wouldn't touch it with a barge pole,' Balfour said firmly. 'Not after the hash the Beeb made last year. Do you want pickets up and down Frith Street? I want no dramas of that sort, thanks all the same. Ireland is out. So is the Middle East and – '

'That's news,' someone said mildly from down the table. 'I wanted to go to Beirut and you know what you said – that was news, not features – '

'Most news is features these days,' Charlton said gloomily. 'The way they comment you'd think the newsreaders mattered more than what they were reading, and that chat came before fact. Anyway, I don't want politics whether it's labelled news, features or crumpet. Not that sort anyway.'

There had been a long silence then, and eventually Crowner had looked down the table at Joel and said with an edge of spite in his voice, 'How about our new boy? Any ideas, Coplin? You can see we need 'em.'

Joel sat staring down at the list in front of him and then said as easily as he could, 'It's a bit of a problem, not knowing enough yet about the company's drift and the sort of stuff you've done in the past. But – ' He lifted his chin and looked at the window and the sliver of sky and scudding spring clouds that it showed. 'I have wondered about something very close to home.'

'The structure and distribution of the hamburger?' Buzzy said and laughed and Joel, with a considerable effort, didn't look at him. Why was this man being so stupidly offensive?

'This part of London – it's rather special. Always has been.'

'Special? Old, you mean? Most of London's old, dear boy,' Balfour said kindly.

'I know that. Even in the wilderness of North America

we know that.' He still didn't look at Lethbridge. 'But there's more to it than age. There's people.'

The silence that greeted him was polite but there was an undertow of impatience in it and he turned his head to look at them all. Sally gazed encouragingly back at him so he spoke what he had to say to her, very aware of the blankness of the other faces around the table.

'I thought it would be interesting to match the people who live in these streets now with some of those who lived here in the past. I imagine there's some still photographs around of the area. Could be some film archive too, once we start looking. Perhaps matching past and present buildings, street activities, see what's changed, what's stayed the same. It'd be documentary because it's social observation, but it'll be history too. Could give it another dimension – depending on the families we find.'

'Genealogy,' someone said flatly from the far end of the table. 'They did that over at Villiers House when I was with the Beeb. How to work out your family tree in ten easy stages. Bit after eleven at night, if you ask me. Won't get much in the way of a rating, even if it makes the Channel. Too specialised.'

'Family trees might come into it, but that wouldn't be the main purpose,' Joel said carefully. The idea was growing in his head as he talked. He'd not planned to say anything at this meeting; indeed he hadn't realised fully until the lunch had started that it was an ideas session at all, but now it was developing inside him like an organic thing.

'What I want to do is show how buildings and streets and the way a district looks affects people. How it becomes part of the – of the fabric of their lives, makes them behave in particular ways, perhaps. It's why people follow in family businesses. It's why they live where they do, why they are what they are, why they marry as they do, even – '

'Impact of environment on personality,' Sally said. 'I like it.'

'I hadn't thought of calling it anything quite so academic,' Joel said, a little alarmed. 'It's just – people and places. That's all. People and places.'

'Nice,' Sally said again. 'It'll be women, of course. Women and houses – they get stuck together, like it or not – ' And she looked triumphantly at Jeffrey Charlton.

'Tracing families round here?' Jeffrey said, and stared down the table at Joel with an even more than usually gloomy expression on his face, which, Joel was beginning to realise, meant he was interested. 'Why round here?'

'Because we're here,' someone said. 'Like Everest,' and there was a ripple of laughter.

'There's a lot to be said for sticking near the office,' Lethbridge said unexpectedly. 'Keeps the location costs down.' And he laughed loudly. 'You're mad to offer this one, Coplin. You'll never be able to pad your exes on a project like this. Honest people, you Americans.'

'The possibility of padding expense claims is not one of my first priorities,' Joel said and now he did look at Lethbridge and suddenly laughed. 'Thank God, I'm not a money man,' he said feelingly and there was a snigger from some of the other people around the table and for a moment Lethbridge looked put out. But not for long.

'We don't have much evidence so far that you're any sort of man,' he murmured and smiled sweetly at Joel and he opened his mouth to answer and then closed it. Not worth the effort.

'So?' Charlton said again. 'Why here?'

'Because it's – it's Soho, isn't it? And because Friese Green worked here – birth of television and so forth. Why not?'

I'm not going to tell them why, Joel was thinking, staring back at Charlton with his face as expressionless as he could make it. That's my affair. I shan't tell them –

Charlton stared back at him and then nodded slowly. 'Any other suggestions?' he asked in a general sort of way, and there was a long and rather lumpy silence and then he sighed and stood up. 'Well, we never do get much out of this affair, do we Balfour?' he said and for the first time his face looked almost cheeful. 'Not that I didn't warn you – the best ideas never come to people over lunches like this. Still, it was a good lunch – '

'I get my best ideas when I deal with the other end of my

gut,' Crowner said. 'Ought to send everyone to sit in the bogs, Alistair. Then we'd get something we really could turn into product.'

'I thought that was just the sort of product we did have,' Sally said. 'Real shit – ' and a few people laughed. But not Charlton. And there was a little silence, suddenly.

'You want me to forget this idea, then?' Joel said wanting to break the quiet and Charlton looked at him, long faced again.

'Of course not. Thought that was understood. Right, Alistair?'

'Oh, absolutely.' Balfour nodded affably at Joel. 'Could be a goer, that one. Get some preliminary research done, bring it in as an offer. Three or four folios, that's all. Then we'll beat Buzzy around the ears and get you a budget for a pilot.'

'Oh.' Joel was nonplussed and knew it showed.

'Never mind, my boy. You'll get used to us and our funny little ways,' Alistair said kindly. 'On your way then. Have a look round, see what you can dig up. See you in a couple of weeks or so, then, hmm? Don't suppose you'll be in the office much till then, hey?' And in a noisy huddle the documentary department of City Television went downstairs and back to the office in Frith Street, leaving Joel standing on the kerb and thinking.

And feeling, he reminded himself, uncomfortably overfed. 'I think what I need is some exercise,' he murmured into his coat collar, and shoving his hands deep into his pockets he turned and began to walk north along Frith Street.

To be paid to wander these streets and nose around among the people and the buildings – now, that was an agreeable prospect. Perhaps getting involved with this company had been worth it after all, if it meant he'd get to know more about the people who lived here. Even his own people –

But that, of course, was a ridiculous thought.

7

At last everything was clean and quiet again. The tables had been cleared and relaid, the floors swept, the Extras stripped and aired. In the kitchen everything shone with the boys' efforts, the bain marie stand, the hobs and ovens, the big stainless steel tables with their mixers and chopping boards, and the water jets in the steamer hissed gently while the fridges and freezers hummed in counterpoint. In another couple of hours it would all start again. There were salads to be prepared, vegetables to be organised, meat to be marinaded, fish to be boned and sauced ready for the evening's trade, but now all was quietness, a waiting watchful breathing time among the blue and white tables, winking with their silver and crystal, as well as in the quiet empty kitchen.

Laura stood at her desk in the corner and closed the cash box and ledgers. A short walk to the bank in Shaftesbury Avenue to put the cash in the night safe, and then she was free till six thirty. There'd be time to go home to the flat and change, after all; she'd been afraid that with all the extra work involved today it wouldn't be possible, but everyone had worked very hard and got straight again much faster than she'd expected, and she felt a sudden surge of intense affection and gratitude for them all. Her staff; good, caring people who gave her so much more for the money she paid them than she had any right to expect; she hoped she showed how much she valued them, that they knew how important they were to her. She gave good wages, a little more than most of the Soho restaurateurs, and she knew that helped to tie her people to the place, but she hoped it was more than that, and she looked up as Angie came in from the kitchen, pulling on his jacket, and smiled warmly at him.

'Thanks Angie. That was marvellous. Anya adored her liver.'

'Didn't she just,' Angie said complacently. 'I knew she would.'

'I'm grateful to you for working so hard – ' she said, needing to let him see how she felt about him, but he looked at her and frowned.

'How d'you mean, grateful?' he said pugnaciously. 'Like I don't always? It's what I'm here for.'

'Of course you do. It was just that, today, it was a heavy load for you. Roasting geese on top of all the usual stuff and – '

'Listen, when I'm too old to do my job properly, then you can be grateful. Right now I'm well able to cope. You don't have to go making no allowances.'

'I'm not making any allowances. Just trying to say I appreciate your efforts. It was a good lunch we had.'

'Sure it was. Isn't it always? For everyone? The day it ain't, you can talk about it, about whether I'm too old. Till then – '

'No one said anything about being old, Angie, for God's sake! I was just saying I enjoyed my lunch and so did everyone else.'

'That you can always say. Any time, Mizz Horvy. Any time at all. Just don't come out with stuff about grateful. I don't need it. Listen, you want anything out? I'm just going for some cigarettes.' She shook her head. 'No thanks. I've got to go to the night safe, and I thought I'd go home for a while. Get a few things sorted out – '

'You do that. You're looking tired,' he said and grinned at her. 'Looks like you're the one's been overdoing it a bit. See you tonight – ' And he went, letting the door swing imperiously behind him and she watched him cross the yard and go straight into Mucky's shop.

Daft old devil, she thought, her affection for him still well in evidence but tempered now with exasperation. If he doesn't stop whingeing on about his age, he'll drive everyone potty. Sixty-five – not that old; why be so conscious of it? And then she remembered how she felt about the way time was running through her own fingers, and how dispirited she felt when she contemplated her own thirty-five years, and grimaced. Perhaps Angie had a point in being so prickly about the subject and then she grimaced again and went purposefully to fetch her coat. Time she went home to Morwell Street and the odd jobs that awaited her there. Staying here and thinking a lot of rubbish about how old people were would get her nowhere.

'Well, how old are you, then?' Kati asked and tilted her head so that the curls on each side of her face swung against her cheeks. She liked doing that. It made her feel nice. It was the only nice thing about not being allowed to put her hair up, having those curls to swing at people. It was interesting the way people behaved when she did it; the way Mr. Bosquet was behaving now, looking at her with his eyes a bit more round and dark than they usually were.

'This is not a question a little girl should ask a grown person,' he said reprovingly and again she tilted her head and laughed at him. It was a new way of laughing she had been practising, low inside her throat so that it sounded sort of bubbly.

'I'm not a little girl, though, am I? You said I wasn't. You said I was shaping up to be a very special lady. Didn't you say that? I remember, so you can't say you didn't say it. You said it last week – '

'*Tu es une petite diable*,' he said softly and then laughed. 'And now tell me you know what that means.'

She pouted. 'Course I don't. I can talk English and I can talk Hungarian, if I have to – I don't want to though. It's horrible, Hungarian is – but I can't talk French. Don't want to. I'm English now. I'm not French and I'm not Hungarian. I'm English.'

'Of course you are Hungarian. You live here in England like the rest of us, but you are as Hungarian as your Poppa's paprika.'

'Poppa's paprika, Poppa's paprika,' she sang, and then giggled. 'Poppa's poker, Poppa's poker, that'd be better.'

'You are a very rude and naughty little girl,' he said and leaned across his counter and pinched her cheek. She didn't move, just sitting there and staring at him, her eyes wide, and liking the way his fingers stayed on her cheek after he relaxed the pressure of his pinch. Being here with him like this was more fun than anything else she could think of, and she giggled softly, forgetting to use her special new laugh and he took his fingers away from her face as though, suddenly, her skin had burned him. Really, being with him was so much fun, much better than being at home across the yard.

She sat and looked down at her lap for a moment; at the dark green plaid dress which she so much hated and the yellowish calico pinafore over it which she hated even more and the thick black stockings and the heavy boots she could see swinging against the side of the mahogany counter, and felt a great wave of misery. It was horrible to be Kati Halascz. It was the worst thing in the world to be and she felt her eyes fill with tears and she sniffed hard, making her nostrils close, so that the tears went to the back of her throat and she could swallow them.

'Oh, I didn't mean to upset you!' he said, alarmed, and came round the counter to stand in front of her and pat her head awkwardly. 'You are not a naughty little girl, at all, of course you are not. You are a nice little girl, Kati. You must not cry – '

She felt better at once. When she got upset at home her mother just snapped at her and her father took no notice. They only paid any attention when Zsuzske whined; they always fussed over *her*, the horrible thing. Now, with another baby around, it would be even worse. They'd ignore her, Kati, even more or just go on and on at her to do things for them. They never patted her head if she started to cry. They just told her to be her age and that meant doing what they wanted. It never meant being fussed over the way Zsuzske was fussed over, and the way Mr. Bosquet was fussing over her now.

It was really much nicer to be here with him than at home with all of them and she lifted her eyes to him, feeling the tears trembling on her eyelashes but not feeling unhappy inside any more at all, and she smiled at him and he smiled back, his eyes looking round like a fish's, again, and she felt even better. He was a *lovely* man, Mr. Bosquet.

'You still haven't told me how old you are,' she said. 'I told you how old I am. You ought to tell me how old you are.'

'It's different for the grown up people,' he said, awkward again.

'Why?'

'When you're young every new year gives you pleasure. You want to be old, a grown up person. But when you are grown up, suddenly you feel different. You want it to be 1899 for ever. It was like everyone last year wanting it to be 1900 and not 1899 any more. New and shining, a new big number. You are still fourteen, fifteen, inside, so you want to stay fourteen, fifteen outside, the way *you* are. You don't want to say, "I am forty-two – " '

'Is that how old you are?' She looked a little awed. 'That *is* old, isn't it? Two years more than Poppa – '

He went a sudden dusky red and went back behind the counter and though she wasn't sure quite what she had said wrong, she knew she'd said something she shouldn't, and immediately set to work to make things comfortable again. It was important to keep Mr. Bosquet nice to be with now that home was so awful. And would get worse, with that horrible, hateful baby in it. All they talked about was Magda, Magda, Magda, when they weren't talking about Zsuzske, Zsuzske, Zsuzske. She turned her body round and pulled up her feet so that she was sitting right on the counter, her arms encircling her knees, and tilted her head and said softly, 'Mr. Bosquet – do you think I could come here and work for you?'

'Eh?' he peered at her and then went on fiddling with the tobacco he had gone back to chopping when he had returned to his side of the counter. 'Work for me? Doing what?'

She shrugged. 'Don't know. Something. Anything. I want to work and get wages. Don't want to go to school *any* more. I don't have to, you know. Now I'm fourteen, I could stay at home or go out to work, Momma says I should stay at home and help her with the babies and Poppa says I have to go to school but I don't want to do anything they say. I want to work. I want to put my hair up and wear proper skirts and shoes, not these horrible boots and I never want to wear a pinafore again, not ever, and be a lady in a shop. *Your* shop. I could talk to the people who come in and give them their tobacco and talk to them and you could sit in your room at the back and have your feet on the fender and be very comfortable. Wouldn't that be nice? You said to me you wanted to sit and read your paper from Marseilles but the customers kept on coming – '

The door of the shop opened with a little ping of the bell fastened above the lintel and she turned her head to see one of the porters from the Italian restaurant in Old Compton Street, a big man with a very shining, bald head. He looked at her and then at Bosquet and grinned.

'Got a new 'elp, John, 'ave yer? Goin' posh are we, all Freiburg and Treyer, like?'

Kati scrambled down from the counter with a great display of thick, black, woollen stockings and went running round to the other side of it 'Oh, Mr. Bosquet, do let me serve him, please, let me? What will it be, Gian? Tell me what you want and I'll get it for you. I know where he keeps all sorts of things – I bet you I can get it for you!'

'A half ounce o' cut Navy shag,' Gian said promptly and she whirled to look along the drawers behind the counter, reading each little brass label with silent movements of her lips, and bending her head so that the shadows thrown by the gaslight behind her didn't obscure them, and then she crowed delightedly and pulled out one of the drawers.

'Here it is – cut Navy shag – no please, please Mr. Bosquet – let me do it! I can do it, you watch!' And she reached for the little scoop that was tied to the side of the counter and released the hook that held the scales so that the pans swung free.

The two men watched her, grinning. Bosquet, now relaxed and leaning on the counter comfortably, seemed quite to have forgotten what she had said about his age, and smiled in a proprietorial way as, with careful and rather elaborate movements, she picked up a scoop of the dark fragrant shreds that filled the drawer she had pulled out, and set it in the pan of the scales against the half ounce weight. She dropped in a few more shreds to make sure the brass arrow pointed exactly centre, and then reached for a sheet of blue paper to wrap it in.

The two men began to laugh then, the big kitchen porter in his dirty apron and heavy canvas trousers, tied at the knees with string, and the dapper Mr. Bosquet, in his tightly fitted black coat and high starched collar, and she peeped up at them from beneath her lashes and then, with the tip of her tongue showing between her teeth – not that she needed to use her tongue that way when she concentrated, but she knew it made people smile – she tried to fold the paper into the sort of triangular bag she had seen Bosquet make many times.

She failed hopelessly, as the thick blue paper sprang out of her fingers and she made a little moué and shook her head and again tried to make it work, and Bosquet smiled and leaned forwards and then, moving a little self consciously, came closer so that he could stand behind her and reach over her shoulders.

'You do it like this, little Miss Butter Fingers,' he said and took her hands in his and moved her fingers for her, so that the paper was folded and then folded again and made into a cone with a twisted end.

'You see? Now you slide in the tobacco, so – ' And he reached for the brass pan of the scales and held her hand as she tipped the contents into it. 'You see? Now you bend over the top, *so*, and you give it to Gian. And you say to him – '

'I know what to say!' she said breathlessly and lifted her head and tilted it backwards so that her curls swept along his face, for he was still standing with his arms around her from behind and his hands over hers. 'I know! Don't tell me what to say, I know!' And she leaned forwards and held out the screw of blue paper to Gian and said triumphantly, 'That'll be a penny ha'penny, please, sir!'

The other man laughed and held out the money which he had ready in his hand. 'Cheap at the bleedin' price,' he said. 'What with the show thrown in.' And he laughed again even more loudly, as Bosquet, seeming suddenly aware of how he was standing pulled away and came round to the front of the counter. 'So you *'ave* got yourself a new bit of 'elp, then, Bosquet?' he said. 'Goin' to be a big operator, are you?'

Bosquet laughed, uncomfortable again. 'This child – she has nothing better to do than come here and waste my time. So I teach her a little. Why not? Her parents should be grateful I look after their children when they are busy. There is a new baby there – you know how it is. I like to be useful to my neighbours. It makes for happy working, hmm? Good neighbours – '

'Yeah,' Gian said and stuffed his little poke of tobacco into his pocket. 'Yeah – neighbours,' and went away, winking at Kati as he did, and she stared back at him, blankly, the way a child would and he looked at her, boredom appearing on his face now. ' 'Bye, Bosquet – see you soon. Don't do nothin' I wouldn't do – ' And the door pinged closed behind him.

'Time you went home,' Bosquet said after a moment. 'Your Momma, she'll be looking for you.'

'She don't care about me. Only when she wants something done,' Kati said. 'Can I, Mr. Bosquet?'

'Can you what?'

'Work here. I'd like that. I did that all right, didn't I? I'd soon learn how to do the paper. I'd make some ready in advance so I didn't have to keep the customers waiting – '

He shook his head. 'You're too young. Anyway, your father'd never let you work here. He wants you to go to school.'

She made that little face again, and once more tilted her head. 'He'll give in. If I go on enough.' She nodded then, knowingly. 'He always gives in in the end to everything. That's how Momma does it. Goes on at him, you see. I'll go on too, if you say I can work here.'

He looked at her, at the way the gaslight glinted on her

dark hair, making it look tinted with dark red, at the round smoothness of her face and the way her pinafore pulled over her bodice. It was too small for her; time they gave her other clothes to wear –

'I'll think about it,' he said uneasily. 'I'll think about it.'

She clapped her hands delightedly and then turned with a little jump so that she was facing the curtained doorway that led to the inner room where he lived. It was getting darker outside now and they could both see the firelight from the inner room flickering over the red plush of the curtain, and could hear the little clattering sound as a few coals fell in the grate and the flames leapt a little higher.

'Come on! I'll make you some tea and some toast at the fire. You'll see what a good helper I am, and then you'll tell Poppa I'm going to work with you. It'll be lovely, you'll see!' And she went into the room literally skipping, and after a moment he moved slowly to the door of the shop and reached up and pulled the little bolt that held it. It was gone six now; he had every right to stop and have tea if he wanted it, didn't he? Every right –

And moving even more slowly and a little heavily now, he went round the counter and into his little sitting room, with its big wooden table in the middle and the wide divan in front of the fire that doubled as his bed at night, and looked at Kati, who was crouching by the fender holding a piece of bread on a long fork to the glowing coals. Her face was shining in the firelight and she turned and looked at him and smiled and the round eyes glittered a little and seemed to laugh, and he sighed and came in, slowing pulling the curtained door closed behind him.

8

The flat felt both stuffy and empty, she thought, as she let the door swing shut behind her, and she stood there in the tiny hallway, her head up, breathing in the air of the place. It smelled of beeswax and furniture polish and the lily of the valley bath salts she favoured and the daffodils that were wilting in a low bowl in the sitting room and, faintly but not unpleasantly, of cat litter and after a moment she moved into the small kitchen and set the brown paper bag from the grocery shop on the work surface.

It was quite absurd to be so melancholy, she told herself as she stood there and stared sightlessly out of the window. Below in the thin afternoon sunshine, the narrow garden lay drooping and dispirited, but there was a faint flush of green on the privet hedges at each side and she knew that somewhere down there in the cold earth the first bulbs were showing their spikes. Soon it would be March and then the winter would really feel over; there was no need to be so low in her spirits. Everything was fine; the restaurant had never been so popular, the staff never so easy to deal with, today's busy time had run as smoothly as a hot knife going through butter and Anya Zsuzske's party was over safely for another year. What was there in all that to make her feel as she did? As though her own life were as half used and empty as this flat, as though she too was little more than a shell which had a function but no real soul, an existence but no true life of its own –

'This is bloody ridiculous,' she said aloud and went to the glass-fronted door that led out to her small fire escape and opened it. The cat had been sitting on the top step and it turned its ruffed head and looked at her scornfully as she called softly, 'Come on, Scatty – I'm back. You can come in and warm up if you like – ' and then stretched and yawned and with a supercilious flick of its tail went past her and into the kitchen to slide its sinuous shape into the small space beside the cooker which was its favourite spot.

'Idiot,' she said to it as it writhed itself into a comfortable position and then settled with its eyes wide and unwinking to stare at her from the darkness. 'It's not as though it's specially warm there. I haven't lit the damn thing for ages – '

That was the trouble, of course. All she ever did here was sleep and perhaps drink a cup of tea as she stood poised for the ring on the doorbell that would tell her the early taxi had arrived to take her to market. She didn't do any real living here; she stored her clothes, that was all. All her living was done in Little Vinegar Yard, at the restaurant. And that wasn't living, was it?

She began methodically to put away her purchases; some catfood, a packet of tea, some disinfectant for the loo, a packet of corn flakes, a carton of UHT milk, because that sort kept best – it was all so impersonal, so unimportant, so dreary, and she stood and looked down at the pack of toothpaste that was the last thing in the bag and thought – if I died tomorrow and a stranger came to clear this flat, they could know nothing of me from what they found. It's as though I'm no one. No personality, *no* one. Just Laura who runs a restaurant and who, when she isn't there, disappears.

'Ridiculous!' she said again, more loudly this time, and went into the living room to switch on the radio and to collect the bowl of dying flowers so that she could replace them with the fresh ones she had bought from the stall on the corner.

She'd give a small party, that was it. Invite a few people, get some food in and do her own cooking. She wouldn't just bring stuff Angie had cooked; she'd be a real person and give a real party of her own –

Who for? asked a little voice deep in her mind. And when? You're always at the restaurant, reckon you can't be spared. That no one but you can do the work properly. How long since you had anyone you could call a close friend, close enough to come to a party here?

Mary? she thought, standing still and staring out of the

kitchen window again, the fresh flowers held unregarded in one hand. Mary – what was her other name? That girl who used to come into the restaurant, who had remembered her from their schooldays together. Mary – but she's married now, she remembered then. Came and told me – how long ago? – ages – that she had met this super man and was getting married and I must come to the wedding. And that was the last I ever heard from or about her. So who could I ask here? The people from the restaurant? Angie? Leno? Customers? She shook her head vigorously at that thought and went on with arranging her flowers. Not to be considered.

Yet who else was there in her life but the people who touched her through her work? She had her restaurant, the money she made and nothing more. Just the work. A successful capable business woman, that's me, with a complex job that I do superbly and a life as dull and tasteless as a bucket of cold water.

Once again she tried to pull herself out of her mood, but that wasn't easy. She wasn't a person much given to introspection; she'd never had time. In the early days running the restaurant, looking after her old parents, had been more than enough. Then, when Poppa had died, she had had to let go of the old flat they had shared and find this one – and a nice enough flat it was, for all its sense of emptiness – and work even harder at Little Vinegar Yard, to keep her mind off the loneliness of not having anyone to go home to at night; so she had not had time to think much. Why she could choose today to do so was beyond her; and once again she found herself standing still and staring blankly at unseen sights while she tried to work out just what had made her so low today. Not miserable, precisely. Not depressed. Not ill. Just a bit melancholy. It must be the weather, she thought; this first February sunshine reminds you it's still a while yet before it gets warm and easy. It's still winter. That's why you're melancholy.

Stupid, the little voice jeered. It's nothing of the sort. It's lunch that did it. All that talk of people's children and who's marrying who and who's doing what. It reminded you that you're not marrying anyone, you're not having children, you're just old Laura who works and makes money for the others and has no other function. Bloody family! she thought with sudden savagery and then was ashamed of herself, for they were, for all their occasional tiresomeness as individuals, a good family and without them all what and who would she be? Even less than she was.

The phone shrilled and she jumped and stood there in the kitchen with her heart actually thumping, and angry with herself for over-reacting so absurdly and then, as the phone went relentlessly on, thumped the flowers on to the table and went to answer it, luxuriously annoyed at being disturbed when she was so busy, and even angrier with herself for being such a liar.

'Yes?' she snapped.

'Laura?' The voice was familiar yet not immediately identifiable and she frowned.

'Who's that?'

'My dear, why so cross? Did I disturb something madly important?'

'Who *is* that?'

'I did disturb you – I'd better call again.' There was a lift of laughter in the voice now and that made her even more sharp-tongued.

'For heaven's sake, either say who you are or go away! I've better things to do than play silly games with – '

'Oh, lawks, I'm sorry, Laura. It's Philip. Philip Cord. Obviously you *are* busy and I'm making a pest of myself. I am sorry – I'll go away. Just tell me when would be a good time to call and I won't bother you a moment before that.'

She stood and stared at the film of dust on the table where the phone stood and then stretched out one finger and made a mark in its smoothness.

'Philip. Oh. Hello.'

'I *did* disturb you. I'm a wretch. Were you about to step into the bath? Or worse still, did you get out specially for me? Are you standing there stark and dripping and hating my guts? I would if I were you.'

'No – I was just – I'd been shopping. Just got in actually.

Sorry if I snapped at you. I was a bit – ' She left it dangling in the air, furious with her own stupidity and not knowing how to extricate herself. 'What did you want?'

'It seems so feeble now,' he said and she could almost see his face. Not a handsome face but a friendly and agreeable one and she felt some of the tension drain out of her as she saw it break into a smile as vividly as though he had been standing there in front of her. 'I just wanted to say thank you.'

'Thank you? What for?'

'A super lunch. It was all so – I don't know. Not just the food, but all of it. The ambience, the warmth. The sheer friendliness of it all. And it was all your doing. Without you to organise that lunch the whole family would just be a bunch of individuals – some nice, some – well, I can say it to you, some absolutely awful. But you pull them together for this lunch in a way that really is – well, I just wanted to say thank you.'

She felt her face go red and actually put up her other hand to touch her cheek. 'Oh, really, Philip. That is way over the top! It's just a lunch. If anyone makes it – all the things you say it is, it's Anya Zsuzske. She's a remarkable old – '

He laughed again, a soft sound that made her face go even redder. 'Dear Laura, you see what I mean about you? You put the best complexion on everything. Dear old Anya Zsuzske is a dotty old bird who cares for nothing except food and lots of it. You know I'm right. A greedy old – '

'Philip, if you go on like that you won't be asked to any more of her parties.' She tried to sound stern but knew she was laughing. It was true, after all. 'You should show more respect.'

'Oh, sod that!' he said cheerfully. 'I don't reckon this notion of respecting people just because they've managed to stay alive a few days more than the average. It's what a person does that deserves respect, not mere longevity. And I wanted you to know how much respect I have for you. You perform wonders there at that restaurant. And not just for the family affairs. All the time, for everyone. Does Ilona ever say how grateful she is for the money you make for her? Does Paul? Or the Ucherguts sisters?'

'The *who*?' she said, momentarily diverted.

He laughed again. 'The Ucherguts sisters. It's a label I use for that awful pair Evelyn and Dolly. They really are the pits. Remember to make it sound really German and ugly,' and he said it again, rolling the word deep in his throat so that it sounded singularly unpleasant. 'It suits them, doesn't it?'

She couldn't help laughing, though she knew she shouldn't. Tiresome as Dolly and Evelyn were, she really shouldn't discuss them outside the family – and then she blinked at the oddness of that thought. Philip was family, of course he was. What else could he be, her cousin's husband? What else could he be but family?

' – they ought to,' he was saying and then as she said nothing added, 'Do they, Laura?'

'Do they what?'

'Say they appreciate all the money you give them?'

'I don't give them any money, Philip. It's their right. They own shares in the business, so they're entitled to share the profits – '

'Without your efforts there wouldn't be any profits. Of course they should be grateful. I keep telling Ilona that but – ' There was a little silence and when he spoke again his voice was different, a little more guarded. 'Anyway, I'm grateful for today. And I just wanted to say so.'

'Well, thank you, Philip.' She smiled and for the first time let her shoulders, which had been held high and tight, relax. 'That was a very kind thought. Though you did say it at the restaurant, of course, not more than a few hours ago.'

'Well, I didn't think I'd said it enough. So I dropped Ilona off at Harrods and then thought, I'll tell Laura. Tell her right now, what sort of a glow she'd left in me for the afternoon. I wanted to share it with you. The way you share all your work with the family. And, as I said, if they don't say they're grateful, then they ought to be made to. You're something very special.'

He was doing it too. Talking about the family as though

it had nothing to do with him, as though they were outsiders and he were blessedly free, on the outside, and suddenly she liked that picture of him and felt a warm glow inside that was so powerful that it came out in words.

'Thank you, Philip. You've made me glow now. It's a nice feeling.'

'Isn't it just?'

There was a short silence and then he said, 'What are you doing?'

'Hmm?'

'Right now. What are you doing?'

She laughed, a soft sound that even to her own ears sounded agreeable. 'Talking to you.'

'What would you be doing if you weren't?'

'Tidying the flat. Putting flowers in water. Feeding the cat.'

'What sort of flat is it?'

'Hmm?'

'Big and glamorous? Small and cosy? "House and Gardens" or "Woman's Own"?'

'Neither,' she said and let her eyes travel round the square room with its heaps of floor cushions and low chrome tables and art deco lamps that had been her grandmother's and which had been taken from Little Vinegar Yard when the upstairs rooms had been made into the Extras. 'I'm not sure how you'd describe it. Dull and empty – ' And then she added, so softly that it was just a breath, ' – like me.'

'What did you say?'

'Nothing. Nothing at all. It's just a flat. Ordinary.'

'I don't believe that.' He sounded vigorous and busy suddenly. 'I get the feeling that you're not doing anything terribly important. Listen, will you make me some tea? Ilona said firmly I wasn't to pick her up till Harrods closes, and that won't be till seven because it's Wednesday – so I was just going to prowl around town, and fill in the time as best I could. It's not long enough to go home and come out again, you see. So, will you take pity on a poor benighted man and give me some tea? Only tea – I had a rather good lunch somewhere – won't bother you with the details – and I'm stuffed with food. But tea would be bliss.'

'But can't Ilona take a cab home? Why do you have to hang around to wait for her?' she said and then was annoyed with herself for being stupid again, for his voice seemed to become cool and remote.

'Look, I don't want to be a nuisance. If you're busy, then, of course, I'll – '

'Of course you're not a nuisance. It's just that – it seemed so silly Ilona having to be fetched and carried – '

'You don't know your cousin Ilona,' he said after a moment. 'But never mind, Laura. I didn't want to make a pest of myself. If it's awkward, then forget all about it. It was just an idea – '

'Don't be silly! Of course you're not a pest,' she said quickly. 'It was just that – I'm not used to – I mean, there's only me here and – but look, do come and have some tea. I could do with some myself. Eating lunch makes me thirsty. I don't usually have so much – it was just that it was the family and – so, please, do come. I'll put the kettle on right away.'

Stop gabbling! her little secret voice commanded, stop making such an absolute ass of yourself, but she ignored it and went on chattering. 'Where are you now? How long will it take you to get to me? I'm in Morwell Street, in Bloomsbury, you know. I have the top flat at number twenty-two – I'm afraid there's no lift so you'll have to climb three flights. There's an entry phone so I'll buzz to let you in – how long will you be?'

'It all depends on how long it takes to get a cab,' he said, and sounded amused and friendly again. 'Say twenty minutes? The kettle should be boiled by then. Twenty-two Morwell Street, third floor. See you.'

And then she was standing with the phone buzzing in her ear and staring at the dust on the table, amazed and angry with herself and, she could not deny, very excited. He had somehow manoeuvred her into inviting him to the flat for tea. She, who never invited anyone here, who had been glooming about the place for that very reason, to have been so suddenly pitchforked into entertaining, and she hung up the phone with a clatter and in a sudden panic rushed to the kitchen to find a duster. To let anyone see the place looking so tired and unkempt would have been embarrassing; that Philip Cord should be the one to see all the dust and the dreariness was more than she could bear, and she went round like a whirlwind, straightening already straight cushions, dusting ashtrays and generally working herself into a tight coil of anxiety.

She had completely forgotten her decision over lunch to tell Ilona not to be so anxious and tense about her husband, and to smile more as a way of dealing with her fearfulness. She was much too fearful herself about Philip Cord's imminent arrival to remember anything at all.

9

The girl on the stage was revolving in a desultory fashion to the heavy rock music that was thumping out of the record player, and doing vaguely lewd things with the vacuum cleaner hose she was holding. Her costume looked rather odd; she was wearing only a frilly starched pinafore with a bib so narrow that her puny little breasts stuck out on each side of it like startled pimples and nothing else apart from a pair of very thick green leg warmers and heavy shoes. Joe Davriosh stopped in the doorway, holding the tatty plush curtains to one side and laughed loudly.

'Christ!' he said. 'You couldn't turn even me on with that one, Don,' he said. 'And everyone knows I got a fuse as short as a gnat's willy. Where'd you get her?'

'I'm looking for a stand-in for Georgie. She's got the flu – '

'More like bloody AIDS, the way she goes on,' the girl on the stage said loudly, still going through her act and making the vacuum cleaner hose loop and curl around the cheeks of her buttocks with considerable skill as she stared malevolently over her shoulder at Davriosh. 'As for turning you on, Joe Davriosh – the girl'd have to be bleedin' hard up to want to do that, I can tell you. Everyone knows about you.'

'That's enough of that,' Preston said. 'I don't take performers who are rude to my colleagues, young lady, and don't you think it. And take off those godawful leg warmers. You look as tasty as last week's toad in the hole. If you're auditioning, then bloody well audition – '

'If you kept this place a bit warmer, you mean bugger, then I'd be able to audition without 'em. It's as cold as bloody charity in here. Listen, do you want me or don't you? I got offers all down the street, you know. You're not the only vaseline in the jar, and don't you think it. I can get all the work I want. I only said I'd come in to do you a favour. So piss or get off the pot – '

'These girls,' Preston said, looking pained. 'It's bad enough I have to be in such a rotten business. Why do I have to spend so much time with such ill bred people? It's possible to be a lady as well as a stripper, madam, and don't you forget it. No, I don't want you. Go and get yourself one of the other jobs, if you can. If I've seen one Bored Little Housewife act I've seen thirty. Original, that's what I want. Ladylike and original. So on your way – '

'Sod you,' the girl said, but there was no animosity in her tone. 'All right then, you mean bugger. I'll do it at the usual rate. If you was anyone else I'd want double.'

'If I were anyone else you'd get half,' Preston said and got to his feet. 'All right. On your bike. Ten o'clock tonight for the first turn. Three more after that. And for Christ's sake put a bit of colour on your nipples. Let's pretend you've got *something* the customers want, eh?'

The two men watched her go flouncing off the small stage into the even smaller wings, cursing loudly as she went and Preston shook his head as he led the way out of the small auditorium to the office at the far side, picking his way through the bald velvet seats.

'A rotten business,' he said again. 'The sooner I can jack all this in and get myself a nice clean berth in a nice clean set-up the better off I'll be. This isn't good for my health.'

He had reached the office now and went to the high backed buttoned leather chair behind the huge leather topped desk. 'I'm getting ulcers, I swear to you, ulcers. So, tell me, Joe, how goes it? What's happening? Not a word have I had out of you for over a fortnight, and you said you'd keep in touch.'

'So I'm in touch. Don't you offer a drink to a man?'

He looked round the office as Preston went to the cupboard behind his desk and opened it to reveal mirrored shelves and a great many bottles and glasses. There were other cupboards fronted with the same glossy veneer as that on the other walls and between them there was a deep green flock wallpaper. The floor was covered in a thick shag carpet in an even more virulent shade of green, and the looped and swagged curtains at the high window which looked out onto a narrow back yard outshone both with their irridescent emerald.

'You've been doing this place up again,' he said as Preston handed him a tall glass filled with amber and ice. 'Last time I was here, wasn't it all purple?'

'Too depressing,' Preston said. 'Anyway, I got bored.'

'Christ, you must be coining it.' Davriosh settled himself comfortably in the deep green leather armchair that faced the desk. 'Why you want the headaches of what we're doing – it's beyond me – Cheers!' And he drank thirstily.

'I can't stand this business. I told you,' Preston said and drank as well. 'However much money it makes, it's a dirty horrible business. Rotten people on the stage and even more rotten people paying money to see 'em. What sort of a business is that for a grown man?'

'Very tasty, I'd say.'

'Not on your life. You come one night and see for yourself – '

Davriosh looked shocked. 'You know I never come in when the punters are in! That'd never do.'

'You see? Like I said, a lousy business. If a businessman like you doesn't want to be seen here, then how do you think I feel?'

'Then go upmarket. Plush the place up a bit, go for the top end of the trade. Get some class girls and class punters, and then – '

Preston shook his head. 'Not enough gravy at the top end. The sort of punters I'd be pleased to associate with, the ones with the money, they're too bloody fly. They expect value for their scratch. The more they've got the more they want for it. Then you have to start getting good acts and they make trouble, what with their big money and their agents – ' He laughed bitterly then. 'Agents! A ponce by any other name, believe me – I tell you, it wouldn't be worth it. The way it is I make a lot of money. It pays me to keep the shows shabby, use bad acts – I mean, did you ever see anything so dreary as that scrubber out there? Varicose veins, an arse two inches nearer the floor every time I look at her – but she's cheap. Got a nasty mouth on her, no class, but she's cheap. I tell you, it gives you ulcers.' He finished his drink and got up to pour another. 'The sooner I'm in with you and Statler full time, the happier I'll be. Just let me know what's going on, that's all I ask.'

He sat down again, pointedly ignoring the way Davriosh was holding his empty glass and lifted his brows at him. 'So? What's been happening?'

'Not a lot. What do you expect in five minutes?'

'It's been a month since you first came to me, Davriosh. A month. Big talk, big promises, and all I've had so far is one lunch and a lot more talk and nothing else. I've given you good money for this – '

'There always has to be development money for new schemes,' Davriosh said and set his glass down on the desk with a little clatter. 'Or do you think I'm going to run my feet off, seeing people, arranging things, for nothing? Why should I beat my head out for you? There's got to be something in it for me – '

'Listen, Davriosh,' Preston said and leaned forwards and tapped the desk under his nose. 'You're in as an equal partner with me, but you haven't put in equal money or anything like it. My investment is money, yours is work. And I want to know what work you've done for my cash. I've got money earmarked for this project I can't touch because I've made a deal with you, and I've put some hard stuff in your hand. A goodly number of C notes you've had and don't think I don't remember how many. So, I want to know what's happening. Is Statler reliable? Is it all going to happen? What's the progress, for God's sake?'

'So, no need to get excited. There's progress,' Joe said peaceably and pushed his glass forwards. 'Listen, you don't have to be so mean with the whisky, do you? I need a drink. It's been a long day, already.'

Grudgingly Preston poured him another drink.

'Now,' Davriosh leaned back happily. 'Progress report. I've been making the searches, know a lot more about how the properties stand. Both of them in the Yard are complicated. I'll tell you that for a start. *Laura's* – well, I'm still trying to work out who owns what there, though I can tell you it's a freehold. The other one, that's interesting.'

He settled more comfortably in his seat. 'It was a freehold a long time, held by Jean Bosquet, French. It was a bloke, see, not a woman.' He looked pleased at his own perspicacity. 'But in the war he got nervous. First war I mean. It was in 1916, it seems, he got worried the Germans'd win, 'nd come over here and clobber him special, being he was French. Barmy, if you ask me, but there it was. So he sold the freehold to L and CD – you know the people I mean. Got that big parcel of property over at Covent Garden as well as here in Soho – you don't? Never mind – it's not important you should. Anyway, Bosquet sold on the understanding him and his family gets to have a long lease so they can keep the business. As I understand it, he wanted the cash for his freehold so he could convert it to gold, in case he had to run away to America or somewhere, but just in case he was wrong and the Germans *didn't* win and come after him, he wanted to be sure he could keep his business. Canny buggers, the French, aren't they? Anyway, that was what happened. It took some finding out, I can tell you but I got my ways. Got people I can talk to – you get real value out of a man with my contacts, Preston. So don't go thinking you're hard done by, because you're not. So all right! Don't look at me so ferocious! I was just telling you. So the shop's on a lease – '

'How long a lease?'

Davriosh chuckled. 'This'll really get you. The old boy agreed a seventy year lease.'

Preston stared at him and frowned. 'So?'

'So this is 1986!' And Davriosh beamed his delight.

'So, again!' Preston said. 'I'm still – oh! 1916 it was?'

Davriosh bent his head once in an exaggerated nod. '1916. The middle of this year, the lease is up. June 24th. Quarter day.'

Preston rubbed his hand over his bald head and grinned.

'So come June we buy,' he said in great satisfaction. 'That makes it easy.'

Davriosh shook his head. 'Not so easy. There's no way the L and CD won't renew his lease. He's got legal rights there – no, it'll take a bit of wheeling and dealing to get him out. Not so easy, believe me. We want the freehold and we don't wait till any lease is up to buy it. That'd be very bad business. We have to persuade L & CD. to part with it now. They'll want to know why, and they'll want a hell of a price. Unless we can box clever.'

'How clever?'

Davriosh grinned. 'Well, there's the Trust, ain't there?'

'The Trust,' Preston said and frowned. 'The Vinegar Trust? Those buggers who make my life a misery with their fussings and their – yes. The Trust.'

'You got it. What we have to do is find a way to make them make a nuisance of themselves there in the Yard and L and CD'll be so glad to get a buyer for the freehold they'll let us have it for flumpence. The thing is, we got to find a way to get the Trust to make a pest of themselves. And I think I know how they can. That don't mean to say it'll work, mind you. It's a bit dicey. But worth a try.'

'The Trust,' Preston said again and lifted his brows, so that his forehead creased. His bald head remained smooth and easy to see in the reflected light from the mirrors in the cupboard behind him, and Davriosh grinned at the oddity of the effect. It made him feel better to be able to laugh at this man behind his fancy desk in his superior office. Always moaning about his business and how much he hated it, and making so much money he didn't know what to do with it all. A man like that was easy to dislike and easier still to laugh at.

'You said there's a fella there you can handle. Remember?' Preston said.

'I remember. I've got a couple of contracts there one way and another. I've been talking to one of them. You know the bloke I mean. Seems a bright enough sort of fella. He's bloody hungry, I tell you that. I like hungry people.'

'I know,' Preston said absently. 'I told you that about

him.' He sat and stared at Davriosh for a long moment and then said abruptly, 'There may be another way round it all.'

'Oh? Not with him?'

'Oh, yes, use him if you need him. He'll come in useful over the other place. No, I have another idea – ' He sat and thought again, staring blankly at Davriosh and clearly not seeing him at all and then grinned slowly. 'Listen, I have other ways of making people play the game the way I want them to. There's someone else can help.'

'Who?'

'If I told you that you'd be as clever as I am. And I like being the clever one. I'll talk to him, see what I can do. You'll just bugger it up, stupid way you go on sometimes. Meanwhile, you go on with the Trust. See how you can get them going.'

Davriosh took a sharp little breath in through his nose. He wasn't going to rise to the bait. If the man wanted to goad someone, let him find someone different. But he registered the insult and stored it away deep in his mind.

'They'll need ammunition,' he said. 'You can't expect 'em to get interested when there's nothing there to get interested in. That's why I came to see you.

'I told you to come and see me,' Preston said.

'I got no message,' Davriosh said easily. 'I came because I got work for you.'

'I put up money. You do the work. And Statler – '

'Never mind him at the moment. It's what you have to do that matters.'

'Have to do?' Preston said in a soft voice. 'I don't *have* to do a thing.'

'You will if you want to get this thing off the ground. Now, listen. This is what I thought. How many sex shops do you have?'

'What's that got to do with anything?'

'A lot. How many? And do you sell wholesale?'

'Tell me why you want to know, and I'll see where I go from there.'

'That shop – tobacconist, right? Sweets, right? So why not newsagent too?'

Preston shook his head. 'No trade there. Little Yard like that – '

'He sells his sweets and his tobacco enough to keep the business going. So why not a few more nice lines? High profit lines?'

Again Preston shook his head. 'I've looked at every outlet on the whole manor. I looked there years ago. His trade, it's all class. Nice people. They buy quality tobacco, top cigars – they're not into porn. If there'd been any business to be done there I'd have done it. It may be a lousy business I'm in, but I'm good at it. Bloody good.'

'You never talked to him?'

'Of course not. I don't waste time on useless outlets.'

'But there could be another use for it apart from taking money,' Davriosh said and laughed. 'Oh, sometimes, Preston, I despair of you, I really do. Call yourself a businessman! Call me stupid? You got to look a bit further than the end of your nose, you know! There's more value to getting some stuff into that shop than just selling it. Now listen – ' And he leaned forwards confidentially. 'I've been looking into it. Been buying a lot of sweets and cigarettes lately. There's a nephew. Works there sometimes, helps the old boy out. He's the only relation he got. Lives over on the Isle of Dogs. A smart fella is Simmy Bosquet. I've been talking to him.'

'So?'

'Told him if he can get his uncle's shop to start stocking some of the right stuff, displaying it nicely, then maybe we can do business. The old man won't hear of it, of course. Not his class of business at all.'

'What did I tell you?'

'So,' Davriosh said, as though the other hadn't spoken. 'So, when he goes away, which he doesn't often do, the nephew takes over the shop for him. Mind you he doesn't go often, the old man. Hasn't had a holiday for over five years.'

'All very interesting, I'm sure. But where does it all get me?'

'So, listen, will you! So, I told Simmy if he can persuade

his uncle to go on holiday for a month, six weeks, we'd pay for the trip. As long as he tells the old boy it's his own money he's giving him, and then – '

'Why the hell should we pay – '

'It's impossible talking to you – you never listen. Do you want in on this business or don't you? I'm telling you a way we can get the freehold and get it cheap. If you'll listen for five minutes.'

'I'm listening,' Preston said sulkily.

'All right. So, Simmy tells his uncle he's giving him a present. Six weeks in France – the old boy likes to go back to visit the place his father came from – and he'll look after the shop while he's away. Okay. You put in the magazines, the really hot stuff, the day the old boy goes away – '

'And the Trust find out,' Preston said and for the first time began to look interested.

'Find out? I should bloody cocoa! I lay a complaint, as a local resident, with the Council, with the Trust, with everyone I can. I'm a respected local chap, got every right to object. I go in one day, see kids there, right? So I complain. Now, just before all this you go to L and CD and offer for the freehold. You don't mind the encumbrance of the lease, you tell 'em. You know about these things. You just want the freehold. You got long term plans for after the old man retires. You know he's old, and you're patient. They get dubious naturally, think there's something going on and look for their share of the gravy. Only then the Trust starts making a drama. So the police get busy and licence questions come up and there you are. They sell their freehold so fast you don't see it for the usual.'

'And how do we get the old boy out, then? So we're the ground landlords, then what?'

'That'll be a doddle. Just get the freehold and we're dealing from strength. But first things first. Okay, then? You'll come up with the money for this? Development money, you see. It's what your side of this business is. Me, I do the work, get the ideas, make them happen. All you have to do is find a few bob. Peanuts to you, six weeks in France.' And he let his gaze roam around the room, at the thick flock of the wallpaper and the leather furniture and the gold pen and pencil on the desk.

'And what about Statler?' Preston said, and again smoothed his hand over his bald head, as though even saying the man's name made him nervous.

'He takes the freehold off our hands. At a profit. Then he gets the lease refused renewal come June. He'll know a way, you see if he doesn't,' Davriosh said promptly. 'And then – ' He grinned. 'Then him and me've got other people who can sort out Laura. While we deal with this stage, he's getting on with what has to be done there. There's more than one way to skin the old cat. A lot more than one,' and he laughed, the same fat chuckle he had produced when he had seen the girl gyrating with her vacuum hose. 'And he's got the right sort of help.'

Preston looked alarmed. 'Has he brought in more people on this? I thought it was a three way split?'

'It is. If there's anyone else to be paid, Statler pays him. And he will. He's got a lot riding on this. He wants that development at Little Vinegar Yard so badly he can almost taste it. He'll pay all he has to get it going. We'll still be in as thirty-three per cent partners, however much he pays to other people to make it happen. We're sitting in the right place, believe me. We went to him with the idea, didn't we? We showed him how juicy it was, didn't we? Well, I did. So, we deserve what we'll get out of it. Don't you worry. As long as you do it the way I said, we're all right. But it takes money.'

'All right,' Preston said, and opened a drawer in his desk and took out a cash box. 'Let me know how much you need and I'll give you half, with the rest when you can assure me the old man's ticket's booked and he's ready to go.'

'And you'll be ready to shift the stock in?'

'I'm always ready,' Preston said and sighed heavily. 'I've got plenty of the horrible stuff. Horrible. It's the only word for it, but what can I do? That's the sort of business this is. The sooner I get out of it the better.'

And he opened the cash box and pulled out a pile of fifty

pound notes. 'You told them there's no question of cheques, I hope? I never pay for anything important by cheque.'

'Of course not,' Davriosh said. 'Who does, when it's real business. No, cash is fine. Now, here's the way I see it – ' And he took a sheet of paper covered with figures out of his pocket and put it down in front of Preston. 'That's what we'll need – '

Outside in the auditorium the sound of the record player started again, and he lifted his chin. 'Blimey, is the show starting already? Time I was off. I can't be doing with being here while all that's going on.' And he got to his feet, tucking the pile of notes Preston had given him into his breast pocket as he went. 'People talk, they see you in places like this – ' And he hurried out into the auditorium. But it took him a good deal longer to get to the curtained exit.

10

Joel walked slowly up the middle of Berwick Street, his hands deep in his trouser pockets so that his coat bunched up behind him, and let the atmosphere of the place seep into him.

He'd been to street markets before of course; they weren't totally unknown in North America, but there they had always seemed contrived, carefully invented and highly commercial arrangements cunningly designed to make people spend their money whether they wanted to or not. But here it was different. This place felt as though it had grown organically, as though the stalls and the stallkeepers had been here for hundreds of years, growing and spreading haphazardly along the greasy garbage-piled gutters, obliterating the shop fronts that lined the streets with the rickety canvas-draped erections that were the stalls, responding always and only to the demand for goods to buy rather than setting out to stimulate the need. Looking at the men in their sacking-aproned busyness and the women bundled in their thick duffle coats with their hair tied in scarves and their grimy fingers peering out of truncated mittens, he could almost see their ancestors standing in the shadows behind them. Their clothes would have been a little different, though not a lot, and some of their wares less lavish, but they had been here, scrabbling the same precarious living the people of Soho always had, selling their meagre offerings to people who could barely afford to pay for them –

He had to stop himself then; letting his imagination run away was no way to make a good documentary. It was fact he was after, not sentimental surmise, he told himself sternly. Look honestly at what you're seeing; don't fantasise. And he did and saw that this was by no means a place where poor people scratched inadequate livings. These stall holders were prosperous and sleek, and taking and making a good deal of money, he decided, and their customers were anything but poverty stricken.

Stall after stall was piled high with exotic and often expensive fruits and vegetables; richly golden pineapples jostled elegant layered green artichokes, lychees and rosy plums and passion fruit and chinese gooseberries sat side by side with crumpled walnuts and glossy pecans, hazels and almonds, and everywhere tomatoes and onions and peppers, carrots and turnips and great green cabbages spilled their colour into the narrow grey street.

And as if that wasn't stimulation for the senses, the scents of them all tumbled around in the air to assault his nose with excitement; the sharp tang of lemons and the sweeter richness of oranges, the bite of spring onions and garlic mixed with the oily reek of car engines and the heavy flowery scents of the women shoppers who were sauntering from stall to stall, teetering on their high heels and dickering, beady eyed with suspicion, with the stall keepers as they filled their bags with food. Money flashed and tinkled into the capacious leather bags many of the stallholders kept firmly at their sides and everywhere there was a sense of busy self-satisfaction. Berwick Street was doing what it generally did so well – moving money and goods from one person to another very briskly indeed.

He lingered by a stall where the display was particularly elegant; fruit had been piled in geometric structures with screws of blue tissue paper between each red apple, and sprigs of plastic grass had been arranged perkily between the rows of oranges, while the whole was fronted by a sheet of artificial grass of an unbelievable green. The stall holder, a good looking man with his hair cut flat across the top of his head to give him the fashionable aggressive look was tumbling apples into a bag from the back of the stall for a fur-coated woman who was standing alongside Joel.

'Not those,' she said sharply, standing on her toes to peer over the display. 'I want these – ' and she pointed to the apples in the front. 'None of your bruised rubbish from the back for me, thank you very much.'

At once the man threw the apples out of the bag back on to the stall and folded his arms. 'Lady, I don't pull down my display for no one. The stuff at the back here's the same as the stuff at the front. You take it or leave it – '

'Then I'll jolly well leave it,' she said loudly and turned and went and the stallholder shouted after her, 'Gawdelpus, lady, wouldn't like to be your old man! What d'you feed 'im on? Rice?' And he guffawed loudly and a couple of the stall holders across the narrow street joined in his catcalling and whooped loudly after the woman who was stamping furiously away across the littered tarmac, clearly mortified with embarrassment.

'That'll show 'er,' the stall holder said with great satisfaction. 'That one – comes down 'ere from bleedin' Mayfair, togged up like a tart on the toot, dickers to the last 'a'penny and then grizzles if you don't give 'er the best you got. 'Igh time she was sent on 'er way. Right, Guv, what can I do yer?'

'I'll have some of those strawberries,' Joel said. 'Strawberries in February – where do they come from?'

'Not South Africa,' the man said promptly. 'You a Jew or an Arab?'

'Neither,' Joel said, startled.

'That's all right then,' the man said cheerfully and thrust the brown paper bag with its punnet of scarlet berries at him. 'Then I can tell yer the truth; Brentford Market, mate, that's where they're from. If you'd 'a' bin a Jew, I'd 'a' said they was Israeli, if you'd 'a' bin an Arab I'd 'a' said they was Tunisian – they'll believe anythin', they will – an' – if you'd bin anyone else I'd 'a' said the South of France. Bleedin' politics – what's they got to do with what you puts in your belly, I ask yer?'

'Do people worry a lot about politics when they buy from you?'

'An' the rest! That'll be eighty pence mate – ta – yeah, they go on an' on about it. There's them as won't buy Spanish on account of it used to be Fascist and them as won't buy Greek on account of – I forget what on account of – and them as won't buy Californian on account of the grape pickers. Me, I'll sell anything, on account o' meself. Anythin' else, guv?'

'How long have you been running this stall?' Joel had picked out one of the strawberries and started to eat it. It didn't taste of anything very much, but it was cool and pleasant on his tongue.

'Since the old man 'anded in 'is lunch pail,' the man said. 'Last ten years, on me own. What's to do with you?'

'I'm – I'm interested in local history. The way families keep businesses going. That sort of thing. Did your father start the stall?'

'Nah – ' the man said cheerfully. ''E got it from 'is dad. and 'is 'ad it before 'im – yes, lady. What'll it be, then? Seventy pence a pahnd, lady, and worth twice that. Go lovely they will with a nice bit of lamb – fresh in this morning, flown special from the fields o' France.' And he winked at Joel as he served the woman who had joined them.

Joel lingered, eating his strawberries because that was easier than carrying the bag away with him, and watched as the man served several more customers, and then blinked as, when the last one went, the man said to him belligerently, 'Well? What else d'you want? You got somethin' to buy, then buy it. Otherwise don't go cluttering up my displays.'

'Sorry if I'm bothering you,' Joel said. 'It was just general interest – I meant no harm.'

'You bleedin' tourists – never do mean no 'arm.' The man turned his head and spat neatly into the gutter. 'But you don't 'arf clutter the place up. All right for you Americans, but some of us got to earn a livin' in this town.'

'Canadian,' Joel said and smiled at him. 'And actually I'm not a tourist – I work here. That is why I'm researching local history. It's part of my job – '

The man looked blank suddenly, every bit of animation leaving his face. 'Oh, yes?' he said woodenly. 'Then I hope you get all you want. Good afternoon *sir*.' And he turned his back with some ostentation and started to fiddle with a box of fruits behind him.

Damn, Joel thought. I've sent him to earth. I'll have to

press the usual button. 'I'm a television director. Doing research for a film,' he said, and at once the man turned back and looked at him and then beamed.

Jesus, but it was depressing the way that bloody television opened every door and crumbled every defence. You ought to be more wary, not less, he wanted to shout at the man. You ought to withdraw even further into your shell, because television people are a bloody sight more dangerous than the tax man or the police or whoever else it was you thought I represented. If I were unscrupulous I could destroy you with a camera and a half hour in an editing channel. But he just smiled and said, 'I hope you can help.'

'Anything you need, squire, I'm the geezer for you,' the man said and lifted his chin and shouted across the street, 'Watch it, you lot! This week I'm Sam Price, apple king of Berwick Street and surrounding parts, next week I'm Sammywell Price o' *Dynasty* – television 'ere I come!'

'That'll be the bleedin' day,' one of them called back, while another set one hand behind his head in an exaggerated model's posture and the other on his hip and minced up and down in front of his heaps of potatoes and onions and cried in a high piping voice. 'Oh, Mr. Producer, can you make me a star too?'

At first Joel was irritated, feeling he'd do better talking to Price on his own but then as several more of the stallholders came wandering over through the few customers in the street, for it was the time of lull before the home going office workers descended to collect their shopping for their evening meals, he changed his mind. The more people he talked to the more likely he was to get the sort of facts he needed, and he squashed the now empty strawberry punnet inside its paper bag and tossed them among the rest of the garbage in the gutter, and put his hands back in his pockets.

'Right, mister, what is it you want? I don't do no naked scenes,' Price said and winked at his now sizeable circle of friends who were listening with broad grins on their faces.

'That's a pity,' Joel said easily. 'I was hoping for a bit of that. Brings in the customers a treat.' He grinned round at them all and then reached into his breast pocket for his small notebook and a pencil. 'Still we can't have everything.'

'Mind you, it's amazing what that Sam'll do for money,' one of the others said. 'Offer 'im a dollar, mister, see what you get.'

'A sight that'll send the customers screaming,' someone said and there was a general laugh. Joel was feeling better by the moment. They were a friendly crowd who clearly all knew each other well, and might well have at their fingers' ends just the sort of information he needed.

'I'll tell you what it is,' he said. 'I want to do a documentary about Soho. The people who work and live here – but not just the ones like you who are here today. It's the ones who had fathers and even grandfathers who were part of the place.'

'Won't mothers do?' one of the men said. 'There's more than a few of us only ever had mothers. We was too poor to have fathers.' And there was another general laugh.

'Uncles, aunts or cousins,' Joel said promptly. 'It's history I'm interested in. Who came here from where, how the district grew, how it changed people –'

'I could tell you some tales,' one man said. He was standing leaning against the pole that supported the stall beside them, and Joel looked at him. He was a small man with a face as wrinkled as the walnuts piled behind him and was wearing a large flat cap pushed back on his head. He looked as though he was never within doors, he was so tanned and leathered. He could be any age, Joel decided. Fifty? Sixty? More?

'Seventy-three years I bin livin' 'ere,' the man said obligingly as though he had heard the thought. 'And my old dad, 'e was the same as me – stayed young and lovely.' And he cackled, revealing a mouth quite innocent of any teeth. 'Died young 'e did. Only eighty-seven.' And he shook his head with great melancholy while his little black eyes glittered with laughter and Joel picked up the cue and shook his head even more sadly.

'Terrible, terrible,' he said. 'A man in his prime. How about your grandfather?'

'Well, o' course, 'e was a sensible man. Kept all the old ways, didn't 'e? Drank a bottle of wine a day all his life and smoked all 'e could get 'is 'ands on and never let the priest get near 'im till 'e passed ninety-five. Now that's what I call sensible. Doing my best, I am, to follow in the old man's footsteps. It's like a duty, ain't it?' And again he laughed and winked and the other men laughed too.

'What's your name?' Joel asked.

'Vittorio Bonner,' the old man said. 'What's yours?'

'Oh. Sorry.' Joel held out his hand to be shaken. 'Joel Coplin.'

'Glad to meet you,' the old man said and someone on the other side said, 'Coplin? Used to be a family called Coplin over at Frith Street. My old dad's auntie, she was a Coplin. Married one of 'em.'

'Bookshop?' Joel said as casually as he could.

'Can't remember that,' the man said, and frowned and Vittorio Bonner pushed forwards, clearly annoyed that someone else had taken the attention away from himself.

'Not really a bookshop it wasn't,' he said. 'More a sort of magazine place. That and papers and odds and ends. I knew 'em. Shut up and went away they did, years ago – before the war, I think. Or not long after.'

'Nice people?' Joel asked, working even harder at being casual.

'Not as nice as us Bonners,' the old man said and cackled and Sam Price, who had moved away to serve a customer, now came back and shouted at him, 'Your lot, mate? Biggest bleedin' thieves unhung they was, and well you know it.'

'Yeah, but nice,' the old man said and grinned again at Joel.

'Now, my family,' Sam Price said. 'They really was a right bunch of villains. Cut your throat for fourpence and hang you out to dry for another 'a'penny. Wicked, dead wicked.' He sounded proud.

'So, listen, these Coplins – they anything to do with you?' the man who had claimed a Coplin aunt said. 'It's not that common a name I don't suppose. Plenty of Caplans around, but Coplins, that's different.'

'My parents emigrated to Canada from here forty years ago,' Joel said carefully.

Vittorio Bonner nodded. 'Then that makes it after the war they went,' he said in a matter of fact way. 'Told you, didn't I? Daft, really. Should 'a gone before, if they'd had any sense,' and again he laughed, opening that black hole of a mouth unappetisingly, and went back to his stall over the road at which a customer had halted.

The other men had begun to drift away too and Joel said with a sudden surge of anxiety. 'Doesn't it surprise you, then? That my family came from here and here I am all this time later?'

Sam Price shrugged. 'Happens all the time, mate. So all that about a television documentary was flannel then? You ain't doing no research for the television? You could have said you was lookin' for your people. We get used to it. You Americans do it all the time, come looking for your roots and that.'

'Canadian,' Joel said and then shook his head. 'You're wrong. I didn't come here on my own account. I *am* making a programme.' Liar, he thought. Liar. Who are you trying to deceive? 'I'm with City Television. It's just – it's only a coincidence my own family being – ' He stopped because again Price was more interested in his customers than in him and after a moment he put his notebook back in his pocket and turned and went, moving dispiritedly up the market towards the Shaftesbury Avenue end. He'd buggered that up good and proper. No one would help him now; he was just another inept tourist making a pest of himself. He'd have to find another way to get his research started. Spend the evening at his desk in his small flat in Holloway making a plan, properly. To just wander around talking to people in this vague fashion was daft. He'd have to be much better organised than that.

He had almost reached the end of the market when he heard the footsteps thudding behind him; and he turned to see the man who had told him about his Coplin aunt.

'Ere, Mr. Coplin!' he called and stopped puffing at Joel's

side. 'You straight about this television programme you're doing?'

'Straight up,' Joel said.

'An' if we 'elps, you'll put us in your programme?'

'I'll try to,' Joel said cautiously. 'Can't promise of course – '

'Good for business, you see. I reckon anything that brings people in has to be good for all of us. Daft, people are. Just say television to them and they all go on like bloody dogs, the way their tongues hang out, pant, pant,' and graphically he mimed an eager dog, his tongue lolling from his mouth and his hands held drooping at shoulder height. Joel grinned. This man was so vivid and so excitingly alive it was impossible not to find pleasure in his company.

'I know,' he said. 'I get uptight about it, the way people behave when I say I'm a television director. As though – ' He shrugged.

'Yeah. As though you was magic. Well, you needn't worry about me. I don't get excited about nothing but Arsenal. But anything what's good for business is good for me. Listen, you want to know about the Coplins, you ought to talk to old Mucky.'

'Who?'

'Mucky,' the man said and turned to go back to his stall, and called back over his shoulder. 'Bosquet, his name is. Got a tobacconist's in little Vinegar Yard. His lot was friends of your lot, as I recall. You ask him.'

11

'What happened?' the old man said, and stood beside the bed staring down at the face on the pillow. It was a crumpled old face seeming to glow with a look of health in the soft light from the light over the bed, which was swathed in a pink cloth. But the eyes were half open, showing a rim of milky blue iris and the mouth hung lax as the breath moved noisily between the parted lips. It was a very sick face, in spite of the pinkness.

The old man looked away, up at the brass plate over the bed which read 'In Memoriam, Annie Zunz' and studied it as though it was of greater importance. 'What happened?' he said again.

The man sitting beside the bed shrugged, his shoulders, elegant in handsome grey Prince of Wales checks, moving with an air of distaste. 'I don't know,' he said. 'I was out trying to do some buying, left him to keep an eye on the shop. When I came back – a couple of hours, no more – I couldn't find him. Then I looked behind the counter and there he was – '

He looked gloomily at the face on the pillow and his own face seemed unnaturally smooth in contrast. 'Doctor said it was a stroke.'

'Terrible thing,' the old man said. 'Terrible.'

There was a little silence and then they both moved, like startled children, awkward and stiff, as a nurse came importantly through the screens. She ignored them both and went to the bed, and with a quick twist of one hand pulled aside the pink cloth over the light. They could see the pillowed face more clearly now, and it no longer looked healthy. The skin was yellowish and parchmenty and the eyes looked even more dead than they had under the pink glow. The younger man shifted his feet and turned away, but now the old man seemed less anxious and better able to look.

The nurse leaned over the body in the bed and began to pat the sagging old cheeks. 'Mr. Boskett!' she said. 'Wake up! Mr. Boskett!'

'It's a French name,' the old man said. 'Bos*quet* – he won't answer if you don't say it right. It upsets him.'

The nurse threw him a look of cold dislike and turned back to the patient and this time pinched his cheek. 'Mr. Boskett – ' she said. 'Wake up, Mr. Boskett!'

The uneven stertorous breathing went on and there was no movement of the eyes and she straightened her back and reached up and twisted the pink cloth back into position and went rustling away, and the old man moved nearer and said softly. 'Jean? It's me, old chap. It's Abner Coplin, old fellow. How are you?'

The younger man moved forwards, one hand held out to stop the other, but then he stood still as the head on the pillow jerked slightly and then turned and the eyes opened wider.

'I knew you was there,' Abner Coplin said with satisfaction. 'That nurse, you wasn't going to answer her, were you? No. Nor would I.' And he pulled the little stool that the younger man had been sitting on closer to the bed and sat down so that he could lean closer to the yellow face.

'I told you!' the younger man said suddenly excited. 'When I phoned you. I told you, didn't I? It was only after we got him here he went like that, all quiet.'

The older man ignored him. 'You wanted me, Jean. You wanted to talk to me?'

The head on the pillow turned again, fretfully, and the eyes opened wider and the sound of the breathing changed, losing its rhythm. It was a few moments before either of them realised that he was trying to talk.

'Take it easy, old fella,' Abner Coplin said. 'No need to get upset. We've got all night if you want it. Don't you fret – ' And he began to pat the old man's shoulder rhythmically, as one would pat a restless child.

'He was talking before,' the younger man said doubtfully.

'Honestly, he was, Uncle Abner. I'd never have sent for you if he hadn't, but I heard your name clear as you like, "Abner", he said and then he said it again, and when I said I'd tell you, he was all right. I mean, he stopped being so agitated. So we brought him here and – '

'Be quiet, Yves!' Abner said. 'Can't hear a damn thing, the way you're going on – ' And the younger man frowned and tugged at his tie to neaten it, clearly irritated.

'Where's your sister?' the old man said then, and looked back over his shoulder. 'Go and talk to her, leave me with your dad a bit. He wants to talk, and he can't while you're here. Don't upset yourself. You know how it is, he's an old man, got things to tell an old friend. Go and find Marie.'

Yves frowned, opened his mouth and closed it again and then shrugged and pushed the screen aside. Beyond them the ward stretched dim and silent in the night and he straightened his tie again and went out, his back stiff with self-consciousness. His patent leather shoes glittered in the dimness and his very white shirt shone with an almost fluorescent brightness as he went on tiptoe past each humped red-blanketed bed towards the door at the far end.

There was a nurse sitting in a pool of light at a table in the centre of the ward and she looked up at him as he reached her.

'That person with your father – he's a relation? Even when people are on the Danger List it's only visiting for relations, you know,' she said in a piercing whisper and Yves blinked at her.

'Uncle Abner?' he said. 'Oh, he's – '

'Ah, his brother, is he? Then that's all right,' the nurse said and returned to her writing. 'As long as no one else comes. Can't have hordes of people rushing in and out in the middle of the night, can we?'

'You said he was dying,' Yves said.

The nurse looked up at him, and her face was smooth and professional. 'Even so,' she said with an air of bright reasonableness. 'We can't disturb all the other patients, can we? No. But since he's the brother, there'll be no problems. Are you going now, then?'

'No. I'm going to sit with my sister. She's very upset, waiting outside, very upset. My father wants to talk to – to his brother.' He smiled at her suddenly, enjoying telling lies to this hard faced young bitch. 'Wants to be private with him. So I'm going to sit with my sister.'

'I doubt he'll get much sense out of him,' the nurse returned to her writing again. 'He's in a coma, after all.' Yves looked down on the froth of white lace on the woman's head and wanted to spit on it. But he went quietly down the ward and out through the big whispering double doors to the room where his sister sat, her back slumped and her face blank, waiting for her father to die.

It was a long time before the old man reappeared, shuffling a little, to come and stand in the doorway of the little cold room where they sat, surrounded by the dullness of green and cream paint and shiny horsehair stuffed chairs. They had been sitting talking softly in a desultory fashion, feeling like strangers, as though when faced with the awful reality of death both of them were locked securely inside their own skins and couldn't signal out, not properly. All they could share were platitudes and sillinesses; none of the fear of their own eventual deaths that was filling them, or the pushing, eager thoughts about the old man's property. They were discussable matters but they had to lie lumpen and dead in the air between them. So when the old man stood there blinking at them from the doorway they both jumped to their feet to greet him with a little flurry of enthusiasm.

'Sit down, Uncle Abner, sit down. You must be feeling dreadful – so tired. Time you were asleep, not sitting here with us this way – '

'I'm not that old,' Abner said sharply. 'Your dad and I are old friends, but I'm the younger one.' He blinked again and said pugnaciously, 'Eighteen years the younger one. Seventy next month, I am. Not that old. Your dad – he's eighteen years more than me.'

'Yes,' Marie said and smiled at him. That made her look young again. Usually she looked a great deal more than her thirty seven years. 'I remember, of course. But sit down all the same. How is he? Should we go in now?'

Abner shook his head and came to sit down and as he folded his lanky shape into the high backed stiff chair he seemed, for all his protestations, to look as old as the man in the bed behind the screens. His face was drawn and greyish and his eyes seemed dull.

'I wouldn't,' he said. 'He's gone back to sleep.'

The euphemism joined the unspoken words to lie heavily in the air and the three of them hovered there, still and silent; Yves in his natty suit and shiny shoes and eloquent tie and Marie in her rusty black widow's clothes, holding her big bag awkwardly in both hands, and the old man in his crumpled grey raincoat.

'Oh,' Yves said and sat down again.

The silence grew between them and then Marie said carefully, 'It could go on like this a long time, couldn't it? When Maman died, I thought then – ' Again the silence fell and then she said loudly, 'I have to think about Simmy. He'll wake up and if I'm not there – '

'You go, Marie.' Yves seemed to rouse himself. 'I'll stay here till morning. I'll have to go then to open the shop of course – ' He stole a look at Abner then. 'Did he say anything about the shop?'

Abner had been sitting slumped a little forwards, his arms on his thighs and his hands dangling between his knees. 'Mmm?' he said and looked up.

'Did he say anything about the shop, Uncle Abner?'

Abner looked at him, his eyes dark in his lined face and seemed to be looking a long way through and beyond him and Yves said, 'Uncle Abner?' again, carefully, as though he were speaking to a child.

'How old are you, Yves?'

'Me?' Yves was mystified. 'What's that got to do with anything? I'm thirty six, since you ask.'

'Not married yet,' the old man said and Yves went a rich and sudden crimson.

'He's got time,' Marie said, quickly. 'Like Dad. He didn't get married till he was past fifty, Dad didn't. Did him no harm.'

'No,' the old man said. 'I suppose not.'

'What did he say about the shop?' Marie was brighter now, her eyes losing their shuttered look. 'Obviously he said something to you.'

'Oh, yes,' Abner said, not taking his eyes from Yves. 'He said something.'

'So?'

'So it was private,' Abner said and now he did look at her.

'Private? What can be private? This is our shop, isn't it? Our living – '

'My living,' Yves said swiftly. 'Mine. You got your share when you got married. Your dot – '

'Dad didn't know then I'd be a widow so soon,' Marie said and stared at them with her eyes even brighter now, almost eager. 'He must have taken that into account when he – after Malcolm was killed, he must have taken that into account.'

'He did,' Abner said. 'Right after your Malcolm was killed, God rest him, he told me, he'd taken it into account. He was insured well, wasn't he? Malcolm?'

Marie looked guarded suddenly. 'Well enough. What's that got to do with – '

'What it's got to do with me is I got your father's will.'

'You – what did you say?'

'I got your father's will,' the old man said wearily. 'He made it a long time ago. Kept adding bits, taking away bits, but the last one he made was when he had that pneumonia. It's the same one now that he made then. It was after your Malcolm died, God rest him, Marie, so he knew what he was doing.'

'What was he doing?' Yves said, and his smooth round face looked pale and hopeless suddenly, and he smoothed his hand over his glistening head and then wiped the brilliantine from his palm on to the very white handkerchief he took from his pocket.

'Looking after you,' Abner said gently. 'He's left the shop to you, for your lifetime. After that it goes to Simmy.'

Marie took a sharp little breath in through her nose. 'To Simmy?'

'To who else? His only grandson.'

'I'm his only daughter – ' Marie said, and her voice had risen now to a sharpness that was quite new. She looked alert and eager and far from the drooping tearful creature she had been.

'A comfortable widow,' Abner said. 'He said to me, a comfortable widow. In your lifetime you've got the pension from the army, the money from his family and the house. For your life, right? Jean told me you were all right. And you're a young woman. You could marry again. And if you did, and you have more children another man won't care for Simmy the way his own grandfather would. So he said, the shop to Yves and then to Simmy.'

'Marry again!' Marie said bitterly and lifted her chin. 'Is it likely? I ask you, is it likely? Men like Malcolm – there aren't a lot of men like Malcolm. All of them killed in the war, men like Malcolm.' And she stood there, her small dark eyes glittering at them from her white face and they gazed back at her and saw what she meant them to see; a plain woman, with a sharp meandering nose and a broad chin that unbalanced her face, and a muddy complexion that seemed to have no life in it at all and after a moment Yves said awkwardly, 'When you come out of mourning, Marie, feel better, get some new clothes – '

'New clothes!' she said, and her disgust was even greater. 'What difference would that make? Even if I could get them – who's got coupons for clothes? Who gets married with *clothes*? I'm going home to Simmy. He'll wake up. Let me know if anything – I'll be back in the afternoon, if I can get someone to look after Simmy.' And she went, letting the green painted door swing behind her so that a great wave of hospital scented air, rich with carbolic and ether and ailing people, come washing coldly over them.

They sat on for a while and then Abner said carefully, 'Did he ever talk much to you, your father? About himself, I mean?'

Yves lifted his head and looked at the other man and his face was smooth, carefully clear of expression.

'You know we never got on,' he said after a long moment.

'Him and me – we never got on. Not after my mother died, especially. He never talked to me much, before, but after – We ran the shop, that was all.' His eyes glazed over and he seemed to be staring back down the long corridor of the years. 'Pity, really. He wasn't so bad, I suppose.'

'He's not dead yet,' Abner said sharply.

'Might as well be,' Yves said. 'You know as well as I do – a man his age, a stroke like that. Do you want him to live?'

'No,' Abner said after a moment. 'He's too good a friend for that.' His eyes filled with tears suddenly. 'I'll miss him. A good friend. We talked a lot.'

'You talked for me, eh?' Yves said and smiled, a little crookedly. 'No, don't feel bad. It wasn't your fault. Nor mine. Not even his, really. We just didn't get on. He seemed to like other people better than me, and other people's kids. Always did. I remember, when I was little, the way he used to be with the other kids in the Yard. Ask those Hungarians, always coming over they were. The mother and the kids – my mother hated them, you know that?' He grinned, suddenly reminiscent. 'She said they were peasants.'

'Your mother was more French than anyone in France,' Abner said and grinned too. 'And the longer she lived here the more French she got.'

'A snob. A terrible snob,' Yves said fondly and his eyes filled with tears and he shook his head. 'It was bad enough with him before she died. After, when I had no one – ' And he took out his handkerchief again and fastidiously but without any embarrassment, dried his eyes and patted his nose. 'Still, I mustn't talk ill of – '

'He's not dead yet,' Abner said again but not sharply now. There was resignation in his voice.

'What was it he wanted so badly?' Yves said after a long silence. 'When I found him he was in such a state – kept on about you, on and on. Not till I told him you'd come to the hospital to see him did he go like that – ' And he jerked his head towards the door. 'It must have been important, he got so upset.'

There was another pause and then Abner said carefully, 'Not that important – just something he wanted to get off his chest. Confession and all that – you know how old men are.'

'No,' Yves said with a little edge of spite in his voice. 'I'm not that old. Thirty-five isn't that old.'

'You know how fast that thirty-five years has gone?' Abner said. 'Well, I'll tell you something. The next thirty five'll go in half, a quarter the time and then you'll be where I am. Seventy. Remember I told you.'

'What did he want? It was more than just talking. It was urgent. I know urgent when I see it.'

The door opened with a sharp impatient sound and the nurse put her head round. 'Mr. Boskett? I think you'd better come now. I'm afraid your father is moribund – he will pass away very shortly.'

'Die,' Abner said loudly. 'He's going to die. Not pass away, *die*.'

The nurse ignored him. 'You can stay for a few minutes if you come now, but I'm afraid you have to go then. The day staff will be here at seven thirty and you can come back, but soon the patients will be waking, so you'll have to go.' She looked at her watch and pursed her lips. 'Almost half past four, I really must get going.' And she vanished and Yves went to the door to follow her back to the ward.

'So you can't say what he wanted?' he said to the old man as he stood there, holding the door knob.

'It's not important,' Abner said. 'Trust me, Yves. It's not important. Just something from years ago. Before you were born. Not important.'

He watched Yves go, and sat there in the silent cold room and stared at the blackness of the window. Who could say what was important? Who could ever say? It had been important once, long ago. It was important still to the old man in the bed in there, sliding out of life as fast as he decently could. But important now?

Abner Coplin shook his head at the dirty black window and said aloud, 'Not important.' Certainly not important enough to upset so many people over it. He'd told the old man he'd sort it out so that he could die happy, and so he would. By saying nothing at all about it to anyone. Ever.

12

'Do you know,' Laura said, 'you never did tell me what it was you wanted to talk to me about.'

He tilted his head at her in a way she now knew was characteristic of him. He would never say as others did, 'What did you say?' or, 'What do you mean?'; he would just tilt his head into that alert birdy posture and look at her, and it made her smile now, as it always did.

'After Anya Zsuzske's lunch, you told me there was something you wanted to talk to me about. And you still haven't.'

He smiled, lazily, and reached for the bottle in the ice bucket beside them and refilled both their glasses. 'Yes I did. I wanted to tell you what I was sure that no one else ever told you. That you do a marvellous job, and I for one appreciate it if no one else does.'

The glow that seemed always to be there within her these days intensified, reaching her neck and cheeks, and she bent her head to stare into her glass of wine.

'Thank you kindly, sir, she said.'

'All right, I get the message. No more praise. It makes you uncomfortable and you'd really rather I bit my tongue, thanks all the same. It makes you blush to be admired and so on and so on. It shouldn't, of course. If you'd been treated all along as you ought to have been, then you'd be able to accept a compliment as your just due and relax and enjoy it. As it is – ' He shook his head. 'As it is, I've got to work hard to make you change your view of yourself. Are you enjoying this?'

'Mmm?' She looked up at him, startled, and he was still smiling and she liked that and smiled back, not caring any more whether or not he could see the pink on her cheeks.

'The restaurant. Your dinner. The evening. Are you enjoying it?'

'The wine waiter's a bit slap-happy,' she said. 'You shouldn't have to pour your own wine. And I'm a bit suspicious about the vegetables – frozen peas this time of the year – not quite the thing, is it? And the – '

She caught his eye, amused and gleaming, and this time the pink became a flood of embarrassment that made her cheeks feel as though they were burning.

'Oh, God, how awful! I'm so sorry, Philip. It's lovely. I'm having a super time, the food is divine, the wine is superb, you're a superb host and excellent company, and I do beg your pardon.'

He laughed so loudly that other people in the restaurant turned and stared at him, but he wasn't at all put out.

'I do *like* you, Laura. You're funny as well as nice. Of course you can criticise the place, even though I chose it. Dammit, you're a professional. I wouldn't be at all impressed if you were the sort of person who just bleated, "Yes sir, no sir, three bags full, sir." Vigorous and intelligent opinions, that's what I like.'

'Then that's all right,' she said. 'I'm not a lot of good at being polite. Mostly, I keep quiet. It's safer than talking. I've talked my way into too much trouble in my time. It's safer to bite your tongue.'

He shook his head irritably and then leaned forwards and put his hand over hers. 'That's ridiculous, Laura. Why should you bite your tongue when you have something to say? I'd always rather be with people who took risks than people who play safe, and so never do any real living. Wouldn't you?'

She stared down at his hand on hers, amazed at the fact that she hadn't snatched it away. This was all getting ridiculous, she told herself. Absolutely ridiculous. Here's a married man, married to my own cousin at that, and I'm flirting with him. And liking it.

For once, she left her hand where it was. Usually she pulled away quickly when he touched her, but not this time. 'I'm not sure. People who take risks for themselves may be all very well. But so often they don't just take them for themselves, do they?' She looked at him now. 'When you play dangerous games you could be hurting other people.' She made her voice sound as deliberate as she could. 'And I don't think I'd be very comfortable doing that.'

He seemed to pick up the message because, moving very casually, he took his hand away. 'It depends. On the person who might be hurt and *their* behaviour. Some people deserve it.'

She shook her head. 'That's not really the point. The fact that someone behaves – oh, I don't know, in a way you don't like, say. That doesn't give you permission to hurt them, does it? You may not like what they do, but that doesn't make them wrong. Just different from you.'

'Don't make judgements, you mean? Fair enough. But surely you must agree that sometimes you have to work out who is going to be hurt the most and who the least by a particular course of action, and then choose? In some situations, pain is inevitable, isn't it?'

'Well, yes, I suppose so. But in that case I reckon I've no right to – to satisfy myself at someone else's expense. Not unless they know I'm doing it.'

'That would make it better?'

'Yes,' she said and picked up her glass and began to drink, carefully not looking at him.

These conversations, elliptical, apparently casual, yet laden with personal meaning, were becoming a feature of their evenings together, and she knew soon they would have to move away from them and start to be honest, talking about what was happening to them in direct language. But she shrank from being the one who pushed them to that stage; it was all too complicated, too difficult. Enough to enjoy the moment, surely? Couldn't she be allowed to have just a little fun and not have to worry all the time about the effects of her fun, the way she did? And for a moment she felt maudlin tears begin to rise and thought – I've had too much wine. Careful.

Across the table he leaned forwards, and offered her a small cigar, and she shook her head, amused and yet gratified. She didn't smoke and never had, and he knew she didn't, yet he was punctilious always about offering her one of his little cigars and she sat and watched him light it, giving it as much care as he would a Corona Corona, and let her mind slide back over the past six weeks.

Only six weeks – it seemed so much longer since that afternoon when he had come to her empty little flat and settled himself into the sofa and talked so lightly and amusingly over the tea she had made for him and made the whole place light up with excitement. For the first time the flat had felt real to her, a true home and not just the place where she washed and slept and kept her clothes. She couldn't remember a word of their conversation; only that they had talked at a great rate, she almost as much as he, and had laughed a great deal. It had all been so relaxed and comfortable that not until he had left, after making a plan to meet for dinner the next evening, 'Because it is quite absurd that you can't ever take an evening off – of course you can have more than just Mondays' – that she had remembered with a small shock that he was Ilona's husband.

She had struggled with herself a good deal over that; to spend time with a married man seemed wrong, even in these enlightened modern times. It might be all right for other people to swan around, not caring whether people they liked had commitments to others or not, but that wasn't her way at all, Laura had told herself fiercely over and over again as she had gone through the evening's work at the restaurant. All the time as she welcomed her customers and talked platitudes with them and recommended dishes and kept Angie soothed in the kitchen and made up her ledgers, she had thought about the plan they had made.

They were to go to the theatre and then have dinner ('somewhere totally un-Hungarian!' he had said gaily. 'I'm not sure where yet, but I promise you not a hint of paprika, not a whisper of gulyas. It's time you had some variety in your life. Culinary variety I mean. I bet you haven't eaten any food but Angie's for years!') and she hadn't been able to deny that she very much wanted to go with him. It would be lovely to see a play; it had been years since she had, years and years, because of the pressures of the restaurant, and as for eating in someone else's establishment – the idea was breathtaking in its unusualness. But still she had struggled with her conscience, seeing Ilona's forehead with those two sharp lines between the brows every time she closed her eyes.

But even while the struggle was going on behind her smiling polite professional face she knew what the outcome would be. She would go. All right, so he was married. What had that got to do with anything? She wasn't planning any sort of siren act. She wasn't going to have an affair with him, for heaven's sake! He was just a nice man who was comfortable to be with and who had taken pity on her solitary state and decided to give her some fun – that was all.

But of course it wasn't. That first evening out had been so delightful that it had seemed inevitable that it should be followed by others. She had managed to insist that they restricted their meetings to Mondays, when she was normally away from her work, and had refused to allow him to take her away from the restaurant at any other time, but that had been as far as her protests had gone. She had tried to talk about Ilona, and what she might feel about the fact that her husband was taking out her cousin, but he had brushed that aside, laughing at her a little.

'My dear Laura, what sort of people do you think we are, for heaven's sake? Suburban drears who live in each other's pockets? You mustn't let your view of how married people behave these days be governed by your memories of your parents! The old Hungarian ways aren't the new ones. Ilona has interests and friends of her own, and so do I. To suggest otherwise would be to insult her, don't you think?'

She had capitulated at once, embarrassed to have displayed so much naivety; it was dreadful to have reached thirty-five and not to know more about how people behaved. If she'd ever thought about marriage at all – which she hadn't – she would have assumed, she realised now, that indeed modern married couples *were* like her parents had been. Her mother always subservient to her father's control in public, however much she managed to run their private life behind the scenes, and, certainly, she had taken it for granted that the two of them were always together. Except, of course, when men's affairs and interests demanded that Tibor should be free to spend an evening with his cronies, which he did often since that was what men did, and who would dream of arguing with that? Clearly, Laura told herself, she had a lot to learn, and so stifled her doubts about Ilona when she agreed to accept yet another Monday arrangement.

But she couldn't stifle her doubts about going any further than that. Inexperienced though she was, she was still able to realise that Philip found her more than just good company. He had a way of letting his hand linger on hers when he shook it, or on her arm when he walked beside her, that made her feel very odd indeed and it was obvious he felt the same way. But she made it as clear as she could that she would not, indeed, could not, have a full blown affair with a man who had a wife with whom he lived. Whether she would go further if that wife were living away from him was a thought she refused to entertain; all she knew was that now she had to be careful. Philip was getting more and more important to her, and that meant it was more and more essential to keep the barriers up between them. But, oddly, it was these very constraints that made their evenings together so memorable and so charged with excitement and feeling.

They would meet at the Waldorf Hotel; he had wanted to collect her from her flat but she had felt obscurely that would somehow be wrong, more risky, and more cheating of Ilona. Quite why she had this idea she didn't know; it was probably irrational, but she didn't care. That was how she felt, so the Waldorf it was.

They would sit in the big central lounge where bored waiters served large afternoon teas to large American tourists and an even more bored pianist tinkled pretty nineteen thirties and forties tunes on the piano, and talk and laugh and talk again, licking the cream from the cakes from their lips and protesting that they were eating far too much and it wasn't healthy and then eating more.

They would embark on elaborate guessing games about the people at the neighbouring tables, giving them names and places of origin and then listening in to their conversations shamelessly in order to check on how close they had come to the truth, Philip in particular going to such lengths to hear what was being said that he almost fell out of his chair sometimes, he tipped it back so far; and Laura would stifle her giggles and egg him on and enjoy herself more than she could remember ever doing.

It was as though she were now able to do the silly things she should have done when she was sixteen, but never had, and to have found in Philip someone who would share the fun was more than she could ever have hoped for. He did outrageous things, smuggling spoons and forks out of the lounge by tucking them into his socks, and then solemnly presenting them to the mystified hall porter as he left, telling him he'd found them in the men's lavatory; or writing passionate notes, pulsating with emotion and innuendo and arranging for them to be delivered by marking them for various room numbers and leaving them in the pigeon holes at the desk for unsuspecting guests to collect and explain to their amazed spouses. It was adolescent, it was silly, and it was wonderful.

She found, too, that she had a greater taste for the theatre than she had ever known. She had seen plays in the past of course, when her brother Alex or her cousin Paul had had small parts, but that was rare, for both of them worked mostly in television, when they worked at all, but never had she been a regular theatre goer. Now, as Monday succeeded Monday, she became more and more knowledgeable about the shows he took her to, and enjoyed them more in consequence. Whether it was 'Forty-Second Street' at Drury Lane or 'Me and My Girl' at the Adelphi or something serious at the National Theatre over the river, she revelled in it.

And then of course there were their dinners; he went to a great deal of trouble to find new places for her and new taste experiences. They had eaten sushi in a Japanese restaurant which she had noted interesting but lacking in substance, and Italian, which she felt was inferior to her beloved Hungarian but had some useful features, and Greek which she adored and Indian which she didn't. Altogether he was educating her in ways she now knew she should have been long ago; to be a restaurateur and to be so busy about your own establishment that you never paid any attention to others – silly in the extreme. There were ideas to be gathered, new methods of business to be learned by watching others. So watch she did.

But mostly she concentrated on Philip. As the weeks went on she found him more and more amusing, more and more easy to be with. She would have found it difficult to tell others what it was he said that made her laugh so much. Often she knew the jokes would have been banal if they had been repeated and that the conversations that reduced her to tears of mirth were downright silly, but it wasn't the content of his speech that delighted her so much. It wasn't even his manner of talking. It was a combination of those and something else besides which she couldn't define.

She would lie awake at night sometimes, trying to do just that, to itemise what it was about him that made her behave so foolishly. For she felt foolish, gloriously foolish. She would whistle tunelessly in a soft happy hiss as she worked, and smile at her guests and chatter to them in a much more animated way than she usually did, and it had been noticed. There were some who asked her if she had been on holiday, to look so well, and others who commented on how much her new hairstyle suited her (she hadn't changed it at all, of course) and one prescient man who said jovially, 'You look as though you're in love!' who made her blush so furiously she had had to make an excuse to go out to the kitchen till she cooled down. If that wasn't foolishness what else could it be?

Because of course I'm not in love, she would say to herself, staring up at the dark ceiling of her bedroom. Of course I'm not. It's just that I was bored, had got into a dreary rut, and Philip has pulled me out of it. I'm having fun and it's that that makes me look different. It's nothing to do with the way Philip is. Not really.

But tonight, she was finding it difficult to believe that. It had been an even better evening than usual; they had gone further afield, for a start, than they generally did, to a jazz concert at the Barbican, and he had chosen a restaurant that was deep in the City, well off her usual Soho track, and from the start there had been an extra tension between them.

She had sat beside him in the dimness of the big concert hall, very aware of the pressure of his thigh against hers. The seats were different here, long and benchlike and though roomy it was possible to sit very close to one's neighbour and he had chosen to do just that. The fact that they were listening to music rather than concentrating on a play meant that she couldn't take her mind away from him. For the whole of the two hours she had been constantly aware of him, of his touch, his smell, his nearness, in a way that had been at first exciting, then alarming and eventually deeply disturbing. She wanted more than this closeness; quite what, she didn't want to think about, but she definitely knew she *wanted.*

And then, over dinner, the repeat of one of those circular conversations in which she repeated her refusal to please herself at Ilona's expense and he tried to suggest that it would do no harm, an argument which she was beginning to want to believe, had unsettled her even more. She sat now staring at her wine glass and literally biting her tongue to stop herself from blurting out the words that were pushing against her tightly closed lips. I want to tell him I like him a lot. I want to tell him I want to go to bed with him. God damn it all. I want, I want – I want –

'Laura,' he said and then, as she remained with her head down, said again, 'Laura?' and now she looked up.

'It's time we talked more, don't you think?' he said. 'It really is getting very difficult, all this politeness. There are things I need to say to you, and I want to be reassured that if I say them and you don't like them we can stay friends. What do you say? To talk or not to talk?'

That was when she stopped biting her tongue.

13

The door had been propped open with a chair, so that the floor could dry more quickly. It had been scrubbed clean of the old polish, and the men from the contractors had gone to spend an hour at the *Dog and Duck* before coming back to put down a new skin of fresh polish, leaving the tables and chairs piled high in the sunshine on the old cobbles outside. Angie had seized the opportunity to give the plants hanging against the window one of his special goings over and each leaf glittered with drops of water in the brightness of the May sunlight. And Laura, her ledgers complete and the orders from the markets not yet arrived to be checked off with Angie, had time to relax for a moment.

She stood in the doorway, leaning against the jamb and enjoying the smell of the day; dust from the Yard, daffodils from the window boxes outside the upstairs windows, the faintly disinfectant overtones of the stuff used to clean the floor and the aromatic paprika and onion smells drifting along from the kitchen. She breathed it in, deeply, and relished its familiarity.

The small side door that led directly into the kitchen and which they were rarely able to use – Angie objected strenuously to the way the occasional passer-by peered in – was open so that the kitchen boys could bring out the bins and carry them to the end of the Yard for the dustmen to collect. Everything looked fresh and clean and new in the brightness and Laura pursed her lips and whistled softly, deeply content with being Laura. It was a good way to feel.

She let her mind slide away to last night, the first time that Philip had stayed over at the flat. Up to now, their lovemaking had been punctuated by the need for Philip to get back to Harrow but last night had been their own. Ilona herself had arranged it for them, all unwittingly, going off to a health farm for a couple of days, and though Laura had demurred at first, all her old conscience pangs rearing up like frightened horses to threaten her, the prospect of having so much uninterrupted time had been more than she could resist.

So, they had eaten at the flat, Philip making dinner (he was an indifferent cook, and the steaks were tough and the spinach salad gritty but that didn't matter in the least) and then sitting silently and contentedly twined on the small sofa, listening to Radio Three. The fact that they had so much time seemed to make them less eager for each other. There was none of the desperate grappling and hunger that had been so essential a part of their first lovemaking, the night after the Barbican concert, when he had taken her home to the flat and stayed until two in the morning. Last night they had been tranquil and quiet and gone to bed as offhandedly and contentedly as a long married pair. She had slipped into his arms with none of the shyness that had so bedevilled her on the three previous occasions they had been together and had lain curled up with him for a long time before, at last, gently and very slowly, he had begun to caress her.

Now, standing against the door staring wide eyed and unseeing at Mucky's shop across the way, she remembered that touch and her skin moved under her summer dress and her belly ached with desire. She had to take a deep breath to make the tide that had lifted in her sink down again and she smiled at Mucky's shop, her wide eyes watching the way she had, last night, responded to Philip, almost feeling again the great glorious ending of it all when she had thought, just for a moment, that she was going to lose all awareness of who or what she was, and would for ever exist only as a sensation of such intense pleasure that it was agony.

Joel, coming out of Mucky's dim shop to stand blinking in the vivid sunlight, caught sight of her, a curving shape in a yellow dress with sturdy brown legs in ivory sandals and a smile on her face so wide and warm that it lifted his mood at once and he smiled back and came straight over to her.

'Hello,' he said and stood there waiting for the smile to

widen even more, if that were possible. But she just stared at him, still with those glittering eyes, very dark beneath her curly hair, and then, slowly the glitter faded and the smile went too, gradually and yet so obviously that he thought absurdly, she's a Cheshire cat –

'Oh!' she said blankly. 'Er – Good morning.'

'I remember now,' he said and tried his own smile again, wanting to bring back to her face the look that had pulled him so sharply across the Yard. 'You're – Laura. I came here for lunch with City Television a few weeks ago, and I was introduced. I hope you remember, though there's no reason why you should.'

Her smile was quite gone now. She looked cool and business-like and her eyes had lost their darkness. They were just pleasant green eyes that looked at him with no more than polite interest.

'A great many people come here for lunch. Forgive me if I don't exactly recall – '

'There's no reason why you should,' he said again. 'It was a busy day, I remember. There were private parties going on all over the place.'

'Oh, yes!' she said then and now seemed for the first time to be giving him all her attention. 'City – you all came on the same day as Anya Zsuzske's birthday party. A busy day – I'd have remembered you otherwise. Did you want something? I'm afraid we're already fully booked for lunch today – '

'Oh, I'm not nearly important enough to come here for lunch,' he said with a mocking note in his voice. He wanted to irritate her now. She had smiled at him with so much warmth and excitement that she had lifted his spirits wonderfully and now was treating him like some boring passer-by, and that rankled. 'I've been warned that only the elite come to you.'

She lifted her brows. 'Hardly the elite. Just my regulars. But we usually manage to find room for people who want to try us. Perhaps for dinner one evening?' She turned as though to go back into the restaurant, to her desk.

'No, thank you,' he said. 'I'm afraid I can't make any such

plans at the moment. Actually – ' He too had turned to leave and then came back. To be annoyed with her was really silly. He'd imagined that blazing smile or else had imagined it was aimed at him. And, he remembered now, he had other reasons to want to talk to her.

'Actually, I'd love to some time. Not in the immediate future, though. I'm working on a project, you see, and it's taking rather a lot of time.'

'Oh?' She looked over his shoulder towards the entry to the Yard that led out to the *Dog and Duck* side, and then at her wristwatch. The floor behind her was dry, and it was time to get the polish on, so that it would be finished in time for getting the tables ready for lunch.

'Mmm. I'm doing a – oh, a sort of social history. I want to know what it was like for families living and growing and developing in this area, over the last hundred years or so. Families like yours.'

She looked directly at him now and there was a thin line between her brows. 'Oh?'

'Dammit, why does everyone look so suspicious when I say that?' he said angrily, letting his earlier irritation at her return, and mix with the dispirited way he'd been feeling when he'd come out of Mucky's shop. 'All I want to do is make a good film, and the way everyone reacts you'd think I was some sort of detective and everyone had a guilty secret to hide! Have you got a guilty secret?'

'I really don't know what you're talking about,' she said coolly and stepped aside to go round him. 'And if you'll excuse me, I have to go and find my workmen. It's getting late – '

'No, please – let me explain.' He put his hand on her arm and she looked down at it, and then with a very deliberate movement of distaste pulled herself away.

'I don't think there is anything to explain,' she said frostily and stepped forwards just as the three workmen came in through the archway, laughing and gossiping. She looked at them and called brusquely, 'Joe! It's high time you got this job finished! It's ten o'clock and we've got a full list of bookings getting here in under three hours. Please, let's have some speed on it – '

'Now, come on, Miss Horvath! When did we ever let you down? Been doin' your floors this past ten years and gone, and never once done 'em anything but perfect. And quick. Come on, you two idle buggers – get on with it – ' And he winked at Laura and Joel and pushed his men past them into the restaurant.

'I'm sorry if I was offensive,' Joel said, not enjoying having to apologise but knowing he had to, if he was to carry his researches any further. It was getting more and more important that he did. 'My name's Joel Coplin. Does that mean anything to you?'

She looked at him, her brows raised again in that slightly supercilious way. 'Should it?'

'I'd hoped so. My great grandfather was a friend of your family's. Or so Mr. Bosquet says.'

'Who?' She seemed startled.

'Over there,' Joel jerked his head. 'The old man in the tobacconist's. Mr. Bosquet.'

She smiled at last, and though it wasn't as it had been when he'd first seen her from the doorway it was at least friendly. 'Oh, Mucky! D'you know, I forgot that was his name. Isn't it ridiculous? Known him all my life and only ever called him Mucky. Like everyone else.'

'Why?'

'Why what?'

'Mucky. He's the cleanest and most dapper old man I've ever met. It's been a long time since anyone wore spats, but there he is, and a suede waistcoat too, the whole shebang.'

'What else would you call someone like that?' she said with great reasonableness and again the smile lifted her round face. 'As far as I know he's never been called anything else, except by his own family. And even they say Mucky sometimes. Simmy does.'

'Simmy?' Joel said hopefully, knowing who he was, but hoping to make her relax even more and forget her earlier suspicion of him completely. But she became cautious again and shook her head.

'Forgive me, but I really have a lot to do, Mr. Coplin, you say?' She had gone in through the door but now came out again and looked at him with her lips pursed. 'Coplin – ' she said again in a considering voice.

'Alleluja. You've remembered,' he said.

'Not really. But I do know my grandfather had a friend – what did you say your grandfather's first name was?'

'I didn't. My father's name was Samuel and my grandfather was David.'

She pushed her lower lip out even further and thought, and then shook her head. 'No, sorry. I thought for a moment – but no.'

'My great grandfather was Abner. Mr. Bo – Mucky remembers him. He said he thought you might. Not remember him yourself, of course. You're much too young. But you might remember that he was a friend of your family. Istvan, Mucky said. That was the one my great grandfather knew.'

'Uncle Istvan,' she said and her face changed and settled into heavier lines. Joel remembered a phrase he'd come across in a historical novel and liked; 'she has a speaking countenance,' he thought.

But then her face smoothed, and she said politely, 'Yes. My Uncle Istvan had a great many old friends. He'd spend hours sitting there with them. In the corner – ' And she turned her head and looked into the restaurant where the three men were busily at work on the floor, making it shine a rich ruby red. 'But I can't remember them all. Though the name Abner – it's an unusual one. And perhaps – ' But then she shook her head decisively. 'Really, you must forgive me. I've got a lot of work to do and though it would be nice to stand and talk to you – '

'Entrancing though it is to wander through a garden of bright images are we not enticing our minds from another subject of almost equal importance?' Joel said with an edge to his voice and she lifted her hands and clapped them together like a child.

'*Kai Lung*!' she cried. 'Oh, do you like them too? Aren't they the best books in the world?'

He had turned to go, feeling defeated, but now whirled back to stare at her. 'You too? I thought everyone but me had forgotten them.'

'Not me! I loved them – read all of them when I was a child. I've still got them all. *The Wallet of Kai Lung*, and *Kai Lung's Golden Hours* and *Kai Lung Unrolls his Mat* and – '

'I've still got mine. I brought them with me. Left a lot of books in Canada of course, but those I brought – '

'But I thought you said – your grandfather was a friend of my family? I don't remember anyone from Canada.'

'They went there after the war. My parents. I was born there.'

'That explains the accent.'

'Oh. What did you think it meant?'

She paused and then said with a little rush, 'I thought it might have been a pose.'

'How do you mean?'

'Oh, there are so many of them. Busy chaps trying to raise money for films all talking big about the stars and millions of dollars, and sitting here counting up the bill and praying they can manage it – they usually have phoney American accents of that sort. I get rather used to them.'

'That's me put in my place,' he said trying to look amused but finding it a little difficult. He was accustomed to the way people outside the television business sneered at it, even while they were fascinated by it, but this was a new insult.

She reddened, clearly aware suddenly of how rude she had sounded. 'Look, I mean no harm. It was just – anyway, what can I do for you? Not now. I really must leave this garden of bright images – ' The smile flickered over her face again. 'But perhaps if you wanted to come back – '

'Yes, please,' he said. 'Look, let me lay it on the line, as we television people say. I want to make a film about Soho and I thought I'd use the families which have been here for ever as the plot of the story. My own – I can't get much help from them, because they're all dead. My parents, I mean.'

'I'm sorry,' she said and without thinking put out her hand to touch his arm. 'That's awful. People think it doesn't matter once you're an adult, but it does, doesn't it? I miss mine dreadfully. My parents died in the same year. Only two or three years ago. I still miss them.'

'My father died when I was seven, so I can't pretend I miss him. But Ma died last year and I *do* miss her. Like the very devil. I feel rather a fool for that.'

'Don't. For my part, I think people who love their families are much nicer than the other sort. The modern ones who don't care tuppence for anyone but themselves.'

'That's very kind.' He smiled at her and she seemed to become aware of her hand on his arm for the first time and pulled it away.

'So you want to talk to me about my family?' she said after a moment. 'For your film?'

'Yes, please. And not just for that, though it is important. Work's always important. But it's not the only thing.' He lifted his chin and looked round the Yard, at the little huddle of buildings pressing down on the small sunlit square in which they were standing and the grey bricks of the walls and the glittering windows with their splash of daffodils, and shook his head. 'It's for me too. I'm not sure sometimes who I am. Or what I am.' He looked back at her. 'That sounds stupid, but – it's just working in television. It makes you feel shaky. It's not pinned to anything, you see. It's just images. Nothing real.'

'I sometimes think it's only images that *are* real. What happens inside my own head is sometimes much better, much more real, than what happens outside me.' She was leaning against the door jamb again, apparently quite free of her earlier anxiety to get back to work.

'Oh, yes. What happens in your *own* head – I quite agree! But television doesn't happen inside your own head, does it? It happens in someone else's and then gets shoved into yours. It's an assault, in a way – ' He stopped and smiled down at her, a little shy suddenly. 'I was just trying to say that I feel the need to sort out who I am. What I came from, you know? That's why I'm doing more than just research for a programme. I'm doing research for me.'

'Looking for your roots?'

There was no hint of mockery in her voice but he felt embarrassed at the corniness of what he had said and that made him a little brusque. 'Not at all. I'm just interested, that's all.'

'It's nothing to be ashamed of,' she said mildly. 'Needing to look for roots. I never left mine. They're still here, but I know what you mean all the same. I sometimes think it'd be good to go to Hungary, find the village where my great grandfather came from, back in the nineties. Almost a hundred years ago, now, but I still think I'd like to go.'

'Why don't you?'

'Not sure what I might find there,' she said and laughed, suddenly awkward and a little shy. 'Heavens, this really won't do! I've got a restaurant to run here. Angie'll be out in a moment and after my blood – '

'Angie?'

'My chef. Rules me with the proverbial rod of iron. Look, I'll help if I can. With your film and with your – with the rest of it. But it'll take time. It always takes time to remember. Come and have dinner here one night? It's all right – my guest. I can talk to you then. Ring up and let me know which night suits you – ' Now she did go inside, picking up the door stop as she went so that she could close the door behind her.

'Thank you,' he said and stood there looking through the glass at her and then lifted his hand in farewell and turned and walked away.

He had a lot to think about; Mucky's very suspicious rejection of him and the way he had been hustled out of the little tobacconist shop, and then this Laura's odd swings of mood, first brilliantly smiling at him and then hostile and then friendly and then –

Behind him he heard the restaurant door rattle and she called his name and turned and looked back from the shadow of the archway to where she stood in the sun, looking as bright as the daffodils above her head.

'I'm sorry if I was a little rude,' she called. 'I was a bit – I'm sorry!' And she looked at him for a long moment and then lifted her hand uncertainly and turned and went back into the restaurant, closing the door behind her with a little snap, leaving him staring at the empty Yard and wondering how soon he could take up her invitation. Tonight? Tomorrow? He'd try. Suddenly it was very important indeed to talk to this odd woman, and to do so as soon as he possibly could.

14

'Item four on the agenda,' Leo said, and looked over his shoulder hopefully at the door; but there was no sign of anyone arriving with the tea tray and with a small sigh he returned to his papers. 'Our newsletter – '

'What newsletter?' Mrs. Capitelli said, immediately on the offensive again. She'd reacted like that to every item that had come up for discussion this morning, aggrieved, aggressive and suspicious. 'We don't have a newsletter. We've never had a newsletter. What is all this about newsletters?'

'I decided we should have one.' Leo too took on what was becoming a familiar stance; pugnacious, patronising and weary. 'I have the right, you know, as Chairman. You should have done it when you were Chairman, but you chose not to, and that was entirely *your* right. Now I've chosen to do otherwise. Edward? Perhaps you'd care to report?'

'Gladly, Mr. Chairman,' Edward said, and began to hand out piles of duplicated sheets, stapled together at one corner. 'These are the drafts for your approval. If you're happy I'll get quotes for printing. I don't propose the committee should vet every issue, mind you. That would be much too tedious for you all. I just want you to read it regularly. But you should check just this first one, before we print, so that you all know exactly what Leo had in mind. I thought the concept rather good. I hope you all agree – '

The tea tray at last arrived, carried into the overheated and cluttered room by one of Mrs. Capitelli's many plain daughters and at once the old woman got to her feet and began to fuss with cups and milk jugs, much to Leo's patent relief, as the rest of them leafed through the papers in a half hearted fashion, one eye cocked eagerly on the cups as they were handed out and the other on the tray of paper-wrapped amoretti that were being handed round after them.

Edward, who had been a little tense, watched them and allowed his shoulders to relax; there'd be no problem with it. Leo had, in his innocence, timed it exactly right.

'There you are then,' he said easily as the papers rustled and the teacups rattled. 'Our first newsletter. Took a lot of sorting out, those recent sales of properties. Still, I managed to get the facts. Interesting, isn't it, to know how much property's appreciated in the past year? We all know of course that the area's a goldmine – but it's comforting to have an actual figure put on your neighbour's place. It shows you what your own stake is worth, hmm? Wish I had more than that small rented room of mine, I can tell you. Not like you, Mrs. C. sitting on this lovely place. Lovely – '

Mrs. Capitelli who had opened her mouth to protest at the newsletter, closed it again and went back to noisily chewing her biscuit as she looked at the place on the page which Edward leaned over to show her. Her brows lifted in surprise as she stared at the figures and then slowly she opened her full mouth in a gaping grin. Edward averted his gaze and looked at Olaffson. 'You'd agree, Mr. Olaffson? Nice information?'

'Very nice,' Olaffson said and nodded vigorously. 'Very nice indeed! A useful service this. I propose we accept the newsletter – good to have an update on this sort of thing as often as we can get it.' He looked down at his copy and shook his head in happy disbelief. 'Did you see what that chap Pritt got for that little place of his in Rupert Street? Half a pocket handkerchief, those rooms, I swear to you, and do you see what he got? My place is twice the size and got better access. A *useful* service this. I definitely propose. Basset here'll second, eh Basset?' And he nudged his neighbour who blinked and said, as he always did, 'Hmm? Oh, yes, absolutely. Yes.'

'Good, good,' Leo said briskly. He hadn't even looked at the newsletter, feeling obscurely that to do so would be infra dig in some way. After all, hadn't Edward implied that the thing was his idea? In fact, wasn't it? His memory was hazy on the point but the more he thought about it the more it seemed that it had been; in which case to look at the thing and to discuss it would be absurd. They'd all think he'd forgotten his own work. 'Put it to the vote – those in favour? Hmm. And those against? Well, I'm sorry, Mrs. C – carried by a majority. My casting vote, you see. The newsletter becomes a regular part of our service to the members of the Trust and Edward Malplackett is the Editor. Any items for inclusion to be sent to him, yes Edward? Splendid, splendid! Right. Item five.'

'Yes – item five,' Mrs. Garcia said suddenly. 'This one amazes me. Someone must have it wrong. Old Mucky with porn in his shop? This I find hard to believe.'

'I've got chapter and verse here,' Leo said and patted the pile of papers in front of him. 'No doubt about it. Two separate complaints laid. And that means we have to do something about it. It's in the Constitution – two or more complaints from the public and we lodge a formal complaint by the Trust to the Police and to the licensing authority – it's all in the Constitution.'

'*My* Constitution,' Mrs. Capitelli said. 'That was the Constitution I got in my first year and – '

'Indeed you did, Mrs. C, indeed you did,' Leo said quickly. 'And very good too. So, it is agreed that under the terms of the Constitution of the Trust, para Seven, subsection (e) we take the usual steps to deal with the matter? No objections?'

'I still think it's peculiar,' Mrs. Garcia said stubbornly. 'I've known Mucky more years than I can remember. He hates those porn shops, always did. Signed my petition, you remember? When they wanted to open a strip show next door to me. I just don't see that – '

'I've seen it,' Miss Foster said suddenly. She spoke so rarely that everyone immediately stopped the undercurrent of talk between themselves that was always part of Trust committee meetings and stared at her. Her nose went pink and she bobbed her head, embarrassed.

'Seen what, Miss Foster?' Leo asked.

'Magazines. In the tobacconist in Little Vinegar Yard,' she

said, and bobbed her head again. 'Went in for some snuff. For my sinuses, you know. Excellent for sinus trouble, snuff is, and Mucky's the only place I can get the sort I need. Went in, saw the magazines. I was surprised – '

'What did you do about it then?' Mr. Olaffson said.

'Do? Nothing. What could I do? I bought my snuff and went out. I didn't look at the magazines. Not to say *look*, I mean. I didn't pick them up or anything.' The pinkness on her nose seemed to spread to her eyes as her anxiety increased. 'I saw the covers, though. Dreadful covers. Really dreadful – so I bought my snuff and left – ' Her voice trailed away.

'You didn't think to report it to the Trust?' Leo said sternly.

'I just didn't think about them at all,' Miss Foster said wretchedly. 'So nasty, you see. They always are, and they're everywhere. It was never like that before, when I was a child and my mother ran our shop. We never had things like that, and I never will now. But everyone else does so I just hurried out and thought, I'll get Mucky to bring my snuff to my shop next time, when he comes back.'

'Comes back?' Mrs. Garcia said.

'Seems he's on a long trip to France, his nephew told me,' Leo said. 'I went in to warn him I was going to have to take this matter up – phoned him and warned him and he didn't seem at all concerned.' It was his turn to go rather pink. 'In fact he was quite unpleasant about it. So there you are. The Constitution rules we take action. The evidence is there, so we have no choice. Right, I'll see to it – or rather Mr. Secretary will – Edward? Yes – All right. Item six – any other business. And I hope there isn't too much, I must say. I have a lot to do at my shop this afternoon and I've been asked to lunch with the Chairman of the General Purposes Committee of the Council – ' He seemed to swell a little as he said it. 'So I do request we keep AOB down. Well, Mrs. C? *What* is it?'

'I thought it might be better to get off the patch,' Davriosh said. 'The way people see you and talk around Soho, it makes you sick. You don't get 'em here. Too far over, you see. Nice place, hmm? Not fancy, but stylish. All the stars come here, you know. Not now, not lunchtime so much, but every night after their shows, they all come to Joe Allen's. This table we're at, it used to be Ingrid Bergman's regular one. Imagine that, Ingrid Bergman!'

Statler looked round at the checked tablecloths and the brick walls and the menu chalked on the blackboards and smiled thinly. 'Very nice. Not the Connaught Grill, I agree, but I dare say very nice.'

'Why should it matter people see us?' Preston said, and smoothed his bald head with one hand. 'We're not doing anything we shouldn't.'

'I've got someone joining us,' Davriosh said and winked at Statler who looked woodenly back at him and said nothing. 'Sort of progress report, you know? It could cause problems if it got around we was talking. Him and us. It wouldn't be a disaster, you understand, not for us, but it could cause problems. For the other fella.'

'Who is he?' Preston asked and leaned back as a very skinny young waiter arrived with his arms stacked with dishes. They were silent as he slapped plates of ham and eggs in front of Davriosh and Preston and a frugal salad before Statler and then as he went Preston said again, 'Who is he? This fella you're on about? Why isn't he here now?'

'He'll get here, he'll get here,' Davriosh said, his mouth already full. Not for him the unnecessary mannerliness of waiting for the others to be served. 'Let's get our own business sorted out first. A progress report, that's what I got for you, Mr. Statler. You'll be pleased, I reckon.'

'I hope so,' Statler murmured and wiped his lips fastidiously and pushed aside his wooden bowl of salad almost untouched. Clearly he was regretting not being at the Connaught Grill.

'The smaller property – the tobacconist's shop and flat, that we got sorted out. The offer for the freehold is in, and by the end of next month, we'll have it. No problem. The other property, though, that's not going to be so easy.'

With a sharp little movement he mopped the remainder of the egg from his plate with a piece of bread and leaned back in his chair, clearly disappointed that his plate was empty, and looking round for the waiter.

'What's the problem with it? Who holds the freehold?'

'That's the problem,' Davriosh said and catching the waiter's eye at last, beckoned. 'It's a family trust. There are a lot of people involved, a lot. All of 'em got different sized pieces, depending on who they got it from. I mean, it's inherited, you see? They inherit their shares from their parents, you know the sort of thing. Still, it's not impossible. We can sort it out. I've got my ways of sorting things. It's what I'm for – '

He grinned at Statler and said to the waiter, 'Side order french fries,' and took another piece of bread from the basket and buttered it lavishly. 'And when I say I can arrange things, believe me I can arrange things. Leave it with me – Ah, here he is!' He pushed back his chair noisily. 'Come and sit down ol' man. We didn't wait. The ham and eggs are good – not a lot of it, but good. I'll get the waiter, order for you – '

The other men half rose in acknowledgement as the tall thin man in a grey suit slid into the fourth chair at the table. He was a neat figure with hair as grey as his clothes and he bent his head in a polite but unsmiling acknowledgement as Davriosh introduced them.

'Secretary of the Vinegar Trust,' Davriosh said importantly as Statler and Preston murmured their acknowledgements. 'That's the thing, you see. Ed's the Secretary of the Trust. Been very helpful to me in many ways.'

'And I hope will continue to be so,' Statler said and for the first time smiled. 'A drink, Mr. Malplackett.'

'Thank you,' Malplackett said. 'Just Perrier, please. Healthier, you know. I need to watch my health.' And he smiled at Statler. The two seemed to have taken a liking to each other on sight.

'So, Ed?' Davriosh said expansively. 'How have things been going?'

'Rather well!' Edward murmured. 'I've just come from a

Trust meeting. The newsletter went down well. Thanks for your help with it. Seeing those prices concentrated their minds wonderfully. It could well work, this scheme of yours. Tell people the going rate you'd like it to be and it turns into it, doesn't it? You'll be pushing up the values nicely – '

'And the other business?' Davriosh said, glancing proudly at the other two men, like a mother showing off a precocious child. 'Have you got that done the way we said? Tell 'em what you've done, Ed. Just tell 'em.'

Edward glanced at Statler almost conspiratorially and smiled. 'It's agreed that the complaints be laid. I've already seen to it that the police have been told, and I rather think they took a look yesterday. Simmy Leach took the day off, arranged for someone to look after the place. He's a bit anxious about his uncle finding out his connection with all this, you see. He stands to inherit a good deal, he reckons, when the old man dies. He used to have a right to the reversion of the place, it seems, under his grandfather's will, but Mucky bought him out. Gave him a lot of cash, years ago, and had the holding rearranged to help the boy. But he's got expensive tastes, has Simmy Leach, and went through the lot in under five years. So now he's dependent on the old man's goodwill. Expects him to leave the property to him – and he's an old fella, after all. Can't be long before he turns in his chips. And if Mucky discovers after he gets back from France what's been going on he might leave the lot to a cats' home, which would upset Mr. Leach a good deal. He fancies the idea of being a property owner. He's bored with his council flat on the Isle of Dogs.' He smiled briefly. 'So keeping the old man sweet is important. He's glad to take our money, but doesn't want to lose the old man's. It's understandable.'

'I hardly see how the old man can fail to find out,' Statler said dryly. 'Considering that he'll come back to discover he has a new landlord – '

'No he won't,' Davriosh said and produced a fat giggle. 'Of course he won't. That's where I come in. I've arranged with the old letting agents, the people who've been collecting his rent for years, to sell me a piece of their business, including his piece. They owed me a favour, so – anyway, he'll come back, he'll find a letter from Joe Early to say he's taking his retirement, sold the business to me, from now on to pay me the rent. *I* won't tell the old boy he's got a new landlord as well as a new agent, now, will I? The magazines'll be out of the shop by then, so who's to tell him there's been any trouble? It'll never come to court or anything, that's for sure. The mere fact there's trouble with the tenant'll be enough to make L and DC part with the freehold. The tales I'll tell 'em and that Edward here'll tell 'em about the trouble that's brewing with the Trust, they'll be glad to part. At our price. I tell you, this one's okay. You'll be laughing, believe you me.'

'I'll look forward to that,' Statler said dryly. 'When you show me the documentation will be soon enough for hilarity. Now, about the other property – the family trust. I'd like a little more information on that. On how you're planning to – what was it you said? Sort things out.'

Davriosh winked and leaned back in his chair. He'd eaten all the bread in the basket and for the first time seemed reasonably content with the state of his stomach.

'Now, that's not so easy to explain. It's been my pleasure to introduce you to my friend Edward here. I've no fear about showing my hand, including the honours cards, to you. And Edward, believe me, is one of the honours. A real ace, and I'm glad to have him. I've told him, stick with us, we can do you a lot of good, so that you can do us a lot of good. We can be very good for each other – '

'The other property, Davriosh,' Statler said. His voice was the same; quiet, a little flat in tone, colourless, but there was a warning in it that Davriosh heard very clearly and he sat up and smiled at the smaller man a shade too widely.

'The other property. Yes, well, I have another card to play. A trump card, believe me. But it's got to be played very close to the chest, you understand. If it ever gets out this man's got an involvement in what we're trying to do the whole thing is off. He'll tip his hand to the rest of them, and they'll know they're sitting on a gold mine. They won't sell – or if they do, they'll want twice the rate you're going to get it for if we leave him to do what he has to do in his own way. I promise you, once he's got control, he'll see to it we get the freehold for a quarter million, maybe, at worst no more than three hundred grand. But if we drop him in it, let our mouths make overtime, then no way. He tells 'em what's on and they won't settle for a penny less than the half. It's a difference of two hundred grand, maybe. Isn't it worth keeping shtoom for the possibility of saving yourself two hundred grand?'

'If I can be assured I'll get it at the price, then, yes, it is,' Statler said. 'But I want it anyway. If I have to go to the higher rate, then I have to – '

'Jesus, but the pickings on this must be good!' Preston said and Statler flicked a glance at him and then looked away, bored.

' – if there is no other way to get it,' he said as though there had been no interruption. 'Obviously I'm a businessman and if I can shave my costs I like to do it.'

Preston, not in the least put out by Statler's obvious dismissal of his opinions, shook his head in admiration. 'Such shavings I'd like to find in my bathroom every morning! He'd like to shave two hundred grand off the price of the property, but if he can't he'll still buy – it's a pleasure to listen to such talk.'

'I need to know,' Statler said, this time not even bothering to look at Preston, 'whether I can be assured of getting the property this way. I appreciate the effort you're putting into making all your little arrangements, and I can quite see that from your point of view they must be profitable – '

'Now, listen Mr. Statler, I'm dealing straight with you!' Davriosh protested. 'I'm not doing any till dipping, believe me! The price my man wants for this property is the price I'll ask you. There'll be nothing in it for me! Apart from my share of the deal I made with you – a third, remember. I'm in for a third with you – '

'I remember. I also remember that all men are greedy, and want more if they can get it. And I have no doubt that you will get some – shall we say commission? – from this arrangement you're so busy about. I have no objection to that – unless it loses me the property, you understand? I want it, and I have to have it by the end of the year, so that I can get my planning applications settled. After the end of the year, my own special arrangements with the planning committee become less advantageous – '

'Retirements?' Preston said owlishly and getting no reply, nor expecting one, nodded. 'That'll be it. Chairman of the committee retiring. No elections due so it's got to be that. Damn nuisance the way these people retire. You sort 'em out, get 'em nicely settled to your ways and they go and retire. Same with the licensing people, you know. And the police. Bloody police.' He sat and stared broodingly into his glass. He'd filled and emptied it more often than any of them, and now he refilled it yet again, and Davriosh looked at him uneasily, but Statler still ignored him.

'So you see,' Statler went on in his dull flat voice, 'it's important that we get this matter sorted out as soon as possible. *Safely*. So keep me informed.' He looked at his watch and pushed back his chair. 'Thank you for lunch, gentlemen. We must come here again. I like it. Good salads.' And he went, weaving his way past the red checked tables and the gossiping lawyers and journalists around them, leaving the three men staring after him.

'I hope you know what you're doing, Joe,' Preston said after a moment. 'Lose that property, and there'll be all hell let loose, you understand that? Are you sure this bloke, whoever he is, can deliver?'

'Of course he can,' Davriosh said stoutly. 'Of course he can.' But he looked uneasy, all the same.

15

The phone rang just as he was settling Anya for the night. It was a complicated process, involving a series of carefully orchestrated heaves and pushes to get her from her great arm chair on to the high brass bed. For years he'd been trying to persuade her – had even begged her – to change to a modern low divan to make it all easier for both of them, but she wouldn't hear of it, clinging to her familiar old bed with the tenacity she normally used only when dealing with food. It had been her marriage bed and had accommodated her for almost seventy years; she wasn't going to be bullied out of it. So, the getting-into-bed ritual remained what it had been, a matter of prolonged sweating and puffing and grunting on the part of both of them. And tonight the phone had started shrilling just as they got to the stage where Anya was holding on round his neck and he was trying to get her to her feet.

For a moment he contemplated dropping her back in her chair, and going to answer it. All his instincts were to run when the phone rang; it might just possibly be his agent, or a management with the offer of something good, even at this time of night; if he didn't answer at once they'd give up, go away, ask someone else and he'd have missed his great chance –

But one glance at Anya's face made him abandon that idea; she hadn't heard the phone of course, and to try to explain to her why she had to sit down again and wait to be put to bed would take up more time than finishing the job and then answering; so he redoubled his efforts, trying to speed the old woman to her place beneath the great feather cover, and succeeding only in making her grunt with irritation at being hustled and deliberately slowing down in consequence. And all the time the phone went on shrilling –

He left her sprawled in the bed like a stranded whale,

shouting despairingly into her ear. 'The phone, Anya – I'll be back in a minute – THE PHONE!' and she lay there helplessly with her brushed cotton nightdress rucked up to show her surprisingly scrawny feet and legs and he ran to the other room.

Even in his panic he felt again the shock of pleasure the room always gave him; it was *his* room, the one place in the big old flat he could regard entirely as his own domain and his own creation. In the dining room, in the sitting room his mother used, in her bedroom, it was all as it had been for years; heavy mahogany furniture, dull brown carpets, the walls and tables and shelves cluttered so thickly with bric-a-brac and mementoes of Hungary that the heavily patterned wallpaper was almost – mercifully – invisible. But here in this room where he slept and lived and dreamed his private hours all was elegance and charm; the black and silver furniture carefully and lovingly collected over the years from antique shops which specialised in art deco, the great swathe of silver curtains at the window, the bellying loops of black fabric that obscured the ceiling, the mirrors everywhere winking and glittering in the glow of the half dozen deco lamps scattered around, all cried their welcome to him and even as the phone shrilled he stood poised at the doorway for just a fraction of a moment to let the pleasure sink in. And then hurried across the thick pile of the scarlet carpet to pick up the phone from the table in the corner.

It was a thirties telephone, a stick and separate earpiece affair, and he sank down on the black leather pouffe beside the chrome and glass table to sit hunched with the earpiece held hard against his head and the stick clutched so tightly in his other hand that his knuckles whitened. He always answered the phone like that; always believed that maybe, this time, it would be the big offer, the special offer, the magic breakthrough offer he'd waited for for so long a time.

But it wasn't. His face seemed to change in the soft yellow light as he listened, settled into tired lines as his mouth drooped and his eyes half closed. He looked suddenly as though he felt cold.

'Oh,' he said in a flat voice. 'Hello.'

He listened as the small voice clacked in his ear, staring unseeingly at the facing mirrored wall in which his own reflection appeared and reappeared, as it was thrown back by the mirrors on the other side. His shape was outlined by reflections of itself, over and over again, and it seemed to him that the words that were being said in his ear reverberated in the same ominous way, and he took a deep breath and tried to cut in, tried to stem the tide of sound that was pouring into his head from the little trumpet of an earpiece.

'I can't,' he said. 'How can I? It's just not possible – I've been thinking about what you said carefully and it's just not possible – '

But the voice was inexorable and he felt as well as saw himself shrink even lower on the pouffe, and he began to shake his head, slowly, over and over again, as though the voice could see him refusing.

'I just don't see that they'll agree – why should they agree? They'll think it's crazy if I – '

Again he was interrupted and again he listened, still looking cold and miserable.

'But it's no use saying that! They'd never believe that. They all know me – know I'm an actor, that acting's all I ever cared about. If I were that sort of businessman wouldn't I have shown it years ago? Of course I would! And – '

Again he was forced to stop and listen for a while.

'Yes. Yes. I see.' He sounded less wretched now. 'I suppose that would be – I can't be sure, mind you, but I could try – '

The voice seemed to change, become less threatening, for now he sat up a little more, and his face seemed to lift, too.

'Yes, I see what you mean. And you're sure that they'll come to no real harm from it? I mean, why? Why are you so – '

Now the voice talked for a long time, and he watched himself listening and after a while tucked the ear piece between his head and his shoulder to release one hand so that he could twitch at the black silk scarf he was wearing tucked into the neck of his dressing gown. It was a scarlet dressing gown of exactly the same shade as the carpet and against it his silver hair showed a rich deep gleam that lit his face which was lightly tanned from the regular sessions he had on the sunbed at the health club he went to every morning. He looked good tonight and as he listened to the little disembodied voice began to feel better, too.

'I suppose you're right, my dear chap. I suppose you're right,' he said at length. 'It's just that – I'm really rather stupid about these things, you know. Just an actor, not a businessman. But if this is going to be of help to you and can't hurt Anya or any of the family – what?'

He listened and then laughed, and now he was a quite different man from the one who had picked up the phone. He looked ten years younger, wise and amusing, charming and relaxed.

'My dear fellow, how on earth do you expect me to know all that? I've never asked! I'm happy enough to have my own share – never attempted to sort out the facts about anyone else's! All this is ancient history, and though one is of course as fascinated as any other man by one's personal history, there comes a point where one is really dreadfully bored by the subject in general. Can't you ask? Hmm? Oh, I see what you mean. I suppose not. Well I'm not sure what more I can do – ' And then his chin came up to tighten his jawline and he smiled as he listened.

'That would be lovely,' he said and now his voice seemed to have changed too, becoming deeper, a little richer. 'You see? There's no need to be unpleasant about things, is there? All you have to do with me is – well, all right, all right! Not another word, my dear chap. When?'

He turned his head to glance at the curved silver clock that sat dead in the centre of the black marble fireplace and his smile widened even more.

'That will be delightful. Hmm? Oh, heavens no! Bless her, once she's asleep that's it – ' His face changed ludicrously suddenly. 'Oh. Ye Gods! Poor Anya! You rang and I left her – my dear chap, I must go! She'll be in such a state – see you in an hour then! – ' And he hung the phone up with a clatter and thrust it onto the table and fled back to Anya.

She had somehow managed to manoeuvre herself up the

bed a little and now lay with her head on the pillow, staring up at the ceiling, her legs still partly uncovered, and he hurried over to the bed and tugged on the big feather quilt which was crumpled beneath her, in order to cover her.

She turned her eyes towards him and said in her deep voice, 'Paul?' She pronounced it in the Hungarian way, Pol, and he smiled at her, liking the sound. It reminded him of his childhood when she had still been able to hear, though already her deafness had begun, and would sit and tell him stories as he sat curled up on her big accommodating lap, and his father would shout and complain at him for being such a baby, sitting on his mother's lap at his age. She would hold him closer then, and murmur, 'Never mind, Poly, never mind. Stay here with your Anya – *Na ezt aztàn szèpen megsinàltad* – you're my beauty – never mind what your father says – stay here with your Anya – let him go with the others – let them be *apya fia* – ' And he would giggle at that, for he knew what that meant.

They were chips off the old block. She would say it sneeringly, not liking her husband and his blustering, not much liking her older boys who were so similar too in so many ways, much preferring her Poly, who was so much like her.

'Poly,' she said again now. '*Ennek mar féle sem trefa or ez trefának már sok* – '

'Darling Anya! You know I don't understand when you speak Hungarian – ' he shouted, automatically lifting his voice to the level at which she was able to hear most of his words.

'You understand when you want to,' she growled, and turned her head away, and he came to the other side of the bed and bent over her, placatingly. She was annoyed and when she got annoyed she could work herself up into such a lather that she didn't sleep. And tonight it was important that she went to sleep, for his sake as well as her own.

'Darling, I'm sorry I left you.' He spoke right into her ear, setting his lips against her thin old skin and pettishly she pushed him away; but she wasn't as angry as she had been and he stroked her face with one hand and shouted, 'I'm sorry, darling. It was an important call – '

'Who was it?'

He opened his mouth to speak and then stopped short 'No one you know,' he bawled and then as she turned her head to look at him said again. 'No one you know,' and patted her cheek.

'I'm hungry,' she said as he began to haul the quilt out from beneath her and pull it over her. 'I want some cholla. And coffee.'

He stared at her, debating with himself. To refuse her might make her sulk, and could add to her still simmering irritation at having been left alone so unceremoniously. On the other hand, fetching the food, helping her with it, settling her again would take time and then maybe he'd arrive before she was asleep and –

He leaned over her and shouted, 'Anya, not coffee. Keeps you awake. Milk and cholla, all right?' And she grinned at him so that her pudding of a face split wide and for a moment there she was again, his childhood Anya, jolly and big and funny and sharing titbits with him and laughing and teasing him and then laughing again so much that it drove his father and brothers out and left them in peace – and he grinned back and kissed her and hurried to the kitchen to fetch her snack.

He watched her gobble the slice of sweet chocolate- and vanilla-flavoured bread, which he had spread with a little of her favourite honey, and shook his head a little. Her greed was touching rather than disgusting. She ate with all the relish of a naughty child and when she had finished licked her old lips with so much satisfaction and pleasure that it made him laugh aloud; but it worried him all the same. He was afraid, so very afraid that one day it would all overcome her, that her bulk would become more than her old heart could handle, and that she would die.

That one day she had to die was a fact he tried very hard to forget. Ninety-one seemed somehow less aged than eighty-nine had seemed. That had been a bad year for him, her eighty-ninth. He was so frightened she wouldn't get through it, but when she had, his spirits had lifted and had remained elated ever since. A number with a zero on the end and then with a one somehow seemed less than a number followed by a nine; it was illogical but there it was. She had passed ninety so there was no reason why she shouldn't reach her hundredth birthday.

And it was desperately important to him that she should. He had no one but his Anya; no one to care about, to fear for, to be angry with and irritated by. His brothers bored him, and he loathed them as much as he knew they despised him. Without Anya life would be intolerable, and watching her eat reminded him all too vividly of the way his father had died ten years ago, his face purple with the effort of breathing, his eyes bloodshot and frightened. He too had been a heavy eater, he too had been vast and ponderous, but he had not had his wife's tenacity and pleasure in living. He had not had Paul to love him and care for him, so he had died too soon.

Only eighty-five, Paul thought now, watching Anya gobbling her chollah. He was only eighty-five. Anya's stronger than he was, better than he was, cleverer than he was. She'll live for a long time yet – she must live for a long time yet – this whole family has good genes when it comes to long lives. His grandmother Maritza had lived to be eighty-eight, hadn't she? And that had been in the old days when there was less good medical care about. And Uncle Istvan, he'd been – what was it? Almost eighty –

He tried to close his mind to memories of the others who had not done so well, to Aunt Magda who had been well under sixty when she had died, the day before his own birthday. But he couldn't succeed. He couldn't help remembering how they had all spent his party at the restaurant weeping and then eating and then weeping again, just as he had to remember too Aunt Kati who had died when he had been a teenager. She had been under sixty, as well –

He shook his head now, as though the movement would send the ugly frightening thoughts deep into the bottom of his mind where they couldn't hurt him and took the tray from Anya and wiped her mouth and hands with the cologne-dampened chamois leather he always kept beside her bed for her in a little china bowl, and helped her turn on her side so that she could sleep. He had read somewhere that big people who slept on their backs sometimes stopped breathing when they were deeply asleep, and ever after he had insisted on making her lie in the proper way, and she let him, obedient as a child when he pushed pillows behind her back to keep her in position and allowing him to arrange her arm so that she didn't crush it under her body and wake with pins and needles. All the time, as he fussed round her she watched him with those dark and intelligent eyes, loving what she saw and he caught her glance as at last she was settled and he reached for the bedside light switch.

'Nice Poly,' she murmured. '*A csodàlàtos fiam. A nàgyszèru fiam.* Nice Poly.' And he smiled back at her. A wonderful son, her special wonderful son, he was, and never ceased to find delight in being told so.

'Goodnight, darling,' he said and bent and kissed her, but her eyes were already closed and he stood there and looked down at her as her breathing softened, deepened and became a light snore, and then switched off the bedside light. At once the small nightlight, which always burned on the corner bureau, throwing its weak gleams across the foot of the bed, sprang into view and he made his way quietly out of the room, tying the specially prepared thick bundle of fabric to the door knob to keep it open. She would hear nothing but he could hear her and that was what mattered.

Now he could concentrate on himself, and as he washed up the plate and tray he'd taken from Anya's room and checked that the old-fashioned kitchen was clean and tidy, ready for the daily woman's ministrations tomorrow morning, he let his mind drift back over his telephone conversation.

The trouble was, he understood so little of such matters as leases and freeholds. That someone should be interested in owning just the ground on which the family restaurant stood made little sense to him; that there might be interest in the place itself seemed very possible; he was well aware of the fact that it was a lucrative business. He had his own steady income to show for it, after all. But to own just the land? Why? He puzzled over that and then sighed softly. He had been assured that no one wanted to interfere with the business in any way. There was no interest of any kind at all in the restaurant, he had been told. None in the world. It was just a matter of freeholds and leaseholds. And if he helped with that, there'd be no harm done to anyone at all. Everything would go on as it always had, ticking over happily, with Laura content and everyone else content too. He and his Anya and the awful sisters-in-law and the Cords, everyone would be happy. It had all been explained to him. And yet still he felt that undertow of doubt. If only he understood it better –

And if I refuse to help, then what? Will he really do as he seems to threaten he would? He's never actually put it into words of course, Paul told himself now, slowly wiping a tea cloth over the same plate again and again, but still he seemed to threaten it – and though it shouldn't matter, it did. He knew it shouldn't, that he should be able to lift up his head and say to everyone, 'The hell with you! The hell with all of you! I am what I am, and I don't give a damn who knows it!' But even as he thought it he felt the jolt in his belly that made him feel sick and dizzy with terror; after all these years of such care, of such watchfulness over every step, such careful choice of every place he went, every person he spoke to, to say, 'I don't give a damn'? He couldn't do it. It was impossible. Not now. Not after so very long –

And then the doorbell rang and he jumped physically and only just avoided dropping the plate. He put it back carefully on to the old dresser in the corner and hung up the tea towel equally carefully and switched off the light before going with a steady tread towards the front door. He paused for a moment at the door of his own room to take a reassuring and comforting look inside and smoothed his hair and tugged his scarlet robe straight as he saw his reflection in the mirror and then, with a relaxed and easy movement and with one hand tucked into the pocket of his robe, the thumb carefully arranged on the outside, opened the front door and stood there, smiling easily.

'My dear chap,' he said and again his voice was deep and rich. 'How delightful to see you! Come in, come in. I was just about to get the ice for your vodka. Come *in* – '

16

'Enjoy it? That's hardly the word,' Joel said solemnly. 'It was a religious experience.'

'You don't have to go right over the top,' Laura said. 'Just say it was magical, wonderful, superb, something simple like that.'

'It was magical, wonderful, superb,' Joel said promptly. 'And a religious experience,' and she laughed.

'I'll tell Angie,' she said. 'He'll like to know that. As a good lapsed Catholic it'll give him something to be shocked about.'

'Angie?'

'My chef. Remember? You asked about him before.'

'I'm sorry. I'd forgotten. What does his name come from? I mean, I'm beginning to realise that most Hungarian names have English equivalents – I've been doing my research, you see. Karoly is Charles and Istvan is Steven and – '

She laughed again. 'Oh, Angie isn't Hungarian. He's Angelo. Angelo Alzano. Italian. But he started to work for my father when he was a boy and he's more Hungarian than any of us now.'

'Does he do all the cooking?' He looked round the restaurant, busy and happy and humming with the noise of replete people talking and shook his head admiringly. 'I've been watching the way things work. Everyone seems to have totally different dishes – there's no overall favourite as far as I can tell – but no one seems to have to wait very long and everyone seems more than content with what they're eating – '

'I should hope so!' Laura said and bridled a little. 'The day everyone isn't happy with what they get here, and the day anyone has to wait too long for a meal, is the day I shut up shop. It'd mean we had no right to be in business any longer.

It's always been like that here. The best of food, served in the best of ways. And yes, Angie does do it all. With assistance of course. But he's the one with his spoon in the pot – excuse me – ' And she was gone, weaving her way through the tables in response to a signal from a customer who wanted her that had been so slight that Joel hadn't noticed it at all.

He watched her go and relaxed. He'd spent a lot of time thinking before he'd actually been able to bring himself to accept her invitation to come to the restaurant for dinner. All through the days that had followed their encounter in the Yard he'd argued with himself about what he was doing. He almost decided to go back to Balfour and Crowner at the office and tell them that he'd changed his mind after all, that his preliminary searches had shown him that there was no way he could make the film he'd suggested. What was more, he'd also come to the conclusion that coming to work in London at all had been lunacy. It was time he faced the fact that he'd made a big error of judgement and took himself back to Toronto with his tail between his legs. There were plenty of people there who would be glad to let him pick up where he left off, who would give him a chance to make the sort of films he was interested in, plenty more who would seize on him to make commercials because of his track record. And there were more important things than bloody film-making after all. Like just being relaxed and happy and being with friends –

And he had sat in the small dull flat he had rented in Kilburn and remembered with a considerable amount of dripping sentiment the good old pals he'd left behind him and the super girls who'd been such fun and especially Liz who'd clearly been so unhappy when he'd announced his departure for London, and made himself thoroughly miserable.

And then inevitably he had experienced a total turnround. He'd woken up the following morning full of anger at his own mawkishness and stupidity. He was over-reacting at being back in his parents' home, that was the thing. The place he'd heard about all through his childhood and about which his mother had never ceased to talk with yearning home-sickness had overwhelmed him, that was all. It had flooded his mind with its strangeness and ordinariness and its shabbiness and its age and its noise and its colour and its excitement and its dullness. Quite what he'd expected to find here he hadn't known; whatever it was, it wasn't this amalgam of suprise and odd emotions and self doubts. But he could cope with that, he'd told his reflection firmly as he shaved. He could, he could, and he would. And the first thing he'd do would be to go and have dinner with that interesting woman with the blazing smile which had turned out to be not quite so blazing, but still interesting.

Even so it had taken him over a week to find the courage to pick up the phone and remind her of her suggestion, and even then he had almost backed down. She had replied by saying simply, 'Hmm?' and he'd found that disconcerting and asked sharply who that was even though he recognised her voice perfectly well. And the cool tones had said, 'This is Laura Horvath. Can I help you?'

'Oh! I wasn't – ' he said. 'I mean, I didn't think I'd got the right number. You didn't say it and – '

'I never do,' she said. 'Who is that?'

'Joel Coplin,' he said, knowing she was going to say, 'Who?' and determined to slam the phone down on her when she did. But she said at once, 'Yes, of course. You're coming in as my guest to have dinner and talk about your film. When can you manage?'

'Tonight?' he'd said.

There had been a little pause and then that cool voice said, 'Tomorrow. Tonight I have people in who will do all they can to monopolise me, and that means not only that I'll be rather bored but that I won't have time to talk to you. Will tomorrow be all right?'

'Fine,' he said. 'And thank you,' and hung up, furious now that he had to wait so long. Having managed to bring himself to the point of calling her, it now seemed outrageous that he should have to sit and twiddle his thumbs for a full twenty four hours. But her explanation had been clear and believable. There was no need to be paranoid, to tell himself, as a small inner voice somewhere was trying to, that she didn't really want to bother with him at all, that she had only agreed to tomorrow night out of pity, that she'd be getting rid of him as fast as she could –

But fortunately he had been able to suppress such foolish notions and had arrived for his dinner promptly at eight, and bearing for her a box with one rose in it.

He'd worried a lot about that; she'd invited him as her guest and he couldn't possibly offer to pay for his dinner without offending her; yet at the same time he couldn't arrive bearing huge gifts and over-lavish offerings. That would be just as offensive. He'd thought that the rose was just right until just before he'd walked into the Yard, at which point he realised despairingly that it was puny, meagre, mean, picayune, every diminishing word he could set tongue to; but since it was too late to get anything else, he'd given it to her anyway; and been rewarded with a moment of total silence and then a look of plain amazement and finally a wide smile; not like the smile that he had first noticed on her face, but a warm one for all that.

'How very charming!' she had said as she had taken it from its box, a tall yellow rose with petals so dark inside they looked like apricot plush. 'This is the nicest thing that's happened to me today – ' And she had put it in a tall vase on her desk, in isolated splendour, and he had seen her touch it several times as he had eaten his solitary meal, watching her as she moved between her tables and talked to her customers and generally kept the place running with ball-bearing smoothness.

He hadn't ordered his meal; just asked her to give him what she thought best and he was glad he had. It had tasted wonderful. First the Hangover soup, a melange of vegetables and broth that was the best he'd ever had, and then a pile of meat and onions with tiny dumplings in a fragrant thick sauce that seemed to melt into his mouth and fill his whole head with taste. He had managed to talk to her after he'd eaten that and asked her what it was.

'Goulash?' he ventured. 'Is that the famous Hungarian goulash that everyone goes on about?'

She laughed. 'You mean Gulyas – I suppose goulash is as close as most people can come to it. No, that's a soup, really. Meat of course. But lots of potato and little bits of *csipetke* – that's tiny bits of dough, cooked with it – like dumplings but not exactly. What you had was paprikash which is a sort of elegant stew.'

'Stew?' he said. 'You can't call that a stew! Such a dreary label for something that tastes so extraordinary.'

'Not really stew, I suppose. That's what we call *pörkolt* – a paprikash has paprika of course, but also sour cream and – look, if you want a cookery lesson, it's the kitchen you need. Angie'll explain all this.'

'You're doing fine,' he said and lifted his glass to her. 'I wish you had time to sit and talk.'

'Have some plum pastry to finish with and then I'll come and sit with you when you get to coffee. Another fifteen minutes, no more. Then everyone'll be settled – ' And again she left him, but he was content enought to sit and watch her as he finished his wine – and he'd found that half a bottle had been no effort to deal with, which surprised him because he had never been a great drinker – and wait.

When she came at last she was carrying two glasses of amber wine and she set one in front of him as Miklos poured coffee for them both. He looked at it doubtfully.

'I've already had more wine than I usually do.'

'This is different. This is Tokay. The Wine of Kings and the King of Wines,' she said. 'Try it.'

He did and liked its sweet fruitiness with an odd and interesting undertaste that was faintly bitter, and said so and she bent her head like a duchess accepting a compliment.

'Of course you like it,' she said tranquilly. 'It's Tokay,' and sipped her own.

They sat in silence for a moment and then she said surprisingly, 'Heavens, but it's good to sit down! I don't usually get so tired, but today – ' She shook her head. 'It's been fearful. Maxie had a row yesterday with Dan and decided today he had a migraine. It happens about once a year, with those two. It's part of their lives now. Dan niggles at Maxie and eventually Maxie gets a migraine and Dan feels lousy about it and goes to see him and they make it up till the next time. Tomorrow they'll walk in here with their arms round each other's necks, but today – ' She stretched her shoulders and rubbed the back of her neck with both hands. 'Today's been murder.'

He was all compunction. 'I shouldn't have come!'

'Don't be silly! We'd made an arrangement.'

'You should have let me know it was a bad day.'

'Ridiculous,' she said and dismissed his protestations with a wave of her hand. 'I'd have put someone else at this table, wouldn't I? Don't be silly. Now, let's talk about your film. What do you need to know?'

'Everything. Anything. Whatever you want to tell me.'

She lifted her brows. 'That's impossible. I need questions to answer.'

'All right. Questions.' He set his glass down, already half empty. The Tokay tasted much more agreeable than he would have expected so sweet a wine to be. 'Who was the first of your family to work here in this restaurant?'

'My great grandfather,' she said at once. 'And great grandmother, of course. Though she didn't actually do much in the restaurant as far as I know.'

He folded his arms on the table and leaned forwards so that he was closer to her; the other diners were getting a shade noisier now as they reached the brandy and cigars stage and he didn't want to miss a word. 'What were their names?'

She leaned forwards too, copying his posture and their heads were close together as she began to explain. Her eyes seemed to be looking at him but they weren't seeing him, of that he was sure. She looked blank as she talked, as though she were watching scenes far away down the end of a long reversed telescope.

'Their names? Viktor and Maritza. I can remember my grandma telling me about them. I was only five when she died. But still I remember – she used to talk about the old days a lot. Not that she remembered the old country, of course. She was born here. Only Aunt Kati was born in

Hungary. The others, they were all English born. But still Hungarian.'

She smiled then and her blank gaze sharpened and she looked at Joel directly. 'My family really is terribly Hungarian. They all behave as though they've only just got off the boat, even though we go back so far here in London, peppering their talk with Hungarian whenever they can. I don't, I must admit. I've forgotten so much – when I was little I understood a good deal of Hungarian, but it's all gone now. My Uncle Istvan and my father – they used it a good deal. I sometimes think my father spoke it to annoy my mother.'

She smiled fleetingly. 'They loved each other in their own way, but they got at each other a lot. You know what I mean? And she was so very English that he used to put on a great Hungarian act to irritate her. It used to make me laugh, I'm afraid, though it annoyed my mother dreadfully.'

'Would you mind if I wrote some of this down?' he said, not wanting to damage the magic web of intimacy that he felt had grown between them, but knowing he'd never remember it all without notes. 'Not about your parents irritating each other, of course. Just the important details, names and dates, you know?'

'I suppose so,' she said and leaned back and he cursed inside his head. He had damaged it after all. 'If you really need to.'

'It would help.' And he reached for his notebook and pen. The sooner he sorted out the impediments of his trade the sooner she'd be able to forget them and relax again. 'When did Viktor and Martiza come here!'

'1888. It's the sort of date you remember. They came from Buda. Not Pesth, and not Budapest. From *Buda*. They were always very fussy about that, apparently. It makes a difference, it seems.'

'How old were they?'

'Oh. Quite young. Viktor was twenty-eight. Big man, even then. Square sort of face, curly hair. I have a picture somewhere.'

'I'd love to see it.'

'If I can find it some time,' she said vaguely and looked down at her hands, wrapped round the glass of Tokay. He felt that she was regretting opening out so much to him and he leaned back, attempting to be casual.

'And his wife, Martiza?'

'She was very young. Only twenty-one. She had a dreadful time, poor thing.'

'How dreadful?'

She lifted her shoulders at him and shot a sharp glance from beneath her lashes. 'In the way women always have had. Too many babies, too soon. Too many dying. Kati was just two when they came here and Maritza had just had another baby who'd died. And there were more who died, three or four. Can you imagine that? All those pregnancies and nothing but dead babies to show for it?'

'No,' he said. 'I can't imagine it.' And that seemed to please her, for she smiled at him.

'Women do better today, don't they? Or I suppose they do, I'm not always sure – anyway, after they got here, Viktor found a job. As a waiter in a Greek restaurant. They weren't badly off, apparently, or so my grandmother used to say. She told me her mother had been very clever with money, always managed to look after it. They got here with all sorts of furniture and goods. Not like some of the people who emigrated who arrived in just the clothes they stood up in. They had silver and linen – all sorts of things – '

'Where did they live?'

'In the East End, where all the Jewish refugees were. They were coming in then in their thousands, apparently. I've never been able to be sure what was what with religion and Viktor and Martiza. My grandmother was a fearful snob and rather prejudiced I think. She always said her mother was a real lady, one of the Catholic aristocracy who had married beneath her.'

She laughed, then, a soft chuckle. 'It's so odd. I feel as though I'm seven years old again and listening to Gran'ma nattering on and on. I used to sit in her lap and she'd talk and talk. I loved it. But now when I listen to what she said – inside my head, you know – I realise she was actually rather awful. By modern standards, that is. By her own, not at all, I suppose – but she used to tell me her father was just a peasant, no good at all, a gambling peasant. What a dreadful thing to say about your own father! She said he was Jewish too.' She grinned then. 'Obviously that was the worst she could say, as far as she was concerned, but I hope he was. I think it's rather nice to be a good mixture. Part Jewish, part Catholic, a bit Hungarian, very English and – '

'And very nice,' he said and then could have bitten his tongue out for she looked suspicious suddenly and her eyes seemed to harden as she stared at him.

'I do appreciate the help you're giving me,' he said then as casually as he could, and bent his head to his notes. 'It's really so nice of you.'

She relaxed as he used the silly word again in so colourless a way, and he breathed again, for he had actually held his breath for a moment. He liked this woman, wanted to get to know her better, to make a friend of her, but it was clear she wasn't going to be an easy conquest. She was more English than perhaps she realized, he thought as he kept his head down over his notebook. Reserved, scared of allowing anyone to get close –

'Hello, Laura!' a voice said behind him, and he lifted his head, startled. But he didn't at once turn to see who was there, because he couldn't take his eyes from her face. She was looking above and beyond him and smiling and there it was again, that blazing dark-eyed look that had drawn him so strongly across the Yard that sunny morning last week. And now he did turn his head as the newcomer came alongside them, and pulling an empty chair from an adjoining table, sat down.

'Do you mind if I join you? he said.

'Oh, no, not at all!' Laura said. Her voice was different too, a little huskier than it had been and a touch breathless. 'I – Mr. Coplin here is doing research for a television film. Social history. He's looking for information about the families of the area. I'm telling him about ours.'

Her eyes lit up even more then, if that were possible, this time with laughter.

'You can help, if you like. This is my cousin Philip Cord, Mr. Coplin. My cousin by marriage. I'm sure he'll be glad to help. He might know more about his wife's side of the family, if you ask him!'

Philip Cord held out his hand to Joel. 'Glad to be of use,' he said and smiled, his eyes crinkling in a very attractive but clearly practised fashion which Joel immediately loathed. 'What can I do for you? Happy to be of assistance – within reason.' And again he smiled, but this time it wasn't attractive at all. It was too watchful to be that.

17

It was, Joel decided, like trying to walk over a ploughed field in the rain while wearing oversized bedroom slippers. Philip Cord seemed to be friendly, with those damned smiles of his much in evidence, yet somehow there was no meat in what he said. He seemed to slither between Joel's questions, missing the point of them over and over again and looking blankly uncomprehending when Joel tried to sharpen and shape his questions even more. And then of course Laura would draw back and look cool and ungiving, not liking the directness of his interrogation, so that after half an hour of apparently animated talk he felt he was no further on, and much more isolated from Laura to whom he had been feeling so comfortably close.

'Look,' he said, almost despairingly. 'Let me see if I can do a family tree, hmm? There are Viktor and Maritza – ' And he scribbled their names at the top of a sheet of paper and drew lines from them to indicate children. 'Here is the eldest – your wife's grandmother, Mr. Cord – and here are the ones who died – how many were there, Miss Horvath?'

She shrugged. 'I can't be sure. Four or five. Does it matter?'

'I think it does. It gives a picture of the hardness of women's lives then. You made that point yourself, remember?'

'Did I?' She looked at Philip Cord and Joel thought – she wants to be alone with him. She's tired of me, wants me to go.

For a brief moment he thought seriously of doing just that, of getting to his feet and thanking her for her help and her delightful dinner and just leaving; he had actually tightened his thigh muscles ready to push back his chair and stand up when he caught Cord's glance on him, suddenly eager, and knew that he too wanted to get rid of him, and at once his feelings somersaulted. Bugger the man. He'd stay put. He had been here first, he was Laura Horvath's guest, he was here for a purpose. Let Cord get the hell out. He, Joel Coplin, was sitting tight.

'All right,' he said smoothly. 'Let's put in four.' And he made his scribbles accordingly. 'Then there was your aunt who was having her birthday party the first time I came here – Anya Zsu – ' He stumbled over the name and Cord said smoothly. 'Mrs. Balog. It is the family who refer to her as Anya Zsuzske.'

'I'm sorry,' Joel said, not looking at him. 'I didn't mean to be over familiar.'

'It's difficult not to be when you're investigating people's families and private lives, I imagine.'

'I'll remember the need to be careful,' Joel said savagely. 'And then, Miss Horvath? There was your grandmother? Mrs. – ah, I imagine Mrs. Horvath?'

She looked at him and then at Philip and out of the corner of his eye Joel saw him shake his head almost imperceptibly and he felt a tide of angry colour lift in his cheeks. Who the hell was this bloody man to try to interfere in this way? A cousin by marriage, that was all. What else was going on here that made the man behave in so overbearing a fashion?

He opened his mouth to speak, almost certainly to say something he'd later regret for its plain rudeness when to his amazement Laura said, 'Yes, there was my grandmother next. And after her there was Istvan. My great Uncle Pishta – that was the pet name we all used. You can use it too if you like when you talk about him. Everyone did.'

He looked at her and she was sitting very straight and her cheeks had small patches of colour on them as she looked very directly at Philip Cord. 'No need to make secrets, Philip,' she said then, seeming not to care that Joel was listening to her private reprimand. 'It's a bad habit in this family, being secretive. You don't want to finish up like Dolly and Evelyn, do you? Always whispering? There's no harm in helping Mr. Coplin with his research, is there? Especially as his family were friends of ours – ' He had been looking at her with his face as usual relaxed into a smile but his eyes had been a little hooded; now he lifted his lids sharply and glanced sideways at Joel.

'What was that?'

'My great grandfather was a friend of Uncle – Pishta.' Joel grinned then, looking at Laura. 'Why does that sound a rather rude name? It's the sort of nickname we'd give to kids who wet their pants when I was at school.'

Surprising him again, Laura laughed, a soft little chuckling sound. 'I used to think that too when I was a child,' she said. 'I said it to him once and he laughed and said it was true – he did use to be a pishta when he was a boy. But it's the usual Hungarian shortening for Istvan, so he didn't mind. You see, Philip?' She looked then at Cord. 'It's quite reasonable that we tell Mr. Coplin what he wants to know. It's no harm to us.'

'Isn't it?' Now Cord wasn't smiling. 'Have we any way of knowing? The way these television people twist things and cheat with facts – '

'And what do you do for a living, Mr. Cord?' Joel asked, his voice silky.

'Mmm? I hardly think that's relevant.'

'Oh, I don't know. I just wondered what sort of stereotyped notion, what sort of clichés, I could trot out about *your* chosen occupation.'

'Oh, I dare say you're an honest enough man personally. It's your bosses who can't be trusted. I've heard some tales of the sort of things these editors and producers do.'

'About my company? About me and the films I make?'

Cord shrugged. The moment of annoyance he had shown at Laura's refusal to accept his guidance had gone. He was clearly content again now that he had roused Joel to irritation, and Joel noted that fact and stored it away at the back of his mind for future use. 'I really can't remember. It's not that important, is it?'

'No, I agree. Your opinion in this matter is very unimportant,' Joel said and thought – touché! That'll show you, you bastard. But Cord smiled at Laura.

'My dear girl, it's of no importance to me whatsoever if

you want to let this television film drag the family's name around. If you don't think anyone else will protest, then fine – '

'Heavens, I haven't agreed to do anything but talk!' Laura said and laughed. She seemed placatory now, as though her moment of resistance to Cord had shivered away and she looked at him appealingly and Joel wanted to lean over and shake her, to tell her not to crawl like that to this nasty piece of work. 'Have I, Mr. Coplin?'

'Not at all,' he said promptly. 'All I need at this stage is some background information about the way families lived and ran their lives and businesses in this part of London over the past eighty or ninety years. We're a long way yet from making our film. I always talk to far more people than I need. Maybe I'll come back and ask, very politely and with all the safeguards anyone could possibly want, for permission to do interviews, but I've a long way to go before we get to that stage. There are many other Soho families to talk to.'

'You see, Philip?' Laura said and again there was that appealing note in her voice that made Joel want to grit his teeth with anger.

'Businesses, Mr. Coplin? What do you want to know about the way people ran their businesses?' Cord said, and now he was no longer smiling but staring challengingly at Joel. 'Are you going to be digging into people's books and ledgers, asking about money? I imagine so. You see, Laura?' He shifted his gaze back to her. 'Thin edges of wedges, that's what. The next thing you know you'll have all sorts of tax people and Lord knows who buzzing around.'

She frowned, genuinely mystified. 'I can't imagine why you're so suspicious, Philip. I don't care how many tax men come! I don't care who sees my books! In fact, I like showing 'em off! I've always run this place the way my father did – the way his father taught him. Everything straight up.'

She laughed then and leaned forwards to set her hand on Philip's arm. 'My dear, don't you know the old story? Poor old Grandfather Zolly got a bit involved with the black market in 'forty two, and as near as dammit was caught. He didn't have to go to court but according to my father it was a very close run thing. And after that, he was so virtuous he could have worn white robes and a halo all day. My father was only a boy at the time but he was already working in the business, but it scared him too. So he was just as careful when he took over. I didn't have to worry about black marketeers, glory be, but I still run the place the way my father did. I don't know any other. So you see, there's no need to be so careful!'

Philip shrugged. He seemed sulky now. 'It's up to you, of course.'

'No it isn't. If the rest of the family object, then I can't involve myself with Mr. Coplin's film, can I? *Do* you object?'

He looked at her and then at Joel and suddenly gave a wide smile that took in both of them.

'I suppose I'm being over-protective. It's just that – ' He shrugged all charming self deprecation. 'This place, it's important to me, Mr. Coplin. It's important to my wife – it's part of her family history and that means it's now part of mine. And we all care a great deal for Laura who keeps it all going – '

And he smiled at her and she smiled back, that great flaming smile that Joel could have warmed his hands at and he thought with a sudden surge of cold fury – they're in love. This marvellous woman's in love with this lousy bastard and he with her – and he wanted to push back his chair and reach round the table and drag the man to his feet and punch him hard.

It took all the self control he had to sit still and he realised after a moment that he was shaking and he pushed his hands down into his lap beneath the table as Laura said, a little loudly, 'More coffee, Mr. Coplin?' in a tone of voice that made it clear she'd said it before and had had to repeat it.

'Mmm? Er – no, thank you. I mean, yes please, I'd love some.' I'm sitting tight, tight, tight, he thought. I'm not letting that bastard have all the running! I'm not letting him just scoop her up from under my nose like that. I've only just found her and I'm not letting go that easily.

The shaking eased and went away, and he was able to pick up his coffee cup when Miklos had filled it and sip with every air of being relaxed and comfortable, but inside he was aghast.

This is crazy, he told himself. This is sheer lunacy. You can't behave like a stupid child, suddenly getting this involved. You've never done anything so idiotic before, not in all your life, and you're a grown man, you're thirty. This is what happens to boys of seventeen, not men of thirty. Falling in love as abruptly as a lemming falling over a cliff – stupid, stupid, stupid, you're even thinking in clichés. Stop this nonsense, stop it at once –

But his mind refused to listen to the commonsense he was hammering at it, and he lifted his eyes and looked at her again, at the way she was sitting with her head half turned so that she could fix her gaze on the other man, and all he could see was a glitter of light around her. She seemed now to be the most beautiful thing he'd ever seen and he forced himself to shift his own gaze and look at Cord, as she was; and he was smiling at her, his mouth curled in a way that seemed to Joel to be positively lascivious. Again he had to push his hands down out of sight to prevent himself from hitting out at that self-satisfied face.

'So,' he said loudly. 'How do we stand? Am I to continue with my research, Miss Horvath, or am I to go away and find other Soho families I can talk to?'

She looked at him, seeming to Joel to drag her eyes unwillingly from Cord and again he felt that shaft of pure hate for the man shoot up inside him.

'Oh, I think we go on,' she said and then smiled. 'I'm a business woman, after all, Mr. Coplin, and I would hate to miss the opportunity of good free publicity for my restaurant if I can get it. I reserve the right, of course, to pull back at any point if I'm not sure that the whole thing will be – ' She pursed her lips in a way that Joel found wholly delightful and said primly, ' – shall we say tasteful. But otherwise I'm glad to help. On the understanding that if you do use us that the restaurant gets a decent showing!'

Joel laughed, feeling a great warm wash of pleasure at the

good sense of her, the wisdom of her, the sheer wonderfulness of her, while underneath the watching sensible part of himself jeered at his childishness. To fall so suddenly into so violent a crush at his age! Ridiculous!

'Absolutely,' he said. 'The word and honour of a Canadian gentleman. There are a few of us in the television business.' And he looked at Cord, enjoying the malice that now filled him. He'd show the arrogant bastard where he got off, just see if he didn't. He'd get this marvellous woman to himself, just watch him –

'Oh, Laura, my dear girl! That's the last thing you need! Publicity? Bless you, you already turn away more customers every day than you can accommodate!'

'That's today,' Laura said. 'Who knows where we'll be tomorrow? You never do know, you see, Philip. Sometimes you can get too sure of yourself, too pleased with the business you're doing and you forget there's another day. Tomorrow isn't always as good as yesterday. Anything can change. So I use whatever opportunities that come my way to look after tomorrow. You see?'

'No I don't,' he said. 'Ever since I've known you – what is it? Fifteen, sixteen years – this place has been the most successful restaurant in Soho – '

'No need to exaggerate,' she said and laughed. '*One* of the most successful I'll go along with. But *the* most? Never! The day I start to think that is the day I'm in real trouble.'

'Hubris,' Joel said and she looked at him and at once his chest tightened with excitement, and he stared back at her, furious at himself for being so absurd.

'What was that?'

'Hubris – insolent or overweening pride that leads to disaster and downfall. The sin of the Greeks who thought themselves above the Gods. You're avoiding it – very wise.'

'Ah!' Cord said. 'Now you're giving us the evidence of how reliable you are, eh, Coplin? No man educated enough to quote Greek at us can possibly be anything but virtuous and upright, hmm?'

'Something like that,' Joel said and stared at him, challengingly. But the other man seemed unaware of the dislike in his tone or in his gaze and grinned at him amiably.

'Well, there it is. If Laura has decided that helping you is good for the restaurant then there'll be no shifting her. What's good for the restaurant is good for the world, in her estimation – '

'It's good for *you*,' Laura said sharply and he shot a little glance at her and after a moment said smoothly, 'Of course, my dear. And for me. Me and Ilona, hmm?'

She went a sudden deep red and leaned back in her chair and Joel thought – that was significant. There was more in that little exchange than I understand. I will one day, but right now, I don't understand. But I will – I have to –

Cord got to his feet. 'Well, I must be away. I've got to get back to Harrow tonight. Good to have had the opportunity to meet you, Coplin.'

'Don't go yet,' Laura said quickly and stood up too. 'There are – I had something I wanted to talk to you about.'

She looked confused suddenly and, embarrassed for her, Joel looked away, collecting up his notebook and his pens and tucking them into his pocket, making a little busyness out of it to cover his awareness of her confusion.

'It's not important, of course,' she said then, and turned away. 'It can wait.'

'I have to go now,' Joel said loudly and stood up. 'I can see myself out, Miss Horvath. Thank you for your help. May I come back some time? Look at the photographs you mentioned? Talk to Angie perhaps about the way the restaurant has developed while he's been here? It could all be grist to the research mill, you see – '

'Yes – yes, of course,' she said, clearly abstracted now. She was still looking at Cord who was humping himself into his coat. 'Philip, just hold on a moment, will you? I'll be right back.' And she moved away, inviting Joel to follow her, and at once he did, letting her lead him to the door.

'It was very kind of you,' he said quietly. 'I greatly enjoyed my dinner. I hope you will allow me to return your hospitality soon. Good night.' And he shook her hand firmly and went, pulling the door closed behind him with a little snap.

He stood out in the dark Yard for a long time, staring at the other diners at their tables, laughing, talking, their heads wreathed in cigar smoke, at Miklos moving ponderously about with glasses of brandy and there, against the window, the two of them, Laura and her cousin's husband, standing close to each other and talking, talking, talking –

Joel watched them, hating himself for behaving like a peeping Tom and totally powerless to do anything else. He saw the intimacy between them in the way they stood so closely, in the angle of Laura's head as she tilted it up to look at the taller Cord, in the manner in which she had one hand laid on his sleeve, apparently unaware of the fact it was there. I'll show the bastard, he told himself again. I won't let him march all over me. I'll show him.

And I don't care if it is hubris, either, he thought then, as at last he found the will to pull up his coat collar to keep out the chill of the spring evening air and turned to go. It's worth the risk. She's extraordinary. Damn her, she's extraordinary.

18

'Seventy pounds?' Abner said. 'You lost *seventy pounds*? No one can lose that sort of money just playing cards.'

'I can,' Viktor said. 'I did. Seventy pounds fifteen and sixpence.' He said it with a sort of gloomy pride that made Abner shake his head and purse his lips into a soundless whistle.

'What did the missus say?' Abner asked after a long pause and Viktor shifted in his chair awkwardly and looked over his shoulder. Maritza was sitting at the desk in the corner with Zolly beside her and that made him add a scowl to his obvious anxiety.

'What she don't know won't hurt her,' he growled and turned round again to sit with his back hunched against her.

'But Poppa, she'll find out!' Istvan said. 'She always does. Better to tell her now than – '

'Shut up, Pishta!' Abner said and kicked him and Istvan lifted his shoulders and subsided.

They sat in silence for a while, the three of them, and then Istvan, who had been looking more and more impatient could contain his feelings no longer.

'Poppa, what do I do?' he burst out. 'If you ain't got it, and I got to have it – what do I do? Here I am with Eva driving me meshuggah with the nagging, thinks I ought to get more. I'm the only man, she says, and the girls are all married and settled and we've got the three kids and – I'm the only man – '

'Don't start that again,' Viktor said. 'It's enough I got the same argument with *her*.' And he jerked his head towards the desk in the corner, as though he were unable to say her name, he was so disgusted. 'Haven't I told her, over and over, haven't I told her? You're the only one got the name, the only Halascz we got in this family now. The girls is all settled, got husbands, haven't I told her? But does she listen? All she can talk about is her lousy Family Trust she wants. Her and her shyster lawyer friends what give her such ideas! Family Trusts! I spit on Family Trusts – ' And he did, aiming accurately for the ashtray full of cigar butts on the table in front of him. 'I don't sign for no Family Trusts.'

'So, why don't you just do what *you* want, Poppa – it's your business, ain't it? Yours to decide. You're the man, the owner. How come she can say yea or nay this way? If you want I should have money, it's *your* business, ain't it?' Istvan leaned back in his chair and stared at the old man. He was dressed in his usual high style, even though there had been no special reason to do so this evening; it had been just a card game, a bit of supper with his father and his father's friend, no more, but he had dressed in his natty grey chalk stripe suit with the wide lapels and the shirt with the fancy buttons and the blue spotted tie and the black and white parti-coloured shoes. His head gleamed sleek and dark with brilliantine, and the heavy gold watch and ring he always wore made his left hand and wrist glitter in the soft light of the restaurant. He looked extremely good and clearly knew it, carefully ignoring the admiring glances from the women at the tables nearby while actually making sure his profile was well displayed as he seemed to concentrate on Viktor.

'Sure it's my business,' Viktor said, but there was uneasiness in him still. 'Sure it is.'

'Then why does Zolly Horvath get to be so busy in your business?' Istvan said sharply and lifted his chin even higher to look at the desk in the corner where the two heads, Maritza's and Zolly's were so very close together. 'So he works here, okay, but does he have to be the cock of the walk as well?'

'Shut up!' Viktor roared and Maritza's head came up with an almost audible snap and she glared across the restaurant at him. 'Shut up,' he said again, more quietly. 'I deal with my affairs in my own way. I don't need you pushing and nagging and driving me crazy as well. Leave it to me. Go on home already. Go back and tell your Eva what she should do the way you tell me to tell my Maritza what she should do, all right? When you're so good at stopping your own hen from crowing you can come and tell me how to do the same with mine. Right now, I got business to arrange. So go away already, and I'll let you know what I can do. I'll fix it, ain't I always fixed it for you? Won't I again? Go home, and leave it to your old Poppa. I'll fix it – '

Istvan stared at him for a long moment and then got to his feet. 'All right, Poppa. All right. I see how it is. So I'll go home. But I tell you, it's a great chance I'll be missing if you can't do this for me. It's not a lot I'm asking for, even. A measly five hundred pounds. What's five hundred pounds to you, with a business like this? To me, it's a future for my family, it's *important*. To you, it's chicken feed, right? You who loses seventy pounds on a lousy card game – '

The two older men watched him weave his way through the restaurant to the desk in the corner and said nothing. He bent his head to kiss Maritza's cheek, studiously ignoring Zolly who stood and watched him with his face quite blank of any expression, and then turned and went to the door to collect his wide shouldered camel hair coat from the stand there. Many people watched him go, as well as his relations; the women at the tables stared after him, seeming to listen to their escorts' chatter but clearly fascinated by this good looking and elegant creature, and he managed to catch the eyes of some of them oh-so-casually, and yet so definitely, that more than one face blushed. And then he was gone, leaving the door swinging behind him.

'Listen, Viktor,' Abner said after a long pause. 'Maybe it's no bad thing you can't give him the money?'

'How do you mean, no bad thing?' Viktor had been lighting another cigar, making a performance of it, circling his head with the curling smoke. 'How can it be no bad thing a boy asks his Poppa for money, and has to be told no? The only boy I got, he is, the only one – ' And he shook his head, almost tearfully. 'My only boy – '

Abner coughed and leaned back in his chair, and spoke carefully, seeming to pick his words. 'How can you say that, Viktor? There's the girls' husbands, don't they count for nothing? They're good for the girls, they are, and isn't Zolly the best son-in-law a man could have? He works here like a mad thing. I've seen him, first thing in the morning, last thing at night – '

'It's all he's fit for, the great idiot,' Viktor said savagely and blew out a great belch of smoke so that his face almost disappeared behind it. 'All he's fit for, a donkey like him. Let him work like a donkey. He's got no brains, no sairchel, nothing – '

'Not true, Viktor, not true,' Abner said mildly. 'He's done wonders here, give the boy his due – '

'He's done no wonders!' Viktor flared. 'If that's the best you can say, do me a favour and talk about the weather. I tell you the man's a great fool, an ox, a donkey, a pig, every lousy creature I can set my tongue to. He's got Maritza where he wants her, she'll do anything the bastard wants. Isn't that enough I have to put up with without my best friend taking his side as well?' He was beginning to sound tearful now. 'I tell you, the man's some sort of devil. First he gets my poor Magda, and look what he's done to her! She looks twice her age, twice! The way he gets round my Maritza so my life's a misery from then on with her nagging over what he wants to change here – and then you tell me I should put one like that in front of my Istvan? The only one that's a Halascz. How can you ask such a thing?'

Abner shook his head, and sighed. 'All right, all right, Viktor, not another word about Zolly. So you hate him, and that's all there is to it. But if it's the boys you're so worried about – the boys in the family – so there's the three Balog lads – Zsuzske's lovely boys. And there's Istvan's Steven and Daniel – ' Prudently he said nothing about Zolly's two sons. 'You can't say Istvan's the only boy you got – '

'He's the only one that's a Halascz. The only one with my name,' Viktor said stubbornly and sat even lower in his chair so that his shoulders came up and made him look like a bad tempered bison, with his great grey head surmounting the heavy muscles of his neck and back. 'He's my special one. You know he is – '

'It don't make no sense to me,' Abner said and shook his head again. 'But it's your business, I suppose.'

'Thank you,' Viktor said, suddenly sardonic and the other old man laughed comfortably.

'All right, all right. So I'm sticking my oar in! So? Don't I have a right, all the years we been friends, all the times we've shared? Don't I have the right?'

'You got the right,' Viktor said after a moment and leaned forwards and punched his friend gently on the arm. 'Who better than you to advise me? Of course you got the right. Listen, Abner. I'll tell you what I think I'm going to do. I'm going to get the money for Istvan, and I'm going to do what *I* want for a change. It's time I went back to the old country, began to have some life of my own. Take my Maritza home, get her away from all this, get a nice farm, raise a few horses, maybe?'

Abner stared at him and then spluttered into laughter. 'You? On a farm? Raising horses? Are you crazy, Viktor? You'll raise horses the way I'll raise devils just by whistling for them! And where're you going to get the money for such a scheme? Sell this place? And then what'll the family do, hmm? You may hate Zolly, but Magda, her children, don't they have any call on you? You can't sell their work from under them.'

Viktor waved his hand airily. 'They'll have more than enough when I've finished. More than enough, for them, for Istvan, for the farm – '

'How?'

Viktor grinned and tapped his lips with one forefinger, looking mysterious. 'Don't I have my ways? Hmm? Don't I have ideas, Abner my old friend? When did you ever know me I didn't have ideas?'

'Terrible ideas,' Abner said. 'Crazy ideas. Listen, Viktor, not gambling again. You promised Maritza, last time, you nearly lost the place altogether and you promised her – '

'Who's gambling?' Viktor looked pained. 'I'm not gambling. I'm selling, that's what I'm doing – ' He chuckled then, fatly pleased with himself. 'I'm selling!'

'You said you wouldn't sell the place!'

'I wouldn't be! Not all of it.'

'Eh?'

'Just a bit of it. At the back there, just a bit of it!'

'At the back? What at the back? All you've got there is the kitchens – what else have you got there?'

Again Viktor leaned forwards. 'Listen, those kitchens – all enlarged and fancy – didn't I say to Maritza it wasn't necessary? For years we did all right with what we had, but this Zolly, it wasn't good enough for him. *He* had to have the big cupboards, the big cold room, the cellar room for wine, yet, all sorts of crazy things. So, Maritza buys the space and he gets what he wants. Only now there's new people in Bateman Street, behind the kitchen. New people, new ideas – '

'So?' Abner said uneasily and looked over his shoulder at Maritza. She caught his eye and smiled at him and he smiled back; a good girl Maritza. Anyone who could put up with a crazy man like Viktor had to be a good girl.

'So I tell you what I'm going to do.' Viktor had poured and drunk another glass of wine and was refilling his glass again, and as usual the fumes reached his head swiftly. He was extra rosy about the nose and cheeks now and his eyes glittered with excitement. 'I'm going to see these new people in Bateman Street. I'm going to tell them I got this place. I can sell 'em extra space at the back, joining on to them. They'll jump at it, jump they will – '

'What sort of business have they got there?' Abner asked. 'Do they need extra space?'

'By the time I've finished with them they'll be pleading for the extra space,' Viktor said and laughed. 'Pleading for it, they'll be. Listen, what difference does it make what business they got? Viktor Halascz tells 'em they need the space, they'll agree. And they'll pay me big money for it, and me and my Maritza'll go to Hungary, find a nice little farm, a few horses. I'll start to live the life of a gentleman, no more sweating over the busy restaurant business for me. I'll see to my horses every day, meet the local gentry – I tell you, it'll be what I was born for – ' And he slumped a little more deeply in his chair and contemplated his glorious future with misty eyes.

'How much money can anyone give you for half a kitchen, Viktor?' Abner said after a pause during which he sat and stared worriedly at the old man who had been his friend for so many years. 'Hmm, Viktor? Not enough for a farm, let alone the horses – '

Viktor waved one hand airily and then refilled his glass. 'I'll get what I ask! These people in Bateman Street'll jump at it, jump at it they will! Just like stinking Zolly wanted more space, so will they – any business would.'

'And what about this business? Hmm? What about the kitchen for this business?'

'He'll manage. Stinking Zolly'll manage. He'll have to. He did before, he can again.'

'I wouldn't be so sure,' Abner said and looked uneasily at Maritza. She was watching them; he had felt her eyes on them for some time now, ever since Zolly had disappeared back to the kitchen. She knew there was something going on she wouldn't like. She had an instinct for it, Abner told himself. Always knew when to get involved with Viktor's crazy ideas, always knew just how much rope to give him. And she was moving now, thinking of coming over here to the sacrosanct corner table where Viktor and his friends always sat, thinking of starting an argument with him, and to hell with what the customers thought. Not that they'd mind unduly; Abner knew how much the regulars enjoyed the cabaret act that was Viktor and his Maritza having an argument.

Across the restaurant, then, he saw Magda and she was standing with a tray full of dirty dishes in her hands and looking at him, an expression of such anxiety on her face that it made Abner crumple his own face in sympathy. She glanced swiftly at her mother and then back at him and as clearly as though she had said it he heard her appeal. And got to his feet.

'Listen, Viktor,' he said quietly, so that Maritza and Magda couldn't hear him. 'I'm leaving. I don't reckon this is a good idea, to tell you the truth, and I don't even want to talk about it. So I'm leaving.' And he moved away, hurrying towards the door and his coat on the stand as fast as he could.

But not fast enough. Maritza caught him as he set his hand to the door that led out to the Yard and said sweetly, 'So, Mr. Coplin? What's the hurry? Why are you rushing off so fast? You usually stay till we have to throw you out. Tonight you're leaving early? So why?'

'I'm tired, Maritza,' he said and leaned forwards to peck her cheek. 'Hard day. Lot to do tomorrow, time I was in bed. Susan'll be wondering where I am. Goo'night Maritza – '

She looked over her shoulder at Viktor who was still sitting at the table. He was staring owlishly at the empty wine bottle now and seemed quite unaware of the colloquy going on behind him.

'Listen, Mr. Coplin – Abner, you're my friend as well as Viktor's, hmm? You care about the whole family, hmm? Haven't you always been good to us, taken care I shouldn't make terrible mistakes in my dealings? Hmm? Wasn't it you warned me about that terrible man, that builder that would have cheated us blind, if we'd let him do the kitchen job. Didn't you save me all that trouble? Quite apart from all the other ways you've helped us.' She looked at him earnestly, her face very close to his. 'You remember the good things you've done for us. Hmm? So save me more trouble. *Now*, Abner. Tell me what he's up to.'

19

'This is nice, Paul!' Laura said and reached out and took his hand and squeezed it. 'I see far too little of you, really. It isn't that I mean to be remote – it's just the way things work out.'

'That's all right,' he said and smiled at her. 'It's the same for me.' He seemed to sit easily, looking relaxed and comfortable but he didn't feel right, Laura decided, watching him covertly over the top of her coffee cup. He's worried about something; is that why he rang out of the blue, suggested this meeting at the flat? Probably. But she knew there was no point in pushing him to talk. Paul had always been the cat who walked by itself. As long as she could remember he had been the one who sat on the outside at all the family parties, watching Anya Zsuzske, smiling and polite when people spoke to him, but always that little bit distant and watchful. As though he expected trouble, she thought now, and again wanted to reach out and touch him. There was something so sad and vulnerable about him, for all his smooth good looks and his neat, well-turned-out appearance. But she controlled the impulse and went on sipping her tea.

'Is Anya Zsuzske well?' she asked after a long silence, and he lifted his chin and said, 'Hmm?' so that he sounded, suddenly, like herself and she laughed, and he looked puzzled.

'You sounded as I do when I answer the phone,' she said. 'And I suspect for the same reason. Because you were thinking of something else.'

He reddened a little. 'I suppose I was. Anya – she's fine.' He made a little grimace then. 'She frightened me after that cold snap we had. Got a cold and wheezed dreadfully – but she's fine now. She's so tough, bless her.'

'Yes,' Laura said, again feeling the emotion in him. He's so scared of losing her, she thought, and that's dreadful. To feel that close to someone that even though they're so old and tired you grudge them the peace of dying when they're ready to – and then she bit her lip as she felt a sudden wave of fear lift over her; suppose it were me, afraid of losing Philip? Would I be as he is? But that was a thought not to be entertained, and she pushed it away.

'I'm glad,' she said gently. 'She can't go on for ever, of course, but every day is important, isn't it?'

'Yes,' he said and now there was real expression in his voice. He sounded miserable and that made her bold.

'What is is, Paul?' she said. 'You're worried about something. Tell me if I can help.'

'I'm not sure – ' he said, and then shook his head. 'It's so difficult to know where to begin. Please, could I have some more tea?'

'Of course.' She took his cup and filled it for him, watching him from beneath her lashes as she did so. He was leaning back in the armchair, staring at the dancing flames of the artificial fire she had just installed in the small fireplace. The flat looked very different now; ever since Philip had started to come here so often she had worked on it, changing curtains here and cushions there, adding a drinks trolley in the corner and new ornaments all over the place. It looked like a home now, she told herself contentedly, as she gave Paul his tea. Maybe that will help him relax, feel easier about what it is that's worrying him.

'Are you afraid because of Anya Zsuzske?' she said after another long silence. 'She is awfully old, you know, and one day – ' She let the words hang in the air between them and he turned his head and looked at her and then, oddly, laughed.

'Oh, my dear Laura, don't you think I've lived with that every hour of every day this past I don't know how many years? She's – you don't have to tell me how frail she is, or how much I need her or – no, I don't want to talk about that.'

He put his cup down very deliberately and with his head

still bent over it said loudly, 'Your brother, Alex. Does it worry you that he's – that he – that he prefers – doesn't have girlfriends? That – ' He stopped and didn't look up.

'That he's gay?' she said after waiting for him to go on. 'Of course it doesn't.'

'Why not?'

'What?'

He looked up at her now and said even more loudly, 'Why not? It's a perversion, isn't it? A disgusting perversion? Why doesn't it worry you?'

'Because I don't think it's perverted at all. It's just the way Alex is. Always has been. I mean, as far as I know. He's – ' She shrugged. 'He's *Alex*. My brother. What he does with his sex life's got nothing to do with that, has it? He's Alex – '

Paul shook his head, still not looking at her. 'It isn't as easy as that,' he said. 'Not really. You can pretend it doesn't matter, but of course it does.'

'Paul,' she said then, and leaned forwards and took hold of both his hands. 'Paul, I don't worry that Alex is gay and I don't worry that you are, either – '

He snatched his hands away from hers as though she had burned him.

'I'm not – I'm – I'm not anything!' he cried and then his face crumpled. 'How can you say that? I've lots of women friends, lead a perfectly normal man's life – just because I never married – but how could I? There was always Anya – my brothers were married, had their families, they wouldn't take care of her, would they? I could never be sure a wife would care for Anya as she should be. How could I marry? I've cut myself off from all that sort of thing for Anya's sake. How can you say – I'm, that I'm such a thing. How can you call me perverted and horrible and – '

'Paul, my dear, dear Paul, I said nothing of the sort,' Laura said, as calmly as she could. It wasn't easy, for he was shaking with emotion and filling the room with his fear. She could almost smell it, acrid and powerful, and it made her own pulses beat faster and filled her chest with tension. 'I don't think like that. I don't think people are perverted or horrible just because they happen to have slightly different needs to other people! I could never think like that – it's you who use those labels, not I. Look, I'm sorry if I've offended you, I didn't mean to. It's just that – well, I wanted to help. I hate to see you looking so miserable and I know that it's supposed to make people feel better if they talk about the things that worry them. And it was you who mentioned it. Well, you mentioned Alex and I thought that was why you – ' She shrugged. 'Look, I'm sorry if I got it wrong, I meant no harm.'

He was leaning back in the armchair again, and in control once more. He even managed to smile shakily at her. 'I'm sorry if I – I didn't mean to get so intense. It's just that – well, Anya had a bad night last night. Couldn't sleep. And that meant I couldn't either.' The smile became a little crooked. 'I'm not complaining, mind you. She's worth every atom of effort I put into looking after her. Just explaining, you see.'

'Yes,' she said and returned to sipping her own tea. She wouldn't say another word, not till he did. Let him explain what he wanted, what it was that had made him so tense that the very air around him seemed to shimmer with it. She'd take no more risks.

The silence between them grew and stretched and then at last he said abruptly. 'There was a reason for asking you about – about how you felt about your brother.'

'Yes?'

'It's – it's because of – I mean, it seemed to me that it made a difference to the way you might feel about other people.'

She shook her head at him, mystified. 'You'll have to explain, Paul. I'm sorry. I may seem dim, but I just don't understand. What has Alex got to do with anything, and other people? I mean, he's my brother, and I'm fond of him, though I don't see much of him.' She laughed then. 'He's a villain really – so busy about his own life he hasn't time to so much as phone. Not that I'm much better. I'm so tied up at the restaurant. We communicate mainly by rumour these days. But I don't mind. He'll call soon enough if he's in trouble, I imagine, just as I'd call him. The less I hear the more certain I am that he's all right.'

'He isn't.'

'What did you say?' He'd spoken so abruptly that she didn't think she'd heard him properly.

'I said, he isn't. All right, I mean. I don't think he is.' He closed his eyes then and said in a tight voice, 'I saw him last week. I thought – he didn't look well. Had the flu, he said. And then he said something about not telling you because it might worry you. And then I thought – ' He looked at her wretchedly, and shook his head and then rubbed his mouth with one hand.

'I'm so afraid he's ill because of – because of how he is,' he said piteously. 'I had to talk to someone about it. I had to, I – ' He shook his head again and then, to her horror, began to weep. The tears slithered down his nose, snail-like and glistening and she sat there frozen with embarrassment and said and did nothing. She couldn't do more than sit very still, trying to take in what he was saying.

'You hear such awful tales,' he went on. 'So many people getting ill, and they have the blood tests and if they find out they've got the thing then they worry themselves sick about whether it'll make them ill, however good they're feeling at the time, and then – ' The tears thickened and his voice seized up and he put both hands in front of his face and wept so bitterly that the chair beneath him shook with it.

She came and knelt beside him, holding his arms above the elbows, not knowing what to do to comfort him, and not knowing what it was that had so frightened him, not wanting to know, just holding on to him and feeling the tension of his muscles through the thin sleeves of his jacket. And then not being able to hold back any longer the word that had come leaping into her mind as he spoke she said loudly, 'Paul! Are you saying you think he's got AIDS?'

The tears increased, and the shaking became even more marked. Now she was angry and shook him hard, and then reached up and pulled his hands away from his wet face.

'For God's sake, man! You've got to tell me! If he has, I

have to know, so that I can – is it true? Or are you just guessing?'

'I don't know.' He managed to get the words out and the sound of his own voice in his ears seemed to steady him, for he took a deep shuddering breath and said in a firmer tone, 'I don't know.'

'Then what the bloody hell are you doing coming here and frightening me this way?' she flamed at him and jumped up and stood staring down at him, holding her elbows bent and her fists tight like a boxer waiting to be attacked. 'How dare you come here and – '

'I couldn't help it,' he said piteously. 'I couldn't. I'm so scared – I thought – ' Again the tears threatened to overwhelm him, but he dragged up some control from somewhere and sat up and took a handkerchief from his pocket and rubbed at his raddled cheeks. 'I can't lie any more, can I? I – there was a man who – I spent some time with him. And then he told me that he'd been with Alex once and then when I saw Alex – Oh, Christ, Laura, I'm so afraid!'

She stood there, very still, and slowly released her fists and let her arms dangle at her sides, trying to take in what it was he was saying. He was gay; he had at last admitted it. She'd always hoped he'd be able to relax enough one day to accept his sexuality and stop being so remote and so icy, but not like this. Never like this. To be told in this way, that both he and her brother – she shook her head in disbelief.

'There's only one thing to be done,' she said, and pushed past him to go to the table in the corner where the telephone stood.

'What are you doing?' He turned and stared at her, his face crinkled again with anxiety. 'What are you doing? Where are you going? Laura?'

She didn't answer him but dialled the number and stood there listening. 'If he's got the bloody answering machine on I'll – ' she began and then her face cleared. 'Alex?'

Paul leapt to his feet. 'No! You can't!' he cried. 'You can't possibly – for God's sake, Laura, you can't!'

But she paid him no attention. 'Alex,' she said crisply into the phone. 'I have to talk to you. I've got Paul here – '

There was a silent moment as she listened and then she said, 'Your cousin Paul. Paul Balog. Who else? What? Yes?'

Again she listened and then she said, 'He frightened me, Alex. Said you were ill. Said it might be AIDS.'

Paul turned away now and moved across to the other side of the small room as though by physically removing himself as far as possible he could leave the situation altogether, and her eyes followed him. But she wasn't looking at him; just concentrating on the thin voice that could just be heard clacking at the end of the phone.

'When did you have the blood test?'

Again the watching silence as the little voice clattered.

'And there can't be any mistake?'

She listened again and then slowly smiled. 'I see. Okay, Alex. You did see I had to ask?'

Paul stood up more straight, and looked across the room at her and she grinned at him and held the phone out. 'Alex wants a word,' she said briefly and after a long frightened moment he moved stiffly and awkwardly, but obeyed, and came and took the phone from her. 'He's had a blood test for it?' he said.

'And he's clear,' she said. 'It seems he wasn't too pleased with having flu. He thought it might be more too. But it wasn't. Talk to him.' And she returned to her tea and filled her cup. However calm she looked there was still fear and tension bubbling in her and the lid rattled as she picked up the tea pot.

'Alex?' Paul said. 'I'm sorry – I shouldn't have – what? – I – someone told me that – Goddam it, Alex, I can't! I can't possibly. Mmm? Well, yes. Yes. No, I still can't. The best I can do is ask him to talk to you himself. No, I really can't. I'm sorry. But it's all right, isn't it? I was so worried that – I'm sorry if I've made waves – ' He stopped short then and Laura looked up and saw the frown that tightened his face as she heard the laughter clearly from the other end of the phone and then lifted one eyebrow as Paul slammed the telephone down on its cradle.

'Why is he laughing?'

'Because he's got no bloody sense of morality, that's why,'

he shouted and then looked mortified. 'Oh, God, I'm sorry, Laura. He's your brother, I know, but – '

She shook her head. 'You don't have to apologise either to me or for Alex. He is what he is, I told you. And I accept him that way. Why is he immoral?'

'It's not for me to say,' he said stiffly and then burst out. 'But damn it all, what a person does is private, a matter to keep to himself and to – to anyone who might be intimately involved. It isn't something to make jokes about –'

'He's laughing because you thought he might have AIDS?'

'No, he's laughing because I thought *I* might have it. And because I thought the same person might have been – ' He went a deep crimson then. 'Oh, Laura, I should never have come. I'm sorry. I really only wanted to help you, to do the right thing, to warn you – damn it, I shouldn't have come. Please forgive me – '

He turned and almost ran across the room to the chair by the door where he had left his coat and hat, and pulled himself into them and then pushed his way out of the door, jabbering as he went. 'I'm sorry, I shouldn't have come, shouldn't have said a word. I'm truly sorry. Forget it, please forget it – '

She tried to hold him back, tried to calm him down, but gave up quickly. It was obvious he wasn't accessible to anything she had to say and she stood at the top of the stairs as he went clattering down them, watching his silvery head disappear into the shadows. She heard the front door slam and then went slowly back to her sitting room.

She had a lot to think about. A *lot* to think about, she told herself. A lot to *think* about. And went on repeating the words as a way of preventing the things she ought to be thinking about from finding room in her mind.

But she couldn't keep that up for long. Eventually she had to face it. Why on earth should Paul come to warn *her* that her brother might have been infected with a dangerous disease? Why hadn't he talked to Alex directly? Why come to her in such a state? Was she seen even by Paul, almost thirty years her senior, as in some sense the head of the family, just because she ran the restaurant? Or was there something more to it than that?

I'll give him a day or so to get over the fright he's had, she thought as she washed the tea things and fed her cat before setting out to go to the restaurant for the evening's work, and then I'll talk to him again. Because there's something here I have to understand, and I don't think I want to.

20

It was as well for his sanity, Joel thought, that Sally Lawrence was ill. She had called into the office to announce in painful detail an attack of pelvic infection which she blamed, with great bitterness, on the lovemaking behaviour of her ex partner, a sound recordist who had been fired from City a couple of weeks earlier after a loud public row with her; Brian Crowner, hanging up the phone on her with a furious bang told anyone who would listen that that was what came of having bloody women in the business. First they got the staff screwed up and then themselves.

Joel, who had been sitting at his desk in the corner of the big production office had started to protest at the stupid injustice of that and then subsided; what was the point of getting angry over the knee jerk attitudes of mindless idiots like Crowner when he had enough problems of his own to deal with? Of course he ought to fight back against such a macho bastard, but feeling as he did at the moment, he couldn't even begin to deal with fools like Crowner. He spent too much time thinking about Laura –

'You'll have to take over the *Thrust* cologne job, Coplin. Thirty seconds with a ten second alternative, and a budget that wouldn't keep me in bog paper. It's all yours,' Crowner said and threw a folder on to his desk. 'The agency handling it are almost as shitty as the client, so enjoy yourself. It's a right Sally Lawrence cockup, this one. I wish you joy of it. You've got two weeks to do it – the schedules are booked.'

Joel picked up the folder and looked at it. 'Ye Gods, who ever came up with a bottle design like this? It's revolting.'

'It's sexy. So they say – can you get the job done in the time? I warn you, it won't be easy dealing with that prat from the agency – that was why I gave the job to Sally. Kept it out of our hair – '

'And then you're surprised she gets ill?' Joel said but Crowner had gone back to his own desk, whistling. His whole career at City was based on buck passing and now he'd done it again, he was a happy man.

And oddly, so was Joel, even though he felt he was walking on the edge of a crumbling precipice. He, who had always been rather amused by the fussing and fuming that went on among his friends when they fell in love, he who had always enjoyed the company of women and had his share of satisfying cheerful girlfriends but had never felt more than comfortable affection for them, to be poleaxed like this? It was mad, it was uncomfortable, it was embarrassing and it was above all very very exhilarating.

Ever since he had eaten his dinner at Laura's he had been obsessed with thoughts of her, and now, looking down at the *Thrust* folder he was grateful for it. To have a rush job to do was what he most needed; there would be little time to spend mooning while dealing with this.

He grabbed his coat and the folder and went, glad to get out into the air, and took a taxi over to the glossy advertising agency offices near Grosvenor Square, and it was a pleasure to sit in the back of the rackety cab which reeked, as they all seemed to these days, of cheap deodorant, and busy himself with the folder. He needed an idea that was quick, inexpensive and effective and which he could bulldoze over a nitpicking agency man and even fussier client. It was just the sort of job he had made his name on, and it was good to have it. The research for his planned film could never have held his attention like this. Now he'd be able to stop thinking obsessively of the compact shape and the round face and curly head of Laura. He'd be able to put her away and get a sense of perspective and proportion about her, and –

But it didn't happen like that. He found his idea – a sudden memory of the stallkeepers in Berwick Street market had come swimming into his consciousness as his taxi rounded a corner where a flower stall glowed vividly and ridiculously frothy with narcissi and roses and mimosa, and he saw a series of sharp, knowing comments from them about the attractiveness of their male customers and passers-by, all of whom, it would turn out, were *Thrust* users to a man – and he had no difficulty in persuading the agency chap, a rather frightened young man with a very shiny new diploma from the Harvard Business School, and damn all in the way of practical experience, to accept it. He had, by the end of the day briefed the casting people in finding his actors, had the location manager at City setting up the permissions to shoot in Berwick Street market, and had even made an appointment to meet the client and soothe him.

Yet all the time this work had been going on, he had been thinking of Laura. Her face was there in the middle of the pages in the folder when he looked at them. Her voice echoed softly in his ears as the agency prat burbled on and on about unique selling points and perceived value and erotic design content, all the clichés he could find. Her presence was with him wherever he went and wherever he turned. It was as though he was operating on two totally different levels, or was perhaps two separate Joels inhabiting the same body. He even peered at himself in a mirror when after lunch with the AP (which was how he now thought of the agency prat) he escaped to the men's room, almost expecting to see himself looking odd. But he saw only the familiar, rather rumpled image that he always did, the same square face and the quiet dark eyes and the full mouth and no sign of what was going on inside his head. And he sighed and went back to the AP to talk again about Thrust – which was beginning to sound like the most stupid product ever invented – and wondered when he'd see her again.

He didn't, but he did see Philip Cord. Only five days after he had been given the Thrust job he arrived at the office of the casting agency, just behind Liberty's in Regent Street, to select the actors who would play his market traders. Tomorrow he would settle down to choosing his Thrust users, who would be of a very different type. And once that was done, the commercial was as good as in the can.

He grinned at that thought. He had made remarkable progress in the time. The script was written and passed – and to the AP's surprise he had insisted on writing it himself and had come up with one based on his remembered conversation in the market that the client liked much better than anything the agency had been able to produce – and the preliminary permissions had been given to shoot film in the street. He had booked space at the open air section of the studios City used over at Hammersmith to build the couple of actual market stalls that would be needed for closeups and had the designer busily at work setting them up. If he could get all his casting done in these two days, he told himself, he'd be sitting pretty; he could even bring this damned thing in under the two weeks, which would be gratifying. And with a little care he might even be able to edge it in under budget which would be even more satisfying.

His lips curled a little as he strode up Regent Street with his hands in his pockets and his raincoat flapping behind him and imagined Buzzy Lethbridge's face when he presented him with a budget underspend rather than a deficit. Heavens, but that would be good! And then he'd call Laura at the restaurant and ask her to – and he began to walk faster, to stop himself thinking about her, and got to the casting people exactly on the dot of ten o'clock.

That was the point at which his careful husbandry of time threatened to fall to pieces. The waiting room was full of actors and he glanced at them with a practised eye as he went through, well used to assessing quickly the quality of what he was being offered, and his brows snapped down. He'd told the agency firmly what he wanted; Soho types, he'd said. The people who live and work in Soho have a stamp about them that you can't miss; he had been thinking of Sam Price and Vittorio Bonner and the other men he had talked to that afternoon when he had gone wandering through Berwick Street market and eaten strawberries from a punnet. That had been not long after he had first met Laura, though at that stage he hadn't yet become so crazily involved with her – and again he had pushed that thought away and repeated to the casting agency girl, 'I want Soho types. People viewers'll believe in as soon as they see 'em without knowing why they do – be sure now. *Soho* people.'

Yet here in the waiting room were a motley collection of

performers who looked far from right. Not a believable market trader among them; and he glanced again at the rows of chairs in the waiting room as he began to close the door of the office and as the latch clicked realised he had seen someone totally unexpected.

He stood very still facing the door, staring at the scratched panels but seeing the scene on the other side quite clearly, as though it had been etched on his retina. On one side of the second row of chairs had been sitting a tall man with a handsome if rather battered face and beautifully cut and shaped silver hair; anything less like a market trader he had never seen, though he had to admit he might be able to cast him as a *Thrust* user. Perhaps he had been called for the wrong day? Perhaps he could get him to come back tomorrow? But more important than him was the man beside him, sitting half turned towards the silver head and hunched over so that he could talk very quietly into the taller man's ear. Philip Cord. There was no mistaking that dark-gold head and that smooth face with its knowing eyes, and Joel felt again the surge of fury he had known the last time he had seen the man, at the restaurant that night when his whole world had flipped itself on its head and come up looking like Laura Horvath.

He put his hand out to the doorknob to open the door again and stare and was just stopped by the trilling voice behind him.

'Morning, Mr. Coplin! Good to see you so spot on for time! Your lot usually keep us sitting here for half an hour or longer twiddling our expensive thumbs before they put in an appearance. It's a pleasure to deal with a real professional – '

He turned and looked at the woman standing beside the desk. She was wearing exceedingly fashionable clothes which looked as though they belonged to someone else, they suited her so little, and an ingratiating expression on her tired and heavily painted face.

'Good morning,' he said and nodded perfunctorily. 'Those people out there – are they for me?'

She lifted her brows at him, and smiled almost simperingly. 'Indeed they are! Every one of them hand picked exactly to your briefing – '

'Exactly to my briefing?' The anger that the sight of Philip Cord had triggered in him was still there and he let it out, luxuriating in his own rudeness. 'Ye Gods, woman, how can you say that? Just one look and it's got to be obvious to the meanest intelligence that there isn't one there that'll be the slightest use to me! Did you *look* at the script I sent you? I'm looking for stall holders. Market stall holders viewers can believe actually know the price of apples! And what you've got out there wouldn't convince me they were anything but very obvious Equity members as camp as a row of pink tents. I told that girl of yours, spelled it out in words of one syllable. I want Soho types, people who look as though they were born and bred in Soho, who've lived there all their lives. If that applies to any one of that crew out there then I'm – ' He swallowed as the woman stood staring at him wide eyed and fearful and took a sharp breath in through his nose.

'Look,' he said more calmly. 'I want to talk to the girl I briefed. Where is she?'

'I'll get her at once,' the woman said, and sniffed nervously and punched the buttons on the phone on her desk. 'Arlene?' she snapped after a moment. 'Come here at once,' and she slammed the phone down and they both stood waiting, not looking at each other as Joel scowled and tried to push his anger back where it belonged, deep inside. The fact that he hated Philip Cord as much as he did shouldn't be allowed to spill over to his dealings with people he had to work with, for heaven's sake – this was ridiculous! But for all his self lecturing, he still smouldered.

Arlene appeared, a blank faced girl with scarlet hair and very tight leather trousers and a T shirt beneath which small breasts did their best to look important.

'Arlene,' snapped the woman who was now sitting behind her desk, also trying to look important. 'What brief did Mr. Coplin here from City Television give you?'

'What, Mrs. Amos?' the girl said and flicked her eyes at Joel.

'I said, what brief were you given?'

'I told you I wanted Soho types, right?' Joel snapped, his anger lifting again as he stared at the girl. She looked as though she couldn't be less interested in him or in Mrs. Amos, or indeed in anything but herself.

'S'right,' she said. 'Soho types. An' that was what I asked the computer for.'

'What did you actually ask it to give you?' Mrs. Amos said, with a heavy sarcasm. 'It's not a person, you know. It's only a machine, you know. Can't think for itself, you know. It produces just what it's asked for and no more. Never heard of the gigo factor? Garbage in, garbage out – '

'Yeah,' the girl said. 'That's right. I punched in I wanted all actors what was Soho types, an' that's what we got. Not one of 'em lives anywhere else.'

Joel closed his eyes in disbelief and then snapped them open again to stare at the girl. 'Are you saying all those people out there *live* in Soho?'

The girl blinked. 'Tha's right. Tha's what you said you wanted, didn't you? Soho types.'

'Oh, Jesus Christ!' Joel said and suddenly the anger went, spluttering away on a sea of laughter. 'Oh, ye gods and a sack of little rabbits. I don't believe this!'

'Arlene,' Mrs. Amos said frostily. 'Go away.' And the girl shrugged and her buttocks gyrated sulkily out of the office. 'I'm so sorry, Mr. Coplin,' she went on. 'I wouldn't have had this happen for the world. But I've been so madly busy I haven't been able to supervise as I should have done. I grant you I should have done. Normally I'd have checked the brief for myself, for a client as vitally important as City, but really, what with all this fuss about the new Attenborough film and all – ' She made a little moue, desperately trying to mollify him. 'I can't tell you how sorry I am – '

'No point in apologies,' Joel said, but without rancour. There seemed no point in going on complaining at the woman. He sat down in the chair beside the desk, and pulled out of his pocket the folded script and the notes he had made about the people he needed to cast. 'Let's just get on as best we can. Wheel 'em in. I can't send the poor devils away without at least seeing them. Bad enough to be put up for commercials, without being rejected in the waiting room. So let's get on with it. But I'll tell you this much – ' He looked at her sharply. 'I expect a decent discount on the bill for the waste of my time. Not only do I not pay for the extra session I'm obviously going to need here, but I also get a reduction in the original fee I agreed. Fair enough?'

'Yes,' Mrs. Amos said after an anguished moment and then pushed the bell on her desk with a sharp gesture as if it were the girl Arlene. 'Of course, Mr. Coplin. We'll begin then. And if you don't mind I'll leave you to get on for a while on your own, once they start, so that I can make sure we've got the right sort of people coming in for you tomorrow. With a little luck we might be able to keep this down to the original two-day schedule after all.'

'I hope you can,' Joel said in high good humour now. The absurdity of the girl's mistake had quite erased his fury. 'I need all the time I can save. But all the same – a cut rate job, Mrs. Amos, a cut rate but first rate job is what I'm getting out of you! Every one of them lives in Soho!' And again he laughed as the first actor, a willowy young man in the tightest and most faded jeans Joel had ever seen came hipping his way into the room.

He worked doggedly through the next two hours hoping every time the door opened to admit the next aspirant that the silver-haired man would come in; or would it be Cord? He doubted that. Surely if he were an actor he'd have been told? He remembered their conversation over dinner at the restaurant, when he'd asked him what he did for a living; what had the man said? He frowned, trying to remember. He'd said nothing, in fact. Had said it wasn't relevant to the matter they were discussing, which was the ethics of television film-making, and had slid over the question completely. And, Joel told himself flatly, there is no way he'd have done that if he were an actor. They always say what they do for a living. Try and stop 'em –

Mrs. Amos came back with coffee for him and disappeared again murmuring something incoherent about having to phone round to collect the people he would need to see next day and he nodded abstractedly and went on, listening to accounts of careers and readings of his script in carefully modulated voices, working class accented voices and twanging mid Atlantic voices and none of them was any good at all; and he would smile and nod and thank them for coming in and assure them he would be in touch if he needed them and watch them walk dejectedly out, each of them knowing perfectly well that they'd never hear another word from him. And he would ring the bell and the next would come in and the whole sad and degrading charade would start all over again.

He hated casting, always had, but never did what some directors did, leaving it entirely to the casting people. And he grinned as he thought of what might have happened this time if he'd done that. Ye Gods, ask for Soho types and what he got were people who *lived* in Soho –

Again the door opened and there he was; the tall, silver-haired man who had been talking to – or rather had been talked to – by Philip Cord. He stood there in the doorway, hovering a little and smiling in a practised style and for the first time Joel stood up.

'Good morning,' he said and lifted his brows at him. 'Now, haven't I seen you somewhere before? I wonder where?' And it was true that looking at the man now there was a familiarity about him; but whether that was because he had actually seen him before today, or because he had noticed him in the waiting room, it was impossible to say. Ever since he'd first set eyes on him he'd been thinking about him, after all.

The tall man smiled even more widely, gratified by the comment. 'I've done a good deal of commercial work,' he murmured. 'The *Mars and Venus* chocolate promotion and that rather odd but effective little ad for *Genesis* floor cleaner – '

'No – ' Joel said thoughtfully. 'Somewhere else.' He sat down and gestured to the older man to sit too. He did so with a great elegance. 'Somewhere social – '

Philip Cord and Laura he was thinking. That man with Laura; and that gave him an idea, a line to the way to bring Cord into the conversation. 'Now, could it be at that splendid Hungarian restaurant in Little Vinegar Yard? I seem to recall – '

The silver haired man smiled even more widely. 'That is very possible,' he said and his voice now was relaxed and silky, with a rich undertone to it that was very pleasing. Very much an actor's voice, Joel registered at the back of his mind. 'It belongs to my family.'

Joel blinked, and said nothing, shocked into silence. He had trawled an unbaited line across a pool he had suspected had no fish in it and come up with a catch so huge it took his breath away.

The other man seemed unaware of the effect he had had, however, and went on, 'My cousin Laura runs it, of course. Everyone in Soho knows Laura, don't they? She's a darling. I'm a *first* cousin.' He leaned forward and pointed to his name on the schedule that Mrs. Amos had left on the desk beside Joel. 'Paul Balog. How do you do.'

'How do you do,' Joel responded automatically and then said without thinking, 'And the man who was talking to you as I came through the waiting room – he's your cousin too?'

The smile vanished from Paul Salog's face. 'I beg your pardon?'

'I noticed you as I came through the waiting room,' Joel said and then, ashamed of his own mendacity, added, 'You're a striking looking man, Mr. Balog. I saw you and thought – you could be one of the *Thrust* users I need for this film. And happened to notice the man you were talking to.'

Paul relaxed visibly, leaning back in his chair, and the smile reappeared, smoother and more winning than ever. 'I'm glad you thought me useful,' he murmured. 'Do you want me to read the script?'

Joel shook his head. 'It's a pleasant job, Mr. Balog. On screen for several seconds and no dialogue. You simply have to walk through the market, collecting admiring glances and being very very degagé and sophisticated. You look the part to a T.'

He was beginning to loathe himself more and more; he who had always been so professional, never employing anyone who wasn't precisely right for the job, who had offended actor friends by passing them over in favour of strangers who seemed to him better for the job, to behave so? And all because of his jealousy over a woman who was quite uninterested in him as far as he could tell. Disgusting!

'Leave the name of your agent, and we'll get the contract out to you. If you want the job. It's planned for a long run, I believe. Should be plenty of residuals in it.'

Paul lifted his chin with a little gesture of pure exaltation. Clearly even a job without lines was something he badly wanted.

Joel smiled at him, friendly and relaxed now. 'So, tell me, this other cousin of yours – I think I've seen him before. Actually met him with your cousin when I dined there the other night, Philip something?

Paul nodded. 'Philip Cord.' He seemed to have lost his anxiety at the mention of the man, but still Joel thought there was a watchfulness about him.

'Is he an actor?'

Paul laughed then, a little sharp sound that had bitterness in it. 'Philip – an actor? Heavens no. I'm not sure what he does, to be truthful. Something to do with art galleries. And he's interested in various other things.' He stood up, and smoothed down his jacket with an elegant little gesture. Then I can tell my agent I definitely have this job, Mr. – ah – Coplin?'

'Definitely,' Joel said. 'We start filming next Monday. I'll send a schedule. Tell me – if he's not an actor, why was he here?'

Paul hesitated. 'I'm sorry about that. I – there was something he wanted to discuss with me. It was important private business. He – er – he arrived at home just as I was leaving and walked along with me, so that we could talk. We hadn't quite finished when we got here. I'm sorry if – '

Joel shook his head. 'Not important at all,' he said, hoping he sounded as offhand as he was trying to be. 'I was just curious. So – we'll see you on Monday then.'

'Thank you,' Paul said and moved to the door. 'I look forward to working with you. Good morning – ' And he opened the door and began to leave.

'I'm glad you live in Soho, Mr. Balog!' Joel said and then grinned. 'I have to tell you you wouldn't have been called for this otherwise. No, don't look like that. I'll explain some other time. It's just rather funny. And – and – give my regards to your cousin Miss Horvath, if you see her.'

Paul looked at him and frowned and said nothing, and went, leaving Joel staring at the closed door and wondering why he had behaved so absurdly. It really was getting to be ridiculous, to be so obsessed with a woman that it made him as obsessed with her relations. And he shook his head at himself and rang the bell again. There was still a hell of a lot of work to get through.

21

'No, no, no,' Maritza said loudly and then started again, her voice rising every time she uttered the word. 'No, no, NO!'

'What d'you mean, no?' Viktor blustered. 'I tell you, I'm the gaffer here. It's *my* business, *my* name on the deeds, you got nothing to do with it. Anyway, why no? Ain't it time we had a better life? Ain't it time we had a bigger place to live in, spent a bit of our hard earned money, enjoyed life a bit? What's so terrible a man wants to retire to the old country, take care of his wife in her old age?' He became pathetic and leaned over towards her, eyes moist, as she sat straight and angry in her high backed chair by the window.

She turned her head away with an expression of distaste on her face at his breath, richly scented with his lunch and the bottle of wine he had had as a little mid-afternoon something and he pulled back, offended.

'Listen!' he roared. 'If you want to be stupid, so be stupid. I'm here telling you what's doing. I'm selling the place, okay? I'm getting a good price from these people. I offered 'em they should have just the kitchen space but that ain't enough. They want the lot and I tell you they'll give me a price for it, a price like you never saw.'

'How much?' she said sharply and he leaned back away from her even more.

'That's not a woman's business,' he said flatly. 'The discussions between me and my business colleagues is my discussions. It ain't to do with you.'

'It's everything to do with me,' she flared at him. 'It's my business too. Haven't I worked and worried my fingers to the bone these last years to make this place what it is? Wasn't it my savings got the place going to start with? And what about my children, hey? You! You might as well not be a father the way you go on, the little you care! This business is for the children, for all of them, for – '

'For your bloody Zolly!' he howled and lumbered to his feet and began to march up and down the cluttered little room, clearly whipping up his anger even more. 'You and your lousy Zolly, I tell you it's enough to make a man spit, he's turned out by his wife in favour of his stinkin' son-in-law! It ain't natural! That's what it ain't. It ain't natural – and – '

She still sat there very straight and then said softly 'What did you say?'

He was still, now. He had reached the window and was standing with his back to it so that his bulk was outlined in the late afternoon light, but his face was shadowed.

'I said, it ain't right,' he muttered, worried now. Maritza shouting was one thing; Maritza quiet was a very different and much more alarming kettle of carp.

'You make me sick!' she said then, and turned her head away so that she need not look at him. 'Sick, you hear me? You and your nasty little mind and your nasty little ideas – sick – '

'Listen, I didn't mean no – ' he began uneasily and then started blustering again. 'Listen, it's all your fault! You nag and push a man so, you make me say things I don't mean. I do say you make too much of that lousy Zolly. I didn't mean no more than that – just you listen to him too much.'

'And why shouldn't I? Isn't it him who keeps this place doing so well? Isn't it him who works and struggles and then works some more to keep it all going? Without him and Magda, God bless them both, there'd be no *Hallascz's* and you wouldn't be able to sit and get drunk every afternoon with your stupid friends the way you do, you and that Miklos and Janos and Yves and – pshht!' And the sound of disgust that came from her lips echoed in the little room.

'And why shouldn't she work, Magda? Ain't she getting the benefit? The others, they don't get what she does, Istvan and – '

'Istvan!' Maritza cried. 'Istvan! If you aren't complaining about Zolly who cares so much for us and for this business we'd be on the street without him, then you're going on about Istvan. He's rotten, you know that? Rotten – I should have known he'd turn out this way, I should have known, I should never have – ah, pshht!' And this time the sound she made was different, hopeless and dull and deeply unhappy.

'Never have what? The only boy we got, you should never have loved and looked after? The only boy after three girls in this house and you regret him?'

She turned now to look at him, and her eyes were dark in their deep sockets. She looked deeply weary and suddenly miserable and he stood there with his face still shadowed and felt his throat tighten at the sight of her.

'Listen, dolly,' he said and came lumbering towards her and knelt in front of her. His knees creaked audibly but he ignored that and set his big hands on her rather twisted gnarled ones. Her arthritis had been getting much worse lately, and that it contributed to her bad temper was something they both knew, though they never spoke of it. 'Listen, dolly. I don't want no trouble for us! What's gone is gone, and all we got now is tomorrow. I want we should enjoy what we got left. I ain't so young no more. Nor are you. Seventy six I am already. And you – '

'I don't need reminding how old I am,' she said tartly.

'So who's reminding? I just want we should spend a few years decent. A nice little farm, a few horses – '

'Horses!' She gave a little snort of laughter. 'What do you know about horses? When Abel told me, horses – I laughed, you know that? I laughed so loud I was nearly choking. Horses!'

He got heavily to his feet. 'So it was Abel started all this.'

'Abel started nothing. I asked him, is all. I just asked him what was going on and thank God he told me. He said horses – such stuff! You can't sell the children's business – it's the family's! It's all our past, all we ever worked for, it's all that we've ever done with our lives! How can you sell it, see it all disappear, so you can pretend you're gentry in Hungary with horses? They'd treat you like a beggar if you try that! You go and buy your farm, sure they'll take your money, but do you think any of those people will talk to you? Have anything to do with you? You're dreaming, you old fool, dreaming. Gambling like you always have. You're throwing away all we've got on a chance, or trying to. But I won't have it. I won't let you – '

'You can't stop me,' he said flatly 'It's in my name. I got the control. It's mine.'

'It's ours,' she said fiercely. 'Yours, mine and the girls – and their husbands. And yes, Istvan and his jumped up Eva as well, it's even theirs. It's *family*, you hear me? I won't let you give away all we got. And don't tell me it's a good price. Whatever price you get, it's giving away the past. Over forty years we been here. Forty years – it's a tradition – '

'A tradition!' he said and laughed loudly, mockingly. 'Such a tradition. A greasy Zolly working in a lousy back kitchen making lecso, this is a tradition? There's money to be taken, I tell you, a good price – '

'It's a tradition,' she said stubbornly. 'A working one. We been here forty years – more than forty years – that makes it a tradition. I'm not letting you lose it.'

'You can't stop me,' he said and turned and went stamping away to the door and out of it, slamming it behind him as hard as he could, so that the shelves in the cupboards rattled and the glass ornaments on them danced. 'You can't stop me!' he bawled from behind the door panels and she heard him go thumping down the stairs and out of the building.

It took her a long time to decide what to do, but once she had she moved with great purpose, going heavily downstairs, and across the mid-afternoon quiet of the restaurant to the kitchen.

Zolly was sitting at the big scrubbed wooden table, shredding marrow on a grater. The light over his head threw the planes of his face into sharp focus and Maritza thought, he looks tired – not wanting to admit that in fact he looked ill. He was thin and his skin was waxy, and his lids were so pale that the darkness of his eyes could be seen shadowy and tense beneath them as he looked down at the grater.

'Zolly,' she said and he lifted his head and grinned at her.

'Hello, Anya Maritza,' he said. 'Come and sit down. I'll make you some coffee and chollah?'

She shook her head. 'No noshing, Zolly, I told you. I got to cut down a bit. Getting too heavy.' And she patted her round belly and he laughed comfortably and made room on the bench beside him for her to sit down. It was always comfortable for them to be together, and today she sat there feeling peace come back into her, anxious as she was, as she watched his strong fingers flashing up and down the gleaming metal grater, moving steadily and unhurriedly yet getting through the great piles of peeled vegetables at a remarkable speed.

'Best son I've got, you are, Zolly,' she said suddenly and he glanced at her and laughed.

'Son-in-law.'

'For me there's no difference. Or yes, maybe there is – that you're better than a son. Better than Istvan, that's for sure.'

'Viktor don't think so.' There was no bitterness in his tone; just a statement of the way it was, like saying, 'The sun rises in the East.' 'Viktor certainly don't think so.'

'Viktor,' she said very deliberately, 'is crazy.'

'Sure,' Zolly said comfortably and reached for a bowl and tipped the piles of pallid greenish shreds into it, so that he could start grating again.

'I mean it,' she said. 'Crazy. I'm not just talking, I'm telling you he's crazy and we have to do something about it. He ought to go somewhere to be treated – '

The long fingers faltered in their rhythm as he stared at her and then, as he bent his head, picked up their steady movements again, up and down, up and down and the green shreds curled out on the other side in sinuous loops. 'Like where? Hungary? I hear he's going to Hungary. With horses.'

'Then you know! How do you know?'

He laughed then for the first time. 'Anya Maritza, what do you think I don't know about what happens here? Doesn't my bloody life depend on knowing? So I know.'

She pursed her lips at his swearing, but without any real anger. 'So you see what I mean. He's crazy.'

'Is it crazy to want to retire? Not so crazy.'

'Crazy to cut off his whole family with nothing. Crazy to put someone else's wanting to build a new place before protecting his own old place. That is crazy,' Maritza said flatly. 'And I know what I have to do about it.'

'It's in his name, the place? Then what can you do? Don't you think I've thought about it? Thought hard? Where do I go if this happens, hmm? What happens to me and Magda and young Zolly and Tibor if he does this, hmm? Do you think I don't worry?'

'No more worrying,' Maritza said and leaned closer to him. 'Just tell Magda what I'm telling you. And I'll talk to Zsuzske and Kati – ' She stopped then and pursed her lips again in that calculating way. 'Maybe *you* can talk to Kati. Maybe we don't need Kati. I'll think about that. But you tell them – Magda and Zsuzske – what I explain. You tell 'em, you see? That Viktor, the poor old poppa, he's ill, he's got crazy notions. We don't want to have to do it but we must protect him against himself. So we arrange it all, he goes to the hospital, the loony bin. We sign the papers and there he sits – '

Now the fingers did stop moving. 'You'd do that?' Zolly said and there was awe in his voice. 'You'd have him put away? How can you do that?'

'It's easy. I tell 'em, the doctors, I tell 'em he's crazy, they should come and see him. And they come and he screams and shouts and they listen at the way he carries on and they say, "Yes, this man is very crazy." And they agree.'

'You'd have him locked up in a madhouse just because he wants to sell this place?' Zolly was still staring at her, awestruck. 'I never thought this of you, Anya Maritza. Never thought I'd hear you say such a thing. What would he do in such a place? He'd go really crazy, poor old Viktor, in a madhouse. I couldn't do it to him.'

'You won't have to,' Maritza said and reached out with her gnarled hand and shook his arm. 'Don't be a fool. Of course he won't have to. But if he *thinks* he has to – '

Zolly sat up and stared at her for a little longer and then bent his head back to his vegetable marrows. 'If he thinks it,' he said flatly. 'Okay, so he thinks it. Then what?'

'Then he does what I tell him, to stop it happening,' Maritza said and her voice was triumphant. 'He thinks if he don't do as I say, he goes to a madhouse. If all of you, Magda and Zsuzske, agree – and you've got to, because this is your business we're talking about, your future, your money – then Viktor has to do what we say. And he'll sign the papers. Ten years I've had those papers ready, ten years, you know that? The lawyers, they got them all fixed up for me ten years ago, a real Family Trust. Like the Rothschilds have and like the Damonts and the Montefiores, all those really rich people. And the Halasczs. They'll have the same. A family trust – ' She sat and contemplated the idea for a long moment, her eyes shining in the glow of the big overhead lamp. 'All this time he's said he wouldn't. Wanted it all for Istvan, didn't want no one but Halasczs should have a share, but he has to understand now, his daughters matter more than Istvan. Even Kati – ' And she sat and stared with her deep dark eyes at her plans for her girls. 'And now I got a way at last I can force him to sign.' She shook her head, suddenly reminiscent. 'The times he's come so close, when he's been drunk and happy, and when he's been drunk and unhappy – but always he wriggled out. Now he's got to. You see, Zolly? If you do like I say and the girls do too – ' And she nodded again, sapiently. 'I tell you, they'll do it. Tell him they will, that is. And he'll sign and you can stop fretting over the future. It'll be yours.'

'Everybody's,' Zolly said quietly and looked up at her and she looked at him, at those pale eyelids and the waxen cheeks and reached out and touched his face.

'Yes,' she said. 'You're a good boy, Zolly. Not greedy. A good boy. Yes, it'll be for everybody.'

'Kati and Zsuzske and Magda and Istvan,' Zolly said, still sitting and staring at her.

She took a deep breath. 'It'll have to be,' she said and her voice was angry now. 'That I know I can't make him shift in. It'll have to be. For my part, the way Istvan wastes money, behaves like he's God knows who, for my part, I'd leave him out. No, don't look at me that way. I'd leave him out. Why shouldn't I? Hasn't he given me nothing but misery and headaches from the very start, from the time he was a baby? Wasn't he born in misery and – '

'Hush,' Zolly said. 'Hush, Anya Maritza. Don't say things you'll be sorry you said.'

'I'll never be sorry,' she said loudly angry, but he knew and smiled at her.

'All right, Anya Maritza. If it's the only way, that's what we do. I won't like it and he – ' He shook his head. 'I've got it in me to feel very sorry for Poppa Viktor. He'll never get over it. You know that?'

She got to her feet, leaning her bent hands heavily on the scrubbed boards of the table. The lamplight picked up the silver glints in her hair and she seemed for a moment to have a halo.

'And I'll never get over it if we don't do it. It's him or me. And you, and the others. And young Zolly and Tibor and the grandchildren and great-grandchildren you'll have one day. It's for the tradition, you know that. Forty years and more we've been here. He got the place with a lousy piece of his stupid gambling, but we're not going to lose it that way. I'm saving it for you. All of you.'

She had reached the door by now and she looked back at him and smiled. 'All right, Zolly? You'll remember what you have to do?'

'Am I likely to forget?' he said dryly. 'It isn't every day I agree to lie my own father-in-law into a madhouse.'

'It won't come to that,' Maritza said confidently. 'Don't you worry yourself. No madhouse, but a Family Trust. What else are families for but to trust each other?' And she laughed and went out and the door swung behind her, and went on swinging as he sat and stared at it and listened to her feet go heavily up the stairs.

22

'Lunching at Laura's?' Preston said as he pulled out his chair and sat down. 'How did you manage that? And I thought you said last time you didn't like the way people gossiped when they saw you on your own patch?'

'Now it don't matter who sees us,' Davriosh said and pushed forward his glass ready to be refilled as Maxie came to take the new arrival's drinks order. 'The man who's doing all the background for me, he won't be here, and he's the only one I have to worry about now. I don't want anyone to know about him, but otherwise it don't matter no more. As for how I managed it – '

He grinned and tilted his head towards the desk in the corner where Laura was standing talking animatedly to one of her customers. 'Sure she tried to keep me out – took a scunner the way she does. But I know how to fix that. I came in here at ten o'clock this morning. I don't phone, I come in well before she gets her book full and I stand there and tell her I have to have a table for one o'clock. That's what I did and there wasn't a thing she could do about it, was there? Not with the blank pages there. I know she'd rather save her tables for the fancy characters she gets in here than have the likes of me – she wants her politicians and the film people and the famous faces. Look over there – see who that is? That woman from the telly – does all the interviews. And that one over there – that's the designer Rhoda Packard – very famous she is. Not sure who she's with, but I think they're from Remingtons. I hear on the grapevine she's involved in some big new musical for Drury Lane if they can get it. And over there – '

'All very interesting,' Preston said. 'But for my part, I couldn't care less. Let them point us out if they want to.

Me, I want to know what's going on. Why all of a sudden a meeting like this?'

'Well!' Davriosh said fatly and grinned. 'I have a progress report to make. A nice progress report, and this afternoon I got an appointment at three o'clock with Reggie Statler to tell him all about it. Only I wanted to talk to you first, because there ought to be a way we can do ourselves a bit of good here.'

'I thought that was what it was all about,' Preston said and nodded at Miklos who had come to take their food order. 'Doing ourselves a bit of good. I'll have the jellied carp and duck with red cabbage.'

'Of course it is. But no reason why we can't do even better,' Davriosh said. 'Fish salad, with extra sour cream and cucumber on the side and stuffed cabbage with a side order of egg barley. And a bottle of seventeen to start with. Now listen to me, Preston – '

'Do I have any choice?'

Davriosh ignored that. 'You'll remember I told you about this place being owned by a Family Trust – '

'One thing at a time,' Preston said. 'Start with the other place, over the yard. What's happening there?'

'I told you that. It's all in hand, the old man's in France, the freehold offer's in and accepted – that's all over bar the shouting. No problem there at all.' He laughed then. 'Not for us, though I tell you, that there Simmy's in for trouble when his uncle finds out. From all accounts the old man can be tart, very tart. And Simmy's so bloody greedy – ' He shook his head disapprovingly. 'He'll fall over himself the way he's going. Still, it's his affair, I suppose. Now, to this place – '

'Keep your voice down!' Preston said sharply. 'You must have been mad to come here if you want to talk about this!'

Davriosh laughed. 'I liked the idea. It gives a sort of relish to it, know what I mean? Don't you worry. They're all too busy talking about themselves to pay any attention to us. Look at 'em!'

And it was true that the restaurant was fizzing with activity. Women were greeting each other with soft little cries of delight and clashing cheeks and kisses in the air, and men were jabbering with the flushed excitement of children on a holiday. Laughter was much in evidence as Maxie moved from table to table with his bottles and glasses and everyone seemed very happy indeed. And totally uninterested in the two grey men at their corner table, watching them.

'I tell you, short of getting down on the floor and starting a bunk up, no one would notice what we said or did,' Davriosh said and Preston said primly, 'Do you have to be so cheap? Isn't it bad enough I have to put up with that sort of thing every day in my office without having to listen to it at lunchtime?'

'Still wanting out, then?' Davriosh said, all mock sympathy. 'Still sick of the sex business?'

'It's sick on its own account,' Preston said with much feeling. 'D'you know what they're doing to me now? The council are shoving up the fee for a show licence. Already it costs me over twelve grand for a strip show licence and now the buggers are saying they can make us pay fifty times more than that. Can you imagine? Fifty times more! God damn it, that'd be bloody near twenty-five per cent of my annual take at the Brewer Street place and it'd make one hell of a hole in the books over at Rupert Street. It don't bear thinking of. And my topless bar in Dean Street, they want to meddle with that too, and the place in Manette Yard. Nicest little near-beer places in the district and they want to cripple 'em. I tell you, the sooner I can go decent the better for me. So I need to know what's the state of play.'

By now the food had arrived and for some time there was no way that Davriosh was going to pay any attention to anything but that, and they sat and demolished the elegantly presented platefuls as the restaurant hummed and laughed and chattered cheerfully around them, but both very aware of why they were here. And it wasn't just for food, delectable though that was.

Not until his stuffed cabbage had followed the carp and he was leaning back, replete and gently belching, did Davriosh return to the subject, and now, for all his early bravado, he kept his voice down.

'The thing is, I've got an agent working for me now. He doesn't know what's in it for me – just that I want the freehold here. And he can get it, by buying their shares from various members of the family.'

'Laura?' Preston said and turned his head to look at her. She was standing beside the table Davriosh had pointed out earlier, where a striking looking woman in extremely elegant clothes was sitting with two men. The dress designer, that was it, he thought and looked at her and then at Laura, who might not be as fashionably dressed as her guest, but who still looked very attractive. There was a glow about her hair and skin that shone even here, five tables away.

'Do me a favour!' Davriosh said. 'Is that likely? No, she's the biggest fly in the proverbial. It's the other people's shares we're after. First things first. And P – my agent – reckons he can get them.'

'Who?'

'Never you mind.' Davriosh sounded pompous suddenly. 'He's my agent. Works for *me*. I throw his name around and he ain't my agent no more, right? So never you mind. Thing is, he reckons to buy up everyone's share but hers.' And he jerked his head towards Laura. 'And under the terms of the Trust, of which I have seen a copy – '

'How did you get your hands on that?'

'I told you, never you mind. He's a good agent, right? And under the terms of this Trust, as long as the majority of the family want to dissolve it and sell the others have got to, like it or not. So, we have to make sure they do it. But there's a catch.'

'There always is.' Preston sound gloomy.

'It's good and bad, good and bad!' Davriosh was jovial. 'The bad is I have to go to Statler and get more out of him. We've had a fair bit already, of course, for the Bosquet property, but now I need a lot more. To sweeten the family members here who own the place. But the good news – ' He laughed now, a bubbling self satisfied little sound. 'The good news is that he has no way of checking how much I need.'

'So?'

'So, we tell him we need a good deal more for the buying up of the shares than we do, and we split the difference. With a little sweetener for my agent, of course.'

'How much difference?' Preston was very alert now.

'I reckon he can get the shares we need for say, a hundred and fifty thousand. Sounds a lot, but for the value of this site, it's nothing. Certainly to Statler it's nothing. And you heard what he said that day we met at Joe Allen's. He wants to shave his costs but he wants the site so bad if he has to pay more then he'll pay more.'

Preston's lips curved. 'I remember. It was a pleasure to listen to the man talk. A pleasure. Such a way with money.'

'As I see it, I can get a quarter of a million out of him easy. The balance between that and what my agent needs to get the properties is ours. A straight split.'

Preston looked at him sharply. 'Why?'

'How do you mean, why?'

'Why should you split with me? You could have the lot. You're not a chap to share anything you don't have to.'

Davriosh laughed. 'Oh, you've got a nasty mind, Preston, you really have. Listen, do you think if I go to Statler, tell him what I need on my own, he'll play? Of course he won't. He wants corroboration.' He rolled the word round his tongue as though proud of being able to say it at all. 'Corroboration. Now, you, he trusts. It's crazy, but there it is. Because I got a small back room and do most of my business out and about in other people's offices, he don't see me as reliable. But you, with your sex shows and your shops and your offices, you he sees as a good businessman.'

'I am. I'm just in the wrong line of business at the moment.'

'Not that wrong if a licence fee of way over six hundred grand is only twenty five per cent of your take,' Davriosh said sardonically. 'Do you think Statler doesn't know to an old threepenny bit what you're worth? And isn't impressed by it? Of course he is. So if you come with me this afternoon and tell him that all I say is so, that I need the extra cash, then we have no problems. I can't expect you to do that for nothing, can I? Wish I could, believe you me!' He laughed loudly then. 'Believe you me!'

There was a little silence and then Preston said, 'All right. I can see the sense in it. But let me say this, Davriosh. If you come a cropper and Statler finds out, then I didn't know you were up to any tricks, right?'

Davriosh looked pained. 'How can you talk that way? As though I'd do anything underhand with you. Aren't we partners?'

'Indeed we are. So let's do it right as partners should. I want a letter from you, telling me the situation as you're going to tell it to Statler. Right? Then a letter from me agreeing with you and that we should talk to Statler, and so forth. All properly dated a week or so back. We can work out what sort of dates we should have on these letters, of course, and then we take copies, one for me, and you can have one too. The important thing is I get covered. On that basis, I'm in. I'll come with you to see Statler.'

'Fair enough,' Davriosh said expansively and waved at Miklos. A tray with plates of raspberry torte had just gone by him and that was a very interesting sight. 'I'll see to it first thing tomorrow.'

'Oh, no, you don't.' Preston smiled at him sweetly. 'You'll see to it this afternoon. *Before* we see Statler.'

Again Davriosh looked hurt. 'Is that necessary? For Chrissakes, Preston, aren't we partners? Can't you trust me? If I say I'll do it tomorrow, I'll do it tomorrow.'

'I'd rather you did it this afternoon,' Preston said silkily. 'We have time. It's only just after two now. We'll go back to your office, get the letters typed and copied and *then* and only then will we go and see Mr. High and Mighty Statler. What a man.' And he shook his head in admiration. 'A real gent. I can't stand him, but what a man.'

'Don't I know it,' Davriosh said and fell on his raspberry torte with gusto. 'Don't I know it. And doesn't he too. But I tell you, the way I'm planning it, nothing can go wrong.'

'The way I'm planning it, nothing can go wrong,' Edward

Malplackett said into the phone. 'I do assure you, you have no need to worry. I have checked the facts on this man. Your information showed the way, but I've checked the facts.'

He listened for a long time, sitting tipped back in his chair with his feet up on his cluttered desk and then grinned.

'Do you think I don't know that?' he said. 'Davriosh is about as reliable as a straw raft in a hurricane. It's not him I'm dealing with. Not ultimately, you understand.'

Again the silence, and then he laughed. 'Would I tell you? Don't be ridiculous. What I know is all I've got. It's my trading balance, my goods on offer, call it what you like. It's mine, and I keep it. Just believe me. The man's as good as settled.'

The thin voice at the other end of the phone rattled on for a long time and Malplackett swung his feet down to the floor and reached for a notebook and began to write, nodding and grinning an assent from time to time.

'All right,' he said at length. 'Tonight at Preston's place in Rupert Street. You know the one I mean? The Queen Freya – that's it. We'll be there at half past eleven – don't be late. And make sure you've got a flashlight. It's important he can actually see those pictures, right? Okay, see you there.' And he hung up the phone with a rattle and leaned back in his chair and stretched.

It was all working out fine. At first it had been a difficult tangle. Leo and the Trust on the one hand and Statler and Davriosh and Preston on the other. He'd not been sure at first he could get away with it, but the whole Bosquet affair had worked out so well that he'd been willing to set caution aside just for once and go for this man's offer. It was a good offer too, and it amused him that there should be so many different interests in the same piece of property.

Sitting now in his messy little back room he laughed aloud as he thought of them all, weaving in and out of each other's paths like dancers at an Elizabethan masque. And there she is, Laura, in the middle of it all and quite unconscious of what's going on. Pity really. It was a nice restaurant, and it was a shame it had to go, but there it was. Progress is progress. The whole district's ripe for renewal. And he got to his feet and went to stare out of his grimy window at the street below.

This could be a whole new career for him. He let his imagination slide; Malplackett and Company – it would look good on those hoardings they put up round new developments. This one would be just the same; there'd be a board on which all the contractors' names were, the architect and the builder and the electrician and the air conditioning and the lifts and God knows who else, all beavering away, but the name at the top would be his. Edward Malplackett. No partners, no one but himself. It was worth taking the chances he was taking now to get that. He had to raise the capital to make it possible, that was the thing. Once he'd done it, then there'd be no more need for chances. He'd be a straight honest businessman.

And he sighed with sheer pleasure at the thought and turned and went back to his desk to pick up the phone. Get tonight's little meeting sorted out and then he'd be on his way.

23

There was a strong smell in the air, like sour wood smoke, and Malplackett wrinkled his nose in distaste as he pushed his way through the crowd of dim figures cluttering up the doorway beyond the red plush curtain and made his way to a far corner.

'Amazing isn't it?' he murmured to the man at his side, and in whose elbow his hand was firmly tucked. 'You'd think they'd be a bit more circumspect, wouldn't you? At least cocaine doesn't advertise itself quite so blatantly.'

'Yes,' gasped the man beside him. 'Er – no.'

Malplackett laughed as he pushed his companion into the rather rickety chair that was behind the table on which a large 'reserved' sign stood.

'Do you know, I have a strong suspicion you haven't the remotest idea what I'm talking about,' he said jovially. 'Admit it!'

'Er – yes,' the man said and slid into the chair and peered up at Malplackett in the dimness. 'Actually, it's a bit noisy in here. Hard to hear anything properly.'

'Well, yes, that is a point,' Malplackett allowed handsomely and grinned at him. 'Now what sort of drink are you buying me?' He waved a long arm and a girl wearing a short frill of a skirt over net tights and high heeled shoes and nothing else came towards them. Her breasts were pendulous and veined and the man beside Malplackett reddened and looked away as she leaned over him to reach for the dirty ashtray on the table and then gave the surface a perfunctory wipe with a grubby cloth.

'I think I need a little something light,' Malplackett said and gave the other man a wicked little grin. 'Feel like stretching to a bottle of bubbly?'

Miserably the other man stared at him and then swallowed. 'If it's not too expensive,' he muttered. 'Didn't bring much out with me.'

Malplackett shook his head, clearly disappointed. 'That's a pity. Oh, well, then. Beer, Jenny. American beer, at least. The sort that made Milwaukee whatever it was.'

The girl grunted and went away and Malplackett leaned back comfortably, gazing benevolently at his companion.

'Well, now, Mr. Hersh. Let me explain. That smell I was talking about.'

The man looked blank. 'Smell?'

'Pot, my dear chap. Pot. Grass. Tea. Marijuana.' He laughed then at the expression of horror on the other face. 'Oh, please, don't look like that! The fact I can recognise it doesn't mean I'm a hopeless addict, you know. Just like a little puff now and again. Like beer.'

'I thought – ' Hersh swallowed and shook his head miserably. 'It's not really something I know much about. Don't understand. There are people at the office know about it, but not me. I just do hygiene, you see, so it isn't the same. I don't get involved with the police like some of them there do and – '

'Well, I dare say there are lot of people, even in this day and age, who don't know the smell of pot when it comes to choke them,' Malplackett said kindly as the beer arrived. 'But I would have thought it's time a chap like you improved his education. The more you know about such things the better your chances of promotion, I'd have thought.'

'I don't want promotion,' Hersh said. 'I'm very happy where I am.' He took a sharp little breath in through his nose that was clearly audible even above the raucous scratchy music that was coming from the stage. 'I like my department and like my job in it. I just want to go on as I am. I don't want anything I haven't got – just a quiet life, Mr. – Mr – '

'Malplackett,' Edward said and smiled. 'It was on the letter I sent you.'

'Yes,' Hersh said. 'The letter you sent me.' He bent his head and drank some of the beer, suddenly and greedily as though he were very thirsty. 'Why me?' he said then loudly. 'Why did you write to me? If you got that list the way you said you did, why pick on me out of it? I'm a very quiet sort of person. I can't see what a man like you wants with me. I just do my job and live quietly and – '

'And walk in the park whenever you have the chance,' Malplackett said softly.

'No, not at all! I mean, well what's wrong with walking in the park? I never hurt anyone, I just walk there and – '

'And watch the old people sunning themselves and the little children running about and playing, hmm?'

'I told you, I do no harm to anyone! I just live quietly on my own, and I do my job and – I never hurt anyone. Why pick on me?'

'Because you do your job, Mr. Hersh,' Malplackett said and then pursed his lips and said, 'Sssh,' as the lights dimmed even more, the music changed and the red plush curtain in front of the small stage leapt into its own bright light. 'The show's starting again! You'll just love this, Mr. Hersh. Great stuff.'

The show started with a girl in a frilly pinny and nothing else but satin high heeled slippers playing at being a Bored Little Housewife with her vacuum cleaner and after ten minutes of tired gyrations during which the vacuum hose worked harder than she did, went off the stage to a spatter of applause that died almost before she disappeared behind the side curtains. And then the music changed to become a sprightly version of 'Three Little Girls from School' from *The Mikado* and Malplackett leaned forwards and said quietly, 'Now, this is why I brought you here for our meeting. All work and no play, you know, not to be thought of!'

The three girls in skimpy old-fashioned school uniforms who came in looked sulky at first, but as they went into their routine the automatic smiles flashed on and they wriggled and gyrated and offered each other skipping ropes with obscene handles and whips and tops that were even more graphically designed and, pretending to argue, pulled each other's clothes off. The audience clearly loved them and shouted their approval loudly, together with a great deal of advice on what to do next, but Edward Malplackett never looked at the stage. He was watching the man opposite him, not moving as he stared at him.

At first, the man kept his head turned away from the stage, concentrating on drinking his beer, but then, slowly, his head turned as unwillingly as though someone had tied a rope to his ear and was pulling on it. His eyes seemed to darken in the light thrown from the little stage as he looked and his face went blank of all expression.

Once or twice he tried to turn his eyes away, but the invisible rope seemed to twitch again and his eyes fastened on the smallest of the three girls almost greedily. She was a skinny little creature with no breasts at all to speak of, and the rest of the audience were shouting hoarse insults at her, wanting to know why she had dimples instead of pimples, and telling her to turn around so that they could see the back – maybe she'd be better equipped there. But Hersh stared at her with his mouth partly open and an eagerness in his eyes that was so intense it made them water a little, and Malplackett's own mouth curved into a grin as he watched him. This was going to work out fine, he told himself. There'd be no trouble here at all.

He knew when the other man arrived, even though he was sitting with his back to the entrance. He turned and raised one hand and Hersh was so intent on what he was watching that he didn't even notice.

'Over here!' Malplackett called over the noise of the music, now reaching a crescendo and the other man gave the briefest of nods and came quickly to slide into the last chair at the table.

The music stopped and a new record was put on; a sixties Tango and a girl in leopard skin with a live snake draped around her neck came on to the stage as the three now completely naked schoolgirls left it, trailing their discarded clothes behind them. Malplackett leaned forwards and said quietly, 'Mr. Hersh!'

The man turned his head and stared at him. The pupils of his eyes were dilated and as he looked at Malplackett and the new arrival they saw them shrink and almost felt the excitement drain out of him; his shoulders resumed their drooping posture which they had lost when he was watching the schoolgirl act, and his mouth drooped.

'Mr. Hersh, here is my friend. The man I explained wants a word with you.'

'How do you do,' Hersh said automatically and after a moment the newcomer smiled at him and said quietly, 'How do *you* do.'

There was another little silence, and Hersh glanced nervously at the stage once or twice and then, very deliberately, pulled his chair round so that his back was presented to it. He looked for all the world like an affronted citizen being forced to demean himself by being somewhere to which he strongly objected. The tense alive man of a few moments ago might never have existed.

'Mr. Hersh has been having a lovely time,' Malplackett said, still keeping his eyes fixed on him. 'The "Three Little Girls from School" number really appealed to him.'

'I know,' the newcomer said at the same time that Hersh cried loudly, 'No it didn't!' and a man at the neighbouring table turned and stared.

'It didn't,' Hersh said more quietly. 'I was just – I was amazed. It's disgusting, it really is. Not what I'm – I've never been to such a place and I never will again, I can tell you. I wouldn't be here now if – ' He shot a glance at Malplackett. 'Mr. – Mr. – he wrote me this letter and I didn't like it. It's stupid, it really is. I don't actually *belong* or anything to this lot, you know! It's just that – my hobby, you see. Pictures. I like photography. Got a little Nikon camera, you see, take a few pictures, dabble in the development and printing – that's all it is. I'm just a hobbyist and it helps to have the chance to see other people's work. But I'm not a member. Not an *active* member, you see. I just – it was the only way to get the pictures and – ' His voice trickled to a standstill as the men sat and watched him and said nothing.

There was a long pause this time and then the other man leaned forwards. 'Mr. Hersh, I don't give a sod about you. I want you to understand that.'

Hersh blinked. 'What?'

'I don't care if your hobby is peeing up lamp posts. I don't care if it's stuffing tigers. I don't care *what* you do. Do you understand that?'

'Who are you?'

'Someone with a job to be done. That's all. A job to be done. And you're the man to do it, so I want to tell you exactly what you have to do so that you can get on with it. But as for what you do with your private life, I don't give a sod.'

'Then what – '

'Perhaps you'd better listen, Mr. Hersh,' Malplacket said kindly.

'I'm damned if I do,' Hersh said with a sudden little spurt of passion. 'I'm not sitting here in this sordid place and listening to men I don't know talking like that! I'm not looking for any jobs! I've got a job – who is this man?'

'You're an inspector from the Department of Environmental Health.' It was a statement, not a question.

'What if I am?'

'You cover this area.'

'So what if I do? What's it got to do with you?'

'There's a restaurant I want you to turn over very thoroughly. You're to find all sorts of problems there. I don't have to spell it out. I want you to make sure that the place needs a lot of money spending on it, if it's to avoid being closed down. Do you understand?'

'You must be mad,' Hersh said and tried to push his chair back to stand up, but Malplackett leaned forwards and gently pushed him down again. 'I can't do that if it isn't true. Why should I? What restaurant? Why do you want me to – '

The other man sighed and shook his head. 'You're really being very stupid, Mr. Hersh,' he said. 'Let's spell it out, shall we? I belong to the same – let's call it a club – that you do. I'm not a hobbyist, I'm not a photographer, I don't pretend to be anything but what I am, which is a very sophisticated man with very sophisticated tastes in sex. I like what I like – which is all sorts. You'll find my name on that list that yours is on – as well as on a great many others which are much more interesting – but the difference between us is I don't mind. I have nothing to lose, you see. I don't work for people who'd chuck me out on my arse, even take me to court if they found out. Also, I'm a lot cleverer than you are. I make sure no one, but no one, ever knows what use I make of the club's facilities or of anything else. Not like you. You aren't at all clever, are you? There was that evening last month down at Cookham, do you remember? A lovely waterside picnic with such lovely children – oh, good, I thought you'd remember. I've got photographs of you enjoying yourself there in case you'd forgotten. And then there was that party over at Wimbledon – I've got those pictures too somewhere – '

He reached into the breast pocket of his overcoat and brought out an envelope, and a small flashlight and he leaned over and handed them to the other man who, without taking his eyes from his face, reached for them and took them. 'No need to worry – I've got plenty of copies. If those get damaged it's not important. I can get you another set. As many as you like.'

The Tango number was over and the stage had been covered again, and the waitresses were bustling about, breasts swinging, to serve more drinks. Malplackett gestured and the girl Jenny brought three more beers as Hersh slowly opened the envelope, and, gingerly, switched on the little flashlight.

'Watch out,' Malplackett said suddenly and reached out and took Hersh's lapel and held on to it. He'd gone a sick white and his eyes had seemed to roll up for a moment as he had looked down on the glossy photographs the envelope contained.

'Don't bother with them any more, now,' the other man said kindly. 'They'll only get you worked up one way or another.' He laughed then, an odd little sound. 'Look at them, as they say, in the privacy of your own home. Let's talk about the work that has to be done. That you have to do.'

Hersh looked up at him, his eyes wide and staring. 'If I do it, whatever it is – what happens then?'

'Nothing. That's the whole point. Nothing at all. If you

don't do it, of course – ah, then that's different. A set of those photographs might find their way to the department offices, mightn't they?'

Hersh nodded miserably and then, amazingly, tried to grin. 'I never thought anything like this could happen to me,' he said and looked down at the envelope again. 'I'm so ordinary – '

'You have a far from ordinary job. You inspect restaurant kitchens and exert control over the way they're run. That's not ordinary.'

'Which restaurant?' Hersh said and picked up the envelope with fingers that were still shaking but which seemed to be stronger now.

'Laura's. Hallash's, you know? In Little Vinegar Yard.'

Hersh stared and then, incredibly, burst into laughter. 'Laura's? Angie's kitchen? You must be potty! That place – it's one of the ones I use as an example to others! It's the cleanest – '

'No doubt,' the other man said sharply. 'But the building's old. I'm not talking about such tuppenny ha'penny things as inadequate washing up or snotty-nosed vegetable cooks with the runs. I'm talking about real problems. Money problems. Dilapidations. Cracked walls. Cockroaches and worse getting in. Drains and rats and so forth. That is what you're going to find there. The sort of work that's going to take a lot of cash to put right. A lot of cash. A lot of work, the sort of things that'll mean she had to shut down for a few weeks to get it done. You know exactly the sort of things I mean. It can't be that unusual.'

'No, I suppose not,' Hersh said and then shook his head. 'Old Angie! Known him for ever, I have. He's a good friend. He'll never believe it – '

'He'll have to believe it,' the other man said shortly. 'Strip the tiles from the walls, check the state of the floors, I don't have to tell you – but do it. And soon – '

'I'm not due there for another month,' Hersh said. 'I've got a routine, you know – '

'Then change it,' the other said curtly and got to his feet. 'I've work to be done and I'm an efficient man, so I want it done as soon as possible. And that means right away, Mr. Hersh. No messing about. I give you a week. After that, the double of that envelope and its contents lands on Mr. Beeton's desk. Oh, yes, Mr. Hersh. I know his name, your head of department. I told you I'm an efficient type. And now I must be going.' He grinned suddenly. 'I've a date with a rather nice lady.'

'Who are you?' Hersh said again and peered up at him. The lights had changed again, dipping lower, ready for another show. 'I've a right to know that much. I can always check the list of club members for myself, after all.'

'As if you could work it out from that!' The man laughed and leaned over and patted him on the shoulder. 'My dear chap, you'd never do it! But I've nothing to be ashamed of. I just do as I do, and as long as I stay within the law I'm all right. And I'm well within the law, I see to that. And unlike you, Mr. Hersh, I don't care who knows who I am. My name is Philip Cord. Good evening!' And he turned and went, disappearing into the crowd by the doorway as the curtains parted and once again the Bored Little Housewife appeared.

24

Three days of hard work and he'd done it. There was just one last shot to get in the can and he ought to have that in the next couple of hours even though it was a tricky one. He had to line it up so that the graphics boys could pull in the image of the *Thrust* bottle and bring it sweeping up between the market stalls and the people, and they had to be gathered round it to sing the final jingle – which Joel regarded as quite the worst he'd ever heard, which was saying quite something – in a shot that pulled back to take in the whole of the street, and which could be used as the ten second special; not easy. But so far, he'd enjoyed himself and, he felt, had made a thoroughly craftsmanlike job of some very unpromising material. In spite of all his coaxing and soothing the client had insisted on a massive packshot – his wife, it turned out, had designed the dreadful bottle – and all Joel could do now was follow his brief. But all the same, he wasn't ashamed of the work he'd done.

Now, as the tension eased up, and his assistant was busy lining up the preliminary shots he could lean back against a strut of one of the stalls and watch the people around him; and the one he watched most was Paul Balog.

He'd been agreeably surprised by him; he'd cast him out of embarrassment and his own obsession with Laura more than anything else, and had had small hope of getting much more out of him than the effect of a walking tailor's dummy, but Paul had actually managed to make an excellent little performance out of what he had to do. Just walking into shot, stopping to buy a carnation for his buttonhole, looking at camera and strolling off; but he'd done it with style, casting at the camera a look so genuinely droll that the cameraman had chuckled appreciatively from behind his lens, and that had made Joel sit up and take notice. To make a cameraman laugh was a very rare achievement indeed.

But it was clear Paul wasn't happy, even though he was working well, and late in the morning when they had been hard at work for several hours Joel had discovered why. He had seen Philip Cord again.

The morning had been tedious in the extreme, with the real market men making it as difficult as possible for him and the actors who were playing their parts, egged on by Sam Price who jeered and, accidentally on purpose, came strolling into shot just at the wrong moment or shouted something outrageous as soon as the sound was rolling, but by lunchtime the novelty had worn off. They paid no more attention to what he was doing and got on with dealing with their customers and grumbling to each other about the way these bleedin' telly people got in the way and never paid no one a penny for the trouble they was causing. And Joel registered their irritation and ordered a small cask of beer for them to be brought out at lunch time.

It was during the lunchbreak that Philip appeared. There wasn't enough going on with this shoot to justify hiring a location caterer, and there were plenty of cafés and sandwich bars around, so most of the crew and cast had scattered. Joel was sitting on the kerb between Sam Price's stall and his neighbour's, eating a salt beef sandwich and enjoying the cool of the shadows there and the comfortable awareness of a job going well. He wasn't precisely hiding, but at the same time he wasn't easily seen and when he saw Paul Balog across the street, standing beside a fruit stall and looking at the raspberries, he considered calling out to him to come and join him. To talk about Laura perhaps – and set the idea firmly aside. He was here to work, not to indulge his own interests, even during the lunch break.

He didn't actually see the other man arrive, but suddenly there he was, standing next to Paul, and talking to him, looking very cool and relaxed. He was wearing a grey linen safari suit and looking pleased with himself, as though he was aware of being more fashionable than anyone else within sight, and again Joel felt that great wash of loathing. It wasn't a feeling he disliked any more, though; to feel like that about so unpleasant a man was positively exhilarating, he decided, and considered getting to his feet and calling the crew and cast together to start work again, thus sending the bastard packing. But it was still ten minutes to the end of the official break and less than half of his people were around; he'd only make a fool of himself if he tried that –

That Paul was distressed was soon obvious. His back, which was all that Joel could see of him at first, was rigid, and his head seemed to shake a little, and Joel stared and frowned. Dammit, what was it with these men? It was none of his business but he was fascinated all the same.

And then to his intense embarrassment they turned away from the stall on the other side of the street and came towards him, and he shrank back further into the shadows of the tarpaulin on Sam Price's stall feeling passionately that it was extremely important that he shouldn't be seen. He hadn't been spying on them, not deliberately, yet he felt as though he had and the thought of being flushed out and stared at by that cool and hateful man was more than he could bear.

But they didn't see him. They stopped on the other side of Sam's stall, which was being looked after by his neighbour because Sam had nipped off for a sandwich, and Joel heard Cord's voice clearly above the hubbub of the market.

'These look better,' he was saying. 'Much less tired. I'll have three punnets of those. When the man's here to take some money that is. Then you can give them to Anya Zsuzske with my love – '

'I will not,' Balog said in a low voice, but it was a tense one, and full of – what? Joel couldn't be sure though it was clear that the man was in the grip of a good deal of very strong feeling. 'She doesn't need your damned – '

'Oh, Paul, do stop being so stuffy!' Cord's lighter voice was jovial and full of laughter. 'She's a dear, darling old glutton and she'll adore them, you know that perfectly well.'

'She is not! And even if she were it's none of your affair. And don't call her – she's Mrs. Balog to you. You're not a relation – '

'Oh, don't try that on, Paul! I'm married to your cousin Ilona! Of course I'm a relation. And that means – '

'It doesn't give you the right to call my mother Anya.' Balog's voice was shriller now. Goddamit, Joel thought, he's almost in tears. Because the man is too familiar with his mother? Surely not?

'As if it makes the slightest difference, my dear chap. Do you think you can stop me just by telling me I'm not a relation? Do you think I'll just say sweetly, 'Oh, all right then. Let's forget all about it. I'll pop off home now? Do be your age! I'm on to something good here and I'm not letting it go whatever you or any one of them say, so there it is. You got yourself into this corner on your own, so you pick up the pieces. And I'll pick up the cheque and the documents tonight.'

'I won't give them to you,' Paul said and his voice trembled now. 'I won't sign them – '

'Oh, Balog, do stop being such a bore! We've been all through this till I'm sick and tired of it. Am I to tell your family all about you? About your interesting tastes and the sort of men you – '

'Christ, I'll kill you, Cord,' Paul said and Joel almost got to his feet. Even at the risk of being labelled an eavesdropper he couldn't let this go on, whatever it was. Paul was at the end of his control; at any moment now he'd either explode or collapse, that was very obvious. But then Cord laughed softly and said, 'There you are at last! Three punnets of those raspberries please – the best ones, mind. They're for a very dear old lady, my aunt, you know, mother of my dear cousin here – gone ninety, you know. Remarkable isn't it?'

'*Re*markable!' Sam Price's tones were unmistakeable and as he heard the scales clash gently and the tinkle of coins going into the cashbox Joel subsided back on to the kerbstone, and listened as the two men moved away, hearing the footsteps disappear into the hubbub of the street.

There was no sign of Cord when five minutes later he made his way round the back of the neighbouring stall to reappear a few yards further down the street. He felt ashamed of being so devious; he could just as easily have stood up and walked straight out into the street, for he had done no wrong in sitting there, but all the same – and as he left the shadows and emerged into the vivid sunshine he looked round covertly. But all he saw was Paul, standing at one side of the shooting area and looking as he had all morning; quiet and composed and ready to work.

Joel hesitated a moment and then very deliberately walked over to him.

'You all right, Balog?' he said and looked closely at the man. His face was expressionless as he stared back, and he lifted his brows in cool and rather dismissive enquiry.

'I thought you looked a little – put out. As though something was worrying you.'

'Not in the least.' He smiled faintly. 'This isn't exactly a taxing part, is it? I hoped I was doing what you wanted?'

'Oh, yes, yes,' Joel said heartily. Too heartily. 'Great stuff. As nice a little piece of work built on no foundation as I've ever seen. I'd like to see you with a part you can really work on, believe me I would. It wasn't work I meant – I was just – '

'As long as I'm working as you want me to,' Balog murmured and drew away, slightly but unmistakeably and, snubbed, Joel turned and went back to the camera man who was waiting with ill concealed impatience for him. Sod the bastard, he thought savagely, sod him. I wanted to help, that was all. If he wants to chuck it in my face let him get on with it. See how much I care.

But he did care. All that afternoon as he got the final shot together – and it worked magnificently in spite of all his preoccupation – he was aware of Paul Balog. He watched him walk faultlessly through his section of the complicated saraband that had been worked out for all the actors playing both stall keepers and the passersby, watched him when they broke as usual after two hours for a cup of tea, brought from a neighbouring cafe, watched as people chattered at him, and he seemed to reply courteously if unenthusiastically. It was all so normal that he began to think he'd imagined that little episode at lunchtime, had drifted into a fantasy in which Cord, the man he so much hated, played the part of a Bad

Person. The way he was feeling about Laura and this man's involvement with her was quite enough to have that effect, he told himself. But he knew, at bottom, that he hadn't imagined it. There was indeed something going on between these two men that was unpleasant, even, he told himself, sinister, and then was furious at his own dramatising of what was probably a perfectly normal situation. Whatever documents and cheques they had been talking about it was none of his affair. If he had any sense he'd forget the whole thing and get on with his own life.

Quite when he made the decision to go and see Laura he wasn't sure. It seemed to grow on him so slowly that one moment he was unaware of it and then there it was, full blown in his mind.

They were doing the last few cutaways as the market began to close up for the day, hurrying to get them into the can before the light changed completely and the backgrounds lost their animation as the stall keepers pulled down their tarpaulins, when he found himself thinking – tonight, I'll go and see her tonight, have dinner, tell her I'm worried about her cousin who by a coincidence has been working for me this week.

Coincidence, he thought and frowned. Will she believe me? It *is* a coincidence and they do happen all the time, but so often when you try to explain it, it all sounds so contrived. Well, he told himself sturdily, he couldn't help that. He'd go and see her and tell her about Paul and this man Cord. Maybe she'd listen? Maybe she'd see what he saw, that Cord was very bad news for her?

The more he thought about the plan the better he liked it, and even took time out to send his P.A. to phone the restaurant and try to book a table for him. It was late in the day and it might be difficult but he had to try; and when the girl came back and told him that she'd managed to get a table for him, because they'd had a cancellation, his spirits lifted absurdly. Maybe today was going to turn out to be one of those magical ones that happened sometimes when everything goes right; a good job of work finished, and a chance to talk to Laura. What more could a man ask for?

And indeed the work did finish well; they got the final difficult shot in just four takes, which was amazing, though he did a couple more to be on the safe side, and at five thirty sharp was calling the wrap. Inside the budget, he told himself joyously, and Laura tonight. Oh, but life was good to him this warm summer day!

'Why?' Laura said and set her elbows on the table and rested her chin on her fists. It was the only way she could find to keep herself steady, her hands were shaking so much.

'Some men are made that way,' Alex said and leaned forwards and touched her face gently. 'Darling, don't look so bereft! It's not the end of the world, is it?'

'No. No, of course not.' She managed to smile then, and even kept her gaze on his face, though her eyes felt sandy and hot. 'Of course it isn't – it's just that – '

'The man's a shit,' Alex said cheerfully. 'But then everyone in the family's always known it, so it can't exactly be a surprise to you. Just you watch out for him, my duck, that's all. Don't let him get too close – word to the wise and all that sort of thing, eh?'

Still she sat with her chin on her fists, staring at him, but she could control her eyes no longer. The pain was pushing against her throat and her nose, as sharp as needles, and the tears appeared and began to run down her face.

At first Alex didn't notice; she had sent Miklos to fetch him a bowl of cold wild cherry soup and he was drinking it greedily and didn't look at her. But then he did look up and at the sight of her ravaged face his own became a mask of amazement.

'Laura! For God's sake, girl, what on earth – '

'Nothing,' she said huskily and now she did move, thrusting her hands into her dress pocket to find a handkerchief and rub at her wet face. 'Nothing – it's just that I'm – '

Alex pushed his soup bowl aside and reached across the table to take hold of both her hands. 'Laura? Why are you so upset? I mean – there wasn't more to this than a bit of chatting up, was there?'

She shook her head, speechlessly and extricated one hand so that she could rub her face again, and he almost shook her other hand with impatience, 'Laura! Will you tell me?'

'It's not important,' she said dully. 'It really isn't. Now that I know I'll keep away from him. It's as simple as that. Now that I know.'

'Of course it's important!' Alex said. 'Godammit all, I have to know! Has that lousy shit been – I mean, has there been a – oh, Christ, I hate all this! It's all wrong – but has he been screwing you?'

'Nice way to put it,' Laura said, with a sudden spark of her usual self emerging. 'I saw it – to me it was different.'

'I'll murder him,' Alex said and his voice was very flat, with no histrionics in it at all, and he pushed his chair back as though he were going to get up and go and find him then and there and she pulled him back.

'Don't be so stupid,' she said sharply, and again rubbed her face though the tears had stopped now. 'I'm not a child, nor am I some kind of possession of yours you have to take care of. I'm a grown up person, Alex. Anything I did I did of my own free will. Eyes wide open and all that. So don't insult me by making a great drama over it. Just let me get over it in my own way. Privately.'

'The man's a bastard, a shit. I could – '

'Yes, yes,' she said wearily. 'Call him names if it makes you feel any better. For my part I'd just like to be left in peace.'

'Christ knows I'm no bloody angel,' Alex said, and he made fists of both hands and beat them lightly on the table in front of him. 'I've run both ways and thought it fair enough – but you don't do this to one of your own.'

'Do what?' she said and took a deep breath. 'Don't find you have needs other people don't? Are you being all moralistic about homosexuality all of a sudden, Alex? It doesn't suit you.'

'Of course not! But it's possible to be gay and to be a decent sort of bloke as well. I thought you of all people would know that – '

'I do,' she said shortly and then leaned forwards and

touched his cheek. 'Listen, Alex, never think I feel like this because – because Philip happens to be gay as well – because he is what he is. It's not that. I'm upset because he didn't tell me. And I thought well – I had thought it was a worthwhile thing. Important, you know? And it couldn't have been important or he'd have told me – about Paul. That's what hurts. But I don't blame him. He – he prefers someone else to me. And it happens to be a man. Well, it happens. Happens all the time, they tell me. And now it's happened to me. It's just my bad luck – it's no – it's not his fault is it? I just wish he'd told me about Paul – '

'And about me as well?'

She sat and stared at him, her face quite still and then closed her eyes suddenly.

'Oh, God,' she whispered. 'Oh, God.'

'Is that worse than Paul?'

'Yes,' she said, and opened her eyes. 'Of course it is.'

'It was a while ago,' he said and looked away, embarrassed, and that she found very touching. Alex had always talked to her cheerfully and easily about his lovers, about the boys he fancied and the ones who fancied him and though she had not liked thinking of him as promiscuous – which clearly he was – she had been glad he had trusted her so well, and had been particularly glad that he was never embarrassed. But now he was.

'It was odd,' he said then. 'I mean, one minute he was all over me and then phtt – it was over. I hadn't minded. I mean, I know he's Ilona's husband and all that, but it wouldn't be the first time I had an affair with a married man – ' He grinned a little crookedly then. 'It sounds so wonderfully "True Romances" doesn't it? I like that. But it was him who got bothered, I think. He was talking about the family one evening and then suddenly, that was it. He went and never called me again. It wasn't till Paul called me I had any idea that – he seems to be cutting a swathe through us all, doesn't he? Do you suppose there's something about being Hungarian that turns him on and never mind the gender?'

'I don't know.' She seemed to have withdrawn into her own misery now, and was hardly listening to him, but at least she'd stopped crying, Alex thought; and went on talking, needing to give her time to recover even more, for the restaurant was beginning to fill up now with pre-theatre diners.

'He's certainly fascinated by us all, isn't he? Did he talk family history at you? He did it with me, for ever. The way the old people came here and how the restaurant was started and who owns it now – '

'Yes,' she said. 'He's interested. But I'm not. Not in him, not any more. I don't ever want to hear another word about him, do you understand, Alex? I'm grateful to you for coming when I asked you, and grateful to you for telling the truth so honestly. It – at least I know everything now. I thought it was just Paul, but now I know it was – well, that's it. I never want to see him or hear of him again, is that clear?'

'It won't be that easy,' he said. 'What with family things. Anya Zsuzske's party every year and all – ' He seemed to brighten then. 'Maybe she'll be dead by next year. Then you can dodge it.'

She managed a laugh. 'You don't change, do you? You're a complete villain, always were – '

'And I love you. You're the best sister any man ever had, villain or saint. Don't forget that.'

'I won't.' She smiled, shy suddenly. 'And you remember – not another word about all this. Now I know it all, I can cope. As long as it doesn't – as long as people don't chew it over and over. You know what I mean?'

'I know. And I hope we do know all there is to know. I wouldn't trust Philip Cord as far as – all right, all right. Not another word. Can I have the rest of my soup now? It's even better than usual – '

She pushed the bowl towards him and got to her feet. 'I'll see how things are going in the kitchen. I've got a lot to do,' she said. 'Enjoy your dinner – and thanks again – '

He looked up from his soup bowl and opened his mouth to speak and then shifted his gaze to look over her shoulder, and she turned her own head to follow his stare.

'Miss Horvath?' Joel said and held out one hand. 'I've

booked a table so don't worry about finding room for me. But there's something I have to do. I mean I want to talk to you about – well, I was wondering. Could you spare the time to sit down and have a drink with me?'

25

'I really don't think I can,' Laura said carefully, holding the phone so tightly that her fingers tingled beneath her white knuckles. 'I've had a lot to deal with just lately and – '

She listened, her face creased with irritation.

'Well, Dolly, I'm sure it is, but I really can't – what? Well, that's up to Evelyn, of course. It's not for me to – '

Again she was interrupted and now she made no attempt to be polite any longer. 'Look, Dolly, I have to say no. I can't see you today, and that's all there is to it. I'm running a hell of a busy restaurant here and I can't indulge myself with cosy family chats in the middle of it all. What? – Ye Gods, Dolly, who the hell do you think you're talking to? I am not your employee, or anything like it! I run this place because it suits you all that I should and you get a bloody good income out of it. Don't try to pretend there's any more involvement than that for you. You have no right to tell me how to run this business. All you have to do is cash your cheques when you get 'em, which, thanks to me, is very very regularly. And they're large cheques too. So be grateful for that, and stop pestering me!' And she slammed the phone down on its cradle and stood there trembling, her eyes closed, and breathing in deeply through her nose.

She couldn't remember the last time she'd lost her temper quite so spectacularly; it was not the sort of self indulgence she admired, but this last call had been the culmination of so much. Bad enough she had gone through such stress while she was trying to drum up the courage to ask Alex to come in to the restaurant so that she could talk to him about what Paul had said that night at her flat; bad enough to have had to swallow the things he had to tell her. On top of that there had been that unpleasant scene with Joel Coplin last night, and now this – she opened her eyes and stared miserably at the window, where Angie was watering the creepers and very obviously not paying any attention at all to anything but the green leaves with which he was dealing.

'Bloody woman!' she said loudly now and Angie looked innocently over his shoulder.

'Talking to me?'

'Not to the wall, Angie. Who else?'

'Thought you might still be on the phone,' he said and grinned at her.

'You know damned well I wasn't,' she said and sat down on her tall stool and folded her arms in front of her and rested her chin on them.

'That was Madam De Yong, I take it?' Angie said with great casualness, pouring water with finicky care onto the plant at the very end of the row. 'She used to drive your dad potty 'n' all.'

'She's impossible!' Laura said. 'As if I haven't enough to put up with without her nagging as well. And talking to me as though – you'd think I was a dish washer or something, she's so damned imperious. Oh, Angie, I wish I could buy her out! Not that I suppose she'd agree, of course, but wouldn't it be marvellous?'

'You'd have to buy out your Auntie Evelyn as well, though, wouldn't you?' Angie said and at last set down his watering can, unable to pretend to be busy there another moment, and came over to stand in front of her desk. 'They reckon to be at daggers drawn, those two, but they're even more like thick as thieves, as I see it. And don't they have the same share between 'em? Your Uncle Istvan's?'

'Yes,' Laura said. 'If only I could have their two shares, then maybe I could buy – ' She stopped suddenly and her eyes slid away from Angie, but he didn't notice. He was standing looking dreamily at the ceiling, planning.

'Then if you could raise the money to buy Mr. Balog's share and then Mrs. Cord's, you'd have the lot, wouldn't you? What're the chances, Mizz Horvy? Could you raise it? I got a bit set aside I could lend you, and then – ' Now he did look at her, hopefully.

'No,' she said shortly. 'Not a chance. You'd better get

back to the kitchen, Angie. The fish arrived fifteen minutes ago.'

'I know when the fish arrived,' Angie said with great dignity. 'You don't have to give me reminders. Listen, Mizz Horvy, I've been looking at the Vinegar Trust Newsletter. You know that new thing they're doing now? They do these property price lists and last week there was a restaurant over at Frith Street went for –'

'I don't want to to talk about it, Angie.' As if I could go to Ilona and ask to buy her share, she was thinking. I couldn't even ask Paul easily; to talk to Ilona and therefore to Philip even on the most businesslike of terms would be impossible.

'It's a lot, I know, three hundred thousand at least, but I got the best part of fifteen thousand set aside, you know. Careful, I am, always was, and invested a bit of it, and it'd be the best thing I could think of to see you having the whole place. It's not that I don't think the world of the rest of the family. You know I do. But it's all your work and effort, 'n't it? Ought by rights to be your place. If you could raise the rest of it, with my fifteen thousand and the bank – '

'Please, Angie,' she said and her voice was tight in her throat. 'Please don't.' And he looked at her more closely and nodded.

'Time I went back to the kitchen,' he said as though no mention had been made of anything of any interest whatsoever. 'Would you believe me, I've got bloody Hersh coming in this morning? It's not three months since last time but he rings and says new regulations down at his office, he's got to change the schedule, would you *believe*? He'll be in at eleven. Talk to you later, then, Mizz Horvy – '

And he went back to his kitchen in so towering a bad temper that one of the kitchen boys actually burst into tears as well as giving in his notice and had to be soothed back to work with all the tact that Leno could muster.

Laura, alone in her quiet restaurant, let her shoulders slump and worked at relaxing. It didn't seem possible that she could be upright at all after a night like the one that lay behind her. Never in all her life had she actually not slept at all, but last night – and she closed her hot eyes at the memory of the long hours spent rolling from side to side of her crumpled too-hot bed.

It's not as though it had been a surprise, she told herself bleakly now, sitting and staring at the creepers in the window which were waving a little in the draught from the open door and glittering with the droplets from Angie's watering can. Ever since that evening when Paul had come to her in such a panic she had known somewhere deep inside that her precious illicit love affair was threatened. She hadn't wanted to face it, had wanted to go on just as they had been, meeting, laughing, eating, drinking, making love and laughing again, and she had worked hard for several days at blocking out the doubts that had come sliding into her mind because of what Paul had said. Don't meddle, she'd told herself desperately. Settle for what you've got. Fun and – don't *meddle*.

But of course it hadn't worked, that self lecturing. So she had meddled, hadn't been able not to. She had called Alex and he had told her what she had feared for too long was actually true. The man she loved regarded her merely as fun, as someone to play with, but no more than that. To her he had come to be the most important thing that had ever been. It had been as though he had grown and inflated like some vast glorious silver balloon to fill her entire world. And now the balloon had burst.

She had gone on with her work, of course, but it had been round the edges of her life and no longer at the centre of it. Work had ceased to be the magic answer to every fear and every self doubt and every worry about the future; it had become something she did to occupy the dead hours when Philip couldn't be with her; only when he was had she lived and breathed and felt and known. And she had, all on her own, destroyed all that –

I won't cry, she told herself fiercely and moving with sharp little actions pulled her ledgers towards her. Work had to be put back where it belonged, slap in the middle of life. It had to be restored to all its old pre-eminence, to be again all that there was; the one thing above all that mattered, the one thing that could be trusted, the one thing that gave comfort and reassurance.

And for a little while it almost seemed as though it was true; that she could blot out all that was miserable by a mere act of labour, but then the rest of it came pushing back into her awareness. That man Coplin standing there and saying, 'Well, it would be easier to talk over a drink, but if you can't, it'll have to be like this. And the thing is, I'm concerned about a relative of yours. It's ridiculous I suppose, but I've got the notion into my head that he – he's in some sort of trouble and needs help. He's a nice man, and I don't want to interfere, but really, I am concerned about him – '

'Who?' Alex had asked bluntly and then added impatiently. 'It's all right. I'm Laura's brother, Alex Horvath. Who are you? And what's this about a relative of ours?'

She frowned now and tried to push the memory out of her head, concentrating as hard as she could on her ledger, but the scene refused to go away; it played itself out inside her head, pushing its images in front of her eyes so that she watched it happen – shadowy yet dreadfully, painfully real against the columns of figures on her ledger's pages.

'May I sit down?' That was Joel Coplin.

'Oh, yes.' That was Alex being impatient. 'What is it you're on about?'

'Paul Balog,' Joel had said then and had turned and looked at her very directly, 'Miss Horvath, I don't want to start any fuss – I really don't, but he's been working with me this week, and I don't – I couldn't help but notice. And knowing you, however slightly – well, I was concerned.'

'How did you know Paul Balog was a cousin of ours?' Alex again, suddenly suspicious, moving his chair closer to hers, setting his arm protectively around her shoulders. 'What do you know about us anyway?'

'I've been doing research on your family.' Joel's voice had been warm and pleasant. She could remember now noticing that and had wondered why, and now, this morning knew why. It was a way of not hearing the words a person said, to listen just to the sound of a voice. I can't cope with any more, she had been thinking, sitting there in the circle of her brother's arm. I've had a bad day, and I can't cope with any more. I'll just listen to his voice. Won't pay any attention to his words.

But she had to, of course. 'So what's the problem?' Alex being clipped and dismissive. 'And what work has he been doing with you?' 'Just three days,' Joel had said, equally crisply. 'Acting in a commercial. But long enough to see what was happening. And he – I think he's being blackmailed.'

The word had bounced on the table between them and gone on bouncing so that it echoed in her ears. Blackmailed, blackmailed. 'Blackmailed?' That had been her own voice stupidly repeating it.

'It sounds so bloody melodramatic when you actually say it,' Joel had said apologetically. 'And perhaps I'm an ass, but I couldn't help but notice. He looked so – he was so distressed. And then I overheard them talking – '

He'd gone quite white then, an odd effect and she had stared at him, startled, and he'd said loudly, so loudly that other people turned to stare. 'I'm very embarrassed about this.'

Oddly, Alex had laughed. 'I never am, and I listen to other people all the time. Quite shameless about it, I am. It's a useful thing to be able to do. Like reading papers upside down on other people's desks. What did you hear?'

'He was being very threatening. I have to say that, because it was what it sounded like. Threatened something to do with documents and cheques and telling – talking to his family about personal matters.'

Now Joel's colour had come back in excess; he was blushing. 'It's nothing to do with me, and I don't want to know. All I can tell you is that Balog looked ghastly and very upset and said he didn't want to do whatever it was and then the threat was there – "Am I to tell your family all about you? About – " ' And Joel had checked himself and shrugged.

'Who threatened him?' Alex still holding her round her shoulders, still being protective, and at that point for some reason she had been irritated by his solicitude and had pulled away from him so that she was sitting quite unsupported when it came.

'Philip Cord. The man I met here the other night, with you, Miss Horvath,' Joel had said and not looked at her. 'I'm sorry, but there it is. That's what I heard and it seemed to me – ' Again he shrugged.

'What did it seem to you?' She had heard her own voice almost with surprise, not knowing she had meant to say anything. 'That you had the right to come here and make a – to gossip about my family in such a disgusting fashion? Is that what it seemed to you?'

'You've every right to be angry,' Joel had said and then looked at her very directly, ignoring Alex, turning one shoulder as though to exclude him. 'If I were you, I would be angry too. But I – I found myself so interested in you and liking you so much when we sat here and talked that evening that I felt – that it made me concerned for you and therefore for the people you care about. That's all.'

'Oh, prettily said.' Alex had clapped his hands together softly. 'As nice a speech as any I've ever had to learn. Who writes your stuff, my friend?'

Joel had looked at him with a flick of his dark eyes and to her amazement Alex had flushed; her brother Alex who always said what he liked and did what he liked and never gave a damn about anyone's opinion to be discomfited? It was so novel that even in the middle of this dizzying evening where everything in her life seemed to be clattering around her ears like a jerrybuilt shed she noticed it.

'I'm sorrier than I can say, but I still think I was right to come and tell you. You seemed – there appeared to be a closeness between you and this man Cord, and if I'm right and he is blackmailing your cousin then it seemed to me right that you should be warned.'

He had stopped then and looked down at his hands. 'It could be of course that I read more into what I heard than was there, because I was so jealous.' He had lifted his eyes then. 'But I don't think it was that, I really don't.'

There had been a silence between them into which the

sounds of the restaurant cascaded; Maxie's voice extolling the venison on tonight's menu and the freshness of the new season's green peas, and customers booming with laughter, determined to extract every atom of pleasure that they could from their evening's entertainment, and the clatter of dishes in Miklos's hands and she had sat and looked at this odd man with her eyes wide, trying to sort out what he'd said. Jealous, of Philip? Why should he be jealous? What an extraordinary and ridiculous thing to say.

'I don't even know who you are.' Alex said in a complaining voice. 'I mean, damn it, here sits a total bloody stranger, slagging off my cousin Philip – not that I doubt for a moment that he's telling the total truth, Laura, any more than you should, after all the rest of – well after all the rest of it, but all the same, a total stranger – and chatting up my sister too. Introduce me, Laura.'

'I'm Joel Coplin.' He hadn't waited for her to catch her breath, as though he feared she wouldn't even try to speak. 'I'm making a film about Soho and your sister was kind enough to give me some help. Also – ' He had hesitated. ' – also, as it happens, my own family come from these parts, though I was born and raised in Canada. They had a shop not far away and my great grandfather was a friend of your great grandfather, that is. As I understand it – '

'A film maker?' Alex had paid no attention at all to any of the rest of it. 'Christ, you're a *film* maker? Television? Or features? Or commercials?'

'Yes,' Joel had said and looked at Laura. But she was still staring down at the table.

'And I, my dear chap, am the best bloody actor in this country! No one's got round to noticing it, but I am. Time we talked more – '

'Time you left,' she had said harshly then, and had stood up. Now, looking back down from the commanding heights of this morning over the long wakeful night to last evening she saw herself, hands thrust deep into her dress pockets, her face no doubt drawn and ugly, being hard and tough. 'I have work to do and I need this table. There has been a mistake about your booking, I'm afraid, Mr. Coplin. I can't accommodate you.'

'I'm sorry,' he'd said. And then surprisingly, 'Sorry you can't accommodate me. Not sorry I told you. You needed to know.'

'You're damned right she did,' Alex had said with an air of rollicking good humour that had made her want to smack him the way she had when they had been children and he had started to tease her in that tiresome way of his. But she had stood there silently with her hands in her pockets, chin up, willing them to go.

'Come on, old man,' Alex had said and gone round the table and tucked his hand into Joel Coplin's elbow. 'You and I, we have matters to discuss. Like films and television and commercials. You do 'em, eh? So do I, my friend, so do I. When I can get 'em. Isn't that a delicious coincidence? The *Dog and Duck* calls. I'll buy you a large drink and we'll discuss our careers, mainly mine. Come on. Laura's all right, aren't you, my love? She'll cope. She always does. Remember what I said.' He'd kissed her then. 'Best out of it, past is past, to hell with spilled milk, wheel out all the old lines and imagine I said 'em. I'll call you. 'Night – ' And he'd dragged Joel away and she had watched them go and said nothing.

And now this morning the memory had to be put away. The scene had replayed; now forget it, she told herself fiercely. You're over the worst. There's nothing else that can hurt as much as that. Just get on with work now and you'll be fine. It's the best remedy there is –

Behind her the door from the kitchen burst open with a clatter and she turned, startled at the sound, to see Angie standing there with his eyes wide and staring and his hair ruffled as though he'd been pulling his hands through it.

'Mizz Horvy,' he said hoarsely. 'For Gawd's sake, come in here. This bloody man Hersh is here and he's saying – he's saying –' He shook his head. 'You'd better come and hear it for yourself.'

26

Am I going along with this, Joel asked himself, because I really want to get this film made, and because I really think the story of the Halascz family is essential to it, or because he's her brother and now the only tenuous link I have to her? And he couldn't find an answer, and went marching along Frith Street, looking for the restaurant's name, trying not to think about his own motives more than he had to.

'It's the least City Television can do!' Alex had said cheerfully when they had parted last night. 'If I'm going to help you with your research you can at least feed me. Poor struggling actor like what I am, weep, weep.'

'We go to your sister's?' Joel had said, standing on the dark street outside the *Dog and Duck* and looking involuntarily over his shoulder at the dark entrance to Little Vinegar Yard.

Alex had laughed. 'She won't have a table for me!' he said. 'And I got the distinct impression last night she wouldn't have one for you either.' He had chuckled softly in the darkness. 'Fancy her, do you?'

'I beg your pardon?' Joel had said stiffly and Alex had laughed again.

'I thought so. What a waste! Good looking chap like you – ah, well, that's the way the bread slices, I suppose. So, listen. Tomorrow. You give me lunch at – let's see. *L'Escargot*! That'll be nice. Decent French nosh, makes a change after Angie's eternity of paprika. One o'clock then, and I'll bring my scrap book and you can tell me the work you've got for me! I'm determined to work for you, now, so don't be late – ' And he'd gone whistling down the road, leaving Joel to walk slowly home, his head whirling from the gins that he had swallowed simply because Alex had kept ordering them (and for which, ultimately, he had found himself paying) and also from the way events had turned.

I'm not sorry, he had thought as he had showered and at last climbed into bed. I'm not. If that bastard Cord is blackmailing Paul Balog then the sooner he's stopped the better. I spiked his guns; and he had grimaced at the banality of the clichéd thought and fallen asleep very abruptly.

I ought to have a headache this morning, he told himself, after all that gin. But he didn't. His mouth was unpleasant and he had no doubt his breath smelled less than agreeable, but food would put a stop to that; and as long as he stuck to Perrier water for the next few days he'd come to no harm. In fact he felt remarkably good and he stopped and stared up at the pale green snail that was the emblem of the restaurant for which he had been seeking and thought about that. And then grinned to himself as he went up the steps.

The thing is, he told himself as he was ushered up a flight of rather elderly stairs to a room above and was greeted by a pleasant middle-aged woman who made him think, just for a moment, of Laura (not because she looked like her but because she was so obviously in charge) the thing is, I've got rid of the louse. It was dreadful to see her looking like that last night, her face drawn and white and all the fire gone out of it. No sign of that blazing smile there then, no indication that she could look as incandescent with life and happiness as he'd seen her; but the man was gone from her life and in time, he told himself, in time it'll all work out fine. I'll teach her to look like that again, and be happy, I will –

If she lets you, his inner and very sardonic voice murmured, if she'll let you. Last night she was far from keen on you, wasn't she? Seemed distinctly to dislike you. What d'you think will change that?

'Hello Elena!' Alex's voice came up the stairs before he did. 'As delicious as ever. Come and be kissed.'

'Good afternoon, Mr. Horvath,' the small woman said equably and led him to the table where Joel sat waiting. 'Your guest is here.'

'Meet Joel Coplin of City,' Alex said and sat down as

Elena shook hands with Joel. 'Make eyes at him. He'll be tomorrow's Steven Spielberg.'

'Today's Mr. Coplin seems fine to me,' Elena said and deftly set a menu in front of him and Joel thought again – Laura's like that. Unruffled, no matter what people say, copes with all sorts of idiots. Wonderful Laura –

'How are you feeling this morning?' Alex said. 'I was a touch bent when I got up, I must confess, but there's nothing wrong with me a decent lunch won't cure. Elena! – a bottle of – '

'Perrier,' Joel said firmly and looked at Alex with his brows slightly lifted and after a moment Alex laughed and looked shamefaced, in a knowingly beguiling manner, and said, 'Right, Perrier.'

'A wise choice,' Joel murmured and returned to the menu and Alex snickered and did the same.

When they'd ordered, Alex leaned back in his chair and looked around. 'Do you ever get the impression that all people do in this tangle of streets we call Soho is eat? Nothing but restaurants.'

'A few other places as well,' Joel said. 'Sex shops, for example – I want to include them in my film too.'

'Then it's Preston you'll need,' Alex said at once. 'He never admits it but the general feeling is he owns most of the places around here – whoever has his name on the lease – the ones that make money that is. Very canny man. Offered me a job once – ' He reflected for a moment. 'But it wasn't quite my style.'

'No?'

'Minder to a bunch of tarts? Decidedly no, ducky.'

Joel lifted his brows at him. 'Do you have to be so camp? I thought that was getting a touch out of date.'

Alex gave a mock wince. 'Touché! Perhaps it is time I altered my style, at that. I do it to make people notice me, of course. Don't we all? It's not easy being an actor,' he sighed gustily. 'Getting the attention of the people with jobs in their gift – that's the real talent. You can't sit at home waiting for the National to ring and beg you to come and do your Hamlet, can you? If I wait for that, I'll still be waiting when all I'm fit for is Lear. So – ' He shrugged. 'A touch of the outrageous. It seems to help.'

'Some directors might find it a turn off,' Joel said.

'Do you?'

'Not particularly.'

'There you are then. It's worth it. And you've noticed me, admit it.'

'I could hardly fail. You were with Laura last night.'

There was a little silence and then Alex said, 'I'm sorry.'

'Hmm?'

'I think I was rather rude to you last night. About Laura. You do like her, don't you?'

Joel sat and looked at his plate for a long moment and then lifted his chin and looked at the other man. 'Yes,' he said. 'A great deal.'

'Oh, shit! And there was I making awful jokes about fancying her – and – look, if you really – I mean, she's quite a lady, my sister.'

Joel smiled faintly. 'I rather think I've noticed that.'

'And she's had enough hurt for one week, thanks. That shit, Cord – ' Alex's fists tightened and seeing the tense knuckles on the tablecloth Joel suddenly felt a great warmth for him. 'If anyone ever hurt her like that again, I'd – '

'Me too,' Joel said and Alex's knuckles relaxed.

'That's all right then,' he said lightly and laughed. 'Bless our little cotton socks, aren't we getting serious! And if it's serious stuff you want to talk about, let's talk about the most serious thing in this whole world. Little Alex Horvath's career. When do I start work for you?'

'One thing at a time,' Joel said easily. 'Now we're talking about Laura, let's go on for a while. Tell me about her.'

'What do you want to know?'

'Everything?'

'That's a tall order. And not, at the same time. I mean, bless her, she's the restaurant, you know. Nothing else really. That's what made me so angry. To the best of my knowledge Cord's the first chap she ever – I don't think she's ever had an affair before. Not that I'd know for sure, of course. She's not the sort to advertise the facts of her private life in *The Times*, but as far as I know – Always too busy, you see, and too tied up with the family. Looked after my parents till they died, and old Uncle Istvan too, and helps Paul with Anya Zsuzske – if he has to work away from home she stays at his place and takes care of the old lady and arranges for someone to go in while she's at the restaurant – it all makes her sound so dull, doesn't it? But she isn't.'

'You're preaching to the converted.'

'When I knew I was gay, I was just a kid. Fourteen, fifteen. I couldn't talk to anyone about it – I mean, Hungarians? They invented the machismo bit, never mind the bloody Spaniards. As far as my family were concerned, gay was like *dead*. But Laura – ' He smiled then, a secret little smile that made his face look even younger. 'She saved my sanity. And the family's. They take it all for granted now. Not like poor old Paul – ' He whistled then. 'What happened to him, poor darling! Mind you, it turned out all right, in the end, but it was rough – '

'What happened?'

'His dad suspected he was gay. And there was all hell let loose.'

'What sort of hell?'

'It was all a bit before my time, to tell the truth – but I've heard the stories. When the old lady died – my great grandmother, Maritza – then the restaurant had to be shared out. It had been hers, after the old man, Viktor, died, but now there was this Family Trust that came in. A share to all of the children, that was the thing. There were great dramas about it, so Timothy told me – he's my brother. We don't see a lot of him now he's got married and has a houseful of kids, but we used to be quite close and he always had a great thing about family history. Knew everything. It seemed that after she died, Paul's father found out that the poor chap was gay and went meshuggah. Potty. Bananas. Up the wall.' He grinned. 'Wish I'd seen it. But there it is, too young. Anyway, he did the classic thing. Cut off the lad without the proverbial bob. So Anya Zsuzske, who was always a goer from all accounts, she retaliated. Told him if he insisted on leaving his little all – and it was a hell of little all, seeing he was a diamond merchant – to the stuffed shirts – have you ever *met* my cousins Freddy and Leonard? Don't. It's no wonder poor old Paul chose to be bent with brothers like that. Anyway, Anya Zsuzske said, you give it all to those two, I give all mine to Paul. And damn me, that's what she did. So Paul, you see, had a quarter of the restaurant. Nice story, isn't it? Nice to see the lad get something, even though his father was such a shit.'

He looked reflective then, as though a new idea had come to him. 'Maybe that's why it's so easy to blackmail Paul? If he had that to put up with from his own dad, it's obvious he'd move heaven and earth to keep the facts about himself from everyone else. He's always covering up. Takes women out – ' And he grimaced and drank some of his Perrier water. 'It's all a bit sad. I may be camp, but I'm not pathetic.'

'No, you're not,' Joel said. 'And that does explain a lot about Paul. Who owns the rest of the place? If Paul has a quarter – '

'Ah well, Laura has a quarter. Our quarter, that is. The share inherited from our grandmother. She was Magda. Heard of Magda?'

'I think so,' Joel said cautiously. 'Laura mentioned her back in the days when we were talking.'

'You'll talk again,' Alex said cheerfully. 'Anyway, her share came to us three. My Uncle Zolly, the younger one, was killed in the war. Pilot, I believe. So it all went to our parents, Tibor and Louisa. And when Dad died, it came to us.' He looked a little haunted suddenly. 'It was a bad time, then, when he died. A bad time. All the changes and the fuss. It wasn't all that long since Grandpa Zolly had died, you see. Not all that long. It made us all feel – ' He shrugged. 'I ran a bit wild.'

'Wild?'

'Drank too much. Played around a bit with coke, one or two little things like that. Laura was – she was magic.'

'Was she?' Joel said gently but the fountain of talk had trickled to a stop and after a while he said; prompting carefully, 'So then what happened to the restaurant?'

'Mmm? Oh, I gave Laura my share. Not gave, actually. She'd helped me out so much I insisted she buy it. At a fair price to her. And then Timmy sold her his share because he wanted to buy a house in leafy Edgware, the wally. He got a good price for his. So,' he shrugged. 'So, Laura owns a quarter. And if there were any justice, then she'd have the lot.'

'Who has got it?'

'Mmm?' It was clear Alex was getting bored now. He had thumped a large scrapbook on to the table with a rather ostentatious gesture and Joel put a hand on it.

'I'll look in a moment, I promise. But I want to know about the restaurant. For my film. And since I'm thinking of you to do the voice over and the interviews – '

Alex's face caught fire. 'What?'

'You heard. Just give me a little more information. You've accounted for half the property. Who has the rest?'

'Oh, Uncle Istvan's lot, for a start. I think it's been shared between – let me see, there's Aunt Evelyn, the horrendous old spinster – honestly, the way she goes on and the way the others go on about her you'd think it was the end of the world that she's never been fucked.' He laughed. 'Maybe it is at that. I'd not like it if people could say it about me.' He shook his head and then, catching Joel's eye said hurriedly, 'And she shares it with her brother's wife. That's Aunt Dolly. Oh, a goer is Aunt Dolly. Spends every penny she can get out of her old man at Harrods. Amazing lady. She got her share of the last quarter from him, I think. Steven. That's the English of Istvan, did you know that?'

'So Istvan had only two children? Evelyn and Steven?' Joel was making notes of all this in his small notebook, scribbling industriously.

'No, there's another one. Daniel. A sinner, like poor old Paul. No, not gay. He was just randy. Women though. He screwed so many of the local girls they packed him off to Australia. His father gave him a share of money and off he went. And I hear the jammy devil married money and is worth a fortune now. Just shows you, doesn't it? Anyway, when Uncle Istvan died his will said he'd given enough cash to Daniel in his life time, so his share of the restaurant was for the other two. So there you have it.'

Joel stared down at his fingers. 'No I haven't. That accounts for three quarters if your Aunts Dolly and Evelyn share a quarter – they have an eighth each. Who has the other quarter?'

Alex looked doubtful for a moment and then his face cleared. 'Oh, yes, of course. That's Ilona's.'

'Who is she? In the family, I mean?'

'She's the granddaughter of the last of the original four, Kati, it was. I think. Yes, that's it, Kati.' He laughed again. 'How could I forget? It was awful when Ilona's father died, my old Uncle Gyorgy. She was close on forty then, Ilona, when he died, I mean. And like the good Hungarian he is, he provided in his will for his children according to their needs. Because her sister was suitably married and her brother was doing very nicely being a doctor, and she was still a pathetic spinster – that Hungarian horror – he left her all his inheritance from Kati. Her only daughter was his wife you see – she was called Ilona, too – so there it was. Poor Ilona labelled useless for everyone to tut over. It's a nasty business, family life, isn't it?'

'Told in these terms I suppose it is,' Joel said. 'So, Ilona – ' He stopped then and said carefully, 'Is she still a spinster?' He thought he knew who she was but he needed confirmation.

'Oh, no.' Alex sounded surprised. 'I assumed you knew – she married the egregious Philip Cord. He's fifteen years younger than she is, and everyone pursed their lips and gossiped like the devil when she married him but she won in the end. Got her man – and her share of the loot.'

'So Philip Cord owns a quarter of the restaurant,' Joel said slowly and lifted his brows at Alex.

'No, his wife does – ' Alex stopped then. 'I mean damn it, it's been a long time since a man took over his wife's property automatically, hasn't it? It's hers, surely?'

'With a husband like that?'

'You could be right. Look, dear man, I don't want to seem disagreeable, but really must we go on and on about all this? You can't tell me you're going to shove all this in your film.'

'No, I suppose not,' Joel said. But, he thought, it's to do with Laura. Anything to do with Laura and I want to know it. Every little detail fascinates me. And this latest one is the most interesting of all. Philip Cord has his hands on a quarter of her restaurant through his wife. That could mean problems for her. That could mean she needs someone to keep an eye on things for her. And who better than me? With Alex's help – and he grinned at Alex and held out one hand.

'Let's see it, then. Your scrapbook. Let's see what sort of work you've done, and talk about what you might be able to do in the future.' And Alex, happy at last, opened it on the table between them.

27

'This is ridiculous,' Laura said, trying to sound as reasonable as she could. 'If the only way you can reveal the damage is by doing more damage that could let something get in here, how can it be regarded as a health hazard?'

'The law is the law, Miss Horvath,' Hersh said. He was sweating, his face damp and greasy in the bright lights of the kitchen. 'If there's any way that infestation can be caused, then the problem has to be put right. It's the law.'

She took a deep breath. 'Look, Mr. Hersh. You tell me that behind those tiles which are wall to wall, floor to ceiling, and uncracked and undamaged and properly grouted as you can see, you tell me that behind all that there could be cracks in the wall? And that could allow cockroaches and other things to get in and – '

'Yes,' he said and his gaze shifted as she stared at him, so that he was staring owlishly at the wall in front of which they were all standing, he and Laura and Angie, in a row.

'But nothing can get in!' Laura said. 'Look at those tiles, Mr. Hersh. How could any creature get past those tiles?'

'It's not for me to say, Miss Horvath. It's the law.'

'Oh, for heaven's sake, Mr. Hersh, this is ridiculous! You might as well say that the floor might fall in and therefore I have to pull that up just in case – '

'If I believed there could be structural faults to the floor then I could ask you to do that,' Hersh said woodenly and ducked his head to look at the folder of papers he held in his hand. 'You can see for yourself. Here's the Act, and if you look at this section, subsection C – '

'I have no doubt it is the law,' she said and it was hard work not to shout at him. Keeping her tone reasonable and relaxed was becoming a very difficult thing to do. 'None at all. But it's all a matter of – interpretation. As an inspector, it's up to you to decide whether the law's being broken. And for some mad reason you say it is, when it's obvious to anyone that it isn't – '

'It is not obvious!' Hersh said loudly and lifted his head. His face looked as greasy as ever but there were patches of red on his cheeks, uneven and ugly. 'Are you suggesting that I'm – that I'm behaving in any way improperly? Because if you are, then – '

'No, no,' Laura said pacifically and put out a hand towards him. 'I've known you too long, Mr. Hersh. We all have. I'm just saying I don't understand why, all of a sudden, when there's nothing changed about the place, you're being so – such a purist. I dare say you're right. The walls here may be less stout than they should be. The building's old, after all. Eighteenth century – of course it's a bit rickety. But I do all I can to keep it in good heart! The panelling upstairs, all stripped and polished and the cellars treated for woodworm and shored up with new timbers and down here in the kitchen, all the tiling – I had it all done by the best people and you can see it's as good as the day it was put in, only two years ago. I got in the best quality work I could find. Whatever state the walls are in under them, that can't affect the cleanliness or safety of this kitchen – '

'I wouldn't be here if it wasn't perfect,' Angie growled. 'Twenty years you've known me, Mr. Hersh, and you know that for a fact. I wouldn't be here if it wasn't perfect. I'm known for it, perfection – '

Hersh snapped shut his folder of papers and turned to go. 'Can't help how long I've known you,' he said, still wooden. 'Law's the law. And I tell you that these tiles have got to come off and the wall underneath has got to be shored up. Work has got to start within a reasonable space of time or I close you down till it's done.'

There was a shocked silence and then Laura said blankly, 'Close us down?'

'I have the right under the law. Public health risk. I am the representative of the public on this matter. I have the right under the law,' the man gabbled and Angie shouted, 'This is crazy!'

'Calling me names, Mr. Alzano? Are you suggesting that – '

'Now I know he's crazy!' Angie roared. 'Twenty years I been Angie, now all of a sudden I'm Mr. Alzano? Crazy.'

'You can't,' Laura said. 'It's impossible – I'll appeal. Get another opinion from a different inspector.'

'It won't make any difference,' Hersh said. 'I have the authority to close you down here and now if I believe there is a health risk. You'd stay closed while waiting for your appeal to be sorted out. You know that – you've got your copy of the rules, haven't you?'

'Yes,' Laura said dully, staring at him with her face blank with the shock of it all. 'Yes – '

'I can give you a month,' Hersh said, and went to the door. 'I'm trying to be fair – '

'Fair?' shouted Angie. '*Fair*? You lousy, stinking – ' But Laura put a hand on his arm and he subsided.

Hersh stopped by the door of the kitchen but he didn't turn round. 'Look, I'm sorry,' he said. 'There's nothing I can do. It's a new – I have people on my back.' Now he did turn and looked at them with miserable eyes. 'Try to understand. I know it's hard on you, but me – I stand to lose my job.' He swallowed. 'It's a new – and I have to do it. It's the law. I have to apply it, or – ' He shook his head and turned back and pushed on the door which swung wide. 'If you start work within the month, I should be able to – it should be all right. Within the month – ' And he let the door go and it swung to and fro so that his retreating footsteps came back to them in a rhythmic loud, soft, loud, soft pattern.

There was a long silence between them and then Angie said, 'Now what?'

'I don't – ' Laura took a deep breath again. It was strange how short of air she felt, as though someone were trying to stop her breathing. 'I don't know.' She put both hands up to her face and again shook her head, holding onto her cheeks as though she feared her head would fall off. 'I just can't think – '

'Money,' Angie said. 'You're going to need money. We

can get it done. Don't fret you, Mizz Horvy. We can get it done. But it'll take a lot of money. And I told you, I've got some you can have – '

'No!' she said loudly and then seeing the look of hurt on his face reached out and took his arm. 'No,' she said more gently. 'You must see that, Angie. I can't take your money. I have to get it the usual way. Borrow it from the bank, raise it the way other people do. I can't get into personal loans. It just wouldn't be right.'

'And it wouldn't be right to be closed down, either,' Angie said stoutly. 'So just you remember that money's there if you want it.'

'I'll remember,' she said and patted his cheek and turned and went back into the restaurant. Another hour or so and they'd be arriving, today's lunchers, the heart of the place, the customers she existed for, and she stopped as she reached the red tiled floor and looked round at the blue and white tables and the glitter of silver and glass and the green freshness of the creeper clad window and thought, close me down? How could they close me down? This place has been here for almost a hundred years. They can't close me down –

But clearly they could, and once more she took a sharp little breath in through her nose and went over to her little desk. There was no point in sitting and worrying. Better to get matters in hand. The sooner the better –

By the time the first lunchers appeared in Little Vinegar Yard, she had set her wheels in motion. She had made telephone appointments with three builders to come and give estimates for the work, and had arranged to go and see her bank manager that afternoon. He had sounded grim on the phone, and her chest had tightened as she heard his noncommittal voice.

'I have some problems with structural work,' she had said brightly when he had asked what it was she wanted to come in about. 'I don't know yet to what extent, but I've had a tiresome visit from the Environmental people and – '

'Structural work,' the bank manager had said and she could almost see the distaste on his face. 'Again? Very costly.'

'Yes,' she said, desperately bright. 'That is why I need to see you.'

'The work on the stairs,' he said. 'That cost a great deal.'

'I know, but you must agree that the income of the restaurant is such that – '

'Well, we can't discuss it now,' he said dampeningly. 'At four o'clock then. I can spare you half an hour,' and he had hung up, leaving her listening to the buzz of the phone with her chest feeling tighter than ever.

It had been a costly few years, she couldn't deny. It had started with the tiling in the kitchen two years ago. The walls had needed treating for woodworm, because there were old timbers in them, and that had shown the need for rebuilding in places, for the building was indeed old and showing its tiredness. And all that had looked so good when it was finished and had given her so much pleasure that she had become perhaps a little over-enthusiastic.

Looking back now as she sat in the restaurant waiting for her first customers she did a mental sum. The floor in here had come next with the laying of new red tiles because some of the old ones had been showing wear and though it had been a big bill, all the same it had been worth it. Or so she had thought at the time, cheerfully using up virtually all her own personal savings to pay for it.

And then a customer had slipped on the stairs and though he'd not hurt himself, the banisters had shown they were less than secure when they had swayed under the impact, so she had set to work on that, borrowing money from the bank to do it. And it had been the right thing to do, she thought now, defensively. Suppose I hadn't and someone else had slipped and the banisters had actually broken instead of just swaying the way they had? Couldn't that have been much more costly in the long run? Bad for the restaurant's reputation? Of course it could –

You didn't have to do the panelling in the Extras, her little voice whispered. That cost more than the kitchen tiling and the restaurant floor and the stairs all put together. You didn't have to –

'But I did,' she murmured aloud. 'I did,' and knew she

lied to herself. The panelling had been shiny with cracked old varnish and for all the cleaners' efforts, grimy and sticky to the touch, and when the young man from the builders who were working on the staircase had shown her what lay beneath the dull cracked surface that had been there, in her memory, for ever and ever she had been completely captivated. He had set to work with a cloth and a scraping knife and a bottle of evil smelling liquid and uncovered wood of a rich glowing amber, with details on the carving she had never known were there under the thick layer of Victorian varnish, and she had at once agreed to have all three of the Extras done as well as the wall alongside the staircase. It had taken over nine months, but it had been worth it as yard after yard of the satiny wood reappeared to lift the place to a glow that made everyone feel good to be in it, even if they didn't know why.

So now she was not only bereft of her own cash reserves, but was in debt too. The restaurant was taking money, of course, a great deal of it, but three quarters of the income had to go out to pay the others their shares and repaying all that had to be found from her own was going to take time.

I should have gone to the others, she thought now, staring down at the sheet of paper on which she had started to make notes of how much she owed. It was to their benefit too. I should have made them contribute; it was all part of the upkeep of their property, after all. It all enhanced their value of their holding. But she knew why she hadn't, and it was no use being angry with herself now.

She had been childish, that was the thing. Wanting to feel that the restaurant was hers, all hers. To have asked her cousins to pay towards the repairs would have been to admit to herself even more obviously that the restaurant wasn't her special place. That though it bore her name as far as all its customers were concerned, though she ran it, though none of the cousins would actually dream of stepping in and ousting her, only a quarter of the equity was hers. And that hurt.

The plan she had been nursing deep at the back of her mind to raise enough money one day to buy them all out had to go. The work in the kitchen would have to be done – and remembering how much it had cost to have the tiling put in in the first place her eyes prickled with tears – and then and only then, when she had paid for that, and paid back the debt she already carried, *then* would she be able to start to save to buy the family out. Till then she had to go cap in hand to the bank manager and to anyone else she could get money from. It was a galling state to be in and as her first customer at last arrived she tucked her sheet of scribbles into her pocket and went to meet them. Work first. Worry afterwards –

When he appeared, the place had settled to its usual two thirty buzz when everyone was fed, apart perhaps from a sweet course and coffee, and were comfortably wined, and at first she didn't notice him. She had heard the door open and felt the soft blast of summer air as someone came in but she had been standing talking to Alistair Balfour from City Television and his two guests, letting him play his usual game of heavy flirtatiousness – it was always his way of showing off to people he brought – and had not looked round. But then she had moved away from the table as Maxie brought coffee and glasses of Tokay and had turned and there he was and her face went white. She felt it happen.

'I have to talk to you, Laura,' he said and smiled. 'Sorry to drop in like this, but it is important. And I knew I could get you here.'

'Won't it do later, Philip? I'm very busy right now.' She was proud of herself, of her smile, even if it was too bright, of her voice even if it was too casual. No one could possibly have known how she was feeling. 'I said all I wanted to say in my letter.'

'Oh, that.' He seemed to dismiss the painfully written note she had sent to him as totally unimportant. The note she had spent so long in writing and yet which had been so bald and dull when she had finished it. 'I've decided that I must stop seeing you,' she had written neatly. 'I am not happy about the situation. I'm sorry.' And had signed it with just her initials. 'I'm not here about that. You're right, of course. The time has come to stop all that. But that doesn't matter now.'

She stood and looked at him standing there in the middle of her restaurant, with her customers around her, and stared at him. 'Is that what you came to say? That it doesn't matter?'

'You said yourself it had to stop – ' he said, and smiled. The same smile that had made her head explode with excitement once. 'It's business I'm here to talk to you about. Ah! They're leaving.' He indicated a table against the window with an inclination of his head. 'I'll sit there and wait for you.' And calmly he walked across the restaurant, murmuring apologies to other people as he brushed against the chairs, and settled himself at the discarded table.

Maxie came over, frowning until he recognised him and then cheerfully cleared the dishes and replaced the cloth with a clean one and brought him a drink, and she stood there and looked at him and tried to control the dizziness that filled her. He looked the same, yet was so unbelievably different. The warmth that had seemed to come to her from him had changed to a chilliness that made her actually shudder. The amusement that had seemed to be a part of him now felt like the most edgy of malice and she blinked as one of the customers called her and turned away, grateful for the distraction.

Most afternoons there were one or two customers who lingered after the general exodus that happened around three o'clock, but today there were none and by quarter past three when the restaurant was empty and Maxie and Miklos and Janos went off gratefully to have their coffee break before cleaning up, she was standing at her desk when she had finished entering the last of the cheques and bills with her head down, waiting for him to speak. She felt quite unable to trust her own voice.

'Business,' he said then, and she lifted her head to look at him. 'Now it's strictly business, Laura. It's all turning out better than I hoped, so the sooner we settle this the better. Will you come and sit down, please?'

'I'll stay here,' she said and folded her hands on her ledger and sat there, as straight as she could.. It wasn't easy.

'I did think I was going to have to persuade you to sell to me, Laura,' he said, and leaned back in his chair and smiled at her. It wasn't easy to see his face; the green light from the creepers behind him shadowed it too well. 'But as things turned out, I don't need to. You really shouldn't have been so sharp with Aunt Dolly, you know.'

'What?' She was startled into speech. 'Aunt Dolly?'

'She phoned you this morning. Wanted to come and see you. But you refused.'

'What if I did? What's that to do with – '

'Everything. I'd made her an offer, you see, and she wanted to talk to you about it. But you decided not to talk to her, so – ' He shrugged. 'So she accepted me.'

'What are you talking about? I don't understand.'

He gave an elaborate sigh to show how patient he was being. 'I want this restaurant, Laura. I want to buy it. I have Ilona's share, of course. No problem there. I am about to get Paul's share. No problem there either. Not at all.' And he laughed suddenly, the same bubbling joyous sound that had made her so happy when she had used to hear it. Now it made her feel cold again. 'He'll do what I tell him to.'

'What do you want it for?' It seemed so banal a question but it was the only one she could think of.

He shook his head regretfully. 'Can't tell you that, my dear. I just want it. You might as well sell to me, hmm? The others are going to, so you can't stop me.'

'I can,' she said and lifted her chin. 'I can and I must.'

Again he shook his head. 'I know the terms of the Trust, Laura. If one of us wants to sell the rest have to agree.'

'We don't! No one can force me – '

He got to his feet and came across the restaurant to stand beside her.

'Yes, you can be forced. The Trust is quite clear. Do you think I haven't checked it all very carefully? If one of the owners wants to break up the Trust and sell the others have to agree. And I am for all practical purposes an owner and I want to sell. So, what are you going to do about it, except agree? You might as well. You actually can't do anything else.'

28

'I don't see why you won't let him help,' Alex said, his voice distorted by the phone. 'He's a knowing sort of chap and – '

'It's nothing to do with him,' Laura said and shifted the phone to her other ear. Her head was beginning to ache. 'It's a totally family affair.'

'And the bank's affair and the Environmental people's affair and everyone else's as well. At least he's got no axe to grind.'

'Everyone has an axe to grind.'

'Not like you to be so cynical, dear heart! Believe me, he hasn't – and I think – '

'Even you have,' she said wearily. 'You're only pushing him at me because you want to keep on his good side. You think he'll give you some work.'

There was a little silence and then he said, 'Ouch.'

'So please, don't go on about him. I'll cope on my own.'

'You're so wasteful, Laura,' Alex said. 'Throwing love away – it's wicked and wasteful.'

'What?' She was startled.

'The man thinks the sun rises and sets in you, do you know that? He wants to help you and God knows you could do with a good deal of that right now. I'm no use to you – too stupid to walk upright when it comes to money, always broke – and you know as well as I do that no one else in the family will be much better. They've all got feelings about it, haven't they? If you talk to Timmy he'll get agitated about Paul – you know how stuffy he can be – and start making trouble for the poor bastard, and you said you don't want that – '

'Of course I don't. Even after – have you talked to him again?'

He sounded disgusted. 'Of course I have. I've told him over and over again – he doesn't have to put up with Cord's leaning on him this way. Just stand up to him – we're on his side, it won't make any difference *what* Cord says about his sex life – '

'What did he say?'

'The same as last time. Just shook his head, went green, wouldn't say anything but that he had no choice – he was selling his share to Cord. I did my best, ducks, I really did.'

'I know,' she said dully. There'd been little hope in her it would be otherwise. 'I wish he wasn't so miserable.'

'I wish you weren't. Please, Laura, see Coplin. Like I said, who else can you talk to? Paul's brothers? Same thing. More upset for him. Ilona? That'll do you a lot of good, and I don't think. Aunt Dolly and poor old Aunt Evelyn? Hardly – '

'You're wrong there,' she said suddenly, staring at the wall as she held the phone even more tightly against her ear. Her hands were tingling with tension and it was getting harder to keep herself from bursting into tears. It was all such a mess, and she was so tired, so very very tired. It seemed to have been years since she had slept and the fatigue was thickening her body so that it seemed as though it weighed too much to move, even almost to breathe. 'I think I *will* talk to them. I might be able to persuade them to turn him down.' She couldn't bring herself to say his name. *Him*. Philip Cord. And she'd believed she loved him and that he loved her. It was a sickening thought, literally. She felt her gorge rise and swallowed hard.

'Sooner you than me. But, please, Laura, don't be stubborn. Think about Coplin's offer. As he says, he's an outsider so he can be sympathetic without being emotionally involved and he's an experienced researcher. Good at digging out facts.'

'What use is that to me? What sort of facts do I want dug out?'

'Who's behind Philip Cord, for a start,' Alex said promptly.

'Why should there be anyone behind him? He's on his own, isn't he? Trying to get the restaurant from me – ' Now her throat did close up and the little sob that escaped her, made him say quickly, 'Oh, damn it, Laura. Let me come round!'

'No.' She managed to get her voice back. 'No, I've already told you. It was good of you to phone, but I want to be left on my own for a while. I'll sort it out, one way or another.'

'The bank turned you down, so how? How on earth can you sort it out if you've got no money?'

'There are other sources,' she said. 'Other banks. I'll find someone somewhere. I won't lose my restaurant.' I won't, I won't, she shouted inside her head. It's all I've got, all I've ever had and I won't lose it. I can't and I won't. But for all the clamour of that inner shrieking she felt empty and frightened. She could lose it. She very nearly had.

'You are the most obstinate bloody woman!' Alex shouted down the phone. 'You make me livid, you know that? Listen to me, Laura! I want to help and the best way I can is to persuade you to talk to Coplin. Yes, I'm using him and I don't deny it – but he isn't a fool. He knows bloody well what I am, and he doesn't care. It's *you* he cares about. All I'm asking you to do is see him. That's all. Just let me bring him, and hear what he has to say. If he can't help, fair enough. Give him the air. But if he can, take what he has to offer. Like I say, it's wicked to waste. What would Grandma have said?'

For the first time she managed a smile. 'She'd have sent Cord packing, wouldn't she? She wouldn't have let this happen. Oh Alex, how could I have been such a bloody fool? To have got myself into this sort of debt, and to have let that horrible man make such – to use me that way. How could I have done it?'

'The way we all do, ducky. By doing your best and liking people. When you like people then you often do get shat on from a great height. Believe me, I'm an expert in that. But *nihil illegitime carborundum*. Never let the bastards grind you down and let me bring Joel Coplin over.'

'Oh, Alex, do shut up!'

'If you let me bring him.'

'Anything! Just shut up!'

'I'll be there as soon as I can flush him out. Don't budge! Give me an hour!' he said joyously and the phone clicked in her ear and wearily she cradled it and went back to the sofa to curl up in the corner, where she had been when it had trilled ten minutes ago.

It had been, she thought, staring at the dead fireplace, the worst three days of her life. Thank God at least for Maxie and Angie who had kept the restaurant running smoothly even though she wasn't there. She had hurried in once or twice to check on what was happening, and had gone late at night to do the ledgers, but that had been all. They looked at her anxiously whenever they saw her, the old waiters and dear old Angie, and that had made her feel worse than ever about the situation she was in.

But the worst part of all of it was the sense of helplessness that filled her. She had, that first afternoon, been reasonably cheerful; the bank manager would be sensible once he realised what was going on, she had told herself, had to be. And she had sat herself in the man's office and told him all about it.

And discovered too late that she had told him too much. He listened to her account of the demand Philip Cord was making and shook his head gloomily.

'I'm sorry, Miss Horvath, but I don't think the bank can be involved in this. Oh no, definitely not. I had thought about your dilapidations before you arrived – '

'Dilapidations?' she had interrupted, hating to hear such a word attached to her precious restaurant. 'It's not dilapidated! It's beautiful. That's the point. There's nothing wrong with it that – '

'I mean the work that has to be done,' the man said with careful emphasis. 'I had been thinking about it and decided that I could hardly refuse your request, under the circumstances.' He had smiled thinly then. 'Since you already owe us a substantial sum it would make good financial sense to cover your immediate needs in order that the business might continue and prosper so that you could repay your debt. But this new development – ' He had shaken his head. 'That puts a new complexion on it.'

'Why?' She tried to sound cool and businesslike, and knew she sounded desperate. 'Why? It's the same situation. You want your debt paid. I can only pay it if – '

'If you own the establishment,' he cut in smoothly. 'And according to your cousin, Mr. Cord you say – '

'He's no relation of mine,' she said fiercely. 'He's just married to my cousin.'

'A minor point,' he had murmured. 'If he is right and the family Trust is one of those labelled trust-for-sale, then indeed you will have to sell. In which case there is no point in the bank underwriting expensive work, is there? The sale of your portion of the property should bring in enough to repay your debt without our risking any further of the bank's funds. And the new owner may not require the work to be done. He may choose to use the premises in a different way.'

'There is no different way to use it. It's a restaurant. It always has been.'

'Well, that's as may be. I can only, regretfully, refuse your request.' And he had pulled a pile of papers towards him to signal the end of the discussion.

'Please, Mr. Carpenter,' she had said, pleadingly. 'Please try to understand. There is no way I'm going to sell, no matter what Cord says.'

He sighed and pushed the papers away again, elaborately patient.

'If the Trust is formulated as Cord suggested to you it is, then I'm afraid, Miss Horvath, you will have no choice. Your solicitor, I feel, is the person you should be talking to, not me.'

And so the nightmare had gone on. She had hurried to her solicitor directly from the bank, insisting on being seen immediately, so urgent was the matter, and had been told bluntly that indeed Cord was right. If one of the co-owners of Halascz's wanted to sell then under the terms of the original Trust as set up by Viktor and Maritza Halascz, the property had to be broken up so that each and every one of them could have the benefit in cash, if that was what they wanted.

'And,' Miss Jeavons, the tall and angular woman who had been Laura's solicitor for years, but whom she hardly knew since she had so few occasions to deal with her, had been very firm on that point. 'And you would be wasting your time and money to try to avoid that, Miss Horvath. It is quite clear. I have the documents here for you to study yourself, if you like.'

'Then what can I do?' Laura had sat slumped in the chair in front of the woman's desk and stared miserably at her, waving away the proffered documents. 'Do I have to part with my restaurant without a murmur?'

'I'm afraid so. But you will have the money from the sale, of course. Can't you start again, elsewhere?'

'Elsewhere wouldn't be my place,' she had said sharply. 'We've been there almost a hundred years. Halascz's. A hundred years – '

'I sympathise, but I'm not sure what I can suggest. Except perhaps that you see if you can raise enough money to buy out Cord and his wife? If you want to buy then he has to sell to you. As long as the price you can pay is at least the same as or better still, more than, any other offer on the table. That's part of the terms of the Trust, too.'

She had felt a flicker of hope then. 'I could force him to sell to me?'

'If the price is right,' Miss Jeavons had said firmly. 'It is my duty of course to the other owners to see that the best possible price is obtained for the property. They are entitled to that. So, if you can find some £125,000 to £130,000 then it may be possible – '

'How much?' she had said blankly.

'I'm afraid so.' The woman had sounded genuinely regretful. 'That's the market value you know. A half million. You are holding a valuable piece of land there between you. All Soho is valuable of course, but that corner is particularly attractive.'

'And you say I could start somewhere else,' Laura had said bitterly and got to her feet. 'So, if I have to sell, my share would be about £125,000 and out of that I owe the bank about seventy five thousand and what with the legal fees and other costs, by the time the whole thing's over, I wouldn't have enough for a stall to sell pizzas let alone a new Halascz's restaurant. And there's no way I can find enough to buy the whole place.'

'I'm sorry,' Miss Jeavons had said yet again, and Laura had snapped furiously, 'Not as sorry as I am,' and gone slamming out into Bedford Row, knowing she was unjust to blame the woman for the facts she had to impart but not caring. If killing the bearer of bad tidings would help, then kill she would, she told herself.

But that didn't help and her anger had dribbled away and she'd gone trailing back to the flat, dusty and untidy now, for she had neither time nor interest in keeping it looking so pleasant as it had been during those happy spring days when she and Philip had first been together, and tried to raise some money. She phoned everyone she could think of outside the family, feeling obscurely that whatever happened, she had to keep them out of it all, but drew dead cards everywhere.

She rang those of her customers she knew were involved in money, bankers and finance company directors and insurance people, fishing oh so delicately for information and getting the same answer everywhere. Money was expensive these hard times, and what did she want it for? And she, knowing how imperative it was that none of the customers should know just how shaky their favourite restaurant was, for fear they might withdraw their allegiance and with it their custom, hedged and lied and slithered around the truth with all the skilled aplomb of a lifetime liar.

'For dilapidations,' she said over and over again. 'I want to make the place even better than it is – '

'But don't,' they said, one after another. '*Laura's* is lovely as it is, my dear. Don't change a thing. Keep away from money. It's far too expensive for you. Just go on as you are. It's the only safe way to be – '

And now she sat wrapped in her old dressing gown like a tired child, not knowing what to do next. The only person she had told of what was happening, of the way the bricks and mortar of her life were crashing in shards about her feet had been Alex, not because she had thought he could help, but because she had to talk to someone and he was the only person she could think of who could be trusted. For all his sometimes silliness and his selfishness and his glittering chatter, there was a good heart in Alex and she could surely rely on him to keep quiet and say nothing to anyone who shouldn't be told, but, she now thought bitterly, even he lets me down. Nagging about that damned Coplin man. I wish I could crawl away and die. I wish I'd never heard of Philip Cord. I wish, I wish –

The buzzer sounded on the entry phone and moving heavily she got to her feet and padded over to it.

'Mmm?'

'Me, Laura!' It was Alex's voice. 'Let me in.'

'On your own?' she said suspiciously. 'Because I've changed my mind. Honestly, I couldn't see anyone but – '

'Oh, stop jabbering woman, and let me in! It's peeing with rain out here and I'm getting sodden. Come on!' And after a moment she grimaced and pressed the button. Even Alex couldn't have got hold of the man so soon, after all.

She opened the door of the flat and left it ajar and went back to her sofa, and again curled up in the corner as though making herself small would make her problems small too. She heard the footsteps behind her and didn't turn her head as they hesitated and then the door clicked shut.

'Help yourself to a drink, Alex,' she said wearily. 'And come and sit down, and don't nag me for pity's sake. I couldn't handle it – '

'I don't want a drink, thanks. Unless I can get one for you? You look as though you need one.'

She twisted in her seat and looked over her shoulders, wide-eyed with shock. Joel Coplin was standing by the closed door, looking tense and anxious as though he were poised for flight. The shoulders of his light summer jacket were sodden and his curly wet hair was plastered to his forehead.

'I'm sorry,' he said. 'It really is pelting down.'

'Where's Alex?'

'I told him to come up but he wouldn't. Just went. But I had to come even at the risk of annoying you. He told me you weren't keen to see me, but I do want to help, I really do. So please, may I come in and get dry?'

29

It was altogether more than she could handle. She had for a moment considered throwing him out; had actually jumped to her feet and stepped forward to push him physically out of the door, but then, suddenly aware of the shabbiness of her comfortable old dressing gown beneath which she was wearing nothing at all had collapsed back into the corner of her sofa.

'Go away,' she said weakly. 'I don't want to talk to anyone. Go away.'

'Of course I will,' he said. 'Eventually. Is the bathroom through there? Because I really would like to get dry. No, don't bother.' He smiled charmingly as again she moved to get up. 'I'll find it,' and coolly he walked past her to the door that led to the little inner lobby of the flat and her bedroom and bathroom.

She stared after him and heard the taps running and the soft pleasant sound as he began to whistle between his teeth, and tried to be angry. What right had this damned man to come and march into her flat this way, and use her bathroom and whistle in it? But she had used up so much of her emotional energy already that there was none left to feel any anger and she watched him as he came back in, now in his shirt sleeves and towelling his hair so that it stood up in a spiky damp crown, and opened her mouth to tell him again to go. But he spoke before she could.

'I've left my jacket over the hot towel rail,' he said. 'It's a light one so it shouldn't take too long to be wearable again. Look at this – wet right through to my shirt! Is that one of those artificial fires? Good! You won't mind if I switch it on, will you? I really do loathe being soggy like this.' And he crouched in front of the fireplace and fiddled in his pocket for matches and with the minimum of fuss found the gas tap and lit the flames.

At once the room lifted in mood; the dust and untidiness seemed to fade from sight as the light of the fire made the ceiling seem lower and more cosy, and the windows, which had been filled with the pallid lilac of the late summer evening, darkened to a richer blue. And though she hadn't felt cold till now – she hadn't been aware of any physical sensation at all – she shivered a little and lifted her face to the faint warmth that came across the hearthrug to her.

'I know you're not supposed to like these things if you're sophisticated and trendy, but I adore them,' he said. 'I'm glad you do too.'

'What?' It seemed so absurd a thing to say; as though they were sitting here as a couple of casual acquaintances making conversation for the sake of it, with nothing more on their minds but the minutiae of social behaviour.

'I'm told they're too kitsch to be taken seriously. That either it's all high tech and no fires at all or country cottage cosy and real logs. For my part, I like these.' He stretched his hands to the blaze, still sitting on the hearth rug. 'They burn and burn and give heat and light yet they never consume themselves. They just look the same all the time. Like me.' He looked over his shoulder at her. 'When I get involved with people and ideas and things I never stop burning, in a sense. It just goes on and on and stays the same.'

'Please go away,' she said, her voice high and thin. 'I know my brother Alex brought you here, but he had no right to. I'm tired. I've got a lot to cope with and I can't, I really can't, really and truly can't – '

It was dreadful. Quite the most dreadful thing that had ever happened. She who had never been a weeper, and yet who had cried so much this week that she would have been entitled to think she had no more tears left in her, to be so uncontrolled, so overwhelmed by her own feelings that she could burst into floods of tears in front of a complete stranger. Yet that was what happened, and she sat there with her face as crumpled and wet as a baby's and could not stop, could not speak, could do nothing but sob.

She did not see him move, nor heard him. One moment he was sitting there on her rug talking nonsense about her fire and the next he was beside her and holding her firmly so that the tearing sobs that had been making her whole body heave seemed less painful and more contained. He said not a word; made none of the crooning 'there, there' noises so many people seemed to think necessary to comfort a weeper; he didn't rock her, didn't stroke her. He just sat solid as a tree trunk against which she could lean and held on to her till the storm had blown itself out.

She subsided into deep shuddering breaths and then, to her even greater embarrassment, began to hiccup, and now he did move, letting go of her for a moment to slap her hard on her back and she gasped and cried, 'No!' and again he put his arms round her and held on, and she closed her eyes, not knowing what else to do.

But it was better now. The hiccupping had stopped, she realised with a momentary shock of surprise, and she could breathe normally and she moved experimentally and at once he let go and left her and went back to the hearth rug and picked up the towel and started to rub his wet hair again, as though the explosion of tears had never happened.

'Er – thank you,' she said, experimentally. Her voice sounded husky, but it was there and that was a comfort.

He said nothing to that. He just smiled at her and set down his towel. 'I think that'll do now. I'm as dry as makes no matter.'

'I don't usually do things like that.'

'Like what?'

'Cry like an idiotic child.'

'Don't you? You should. It helps a lot. I cried like that when my mother died. It made a lot of difference. For the better.'

'Oh.' She was nonplussed. She had quite liked this man when she had first met him; had found him pleasant and interesting, but no more than that. He liked the same writers she did – or at least one of them – and he talked sensibly.

But that had been all there was to it; a casual meeting in Little Vinegar Yard and then that evening at the restaurant talking about his film. No more than that apart from the unpleasant time when he had talked of Paul's problems. Yet she had wept all over him, and here they sat together as comfortably and as at ease with each other as though they had known each other for years. It was very odd.

He was thinking much the same, sitting beside the fire and its eternal flames and trying not to show just how good he felt. She was in trouble, deep and frightening trouble and to let her know that he had found so much pleasure in holding her while she wept would be insulting at the very least. He had no right to rejoice in being with her when the only reason he was here was her misery. It was a paradox of a situation and he didn't know quite how to handle it.

Ever since he had walked into the room he had been acting instinctively, planning nothing, not really thinking at all. Just reacting. But now it seemed to be time to be more sensible – and he didn't know how to be. But she helped him.

'I can hardly throw you out now, can I?'

'I hope you don't want to any more.'

'Oh, I do. In a way. Not because of you, you understand, but because of me. I mean, I'm grateful to you for being kind. It's awful when people slobber and grizzle all over you and you were very kind about it.'

'Stop that,' he said sharply. 'Never apologise for tears. They're honest feelings honestly expressed, never something to be ashamed of.'

'All right, I won't apologise. But I can be grateful. And I am. Though I would rather be on my own.'

'I dare say you would. But I don't think it would be the right thing for you right now.'

'Oh? You're an expert in what I need?'

'I'd like to be.'

She reddened and looked away from him. 'If you'd like some coffee or a drink or something – '

'Thank God for the sacred laws of hospitality!' he said.

'I'd love some tea. I'll make it. Where's the kitchen? Oh! There. Yes – '

He went and switched on the light and she heard him say softly, 'And who are you?' and open the little back door and she closed her eyes in anger at herself. That poor drowned cat, out there in the rain all this time. She'd forgotten all about him.

'Aren't they incredible?' Joel's voice came from the kitchen. 'It's raining like crazy out there and this creature looks as dry as a dust storm.'

The cat came stalking in, looked at the fire and then at her and after a moment turned its back on her and jumped on to the armchair and curled up, oozing disdain and behind her, Joel laughed.

'Imperious devils, aren't they? I like 'em. Listen, have you had any supper?'

'Mmm?'

'I thought not. Probably no lunch either. You look dreadful – '

She blinked at that and put up her hands to smooth her hair, but she said nothing.

'I'm not hungry.'

'Piffle. Omelette all right?'

'I don't want – '

'Oh, well then, I'll do it anyway – ' And he went back into the kitchen and she heard him crashing around, an agreeable friendly sound and she sat and thought – what the hell am I doing sitting here and letting this strange man prowl around in my kitchen? I must be mad. I ought to be at the restaurant. I ought to be working. I can't go on like this. But she just sat there and stared at the flames. It was as though she had no energy in her to do anything else.

He watched her from the kitchen as he worked, beating eggs, cutting bread for toast, and finding butter and milk in the depleted little fridge. There wasn't much there to use for any sort of interesting omelette, not so much as a sprig of parsley and he stood there by the door for a moment and looked at her and felt a pang of pure sadness for her. This little flat, so bleak, so lacking in any real sense of home, in spite of the brave little touches she had put in it; the almost empty fridge, the scornful cat – all of it seemed infinitely pathetic. But not as sad as the figure of Laura herself.

She sat there in the corner of the sofa in her blue dressing gown, her knees hunched up and her arms around them, staring into the flames. He could see the curve of her cheek and one side of her mouth, drooping now and not lifting in that blazing triangular smile that had first pulled him to her, and the sight of it made the skin across his back move with excitement. She had looked marvellous that brilliant sunshining morning in Little Vinegar Yard, and he had been totally bedazzled by her. But now, seeing her looking anything but blazing, more like an extinguished fire, grey and flat and dull, the feeling was even stronger. She looked, he thought then, the way he would have expected the cat he had let in out of the rain to look; bedraggled and tired and sorry for herself, but the cat lay sleek and content on its armchair, licking its glossy fur into even greater beauty while she sat in the corner of a sofa and looked pitiful. Yet she seemed to him to be so lovely in her sad state that it was all he could do not to go in there and scoop her up again and hold her close. But she wasn't weeping now, so he couldn't. And he returned to his cooking.

'I've done the best I could,' he said. 'Your fridge isn't exactly bursting. But give me a couple of eggs and a heel of bread and it's amazing what I can do. Here you are.' And he pulled a small table forwards, and set a tray in front of her. It looked attractive; a pot of teat and a plate of softly scrambled eggs piled on toast, steaming gently.

She looked at it and then at him and said. 'I'm really not hungry – '

'No doubt. But it's there so you may as well eat it. I've got mine as well – three eggs scramble up quite big, if you talk to them nicely while you do it.'

She smiled faintly and then, as he brought his own tray and sat down on the hearthrug and balanced it on his knees, picked up her fork. It was obvious to him she was only being polite, but that didn't matter. He watched her covertly as she took the first mouthful and then another and saw how the taste and warmth of the food woke up her need for it. By the time he started his own she was eating with real appetite and he ate, too, but with much more satisfaction than scrambled eggs usually created in him.

They sat in companionable silence then, sipping the hot tea he had made and at length she sighed, and set down her cup.

'I owe you an apology. I was rude to you,' she said.

He grinned. 'When?'

'Last time we met.'

'Were you? I didn't notice. I only thought what a – how agreeable I found you.'

'That's kind of you.'

'I'm quite kind. Some men are, you know.'

She managed a small smile. 'Did you think I'd doubt that?'

'You've been ill-treated by one of the breed. I thought perhaps – I'd hate you to become a misanthrope.'

'A – '

'Manhater,' he said obligingly. 'It's the literal meaning. From the Greek.'

'If you lecture me on etymology you could make me misanthropic about *you*. I may be just a restaurateur, but I am literate.'

He reddened. 'I'm sorry. I meant no insult. Please, never think that. I enjoy words and – '

'I'm sure you do.' She smiled then, and pushed the table in front of her to one side and stretched out her legs. She was barefoot and for a moment he wondered if she was wearing anything beneath her robe and again the flesh moved across his back. He went even redder and looked away from her, and she smiled even more widely.

'It's all right. I do it too. Tease out words and play with them – do you accept it?'

'I'm sorry?'

'My apology.'

'It wasn't necessary. Are you feeling better now?'

'Amazingly so. It's odd – I could have sworn I wasn't hungry.'

'When did you last eat?'

She looked vague. 'I can't remember.'

'That's why you weren't hungry. That'll tide you over for a while, but not for long. Soon I'm going to send you to get dressed and we're going out of here and – '

'No!' She pulled her legs up again and set her arms round them in the old defensive babylike posture. 'I ought to be working at the restaurant. I can't just – '

'It's the restaurant we'll be going to. They're entitled to see you there. Your customers. The waiters. Everyone.'

She was looking hunted and tense again and he reached forwards and held out one hand to her. 'No, don't get like that. Listen to me.'

'Well?' she said and stared at him. It was odd, she was thinking. An hour ago he was the last person I wanted to see. I wanted just to be left on my own to think, and now – she blinked at the thought. Now, she needed him to tell her what to do. It was *very* odd.

'You've panicked a little, I think. I know a bit about what happened, but not enough. Whatever it is – and never think I'm diminishing it in any way because I'm not – whatever it is, it's my guess that we can deal with it. As long as we don't get into a tailspin. That never helps.'

'Alex must have told you all about it. Why else were you so anxious to come here?'

He smiled faintly. 'I'd have been anxious to come here no matter what. I like you. Didn't you know that? You're the most interesting woman I think I've ever met. He told me some. Not all, though, I suspect. I need more, if I'm to help properly. Let's pretend I know nothing at all about what happened, and only the barest details about the people involved. Tell me the whole thing from the beginning and then we'll come up with a strategy.'

'A strategy,' she repeated, as though she were savouring the word. 'That makes it sound like a battle.'

'That's exactly how you should be thinking about it. When I came in here I think it was defeat you were dealing with.'

There was a short silence and then she looked at him from beneath her lashes, shyly, like a child caught out in her bad schoolwork. 'I think perhaps – yes, I did think it was all over. That I'd lost the restaurant.' She frowned then and shook her head. 'And I'm not going to be soothed now into thinking otherwise. As far as I can see, I *have* lost it – '

'Not yet. There are things we can do. As I said, strategies. I want to find out *why*. I want the facts behind Mr. Cord and his dealings. Why all of a sudden he wants to close down the family business – '

'He hasn't said he wants to. Just that he wants it to be sold,' she said. 'I – it was just me saying that it would have to close if we sold. I'm trying to be fair, you see. I'm angry with him – ' She caught her breath then, with a little hissing sound. 'My God, I'm angry with him, but I have to be fair. Maybe he wants to run it himself.' Her chin came up then, and she said scornfully, 'He'd make the most awful botch of it. He hasn't a clue. It takes years of learning to run a place like ours as it should be.'

'You have to be born into it,' he said and smiled and she nodded at once.

'Yes. Born into it.'

'My film.'

'Mmm?'

'My film, remember? That's exactly one of the factors I want to consider. Whether there are some businesses a person has to be born into. The effects of family, of traditions – '

'Then you do have an axe to grind.' She managed a grin. 'I told Alex that. That everyone always has an axe to grind. No one's ever totally disinterested in what they do. There always has to be a reason.'

'Of course I'm grinding axes. And knives and scissors too. I want my film and – ' He stopped then and looked at her closely so that she had to lift her eyes and meet his gaze. 'I also want to know you better,' he said very deliberately. 'That's the most important axe as far as I'm concerned. You.'

'Thank you,' she said after a moment. There wasn't very much else she could say, she thought and tried to look away from him. But she couldn't, and he laughed softly.

'So it's agreed. You'll get dressed and we'll go to the restaurant and we'll have a proper dinner – think of the eggs as just a starter – and plan how we're going to save your restaurant and scupper Mr. Egregious Cord, and – '

'Make your film.'

'Thank you. Yes, make my film.' He laughed then. 'And we'll enjoy ourselves. There's nothing quite as exhilarating as having a real villain to defeat, and Mr. Cord is one hell of a villain. And we'll see him off. You'll see if we don't – '

And she went obediently to dress, feeling better than she would have thought possible a couple of hours ago, but wishing she could be quite as hopeful as Joel Coplin was. Because for all his cheerful comfort, inside she remained deeply pessimistic.

30

The lift sighed its way upwards and the suspicious face of the man in the peaked cap disappeared beneath her feet and she relaxed. It was just like Dolly to live in a block of flats so lavishly carpeted and peach mirrored and ornamented about the entrance and hallways and staffed by so paranoid a doorman; to get past him had taken every bit of persuasion she had and finally she had told him tartly that if he wanted to telephone Mrs. Halascz and tell her he had sent away her cousin then on his own head be it; and the man had at last unwillingly let her in.

Now, as she closed the lift gates behind her on the ninth floor, and took in the long corridor with its inevitable coral carpet and pink mirrored walls, she wondered why she had bothered. She had agreed with Joel last night that it would be a good thing to do, to get Evelyn and Dolly on her side, but now she wasn't so certain. Would it work? It certainly hadn't with Aunt Evelyn –

She walked slowly along the hall, peering at the numbers on the polished mock mahogany doors, Nine A, Nine B, and thought about her discussion with Evelyn and felt the anger rise in her again. And then was angry with herself for being angry.

It was pathetic, that was the thing, and more than that; it was frightening. Looking at Evelyn, all sharp edges and suspicion and resentment of other people's happiness, had made her feel cold inside. She had gone to the small house tucked away in a narrow street behind Queensway in a fairly hopeful mood. Her evening at the restaurant had jolted her back into a better frame of mind; she was still worried, still alarmed by the threat to her precious place, but actually being there, among the familiar tables and chairs and above all with Maxie and Miklos and Angie and all the others had comforted her. Halascz's restaurant had been there far too long for someone like Philip Cord to be able to topple it. It was too solid, too real to be spoiled. Evelyn and Dolly and Paul – surely they all cared as much for the family and its traditions as she did? Once they realised what Cord was up to, they'd help her, and support her; of course they would. He had been the object of whispers and gossip ever since he had married Ilona; they had all disliked him. Surely now they would rally round and exclude him and his destructive plans?

But Evelyn had been very difficult to talk to. She had come to her front door and peered round it only after Laura had rung several times, and stood there behind it looking at her with one dark suspicious eye and had only invited her in when Laura had said loudly, 'Hello Aunt Evelyn. May I come in and talk to you? I did phone, remember. I said I was coming.'

'Nothing to talk about,' Evelyn had mumbled, but let her in all the same and led her to a stuffy sitting room on the first floor of the tiny house, which, Laura thought, couldn't have been cleaned, let alone repainted or cared for in any real way, for many years.

She could remember being brought here to visit long ago when she was a child and it had seemed gloomy then. Now it was depressingly grimy and it smelled sour and old and heavy with cats. There were three of them in the sitting room, prowling about among the greasy, overstuffed furniture and glaring malevolently at her, and the smell there had been even more unpleasant; and that had been when Laura had felt the first sharp stab of fear.

Cats, she had thought. I keep a cat. Will I get like this, alone and lonely with nothing but cats? Will I stop noticing they smell? Will I get grimy and defeated and miserable like Aunt Evelyn?

And her fear had made her tongue sharp, she now knew as she remembered, walking along the coral carpets of Aunt Dolly's St. John's Wood fastness. She shouldn't have spoken to her as she did. For she had said abruptly, 'Aunt Evelyn! What's all this about you selling your share of the restaurant?'

The older woman had bristled, her narrow shoulders in their sagging purple cardigan coming up almost to her ears and she had stared at Laura and said loudly, 'None of your business.'

'Of course it's my business! The restaurant only exists because of me! It's my work that gives you your income!'

'It was my father's place, and I have every right to have a share. You can't come here and tell me I haven't! It's mine and I can do what I like with it. It was my father's – '

'And mine.'

'It wasn't! My father was the one who had all the right, who should have had it all. He was a Halascz. You lot aren't! Your father was just the cook, squeezed his way in, got round the old lady, my father told me about him. Oh, I know what happened there! My father, he told me! So don't you go on at me – '

'Aunt Evelyn, let's not fight over this.' Too late Laura caught her tongue between her teeth, began to be placatory. 'It belongs to all of us, of course it does. You and Paul and me and Ilona – ' She had stopped then and bitten her lip and then said again, more loudly, 'And Ilona and – '

'Dolly,' Evelyn said with a little crow. 'And Dolly. Go and tell *her* what she can do with what's hers by right and see where it gets you. She's not a Halascz, mind you, for all she's married the name. She's just a woman who gets her hands in my brother's pockets and robs him. Me, I've more right to my share than she has to hers. Poppa earned it for me, and gave it to me. I don't have to nag a husband for it, make his life a misery the way Dolly got her share – '

'None of that matters, Aunt Evelyn,' Laura had said desperately. 'Does it? Not now. It's the way things are *now* that's important. And Philip Cord – ' She managed to get the name out somehow. 'Philip Cord is trying to cheat us out of our place. You do realise that? That he's trying to cheat us?'

Evelyn had looked sideways at her, her eyes sharp and foxy and the marmalade cat on her lap which she was stroking suddenly tightened its claws on her arm and made her squeal and she pushed it away. But she still watched Laura with that beady eyed gaze.

'I wouldn't say cheating,' she muttered. 'Fair price. Fair price isn't cheating.'

'What has he offered you?'

'That's between me and him,' Evelyn said and tried to look dignified. 'Business, you know. My affair and his. None of yours. You deal with him yourself.'

'I don't want to. I don't trust him. I want to know how he's got legal hold of Ilona's share, and what right he has to try to – ' She swallowed then, making herself control her anger. 'Aunt Evelyn, maybe I can pay you more than he's offering. I want the restaurant to go on as it always has. I don't think Philip will keep it that way, do you? You want it to be the same, don't you? It's a traditon.'

'Tradition?' Evelyn said and then suddenly sat up very straight and seemed to shout it. 'Tradition? What do I care for tradition? It was tradition in the old country a father found a husband for a daughter, gave a dowry, did it right, but what good do that ever do me? It was a tradition people loved each other, so they said, but who ever loved me? No one ever loved me – '

Laura had sat in the smelly over stuffed little room and looked at her and couldn't argue. Evelyn sitting in her armchair looking like a heap of old clothes was so singularly unlovable that to argue with her was not possible. The malevolence in her eyes, the twisted shape of her mouth with its smudged lipstick running up the lines that scored the upper lip, the thin unwashed hair pulled across the bumpy old skull, all looked so depressing and so repellent that Laura felt her hands tighten into fists, and hated herself for being so uncharitable. Aunt Evelyn was a disappointed woman; she had been ill-served by life and she needed all the care she could get from her family. To feel as she did, Laura told herself, was wicked and wrong. And frightening, too, because maybe, one day, if I'm not careful, that could be me. Could I be a lonely spinster, unloved and unwanted by everyone the way she is? The thought had made her feel sick and cold.

She found Dolly's flat at last and she stood poised, her hand ready to press the bell under the elaborate gothic lettering which read, 'Flat Nine M, Mr. and Mrs. Stephen Halascz.' It hadn't worked, none of it, with Aunt Evelyn. She had gone away leaving the old woman stubborn and triumphant in her refusal to budge. How much Cord had offered her Laura didn't know and what he'd promised her to get her to sell she didn't know. All Evelyn would say, over and over again was, 'It's mine. I can do what I like with it. I'm the only one entitled, really. It's mine.'

Only an eighth, though, Laura told herself now optimistically. Only an eighth. Perhaps, if I can persuade Aunt Dolly to sell to me, we can cancel out Evelyn's involvement? And she pressed the bell hard.

The door opened with such speed that for a moment Laura suspected that someone had been standing behind it, watching her through the spyhole she had seen in the middle of the door. But it wasn't Dolly who stood there. It was a round woman in a blue nylon overall who looked at her sourly and said, 'Yiss? Pliss?'

'Mrs. Halascz?' Laura said and stepped forwards, and the woman said, 'To see,' and closed the door in her face, leaving Laura once again filled with anger. Bloody family, she thought furiously. Bloody family!

But then the door opened wide and Dolly was standing there her arms wide.

'My dear Laura! Such a treat to see you! So lovely of you to come over like this – I see you so rarely! I can't tell you how delighted I was you called – really delighted – do come in. You look a little peaky, my dear! Are you working too hard? Time you found a nice man to marry and settle down with. Someone to look after you. Don't want to get like poor Evelyn, do you? Have you seen her lately? Dreadful, isn't it? Really gone to seed. Now, a little drinky, hmm? A little schnapps, just what a girl needs – '

She was wearing a long housecoat in heavy rose brocade that exactly matched the curtains and cushions which were scattered over the long low white leather sofas, of which the room had three. There were glittering chrome and white leather chairs and tables and the carpet was a huge and very thick, washed Chinese, also in shades of rose, and obviously very expensive indeed. Over the fireplace was a six foot high portrait of Dolly, wearing black and pearls, which was so overwhelming in its glamour that Laura could hardly look at it. Altogether the room looked like a Tottenham Court Road shop window, it was so ferociously tasteful, and she felt very intimidated as she sank into the sofa into which Dolly had pushed her before going to a table laden with crystal decanters to fetch her a drink.

'Now, why, I ask myself, why?' Dolly chattered. 'Here am I begging you for years not to make strange, to come and visit your old cousin, to come to our parties, meet some of the lovely men Steven knows, and what happens? Nothing! Yet here you are all of a sudden ringing me up the first thing in the morning when I haven't even dressed yet, begging to come and see me – '

'Not first thing, really, Aunt Dolly,' Laura protested, stung by the accusation of selfishness. 'I mean, it's well past eleven. I've already been – I mean, it's past eleven.'

'My dear, you called at nine, and said it was absolutely urgent you see me – and now it's eleven! But at last you're here. Well, now, settle down and tell me *all* about it. What can I do for you?'

Laura sat and looked at the narrow bony face and the snapping dark eyes under the perfect make up and hesitated. She'd handled Aunt Evelyn all wrong, been much too direct. Would it be wrong to do the same with Dolly? Strategy, she thought. I need a strategy, and felt a little surge of warmth as she remembered Joel's voice saying the same word.

'It's hard to sort out, Aunt Dolly,' she began and then, seeing the watchful look in those boot button eyes knew she was wasting her time being tactful. That would seem to this sharp, smart lady to be deviousness. Better to be just herself, say what she had come to say and see what happened.

'It's the restaurant, Aunt Dolly. You're happy with the income you get from it?'

Dolly pursed her lips judiciously. 'Satisfied? Hard to say.

I don't think about it much.' She smiled and flicked a glance round her luxurious room, taking in the great sweep of window clad in fine net and the expensive ornaments on the small tables. 'I'm glad I don't have to depend on it, of course. Thank God, your cousin Steven's in a nice line of business. But I suppose it's very nice.'

'You think I run it well, the restaurant? You said so when you were last there. For Anya Zsuzske's birthday party. Do you remember?'

'Very nice, dear.' Aunt Dolly looked down at her glass. 'Very nice. So?'

'So you don't want it to close?'

'Are you thinking of closing it?' Aunt Dolly looked at her now, her eyes wide and limpid, or as wide as such small eyes could be, and Laura felt her chest tighten. This bloody woman, she thought. She knows why I'm here and she's already decided. Oh hell, she's already decided.

'You know I'm not. Philip Cord is.'

Aunt Dolly shook her head. 'He didn't say that to me.'

'Then why else is he trying to force me to sell?'

'To get some money, I imagine, dear. It's what we all need, isn't it? Money?'

'I do,' Laura said bitterly. 'For the restaurant. I have to do some major work in the kitchen. But why should Philip Cord want to close the place when it brings you all such a good income for no effort? Look, I've got notes here, last year's figures of all the dividends you all had – ' She dug into her bag and pulled out the paper she had prepared. 'You see? Nineteen thousand last year – that was what you had. Aunt Evelyn had the same and Paul and Ilona had £38,000 each – '

'My dear,' Aunt Dolly murmured. 'I really don't want to hear about everyone else's private affairs! I'm only interested in my own. And yes, I got nineteen thousand last year from Steven's gift to me. He's so good – but the tax situation – it's dreadful, isn't it? I don't see nearly as much for it as I should, you know. Not nearly what I should.'

'You'll see even less if you sell your share to Cord,' Laura said sharply.

Dolly got up and went back to the drinks trolley. 'Oh, I don't think so,' she said sweetly. 'It all depends on your financial nous, doesn't it? On how much I can get for what I have to offer. I'm only a housewife, of course – ' She turned and looked round her room again and smiled, so that her eyes almost disappeared into her pouched cheeks. 'But I have a little commonsense, and it does seem to me I could do quite well for myself with a little capital to play with. I have so many ideas, starving for want of a little air, you know. Capital is air.' And she nodded gnomically as though she had said something infinitely wise and came back to sit beside Laura.

'But you wouldn't sell my restaurant from under me just to get some air, would you? You can get capital in other ways, if you want it. Why take my restaurant away?'

'Because it isn't yours, dear,' Aunt Dolly said with infinite reasonableness. 'It's ours.'

Laura was silent, and then took a deep breath and said, 'I'm sorry. We're talking at cross purposes here. Look, let me put it on the line, Aunt Dolly. I want to keep the restaurant. Very much. I can go on earning with it, make a lot of success. And anyway, I want to keep it. I may sound silly, but it's the tradition of it all I care about as much as anything. Great grandfather, almost a hundred years ago – it would be wicked, wicked to let it go now. So, what do you want to sell your share to me instead of to Philip Cord?'

'How much have you got?' Dolly said promptly, and grinned as Laura reddened. 'Philip, you see, has access to capital and you haven't, have you? He explained it to me so well. And I'd be mad to turn down a quarter of a million pounds for the sake of – '

'He's offering you a quarter of a million for an eighth share? He can't be! The whole site isn't worth more than – '

'It's worth what someone is willing to pay for it,' Aunt Dolly cut in. 'And that's what I'm asking for my share. If you can find it, then dear, by all means. I don't want to be unkind to a woman on her own. I look at poor dear Evelyn and I think – well, dear, I'd put you first if you could raise the capital. I truly would. Dear Philip – ' She grinned then, showing her teeth and giggled. 'He'd never forgive me! But there it is – he'd still have access to Ilona's share, of course, so – '

Laura had got to her feet and had pulled her coat around her. She was near tears again of fury and disappointment and needed to get out, as fast as she could, but now she stopped and stared.

'What did you say?'

'Mmm? Oh, that Philip will never forgive me – '

'That he has access to Ilona's share.' She sat down again, suddenly. 'Do you mean he doesn't actually have control of it?'

Dolly looked sideways at her and then giggled again, but it wasn't as triumphant a little sound now. 'Well, married couples you know, and she was always so jealous. But he says he can make sure she does what he says and he is her husband, after all! So I dare say he'll be all right. If he gets mine and Evelyn's as well, and Paul's – ' Again her eyes slid away. 'Poor Paul. Well, one way or another, Philip will have control, won't he? So I might as well sell to the man with the power. I'm sorry, dear, knowing how you feel, but there – if you sell too, then you'll have your money and you can start again somewhere else.'

'Why does everyone want me to start again somewhere else? I won't. It's the here and now Halascz's that I want. The place that's been here from the beginning. Where else could I be that would be better?'

'It's to be quite a development, I understand,' Aunt Dolly said and again Laura stared at her.

'What did you say?'

'Didn't you know? That's what it's all about. There's a consortium – such a lovely word, isn't it? – a consortium which wants to put a building there on the site. They say they can get planning consent for ten stories and a penthouse, imagine! But even if they can't the site is still worth a great deal. So, there you are, dear. I'd be mad not to go along with Philip, wouldn't I? Seeing he's working with this consortium.'

31

The post came just after nine in the morning in her corner of Soho and she had got into the habit of arriving half an hour earlier these days in order to be waiting for it. The silence from Philip Cord had been ominous, and she expected it to be broken any day. Each time the postman came whistling into Little Vinegar Yard, sorting the letters in his hand as he came, her throat tightened with fear. Would this be the day when an official letter would arrive telling her that the fight was over and that she had to part with her restaurant? But this morning as she stood waiting in the Yard, the postman gave her just estimates from the builders for the kitchen work, and a letter from Hersh confirming in pompous civil service language what had to be done.

She stared down at the sheet of white paper headed only 'Memo to Miss Laura Horvath, from Mr. C. Hersh' and wanted to crush it into a ball in her hands and throw it away, but that would not have helped her at all, and she folded it neatly with deliberate fingers and lifted her chin to take a deep breath of the fresh morning air before taking her letters back to her desk.

The door of the restaurant stood propped open behind her and she could hear one of the kitchen boys singing tunelessly as he crashed among the big pans he was scouring and the hiss of the big water urns that were turned on first thing every morning ready for the preparation of vegetables. There was a smell of fresh coffee in the air, and of bleach from the washing-up and the beeswax polish the morning cleaners used on the panelling of the staircase, and the outside smells as well; petrol and fresh fruit and vegetables from the stalls and bacon being fried at the little cafe out in Dean Street and her eyes smarted with the pleasure it all gave her; so richly familiar, so much a part of the fabric of her life, and now so threatened.

But she had to be strong. She knew that now; knew that curling up and crying helped no one. She had to stand up and keep on going – and she smiled a little crookedly as the silly pat phrases came into her head and she heard Joel's voice in her memory saying, 'Keep on telling yourself you can win. It doesn't matter how silly you feel talking to yourself – you just do it. It makes all the difference –' He was right. It did.

She turned to go in and start the day's work and then stopped as a couple of men came toiling through the archway into the Yard from Frith Street. They were carrying timber and a placard held so that she could not see the front of it, and she paused and watched, puzzled. This couldn't be a builder for her work, could it? Of course it couldn't. She hadn't accepted any of the estimates yet. Nor, whispered her inner voice, nor have you found the money to pay for it, either.

The men stopped and the first of them peered at the order sheet in his hand and then looked round and catching sight of her called, 'Boskett, miss? Would that be you?'

'I beg your pardon?'

'No,' he said as he looked over her shoulder at the restaurant. 'Says 'ere it's a tobacconist. Sorry to 'ave bothered you. It's this side we're after – come on, Sam!' And he jerked his head at the other man and they moved across the Yard to the front of Mucky's shop.

Still puzzled and with a sense of foreboding growing in her Laura watched as the first man tried the door and finding it locked, knocked hard. There was no response and after another moment the man knocked again, harder and stepped back to look up at the front of the building.

'Lives 'ere, does 'e?' he asked, returning to look at Laura. 'Lives over the shop, like?'

'Yes –' Laura came over to stand beside the man. 'What are you here for?' From this vantage point she could see the front of the placard and her brows snapped down hard as she stared at it.

'Acquired for Clients of J. Davriosh,' it read, in scarlet letters on a white ground and there was a telephone number and that was all.

'What are you doing?' she said sharply. 'What does this mean?'

'What it says, lady. Sold 'n't it? Got to board it up to keep out the vandals like, and put up the placard. That's what we're 'ere for.'

'But you can't be,' she said and stared at him. 'There must be some mistake. Mucky's not – he would have told me, if –' She stopped then and took a deep breath. 'Look, leave that stuff there, will you? I'll find out what's going on. It's all right. He's a good friend of mine. I tell you what – come over into my kitchen. Time you had your second breakfast, hmm?' And she smiled winningly at the man.

'Second – well, all very irregular, really, but – seein' we can't get no answer.'

He banged on the door again, but not very enthusiastically. 'Seein' you know 'm.'

'Neighbours, you see. Only two businesses here in the Yard. Known each other for ever,' she said, gabbling a little.

'Right then, Sam. Put that stuff down there and we'll avail ourselves of this lady's kind offer then.' And the two men grinned at her and followed her across the Yard with alacrity.

She settled them in the kitchen with young Fred, commanding him to make toast and coffee for them – a prospect which made them beam – and then went back to Mucky's shop. Upstairs the windows were as blank as always, the net curtains flat and still against the glass, but she stood there and tilted her chin and called, 'Mucky! It's only me. They're in my kitchen. Come down and let me in.'

There was no response, not so much a twitch of a curtain, but she knew her Mucky and stood there patiently waiting, and after a minute or two she heard the scratching of bolts being drawn, and moved closer to the shop door as it opened a crack and Mucky peered out.

'Quick, let me slip in,' she murmured and pushed on the door and he yielded and at once she was in and bolting the door again. She peered through the sliver of glass beside the drawn doorblind but the Yard was empty. It was only just past eight thirty and the first of Mucky's regular customers wouldn't be arriving for a while yet, so there was time to talk. And she turned to look at him.

He had always been a small man, Mucky, but now he looked shrivelled and tiny and she put her hand out impulsively and said, 'Come on. We'll sit down,' and half led him and half pushed him past the counter to the doorway that led to the room at the back. Even under these odd circumstances it was a pleasure to be in the shop, with its high mahogany showcases and broad polished counter glinting with brass fittings, and the rich sugary smell of the tobacco filled her nose with familiar delight. She'd been coming in and out of this little shop for all her life. How could it have been 'Acquired for Clients' of anybody, let alone Joe Davriosh?

The small room was dim, for the curtains were still drawn and she pulled them back with a soft clash of the brass rings as he stood there and looked at her with his wizened nut of a face quite expressionless.

'Come on, Mucky,' she said heavily. 'Put the kettle on and make me some coffee. And tell me what's going on.'

To her surprise he obeyed, shuffling across to the little curtained corner where he had a small sink and a gas ring and a few dishes and she perched on the edge of the table and watched him as he moved through the familiar ritual.

'All right. Now, what's going on?' she said as he came shuffling back and put a mug of steaming coffee into her hand. 'Why are you looking like that? I've never seen you in such a state, and it doesn't suit you.'

He looked down at his shirtsleeved arms, at the trousers concertinaed over his bare feet and said tremulously, 'Didn't feel up to it, this morning, getting dressed.'

'What happened?' she said more gently. 'Tell me, Mucky.'

He began to weep, standing there with a mug of steaming coffee in one hand and letting tears slide down his cheeks as he stared at her, as woebegone as a child, and she reached forwards and took his mug and then made him sit down in the armchair beside the fireplace, ornamented now with dried grasses in a big vase instead of the big dancing fire that had made so many winter visits to this shop such a delight for the young Laura, and then gave him back his mug.

'Drink that,' she commanded. 'You'll feel better then.' Obediently he began to sip and she sat and looked at him and waited patiently.

'It was Simmy,' he said at length and she was shocked at the way his voice sounded. He who was always so chipper and bright to seem so slurred and husky.

'What did he do?' She kept her own voice as gentle as she could, treating him as though he were a frightened child, who needed careful humouring. 'Tell me about it.'

'Sent me to France.' He looked up at her and his eyes were still swimming. 'I was so excited. Going to France – six weeks – it was such – I was so excited. But it wasn't any pleasure at all. They didn't like me. Ignored me. Treated me like a foreigner. Even the Bosquets did, and me a Bosquet, just like them. But they treated me as though I was just English. They didn't like me at all – it wasn't like that last time I went, five years ago –'

'People can be silly, Mucky. Don't worry about that. It's not so bad to be English. I am –'

He shook his head. 'You're like me – different. You're Hungarian. I'm French, and they didn't want me. It was horrid and I wanted to come back sooner, but when I phoned Simmy he said not. Try to have fun, he said, and sent more money and I went to Monaco.' He brightened a little then. 'That was much better. I liked that better than France. They don't hate you if you're English in Monaco. They just like people who play in the Casino. I liked that.'

'I'm glad,' she said.

'Didn't win much,' he said and tried to smile at her and for a moment the old Mucky glinted there. 'Didn't lose much either, but I had a lot of fun, toing and froing, you know, toing and froing.'

'I'm sure you did.' Still she was gentle, still humouring him, though she wanted to shake him to find out why those men were sitting even now in her kitchen eating her toast and drinking her cofee but knowing she couldn't rush him.

'And then I came home and Simmy –' The old man frowned. 'Simmy said there had been a few changes but nothing to worry about. Someone had bought the freehold and there was some extra money for me. Five thousand pounds – five thousand pounds.'

'Simmy gave you –' she began and he shook his head, more vigorously now.

'Not Simmy. The new landlord. I didn't know what had happened. It's always been all right, you see. I just paid the rent every quarter, that was that. Now suddenly it's someone else takes the rent – but I didn't think I was – I mean, five thousand pounds.' He closed his eyes and wailed. 'I should have known. I should have argued! There's never anyone gives you something for nothing!'

'No,' Laura said bitterly. 'No one ever gives you anything for nothing. They just take.' And there was a little silence between them as they stared at each other.

'And then?' she ventured at last and he took a little breath and said, 'They sent me a letter. Said I'd not paid the rent properly – I don't understand it. Lots of papers. I went to the solicitor, of course, and he did what he could. But it was all something Simmy had done. He'd made things happen so that I made the mistakes, you see, when I paid and all that – there was nothing I could do. I had to sign papers and everything so there it is. And they said I'd be left to run the shop as long as I wanted but then last week another letter came and said I had to go today, they were locking up the place. So –' He looked at her and his eyes were dull and miserable. 'I just went to bed. But when it was you calling, I –' He smiled shakily. 'It's all right talking to you. Not like Simmy. My nephew Simmy.'

'Oh, Mucky,' she said. There was nothing she could say. 'Oh, Mucky, I am sorry. I can't imagine the Yard without you.'

'Neither can I.'

Again there was silence and then she said carefully, 'Has anyone told you why? I mean, why the place has to be shut?'

'Developers,' Mucky said. 'That's what it is. I asked the solicitor but he didn't know and I asked some of the customers and they didn't, but one of them said ask Joe Davriosh, he knows everything, so I did. And he knew – it was him who had to close the shop up, he told me. For developers.'

'Which developers?' she asked urgently and he shook his head.

'I don't know. I don't care any more. It's all so –' He set down his now empty mug. 'All such a mess. I'm going back to bed.'

'Mucky, you can't,' she said. 'I mean, if they're going to board the place up –'

'They can board me up too,' he said mulishly. 'I don't care any more. It's a judgement on us, I suppose. A judgement.' He lifted his chin then and looked at her and for the first time there was a spark of something more than defeat in him.

'Why did you come?' he said suddenly after a long pause. 'Why are you here?'

She blinked at him, and felt a little stab of fear; was he losing his mind? Was all this unsettling him, making him talk nonsense?

'Mucky, I told you! I saw the men and –'

He shook his head impatiently. 'No, I mean, why are you helping me? Why are you concerned?'

'Because you're Mucky! I've known you all my life!' she said. 'You're my neighbour. Part of my life –'

'Of course you are!' He was quite different suddenly, sitting up very straight. 'Part of your life, part of my life, of course you are! Oh, I should have thought about it sooner! Oh, I'll show him. I'll show him what he's done! He thinks he'll get it all, doesn't he? He thinks I'll just die and disappear and leave him sitting on heaps of – Oh, I'll show him. It's a judgement on us but it's most of all on him!'

She stared at him, bewildered. 'Mucky, what are you talking about?'

'I owe it to you, you see. Your grandfather Istvan, you see. It's through him, I owe it to you!'

The bewilderment grew. 'I don't know what you mean, Mucky. Istvan? He was my great uncle, not my grandfather and anyway –'

He waved one hand airily. It was incredible to see how he had changed, how alert and alive he was. He was just as Mucky always had been, though untidy in a way he normally never was. 'Grandfather, uncle, mother, aunt, it's all the same after so many years. But debts have to be paid and the right thing has to be done for a family. So I'll do it. And Simmy, my nephew Simmy, my sister's boy Simmy –' And be began to laugh, loudly, hiccupping and coughing and then laughing again, until she was alarmed and thought he would choke himself.

She leaned over and thumped his back and he regained his control and sat there and beamed at her, his eyes alight with the tears of his coughing, but something more besides. 'It's time anyway. I could have died behind this counter, couldn't I? But why should I do that? I'll go back to Monaco, they liked me there and I liked them. Not like France. And I'll take enough to be right there, but there's lots of it –' He giggled shrilly. 'The rest of it goes to you. To Halascz's, where it ought to be, here in Little Vinegar Yard just where it ought to be –' And he wrapped his thin arms around his even thinner chest and rocked to and fro, laughing again, but more softly this time.

'I'll going to get you to the doctor, Mucky,' Laura said decisively and got to her feet. 'All this has upset you too much. Come on now, you get dressed and I'll take you along to see the doctor –'

'I don't need any doctor,' he said. 'Just the solicitor, to make it all right. Oh, I'll show him, that Simmy. I'll show him he can shut up the shop but it won't do him a ha'porth of good, not a ha'porth! I'll show him!' But he didn't argue when she urged him towards the staircase and his room with firm instructions to dress.

She stood in the shop listening to him move around above her head and looked round at it. Small and beautiful and old; a lovely place and it had to go and she felt the same anger that had filled her when she had heard of the attempt to spoil her restaurant. Not as powerfully, perhaps, but still it was there. Who were these hateful anonymous people. these developers as they called themselves who could come and destroy such things as this shop, her restaurant, just for the sake of money? Who were they? How dare they do it? They couldn't be allowed to, they couldn't –

The stairs creaked and Mucky reappeared and it was as though the last half hour hadn't happened. He was dressed as neatly as he always was, with his spats smooth over his ankles and his hat carefully brushed, and he smiled at her as she turned to look at him.

'I'm sorry if I upset you, my dear,' he said. 'I wasn't quite myself. But I'm all right now. Where are these men? The ones who've come to board up?'

'In my kitchen.' She stared at him, puzzled. Had she imagined the way he had been before? He had never looked more normal, more in control of himself.

He nodded. 'I'll talk to them. Send 'em away till this afternoon. It won't take me long to pack my few bits. The bits I want. The rest can stay here, for my part. And I'll go back to Monaco. Yes, back to Monaco.' And he beamed at her. 'I toed and froed before, but I can do more toing and not so much froing if I'm there all the time. You see if I don't. You'll have to come and visit me, my dear. I'll get a little flat perhaps. That'll be fun. And the sun will be nice –'

'But, Mucky –'

'No, my dear, don't you worry. I'll see the solicitor this afternoon, sort it all out and be on my way. There'll be no problems, you'll see. It's the only right thing to do. I know that now. The right thing to do.' And he positively beamed at her.

'I wish I understood what all this is about Mucky. One minute you're so miserable and the next – I don't understand.'

'You will, you will! It'll all be explained, but not now. I've got a lot to do right now,' and he hurried her out of the shop and went bustling across the Yard and she followed him as he made his way through the restaurant to the kitchen.

The men were dubious until he had pushed a five pound note into their hands and they agreed with alacrity to come back next morning and went off whistling and Mucky smiled at Laura and nodded and went out after them. And she didn't say a word to stop him. There seemed no point since she couldn't work out what it was that the old man was talking about. But, she told herself, I can find out. I'll call Joel. That's what I'll do. If anyone can find out what's going on he can. And it seemed the most natural thing in the world to turn to him.

32

At four o'clock, when they were clear of the last lunchers, she phoned again. Ever since the letter had been pushed into her hand just before one o'clock by a bored secretary who was obviously affronted at having to act as a messenger, she had been bursting to talk to him, but it had been impossible to steal so much as a moment, for as well as the usual full restaurant, two of the Extras were in use today. But now at last they were all gone, and the kitchen was quiet and she could perch at her small desk and dial his number.

'I'm not nagging,' she said breathlessly. 'I know you said you'd come as soon as you could, but the most amazing thing has happened. I don't believe it, actually. It's all so incredible – please, can you get here any sooner than you said this morning that you could? I need to – I could do with some advice before the end of office hours. I may need to talk to this solicitor, you see – hmm? No – not mine, Mucky's. He sent me this amazing letter and – oh, I'm sorry, Joel, I don't mean to sound such an ass, but it's totally incredible, it really is. So, please, can you come sooner and – bless you. I'll be waiting.' And she hung up the phone and sat and stared at the window until she could control her impatience no longer and ran to the door.

She walked up and down outside in the Yard trying to burn up her restless anxiety. Mucky's shop stood still and silent on the other side, the blind still drawn on the door, and she watched as one or two people came and tried to push it open, and then peer in and, disappointed, went away, and tried to imagine how it would be when the shop was gone. And couldn't. And tried to make sense of what had been in the letter and couldn't do that either, catching her breath at the thought of it. It was all too much to take in.

He came into the Yard through the Frith Street arch and

she stood and looked at him, at the loping walk and the way he kept his hands shoved deep in his trouser pockets so that his jacket was bunched up behind him and felt a great wash of relief, and almost ran towards him. And then stopped, embarrassed at her childishness. She really had to stop being so silly; bad enough she'd made a fool of herself over Cord. No need to go head first into making herself a double fool with this man. He was friendly, he was sympathetic, he was helpful, but still a man and for a brief moment she wished she hadn't sent for him to help her. And then, as he smiled and tilted his head enquiringly, she forgot her misgivings and held out the letter to him.

'Tell me what that says to you,' she said. 'I want to be sure I'm not imagining it.'

He took it from her and stood there reading it and she looked at his bent head and the way the wind lifted the curly hair on the crown and thought – nice man. Alex was right. Nice man –

'Bosquet,' he said after he had finished reading and looked across the Yard to the tobacconist's shop. 'That Bosquet?'

She nodded. 'Mucky.'

'He wants to give you money, this solicitor says, as a gift?'

She nodded. 'That stuff about death duties – '

'Yes, that makes sense.' He looked at the letter again. 'Plenty of people do that for their children. Give them money while they're still alive so that the children don't have to pay vast sums in death duties after they're dead. But you're not one of Mucky's children.'

'Exactly. It's the craziest thing I've ever heard.'

He grinned at her and held out the letter to her. 'Crazy or not, it's great. It's a lot of money.'

'It's an incredible amount! Twenty thousand pounds, he says. That'll cover the work in the kitchen and improve my overdraft – and – ' She bit her lip. 'That's what's troubling me, I mean. I need it so much that I'm tempted to take it. And I don't see how I can.'

'Why not?'

'Why – do be reasonable, Joel! How can I? Why should I

take an old man's money, just like that? He must have gone mad – how can I?' She looked down at the letter again. 'Mind you, if the solicitor thought it wrong he wouldn't let him do it, would he? I mean if he really wasn't – what's the phrase they use? Of sound mind and body – '

'Something like that. Have you talked to the solicitor?'

'No. That's what I wanted to talk to you about. I mean, he says he has instructions from Mucky to talk to me, if I want to. But I need to make a decision first. Do I take it or not?'

'What are the special circumstances?'

'Mmm?'

'The letter. It says the gift is due to the special circumstances of your situations. What does that mean?'

She shook her head. 'I'm totally mystified. I don't know any special circumstances. Except that we're neighbours and always have been. He knew my family before me – we've always been close. The only two families in the Yard, you see. It was natural.'

'Then maybe it's natural he should give you this money.'

'It can't be. He's got his own family. His nephew.'

'But from what you said when you phoned this morning, Simmy's the cause of the whole problem – ' And he looked over his shoulder at the blank faced shop, standing there with its blind down so that it looked like a sightless man.

'Yes,' she said. 'Yes, he's very angry with Simmy. Maybe he's dong this to pay him out? Rather over the top though, isn't it? To give money to a stranger to punish a relation – '

'Not a stranger,' he said. 'You're as close as family in some ways, aren't you?' He laughed then. 'Forgive me if I sound selfishly interested in my own affairs, but I can't tell you what this means to me for my film. I set out to look at the sense of community here, at the way families interlink and now, look at this! How interlinked can you get? It's really amazing.'

Suddenly she smiled. 'That's better!'

'Better?'

'I was feeling bad about wasting your time. Leaning on

you when after all, why should you be involved? But if thee's something in it all for you then that helps.'

He frowned. 'I didn't think you were an ungenerous person, Laura. It was one of the most warming things about you, I thought. Generosity. Was I wrong?

She reddened. 'I don't know what you mean.'

'Yes you do. To suggest it's only all right for me to be interested in helping you if – what was the phrase? There was something in it for me.' He made a little face. 'I don't like that.'

She looked at him for a long moment and then reddened even more. 'Yes. You're right. It did sound ungracious. I didn't mean to be. I just didn't want to feel – oh, I suppose this'll sound wrong too. Too grateful.'

'Oh, heavens no,' he said vigorously. 'I don't want you to be grateful. Appreciative, by all means. Grateful never.'

'I'm not sure I know the difference.'

'One is generous. The other's just hire and salary. I don't want us to be in that sort of relationship to each other.'

'I – ' She stopped and then shook her head. 'We're talking about the wrong things.'

'Yes we are.' Now it was his turn to look embarrassed. 'Let's talk about the letter instead. You were going to ask my advice. So here it is. Go and see the solicitor. Keep an open mind, but see what he has to say. Then you can decide.'

She nodded and looked down at the letter again. 'Yes – I think perhaps – ' She lifted her head and looked at him very directly. 'Now, be generous to me. Come with me as my advisor.'

'What?' He looked startled.

'He says in the letter he's got Mucky's permission to talk to me and/or my advisors on the matter. So, come with me. Be my advisor.'

'I rather think he was thinking of one of his own kidney. A legal eagle.'

'I don't care what he had in mind. It's my decision,' Laura said with spirit. 'I seek and take my advice where I choose. So, I ask you.' She grinned then. 'Will you be generous enough to accept?'

'Touché,' he said and laughed. 'All right. When will you see him?'

'Now,' she said promptly. 'Let me phone. See if he's there. Wait for me.' And she ran into the restaurant and he heard her calling for Maxie as soon as she was inside the door.

She came out ten minutes later, wearing a yellow duster coat over her dress and with her face newly made-up, and she smiled at him, that triangular smile that was so characteristic of her, and he swallowed with disappointment. He hadn't been thinking about how she looked that day when he had stood here in Little Vinegar Yard and seen her smile at Philip Cord, until she had smiled at him, but now, remembering the glory of that look and comparing it with what he saw before him – it hurt and he had to steel his face so that she didn't see it. Her smile was warm and friendly and open and delightful, but it wasn't the way she had looked at that other man.

'He was waiting for me to phone,' she said. 'Sounds a reasonable sort of person, actually. He's over at Argyle Street. A taxi?'

'A taxi,' he agreed and stood back to let her precede him through the archway into Frith Street. As long as I control myself, he thought as they came out into the sunshine again and looked for a cab with its light on, as long as I keep my head, she need never know what a fool I am about her. As soon as I can I'll go back to Toronto and forget all about her. Because it's obvious I'm wasting my time. And he tried not to pay any attention to the sense of desolation that filled him at the thought.

The solicitor was, as Laura had said, a very reasonable sort of man, tall and surprisingly young. He sat in his office in his shirtsleeves and welcomed them with a broad smile, assurances of being perfectly happy to include Joel in their meeting, and the offer of afternoon tea.

'I am a tea snob,' he said. 'You can have Lapsang or Darjeeling or Earl Grey or Orange Pekoe. I recommend the Orange Pekoe.'

'That'll be lovely,' Laura said and sat on the edge of her

chair, eagerly, as he shouted the order for tea through to his outer office.

'Well?' he said. 'What did you think of my letter?'

'It amazed me,' she said at once. 'Look, Mr. Rose, I'm so confused I just don't know whether I'm on this earth or Fuller's – '

'Oh, lovely!' the solicitor said. 'I haven't heard that phrase since my grandmother died. She said it all the time – '

'And your grandmother lived and worked here in Soho too,' Joel said, with a note of resignation in his voice, and the man looked at him and said, 'Well, yes, actually. She had a shop in Foubert's Place. Corsetière, would you believe.'

'It's beginning to be too much for me,' Joel said and shook his head in disbelief. 'I get an idea for a film, and everywhere I turn the basic premise keeps jumping up and shouting at me. It's really incredible.'

'A film?' The man sounded interested. 'What film?'

Joel shook his head firmly. 'Not now. Later, I promise. I'll talk to you for ever about it when we've got this matter sorted out. But not now. Laura?'

'Yes,' Laura said. 'Look, Mr. Rose, what I need to know is – why? I can't let him do this if I don't know why.'

'I agree with you.' The tea arrived and there was a small flurry as he poured it out and distributed cups. 'I asked him the same thing. He was fairly mysterious about it, but quite clear and very definite about what he wanted to do.'

'Is he – ' She paused, not wanting to be unkind and then said with a little rush. 'I mean he's getting on a bit, and though I never saw any signs that he was not quite – '

'Is he sane, do you mean?' Mr. Rose laughed. 'Oh, he's perfectly sane! Knows exactly what he's doing and why, even if he chooses not to let me have all the details. And when I realised what his nephew had been up to over in the shop in his absence – ' He looked angry suddenly. 'I was away too. Only got back yesterday, so my partner was dealing with it. I might have been able to stop it, because I know so much more about the old man and his lease than anyone else does. He was my father's client before me – anyway, that's all water under the bridge now. The fact is, the nephew did a bit of wheeling and dealing in the old man's absence, started taking pornographic magazines into the shop, risked a prosecution and the freehold changed hands in the middle of a great deal of flurry and fuss over which I had no way of exerting any control. Nor did my partner, to be fair to him. So I can't undo the loss of the shop, but I have to say it's not so terrible. He's got a lot of money for it.' He looked at them bright eyed and cheerful over the rim of his cup. 'He's got a lot of money altogether, the old man. And he's determined, bound and determined that the unpleasant Simmy gets not a penny and you get the lot.'

'The lot?' Laura said. 'But you said in your letter – '

'Yes. Twenty thousand pounds. That's a gift to ease the death duties situation. At first the old chap wanted just to leave you everything in his will. I explained the death duties problem and he at once decided the answer was to give you as much as he could in advance. Hence this first twenty thousand.'

'Do you mean she stands to get a great deal more eventually?' Joel asked.

'A great deal more,' Rose said and set down his cup. 'You have as they say, Miss Horvath, considerable expectations. All rather Dickensian.'

'But why? I just don't understand why!'

'He says – 'Rose coughed. 'He says it is because his family and yours are linked in a manner that makes this right and necessary. That it should have been done long ago. That he is paying the debt his father owed your family. And that's all he will say. So, there it is. If you accept this, then I can put the matter in hand.'

'Where is he?' Laura said. 'I must talk to him.'

The solicitor shook is head. 'No, he doesn't want that. I told him he should see you and tell you himself. It would be a nice thing to do, and so forth, but he wouldn't hear of it. He's going back to his shop to pack a bag, I gather, and then he's going to Monaco. I have to apply for permits and so forth, for him.' He sighed. 'He's quite a demanding client, all of a sudden. For years he's just quietly run that shop and not needed a thing and now suddenly it's all bustle and push. Well it won't do him any harm, I dare say. I'd leave him alone, Miss Horvath. He's made a decision and there it is. Don't try to see him. Write letters, by all means, but at present he wants to be left alone. I think he's entitled to that.'

There was a long silence and then Laura said in a rather small voice, 'Then I should take it, Joel?'

He looked at her and nodded. 'I rather think you should,' he said. 'Mr. Rose thinks so – '

'Oh, absolutely.'

'Then there's no reason why you shouldn't.'

She closed her eyes. 'It's wonderful.' She said it almost in a whisper. 'I thought I was going to lose the restaurant.'

'What?' Mr. Rose looked at her sharply. 'Why?'

'It's a long story.'

'Of course, if you prefer not to discuss it – '

'Not at all,' she said quickly. 'I'm glad to explain. It's just that – well, I ran out of money. And the – ' She took a deep breath. 'I'd better start at the beginning.'

And she did, telling the whole tale of Cord and his deviousness succinctly and without self-pity, and as he listened, some of the desolation began to lift from Joel. He'd been unreasonable to feel as he had back there in Little Vinegar Yard. To think she would get over the way she had been ill used so swiftly, could respond to his own feeling for her as he wanted her to so soon after having been so hurt, had been ridiculous. She needed far more time than that and he let his tense shoulders relax against his chair back and went on listening to her even tones as she told the story.

'And now,' Mr. Rose said when she had finished. 'You have the money for the work in the kitchen and also, you think you could borrow successfully against your expectations in this will.'

'Well yes,' she said. 'It does seem as though I'm out of the wood, doesn't it?'

'It depends on how much money the man Cord has,' Rose said. 'These sites are changing hands at incredible prices, you know. He only has to buy your share, doesn't he? As I understand it, he has control of one quarter through his wife, has bought another quarter from your cousin Paul Balog at a very low price – '

'Wickedly low,' Joel said savagely.

'Still, he has got it. And has just to get the rest from you and from your aunts.'

'Yes,' Laura said. 'That's it.'

'You on the other hand would have to buy three quarters and he is hardly likely to let you have cheaply the half he already controls, is he? Mr. Bosquet has money to leave you, Miss Horvath, but not enough for that. You can look forward to another hundred thousand or so, maybe less. It depends on how much he gets through while he's living his life out there in Monaco. And you know, he's a very lively old man. Seventy-six, but he could live another ten years, maybe more. People do, you know.'

She reddened. 'I want him to!'

'I'm sure you do. But the thing is, borrowing against the will.' He shook his head. 'I wouldn't count on it.'

There was a little silence and then she nodded heavily. 'I was silly. Got excited, I suppose. It's so important to me, you see. I – well, anyway, I can do the kitchen, can't I? That'll be something.'

'Indeed it will.' Mr. Rose got to his feet. 'I'll be in touch with all the documents involved. Meanwhile, I'm glad you feel able to accept Mr. Bosquet's gift. It matters a lot to him that you should have it. But I wish I knew why.' He grinned then and looked very young indeed. 'I'm as curious as the next man. One wonders what sort of villainy his father got up to, that he feels as he did! Ah well, I suppose we'll never know.'

'We could know,' Joel said suddenly. 'We could find out, I think. Without asking Mr. Bosquet. No need to look so anxious, Mr. Rose! There's someone else who'll know, I'm sure.'

'Who's that?' Laura stared at him, her forehead creased.

'Your aunt, Laura. Anya Zsuzske. She's a good deal older than Mucky, isn't she? It's my guess she'll remember a lot. If she's asked.'

33

'No,' Paul said, and sat up even more straight in his chair, as though to give added authority to his words. 'Absolutely no, Coplin. She's an old lady. She can't be bothered over such things.'

'She may be old, but that doesn't mean she isn't interested in talking,' Joel said mildly. 'I've known old people in my time. A lot of them.' He smiled reminiscently. 'I had a great uncle who reached a hundred – and wanted to take out a ten year annuity on his birthday. He liked nothing better than to talk about the past.'

'Anya is different,' Paul said stubbornly. 'She doesn't.'

'Of course, I can't force you to let me talk to her,' Joel said. 'And I wouldn't even try to. But it does seem to me that you're being unfair to her. Never mind me, and through me, Laura – to *her*. She can't have much fun in life.'

Paul bristled. 'Are you implying I don't look after her properly?' He looked angry and frightened at the same time and Joel sighed.

'Stop being so defensive, man! Of course not! I'm only making the point that being old can't be much fun at the best of times. Things you can't do, things people won't let you do – all you've got left is what you remember. It's all there is of your life, isn't it, what you have inside your head? And if no one ever talks to you about it, then you might as well not have lived it – '

Paul stared at him, his lower lip stuck forward in a childishly mulish expression and Joel felt again the deep pity for him that had filled him when they had worked together on the *Thrust* commercial. He looked so very much a man, so tall, so elegant, so adult, with his silver head and craggy face and well muscled body, but it was all the thinnest of veneers. Beneath it lay a stubborn, vain and very frightened child and he wanted to reach out and touch him, and tell him it was all right, he was safe, and had no need to be so suspicious. But he stayed still, relaxing in the big old armchair and just watching him.

There was a faint tinkling sound and Paul lifted his head and listened. It came again and he said pettishly, 'There, you've woken her! I told you it wouldn't be right – ' And he got to his feet and hurried across the big shabby living room and went out and after a moment Joel got to his feet and followed him.

Laura had made the arrangement for him to come here this afternoon; he had tried to call Balog himself but been thoroughly snubbed, and Laura had said she'd ask him and arrange it.

'He's probably feeling awful about me, that's the thing,' she had said. 'Selling his share to Cord as he has – but I can't let him go on being so miserable about it. He couldn't help it, obviously. I want him to know that I realise that, but I've been putting off calling him. I'll have to do it some time. Better now than not – ' And she had called him.

What they had said to each other she didn't tell Joel, and he hadn't asked, but she looked a little less tense after the call than she had before, and told him that Paul had agreed to see him if he came round the next afternoon, so clearly it had been a reasonably satisfactory conversation. So he'd hoped he would have no difficulty with Balog; but the man had been guarded and hostile from the start. Polite but clearly unhappy about talking to him. And even unhappier about allowing him access to his mother.

But Joel wasn't going to give up that easily. The more he thought about it, the more obvious it became to him that Anya Zsuzske held in her gnarled old hands the lines that burrowed deeply into the problems of Little Vinegar Yard, and also, to his film. His commitment to Laura was undoubted; he wanted more than he could have imagined ever wanting anything to see her happy and content, her restaurant safely in her ownership and all her debts paid and all her fears removed from her. But that didn't mean he hadn't at the same time a commitment to himself and his own work, and the idea of his film about Soho was growing and shaping in his mind like a living thing.

He could see the patterns of it, misty but unquestionably there. He would link the past and present in a series of loops that took in three or maybe four specific Soho occupations, and the families who had followed them and still followed them. The Bosquets and their tobacconist's shop; the Halasczs and the Horvaths and their restaurant – and it was Anya Zsuzske with her ninety years of memories to draw on who was going to be the most important source of information for him. After he had talked to her, after he had sorted out these two interlocking stories, then he could go and find two more. In the market perhaps? The Price family of apple sellers? Mr. Rose's grandmother, the corsetière of Argyle Street? Possibly even his own family, the Coplins? But first, Anya Zsuzske and the story of Little Vinegar Yard.

His feet were silent on the old carpets as he followed the sound of Paul's voice out of the room, down the long corridor, with its red runner of turkey carpet and the trim little mats at the doorways, to the last door, which stood ajar.

He stopped outside and disliking himself intensely for being so devious, listened. There was a clink of china and then the old woman's voice said, 'Ah! Thank you Poly – *sàjhalom – bocsanát* – I wish you didn't have to do such things – '

'It's all right, Anya!' Paul's voice came surprisingly loud and Joel stepped back, suddenly fearful he was about to come out and would find him there, listening at the door, like some horrible old landlady in a cheap lodging house. 'You don't have to apologise. We're all made the same – here's your tissues. You can manage?'

The old lady grunted and Joel heard a door open and the flush of a lavatory and the splash of water taps running into a basin and understood, and closed his eyes as another wave of pity washed over him, this time for both of the people on the other side of the door; for the old lady to have to rely on her son for all her most basic bodily needs, and for him to have to look after her in such a way. It had to be misery for both of them, and he wanted to turn and run out of their flat and leave them in peace. It was an appalling intrusion to be here at all, even to want to talk to this old woman against her son's will, and he actually turned to go, when the waft of eau de cologne hit his nose and he stopped. His mother had used just that sort of scent and it was though she were standing here beside him, the physical effect of the smell was so powerful.

He took a deep breath and with his mind made up, stepped forwards and pushed on the door.

Paul was just coming out of the bathroom drying his hands on a small towel and his face froze into a mask of anger as he saw Joel standing there. The face against the pillow, however, looked quite different. The eyes were very dark in the sagging old face and, Joel thought, very intelligent, and he grinned at her and said loudly, 'I'm pushing in where I shouldn't. I'm Joel Coplin, and I wanted to talk to you, Mrs. Balog.'

Paul stepped forwards, his mouth open to speak, but the old lady was before him.

'Coplin?' she said and her voice seemed to rumble as it came out of the great bulk of her. 'Coplin. Abner Coplin's son? Or grandson more like, looking at you – '

Joel grinned ever more widely. 'Great grandson,' he shouted. 'My grandfather was David, and my father was Samuel.'

She managed to nod her great head, buried though it was in her pillows. 'Ah well, I dare say I am forgetting some of them now. Great grandfather, hmm? What's your name?'

'Joel.'

'Always did go in for these bible names, the Coplins,' the old lady said and snickered. 'I told him once, Abner, I told him, if your lot behaved as well as they're labelled, they'd be all right. But there, who could be that good? Abner and David and Samuel – I ask you!' And again she snickered.

'I'd like to talk to you about the old days, Mrs. Balog,' Joel said loudly and she cocked an eye at him and said irritably, 'Don't whisper, boy. You're whispering and mumbling.'

'I'd like to talk to you,' he said even more loudly, but careful not to shout. His great uncle had taught him how to speak to the deaf. Shouting never helped. It was clarity of diction that was needed. 'About the old days.'

'Talk to me about the old days?' She turned her head and looked at her son who was still staring at Joel with his face rigid and expressionless. 'You hear that, Poly? He wants to talk to me of the old days.'

'You don't have to, Anya,' Paul said loudly. 'If it makes you tired and you want to rest – you don't have to.'

'Want to rest? I've got a million years to rest. I won't even have to turn over, I'll rest so well. Dead soon, I'll be. Plenty of rest then.'

'Don't talk that way, Anya,' Paul said, but he spoke automatically, not taking his eyes from Joel.

'Sit down, Abner's boy,' she said then and patted the bed beside her. 'Talk about the old days, eh? This is something I can do. It's the only thing I can do – ' And with a sudden pettish movement she slapped both hands on the bed on each side of her. 'Useless old fool.'

'Don't talk too much, Coplin. She's a lot frailer than you think,' Paul said, and there was no appeal in his voice, but Joel knew it was there all the same. 'Don't make her tired.'

'You don't mind then, after all?'

'What can I do whether I mind or not?' Paul said bitterly. 'You've walked in here and she's seen you. I have no more to say in the matter. She's Anya, you know. I don't tell her what to do – I can only tell you.'

'Then tell me.'

'Don't – I don't want her upset. She doesn't have to know – don't tell her about me. That I've lost my share of the restaurant – ' His face began to crumple then, and Joel looked down at his hands, wanting to protect the man from his own weakness. 'She gave it to me, all those years ago, to keep me safe, she said. And now – now I've – just don't tell her.' And he walked clumsily past Joel and out of the room and closed the door behind him, leaving Joel staring at the old woman in the bed who gazed back gravely.

'He's upset,' she said after a moment and then said something in a language Joel couldn't understand, and he tilted his head enquiringly.

'He's upset,' she said again. 'He doesn't want you to talk to me.'

'He's worried it will make you tired,' Joel said, speaking as distinctly as he could and she said sharply, 'You don't have to shout. I can hear you. It won't make me tired. What's tired about talking? It's more tired to lay here with nothing to do, nothing to work for, nothing but remembering all day. *This* makes a person tired.'

Joel nodded and came across to the bed and perched on the edge of it. 'I know. It's always easier to talk, isn't it?'

'Yes,' she said and wriggled her bulk a little so that she was sitting more upright. 'Give me that over there.' She jerked her head at the tallboy behind him and obediently he went and fetched the biscuit tin she was indicating.

'And there, in the cupboard. Tokay,' she said and grinned wickedly. 'After dinner, he lets me have it, most nights. Today I have it in the afternoon, because I have a visitor. Talking and Tokay – a special day!'

He fetched her the decanter and the glass he found beside it and then, still following instructions, went to the bathroom where he found a toothglass which she insisted on using herself.

'You're the guest,' she said stubbornly. 'Guests get the best. I was brought up this way. Take the good glass.'

So he did and turned the handsome piece of old crystal between his fingers and grinned at her and she grinned back and again jerked her head, and he obeyed the instructions, filling the glasses till the glinting amber winked in the afternoon sunlight.

She had eaten several of the small sugary biscuits and was drinking her second glass of Tokay before she spoke again.

'So, you want to talk about the old days. About your grandfather, and your father, and all the rest of them. A good family, the Coplins. Friends to all of us, one way and another – '

'I want to talk about them, yes. And about your family,

too. About the restaurant, and the way it was shared out between you all – '

She laughed suddenly, a rich bubble of laughter that seemed to rumble deep inside her belly and she made an expressive little sound with her lips too, that sent crumbs scattering onto her bedcovers.

'Poor old Poppa,' she said. 'My mother – my mother, the things she did. She made up her mind we were to have it, you know. The three of us – '

'The three of you.'

'The sisters,' she said and reached for another biscuit, scrabbling in the tin box as eagerly as a child. 'Me and my sisters.'

'And your brother. What about him?'

'My brother?' She looked at him with her face crinkled as she concentrated and he thought – oh, no. Don't let her tire too soon. Don't, don't let her wander off – and controlled the impulse to prompt her with words and sat silently looking at her.

'Anya,' she said suddenly. 'You didn't know my mother, did you?'

'No,' he said.

'Strong, my mother was. Strong,' the old woman said and shook her heavy old cheeks so that again the crumbs flew from her lips. 'She knew how to make Poppa do what she wanted.' She laughed then, the same bubbling chuckle that seemed to reverberate somewhere deep inside her. 'But not all the time. He got his own way too sometimes.'

'Did he?'

She paid him no attention, staring at him but seeing something quite different. 'Oh, Poppa, he wanted to be a gentleman so much. He wanted to have horses and be a gentleman, my Poppa – ' Her eyes focussed then and she looked at him shrewdly. 'But you're too young to remember him.'

'I'm afraid so.'

'You should have known him. Funny and nice and – funny.'

Again the old eyes softened into a glaze. 'But we were

girls and girls weren't the same to him. Not like boys. All the time he told us that. Girls aren't like boys.'

Once again the look in her eyes changed and she sharpened and he thought – it's like watching the sea. The waves come up, urgent and busy and purposeful and then they fall back and disappear into a rattle of shingle and don't know where they want to be. And then another wave comes and the purpose comes with it –

'So it was good Anya was there, wasn't it? If she hadn't been he'd have given it all to him, you know that?'

He said nothing, just lifting his brows at her encouragingly and once again the wave receded and left only the tumble of the shingle, as she closed her eyes and for a moment he feared she had gone to sleep; but then suddenly she opened them again and looked at him and once more she was alert and clearly aware of what she was saying.

'So, tell me what you want to know, I'll try to remember. I like to talk of the old days. I don't get the chance often. It's good to talk. If you don't talk about it, it all shrivels away and then there's nothing left. All that time you've lived and nothing left to show for it.'

'Yes,' Joel said. 'It's good to talk. Talk to me about the things your mother and father did for you. For you three girls and for your brother. For Istvan.'

'Brother,' she said and laughed, and there was a bitterness in her voice. 'I never had a brother.'

He frowned and shook his head. 'Istvan, Mrs Balog,' he said very distinctly. 'Don't you remember Istvan? Your brother?'

'Of course I remember Istvan,' she said pettishly. 'All of us had to remember him. All the time, we had to, Poppa saw to that. The only Halascz. How could we forget?'

'Then why do you say you don't have a brother?'

She pushed the tin of biscuits away, suddenly, and folded her hands on her belly and looked at him closely. 'You won't tell anyone?'

'Tell anyone what?'

'What happened. It has to stay in the family, you see. What else can you do but keep such a thing in the family?

Them you can tell, because they know. But no one else. You promise?'

'Of course I promise. Just the family.' Whatever it was it was important. She had a flush over the places where her cheekbones would have been if they had been visible beneath the fat that blurred her old face, and her eyes now were as sharp as pins. 'Just tell me all about it.'

And she did.

34

Zsuzske had been playing with the baby all afternoon, and was getting tired of it. She wasn't a nice baby, who laughed and played like Mary Garcia's baby brother in Frith Street. He was nice, but Magda was a miserable baby who grizzled and had a nose that ran all the time and who smelled nasty. But Anya had said she must play with her, so she did. It was better than making Anya shout.

The noise that had been so loud and horrible all morning and which had stopped now started again, and Zsuzske put her hands over her ears. It wasn't like crying and it wasn't like shouting and it wasn't like shrieking. It was like all of them together and it hurt her chest when she heard it. It made it feel tight as though she had on the baby Magda's vest instead of her own.

There were footsteps then, and she sat and thought about going out of the room to see what was happening. They'd told her she mustn't, no matter what, that she had to stay in the sitting room and look after the baby Magda, but the baby had gone to sleep all of a sudden, lying down in the middle of the bricks and dolls and falling fast asleep, so there was no reason why not.

Quietly she moved away from the rug by the fire and the toys and the baby, and went on her hands and knees to the door. She didn't have to crawl like that; she was six now, and it had been a long time since she had crawled the way the baby did. She couldn't even remember what it had been like to do it, but she had the feeling now that it was the safest way to go.

At the door she sat up on her heels and thought for a while. The horrible noise had stopped now, and there were grown-up voices and it sounded as though they were on the other side of the bedroom door, the bedroom she usually shared with Kati and the baby, but which they hadn't let her sleep in last night, making her sleep in Anya's bed, and slowly she turned the knob of the door and eased it open. They'd think it was an accident as long as she didn't open it wide. They'd think she'd just happened to notice it was open and had come to close it, like a good girl should. If she did it carefully and slowly –

Now the door was open, even only a little bit, it was easier to hear what was going on and she stayed there, still crouching so that she sat on her heels, and listened hard. Behind her the baby snored a little and the fire crackled, but that was all.

Outside in the Yard it was quiet and there was no one. Why should there be? It was Sunday, the dead day, the one she usually liked because the restaurant was closed and Poppa was upstairs here and sometimes let you play on him, and listen to his big watch from the Old Country.

'Give it to me,' she heard her father's voice so loud that she shrank back, afraid he was going to come out of the room and find her, but the other door stayed firmly shut and she went on listening. 'I want to see for myself – let me see – '

'Poppa!' That was Kati, thought Zsuzske. That was her voice. She sounds funny, as though she's been crying. 'Poppa, give him to me!'

'A boy,' Poppa was saying, and it was as though he was singing. 'A boy, a boy, at last a boy! *Chucheke*, let me look at your little tassel – look at that, Maritza! Will you look at that! He's got little balls like a Turk, this boy, this Halascz!'

Anya's voice then, high and loud and no words she could understand. Anya angry and shouting and Zsuzska shrank back and began to close the sitting room door. Anya shouting was dreadful.

But before the door was closed she heard Poppa again, laughing and happy and then Kati said something in that strange new voice of hers; maybe she had a cold? Zsuzske hadn't seen her since yesterday, and she didn't have a cold then but they'd said she wasn't well today and she must look after the baby and be good, so maybe it was because Kati had a cold?

Suddenly, almost before she realised what was happening, the bedroom door opened and in a great wash of terror she let the door go, leaving it open and scuttled over the floor on her knees and threw herself down beside the baby Magda and closed her eyes. They'd catch her, catch her listening and then Anya would shout even more and – she closed her eyes tightly and as the door opened threw up one arm to cover her eyes. They wouldn't see her eyes wobbling and wouldn't know she was really awake.

'Hush, you fool!' That was Anya. 'The little ones are asleep, thank God. Listen, give him to me – you must be mad, taking him like that. He ought to be with her – give him to me – '

'It's too dark in there to see him properly,' Poppa said and laughed again. 'Look at him! A great lump of a boy – oh, Maritza, such a lump of a boy! Why didn't we have such a one, eh? Never one like this before, a right little Halascz, will you look at the balls on him – '

'You'll wake the little ones, you fool. Shut up!'

'They got to see him, ain't they? Their new baby – '

'Their new baby what?'

There was a little silence then and moving as though she was really fast asleep, Zsuzske turned over, making the sort of soft noises the baby Magda sometimes made when she turned over in her sleep. She arranged herself carefully so that she could open one eye and look through the crack of space beneath her arm and above her nose that she had left there. Now she could see what was happening.

Poppa was holding a bundle. That was what it was, a baby bundle. It was like she was a very little girl again, a hundred years ago, when Poppa had fetched her and Kati from over the Yard where they had been playing at Mr. Bosquet's, and Anya had been in bed and had her hair down instead of pinned up and had looked as though she had just woken up.

'This is your new baby sister,' Anya had said, her voice all bright the way it was when she wanted Zsuzske to eat her dinner and Zsuzske didn't want to. 'This is your new little sister.'

'Another lousy little sister,' Poppa had said in a growl and then Anya had started to cry and Poppa had shouted and then Kati had taken her outside and she had cried too. There had been a bundle like that then. A baby bundle called Magda. And here was another one.

Zsuzske lay there with her arm over her face, and just a small peeping space under it and over her nose, and thought about that. It was a hundred years ago, the last time, but she remembered and it had been different then. They had told her about it before it happened, that was what was different. This time they hadn't.

She thought for a little while and then sat up and rubbed her eyes a lot, to show she'd really been asleep.

'Anya?' she said. 'What's that?'

'I told you you'd wake them!' Anya said and pushed on Poppa's shoulder. 'Take it back to her.'

'Poppa, what have you got there? Is that another baby?'

'Oh, my little Zsuzske, they didn't forget you when they handed out the brains, eh? You see, Maritza? You can't keep this one in the dark. Show her her new baby! See, Zsuzske? A little boy! We got a little boy now!'

Zsuzske looked at Anya who was standing behind Poppa and looking over his shoulder. Her face was strange. Flat and dull and strange.

'Where's Kati?' Zsuzske said, not knowing why she asked because she knew where Kati was. She was in the bedroom. She'd been making all those horrible noises. She didn't know why she was asking, but she knew it was an important question.

Poppa looked at her and then over his shoulder at Anya, who leaned forwards and took the baby bundle from him. Because Anya was shorter than Poppa, Zsuzska could see now, and she went close and stood on her tiptoes and stared at the baby inside the bundle.

It was just a baby, she decided, and was rather sad about that. It was a boy so it ought to look different, but it looked like Magda only a lot smaller. It was asleep like Magda, too.

'A boy,' she said. 'Don't boys look different? This one looks the same as Magda.'

'You're looking at the wrong end!' Poppa said and laughed hugely, the sort of very big laugh he made when he had been sitting downstairs for a long time with the other men. 'At the other end, he looks different, oh boy, does he look different!'

'Shut up, Viktor,' Anya said and then looked at Zsuzske. 'Listen, dolly, go and play, eh? Quietly. Don't wake the baby – '

'Which baby?' Zsuzske said and looked over her shoulder at Magda, asleep on the rug. Suddenly she looked very big and very old. Not at all like a baby really.

'Magda,' Anya said after a moment. 'Don't wake Magda.'

'What's his name?' she said then, suddenly feeling she could ask questions, be cheeky. Anya wouldn't shout at her. It was another of those things she knew without knowing why she knew.

'I – it's,' Anya began and then Poppa said, 'He's my boy Viktor, of course!'

'No!' That was Anya, suddenly loud. 'No. This I won't have. I can – I can't have that.'

Poppa was very quiet, and Zsuzske looked at him and his face had gone still and solid.

'I'm sorry, Maritza,' he said and it was as though there was no one except him and Anya. No Magda, no Zsuzske, certainly no baby boy without a name. 'I got excited. I didn't think.'

'I noticed,' Anya said and looked again at the baby.

'I'm sorry. It's just – a man needs sons. If he can't have sons, what is he?'

'The father of daughters isn't good enough?'

Poppa said nothing but he looked at the baby bundle with his eyes so wide and dark that he didn't look like Poppa any more, Zsuzske thought, and suddenly she felt the crying inside her nose sharp and pushing and the tears came out of her eyes and she heard herself bawling, loudly.

Anya kneeled down then, and put her arm round her. She still had the baby in her other arm but she held Zsuzska close and then at last it was all right. Anya was just being the way she was and the crying stopped hurting and started being a nice feeling and Zsuzske snivelled and sniffled and squeezed her eyes to make the tears come out and felt good inside.

There was a sound then and the door they had shut behind them was pushed open and Zsuzske looked up over Anya's shoulder and it was Kati. She was wearing a dressing gown and she looked tired, as though she'd just woken up.

'Anya?' she said and then the sort of crying that hurt came back into Zsuzske's nose because Anya dropped her, stood up and dropped her, leaving her there alone in the middle of the floor so that she could go over to Kati and hold her in her spare arm.

Zsuzske hated Kati then. She often hated Kati, who shouted at her like a grown up but behaved like a child and made Anya hold and love her instead of Zsuzske.

'Anya,' Kati said again and now Poppa went over and took her arm. 'Back to bed, Kati,' he said loudly. 'You're in no condition to be out here. Back to bed, at once. You want you should be ill?'

'I want to be dead,' Kati said and began to cry loudly and Zsuzske did too and then it was Magda, sitting up on the rug and rubbing her eyes and shrieking, her nose running and her mouth shrieking and Zsuzske tried to cry louder but couldn't. No one could cry louder than Magda, though Kati was trying to.

And then it was evening time. It had been afternoon and now it was evening. Zsuzske tried sometimes, afterwards, to remember what happened but she couldn't. It was just the way it was; it was afternoon and there was the new baby and then it was evening time and the new baby wasn't so new any more and Kati wasn't in her dressing gown any more but was sitting by the fire, with Poppa and Momma, like a grown up person. And Zsuzske was in the big armchair curled up. She must have been asleep. That was it, asleep, only now she wasn't. But her eyes were still closed and she listened to them talk, Anya and Poppa and Kati.

'If you tell me, I promise you, I won't make no trouble.

But a man's entitled to know who makes such a disgrace of his house!' Poppa was saying.

'No!' Kati said.

'Listen, Kati, no one'll make trouble, I promise you, no one will. But we have to decide, the birth certificate, everything – you ought to be married to the man, so the baby gets a decent certificate.'

'Tell them it's your baby,' Kati said. 'I won't say.'

There was silence then. Zsuzske, lying curled up with the light of the fire making orange patterns behind her closed eyes listened to the silence and knew it was best to stay asleep. It was a bad silence.

'What did you say?' Poppa said.

'You heard me,' Kati said. 'I won't say. It's my affair. Mine, you hear me? If I tell you who it was, you'll make such a fuss, you'll make him marry me, and I don't want to. He wants to but I don't, so there's an end to it. So I won't tell you. You can't make me.'

'You said to say it's our baby,' Poppa said. His voice was loud and Zsuzske thought, if he talks so loud I'll have to wake up and I don't want to. I don't want them to know I'm awake. Shut up, Poppa. Be quiet, Poppa.

'So?' Kati again.

'You want us to do that? To say it's our baby?' This was Anya's voice and Zsuzske listened and thought – Anya sounds like me when she says to me do you want another potato and I don't know if I do. She doesn't know what she wants. It was strange to think of grown-ups not knowing what they wanted.

'Why not? No one knows about me. I didn't show much, did I?' Kati began to sound like she usually did, whining and wanting things, and Zsuzske liked that. She'd been sounding all wrong, this past few days. What past few days? She tried to remember and couldn't. 'I've not put my nose outside these rotten walls except at night this past three months, hiding away. You were pregnant – who knows what happened to your baby? Only us. We're the only ones know your baby died. So say this one is your baby. It doesn't have to be mine, I don't want it – '

'Don't want our little boy?' Poppa said, and his voice was big and loud again. 'That lovely boy who – '

'I don't care. I don't care, I don't *care*!' Kati was shouting and crying and now Zsuzske had to wake up, she was making so much noise. She had to and she sat up and looked round.

It was strange being Zsuzske. Sometimes she remembered everything that happened to her in every tiny bit. She remembered how many bites there were on her apple and how many sweets had been in the bag Poppa had brought her. But then there were times when whole days, whole weeks, even longer, just fell into a black hole in her mind and she couldn't ever find them again.

It was like that with Kati. One moment she was there in the sitting room and crying, I don't care, I don't care, I don't *care*,' and the next it was a long time afterwards and she wasn't there. She hadn't been there for a long time. There was the Yard, and it was a hot Sunday afternoon and Anya had come out with a chair and was sleeping in it in the sun and Magda was running up and down with her dog on wheels and Istvan was in the high chair and banging on the front of it with his bricks and throwing them down so that Zsuzske had to pick them up.

'Be a good sister,' Anya had said sleepily, sitting there with her arms folded. 'Pick up your little brother's bricks when he throws them. Be a nice big sister – '

And because she was now seven and getting to be such a nice big girl, she had to.

And there suddenly was Kati again coming through the archway with a tall man with a thin face. She was wearing a white satin dress with a pouched front over a deep white belt and it was trimmed all round its flounced skirt with white spotted net frills edged with baby ribbon. The sleeves were frilled too, and her hat was made of pleated satin ribbon, like her shirt. Zsuzske had never seen anything quite so beautiful and she pulled her blue serge dress over her black stockinged legs and scowled at her sister.

But she paid her no attention.'This is Ferenc, Momma,' she said and Anya sat up and held out her hand and the tall man bent over it and said something and kissed the air over it.

There was a lot of talking and laughing then and Poppa came out and sat in the sun as well, and they sent Zsuzske to the ice cream shop in Bateman Street, where Mr. Ferraro was open even on Sundays, to fetch strawberry cornets, and by the time she came back they were all acting as though they'd been there for ever and that Ferenc, who was the tall man, had been there for ever too. They told her he was to marry her sister Kati and Poppa had cried and looked sour and then fetched wine and laughed instead and Zsuzske and Magda and Istvan had been allowed to eat all the ice cream. A good day, really, Zsuzske had thought. Till all the grown ups went inside to sit at a table in the corner of the restaurant and talk some more and left Zsuzske to look after the little ones in the sunshiny Yard. And Mr. Bosquet had come out into the Yard.

He stood there in the shadow of his shop door and called Zsuzske and she went to him at once, for he was a nice man, a big nice old man who was as frightened inside as she was, sometimes. She knew that because of the way he looked at her sideways and blinked at her and she would smile at him and say, 'Don't worry! It may never happen!' the way her father did all the time when he saw him. And Mr. Bosquet would laugh and not look quite so frightened. But most of the time he did.

'Who was that?' he said, and Zsuzske looked over her shoulder to see where he was staring. They could see into the restaurant from here, see the four shapes sitting round the table.

'That is Ferenc,' Zsuzske said, proud to have the answers to a grown-up's question, even a frightened grown-up like Mr. Bosquet. 'That is Ferenc Kiss and he's going to marry my sister and Anya says I can be a bridesmaid. What to bridesmaids do, Mr. Bosquet?'

'They wear pretty dresses,' he said after a moment and she had stared at him, surprised. He didn't sound frightened now. He sounded angry. 'She's marrying that man?'

'Yes. She says she's going to have the best white dress and lilies of the valley and – '

'Why?'

'She didn't say.'

'What about – ' He had looked down at her then and his face had gone smooth. 'Where is she going to live? She and her Ferenc Kiss?'

'She didn't say.' Zsuzske was mystified. He'd never talked so much or so directly as long as she could remember. Not ever. 'She said they were going to look for a flat. She told Poppa she was going to look for a flat. They're all talking about that now, I think. That and money.' And she had nodded seriously. They always sat round tables when they talked about money. She'd heard it often.

'And they'll be just the two of them in this flat?' Mr. Bosquet said. 'Just them and no one else?'

'I don't know,' Zsuzske said. She was getting bored now and wanted to lick her ice cream more quickly and she couldn't do that while he was talking all the time. It wouldn't be polite. 'Who else should there be?'

'Your – the baby. Istvan,' he said and after a moment looked across the Yard to the high chair by the door in the sun, where Istvan was getting ice cream in his hair, rubbing it in and looking happy.

'My little brother,' Zsuzske said.

'That's right. Your little brother,' Mr. Bosquet said and he sounded angry again. 'That's who. Your little *brother*.'

'I don't know, Mr. Bosquet,' Zsuzske said and now it was important not to talk to him any more. 'I'm going home now. Goodbye.' And she ran across the Yard and started to clean the ice cream off Istvan's face, though it made him cry when she took the soggy cornet away from him. He bawled a lot and Poppa came out and picked him up and soothed him and shouted at her for making him cry and took him inside. She sat on the step of the restaurant and looked across to the tobacco shop. It was quite silent now, with the door shut and the blinds down, but she knew he was in there and watching, though she didn't know how she knew.

There was something else she knew too, though she never

told anyone about it. She knew now that Istvan wasn't her little brother. He didn't have the same Anya and Poppa she had. Whatever they said. He had a different Anya and Poppa and Zsuzske knew who they were.

35

'Are you quite sure?' Joel said and then made a face at his own foolishness. 'I'm sorry! That was a silly question.'

'I wouldn't say if I wasn't sure,' the old woman said. 'That was the first time I knew for sure that afternoon. But afterwards – oh, there were things said, things I saw that proved it. The rows Anya and Poppa had –' She sighed, a ghostly little noise that made her great belly rise like bread. 'He tried to forget Istvan wasn't his son, you see. He tried to pretend there hadn't been any other man. And Kati never said. Poor old Jean!'

'Who?'

'Jean Bosquet. He loved my sister, Kati, poor old man. He told me often and often. He knew it had been wrong, knew she was only fifteen, but couldn't help it. The way he told me, I knew it wasn't his fault. It was hers. She made him do it –'

'He *told* you that? A child your age?' Joel was shocked and didn't care if she knew.

She laughed then, a bubble that turned into a cough. 'No – no – he wasn't like that. He was a good man. He wasn't telling *me* when he talked. Not in so many words. It was just the way people do talk to children sometimes. They talk to themselves really, with the child listening.' She managed a portentous little nod, moving her head heavily on her pillows. 'But I understood what he was saying. He wanted Kati but she didn't want him, and he wanted Istvan but she wouldn't admit he had a right to him so what could the poor old man do? He married Violetta and then Yves was born.' She squinted at Joel. 'You know Yves?'

'No,' he said. 'I'm not sure I've heard about Yves –'

'Then listen,' she said tartly. 'Jean Bosquet, when my sister wouldn't have him and married Ferenc Kiss instead, went and married Violetta – her father had the patisserie in Dean Street. And they had this little boy, Yves – and then they had a girl, I forget the name – and then they died and Yves had the shop after them –'

'Mucky,' Joel said, and nodded. 'Of course. Mucky.'

'What's that?'

'It doesn't matter,' he said. 'Not important. But I know who you mean, now. Look, Mrs. Balog – didn't anyone else in the family know that Istvan was your parents' grandson and not their son?'

'Kati knew,' she said and grinned and a couple of long yellow teeth showed in the dark cavern of her mouth.

'And no one else?'

She was silent for a long time, and her eyes seemed to have glazed and he watched her, not wanting to push her too hard but wanting so much to know all she had to tell him that he could almost taste his own hunger. But he managed to be patient. And was rewarded.

'I can see them still, you know that?' she said almost dreamily. 'When I think of the old days, I see the scenes inside my head and see the people there and I don't say to myself, what are they saying? I just look at the people there and I hear them start talking and I listen.' She chuckled then, a soft little sound that was oddly young. 'I was a wicked child! I sat under tables and I sat in corners and I kept myself small, and I listened. They forgot I was there, and I just listened and listened and I knew everything and none of them knew I knew. A wicked child.'

'I rather think you were,' Joel said and laughed too and she looked at him with a glint of pure mischief in her eyes and laughed with him, and for a moment there was a rapport there into which the vast age gap between them seemed to vanish completely.

'It was sad for Anya, though,' she said suddenly and then started to pant a little as she tried to haul herself up the bed. She had slipped down so that her head was poked forward and at once he got to his feet and leaned over and tucking his arm into hers, the way he had been used to do for his mother when she had been ill, gave a practised heave. And she came up the bed and lay back gasping a little on the pillows.

'Why sad for your mother?'

'She never felt right about it. Poppa, he could pretend Istvan was his boy but she always knew he wasn't. She'd lost so many. So many babies and they were all hers, all special. The last one she had which died just six weeks before Istvan was born, that one was very special. The only time she had a boy, you see. She told me when my Leonard was born – the only time she had a boy it died. She didn't realise what she was saying to me, I think, about Istvan. But she said it. Poor Anya. Poor Poppa –' She looked very directly at Joel then. 'But do you understand? Your own are special, the way no one else's ever can be. My Paul – he's so much more to me than Richard and Veronica and Charles. They're my grandchildren and they're important, but they aren't mine, are they? And Istvan was never my Anya's. He was Poppa's but never hers. She looked after him and loved him, you understand.' She peered closely at him and put out one gnarled hand to tug at his sleeve. It was clearly important to her that he should understand. 'She cared for him and reared him as carefully as she did we three, but she never felt for him as Poppa did.'

'I understand,' Joel said gently though still loudly and patted her hand. 'She was a good lady, your mother. I know that. A good lady who suffered a lot.'

'Being married to Poppa, she suffered,' the old lady said and again produced a little cackle of laughter. 'Oh, he was so wicked, my Poppa. So lovely and so wicked! The gambling, the drinking, the laughing, the stories, the way he talked – oh, he was a wonderfully wicked old man!' And she seemed to light up as she stared back at her father down the long corridors of the dead years.

'I'm sure he was,' Joel said and again patted her hand.

'And he won in the end, though she tried so hard to stop it.' She shook her head and made a little face. 'Well, they both won. Both lost too. The last years that was all they ever talked about. The money, the Family Trust, who should have it, who shouldn't. And then when she threatened to have him locked up in a hospital and made us all agree to help her – that was bad. I was bad –'

'You were bad? How?'

'I let her make me do what she wanted, or at least, I almost did. She wanted it all to come to just the three of us, you see. Kati and Magda and me. We were the only ones entitled, she said. We were his three children, no one else. But Poppa said no, it must be the four of us. All the neighbours, all the friends, they knew there were four children in the Halascz family. It had to be left to us all because of scandal –' She stopped then and laughed, a sharp little sound that was full of contempt. 'Scandal! As though anyone in Soho cared tuppence. As though any of them would have even noticed! But Poppa was determined and Anya was too – and Poppa won really.'

'How?'

'She threatened to have him sent to a madhouse, you know that? No? Well, she did. He drank too much, he lost his temper too much, shouted and threw things too much. He had ideas of going to Hungary to be a gentleman – she could have made the doctors say he was mad on such things. And she told us we must say the same. And the others, they said they would. Magda, because she wanted the restaurant for her Zolly – and they did all the work there, after all. It was natural enough. And Kati – Kati because she was Kati. So greedy, always. So wicked and so greedy.'

'You didn't like Kati?' he asked carefully.

'Like her? I loved her! She was my sister, I loved her. But she was greedy and selfish and so – she was a bad person. But I loved her. Of course I did. How else could it be?' She looked at him as though he were the one who was mad, who needed to be sent to a madhouse, and he smiled at her, eager to be placatory.

'Of course! I'm sorry. I meant no – I didn't mean to offend you. And then what happened?'

'He said he would sign the Trust, said he would leave the money the way she wanted it as long as she stopped all this nonsense about madhouses. So she agreed, and he went to the lawyer –' A smile moved across her old face the way sunshine moves across a field on a blustery cloud-riven day. 'And they were his drinking friends, too. Who was there in Soho who wasn't my Poppa's drinking friend? Even poor old Jean, whose son he'd taken from him, even he drank with my father. And the lawyers fixed it. I don't know how they fixed it so the money was left to us all, Istvan as well. Anya was so angry –' She sighed as she watched her Anya being angry in her memory. 'But she got over it. At least he hadn't left it *all* to Istvan which was what he wanted, Poppa. She hadn't got her own way entirely, but then neither had Poppa. So that made it not so bad for her. Poor Anya! She died as angry as she'd lived. Always furious, that was my Anya. Me, I'd do anything for peace and quiet and no arguments. So I never told anyone about it all. All that I knew I never told Magda. I felt a bit bad about that. Poor Magda, working so hard and getting so little, really. But she was happy and she had a good husband who loved her and was good to her children, which was more than you could say about Laszlo Balog.'

Her voice went hard and loud suddenly and Joel blinked at the malice in it. 'He was wicked to my Poly, so wicked! I hated him. I really hated him, do you know that? But I won. My Poly and I, we're still here, and where's Laszlo Balog? In hell, where he belongs –'

Joel coughed, as embarrassed as if she'd suddenly stripped off all her clothes. 'So, the Trust was made for the four of you, in your own names –'

She laughed then, the flash of malice vanishing as suddenly as it had appeared. 'Oh, no, Poppa and those lawyers – too clever for that. In case Anya discovered what he had done, you see, he made them say in the documents that the property was left to the 'children of the Family'. Anya didn't discover till after she had signed, and it was too late, what it meant. It was the way it was written, you see. If it had been names it would have been different. But "children of the Family" – that made it that Istvan was treated the same as the rest of us, Poppa said. He should have got his share from Kati, shouldn't he? He was her son, not Anya's and Poppa's. But there it was. Poppa won in the end. Poppa always did, really – even when he was dead. Anya died first so she was happy enough. But Poppa – he got Istvan what he wanted for him. Not *all* that he wanted. But more than he had a right to.'

She sighed deeply then and smiled at Joel. 'Enough. I've talked enough. It's good to talk, but it's enough.'

He stood up at once. 'Of course, Mrs. Balog. You've been very good to me, I do appreciate it. To talk to me for so long – it was good of you.'

'So long ago,' she said sleepily. 'So many people, so many angry people –' And she closed her eyes and he stood there and watched her as she fell asleep with the sudden abandon that only the very old and the very young can show.

'I'm not sure,' Laura said carefully, 'what all this means.'

'Nor am I just yet,' Joel said. 'But I reckon we can work it out. Your Uncle Istvan wasn't your uncle. He was your cousin. He had no right to inherit a quarter of this place.' He lifted his head and looked round. It was late in the afternoon and the tables were set and ready for the evening's influx and there was a rich smell of lecso and roasting goose in the air. Angie in a spirit of fury at the way his kitchen was about to be pulled about his ears was producing all the most exotic and difficult dishes he could think of while he had the choice. 'The only people who really had a right, as I understand it, were the three sisters.'

'But Uncle Istvan –' She blinked. 'I have to call him that. He was always called that.'

'It's not important what you call him. What matters is what he is. Which is a grandson of the old pair and therefore not a direct inheritor.'

A slow smile appeared on Laura's face and began to spread until she was beaming. 'Oh, Joel,' she breathed and then began to laugh. 'Oh, Joel, Aunt Dolly and Aunt Evelyn!'

He looked at her and then he too began to grin. 'Oh, dear me, yes. Dolly and Evelyn. They *are* going to be put out, aren't they?'

'More than a little – look.' She ran to her desk and grabbed a piece of paper. 'Here's how it is, as I see it.' She began to scribble. 'Here are the family, all right? Kati and her children – only this time, put Istvan as her son. Right. His descendants and Ilona's, they should share a third. And Zsuzske's sons, they should share another third – and then my grandmother Magda's descendants, which is really just me, because Alex and Timothy – I have their shares. You know about that – so –' She shook her head. 'It's all so muddled! How do we sort out who legally owns what –'

'And how much Dolly and Evelyn owe the rest of you,' Joel said.

'They owe me? How can they – oh! I see,' Laura said and stared blankly. 'You mean all the money they've had for their share –'

'They've been getting a quarter, right?'

'Yes. It's a lot of money.'

'But they shouldn't have had that. They should have had – Let's see, half the share that came down through Kati. A sixth for Ilona and a sixth for Istvan. Because they inherited through him. Half of a third is one sixth. And half of a sixth is a twelfth. Much smaller amounts, aren't they? I can't work out right now just how much money they've had that they shouldn't because it really belonged to you and to Paul Balog, but I'm sure the lawyers can work it out.'

'Have I the right to ask them?'

'With Paul to back you, yes –'

'But Paul has sold his share to Philip Cord and –'

Joel frowned. 'I have to be honest, Laura. I can't help you. I'm no great shakes when it comes to the law. I wasn't at home in Canada, and this is British law. It's probably different. I think you ought to see your own solicitor as soon as possible. Get him to look into this. It could be that Paul sold without enough information and that being so, the sale isn't legal. I just don't know. But someone will. So you'll have to find out and act accordingly.'

She was silent for a moment. 'Will I have to sue my own family?' She frowned. 'I'd hate to have to take all this to court.'

'You may have to, to keep your hands on your own

restaurant. Because he's using the terms of the Trust to get you out, isn't he? Cord? But if those terms have been breached because of a – what's the expression? Miscarriage of justice – after your great whatever it was grandfather died – old Viktor – well, then, it's back to square one. Cord loses his power to destroy you. If you have to go to court to make that possible, then isn't it worth it?'

She seemed to have shrunk a little as she stood there and stared at him, her face creased with anxiety. 'But Joel, imagine having it all talked about. Poor old Aunt Kati and her behaviour – she was only fifteen when Istvan was born, wasn't she? I've worked it out – I know how old Uncle Istvan was when he died seven years ago, and how old she was, so – it would be awful to have people talking about it all and sniggering over them. And old Maritza and Viktor – they're dead. They ought to be left in peace. Not talked about by lawyers in public courts.'

'Yes, Laura, they're dead,' Joel said gently and moved closer and set his hands on her arms. 'And nothing anyone says can possibly hurt them. But if none of this is said anywhere then you'll be hurt. And so will Paul and so will Ilona, won't she? She may be married to Cord and we may both hate him but she's entitled to her just rights. And she hasn't been getting them. Don't be mealy mouthed about this, Laura. Go to court if you must. Isn't it worth it to keep this place going?'

She looked round at her red tiled floor and her creeper clad window and the pretty tables and took a long breath. 'I suppose so. If it will save it – but it isn't just Philip, is it? It's the developers who are the real worry. And they aren't going to be stopped just because we go to court over an ancient family scandal. They've already got hold of Mucky's place, haven't they? They won't stop trying to get mine –'

She stopped sharply then and said blankly, 'Oh!'

'What is it?'

'Mucky, he – oh, this is really so confusing. He's a sort of relation of mine, then, isn't he? He's Yves. The second son of Jean Bosquet. The first was my Uncle – Cousin

Istvan. It sort of makes Mucky into a relation. And he's left me all his money –'

'Do you feel better about that, then? Obviously he knew the truth about Istvan. That must have been what he meant when he kept telling you it was the right thing to do.'

'Yes,' she said. 'He must have known, and always felt wrong about it – do you suppose he felt we were entitled to a share of his shop? Or that he was entitled to a share of our restaurant?'

Joel laughed and shook his head. 'I don't know, Laura. I really wouldn't even like to begin guessing. All I know is he feels he's done the right thing now. And that means your kitchen can be done up to please the damned Environment Officer or whoever the bloody man is, and you can pay off some of your debts. And if you're willing to go to court and claim back the share of your inheritance that is due to you from Dolly and Evelyn then maybe you'll be able to fight off the developers as well. There has to be a way –'

She seemed to be aware suddenly of the fact that he was still standing with his hands on her shoulders and pulled away from him, a little flustered, and went to perch on her tall stool behind her small desk. She was using it as protection, a sort of bulwark against him and he could feel that, and the hurt bit into him. But then he remembered and pushed the pain away. Don't rush her, he told himself furiously. Don't rush her, you damned fool.

There was a little silence as she sat with her forehead creased, thinking, and suddenly she said. 'I wonder if I'd make much of a job of being a liar? A thorough going out and out liar.'

'What?' He was startled.

'Well, maybe I wouldn't have to go to court – if I told Dolly and Evelyn I was going to and would expose the whole family, and the only way to stop me was to sell me their share of the restaurant, without specifying just what size share it was, if you see what I mean, at a price we both agreed on –'

He grinned. 'You can be quite devious, can't you?'

'Well, why not? Haven't other people been devious with me?'

'Counting up how many wrongs to a right?'

'No, of course not. Well, yes. Maybe. A bit. Oh, I don't know. I just don't want anything to happen to this place. Whatever Maritza and Viktor did, whatever happened all those years ago, what we've got now is this. It goes all the way back to them, and it's a good and beautiful thing. To let it die now just because a man like Philip Cord wants to make money out of it and because some anonymous developer wants to do something different here – it's just not on, and I won't have it. I'll fight for this place and use any method I have to do it, even if it means being as bent as one of Maxie's corkscrews. So there!'

'Attagirl,' he said softly. 'Go to it, Laura. Right on, Laura!' And she grinned, embarrassed.

'Well, that's how I feel and that's an end to it. I'll go and see Dolly. And it'll be different this time, you see if it isn't. The things I'll say to her – oh, it'll be different all right. First thing tomorrow, I'll go to see her. And then Evelyn – oh, just you watch me, Joel Coplin. No one's going to take my place away from me. Not now. Not ever!'

36

'Oh!' Joe Davriosh said and stopped short. 'What the hell are *you* doing here?'

'The same as you, I imagine,' Cord said, and reached in his pocket for a cigarette. 'Waiting to see Reggie Statler.'

'Why?'

'Because I want to see him,' Cord said, with insultingly careful enunciation.

'Hmm. More like because he sent for you,' Davriosh said and slumped down in the leather seat beside him; at once Cord moved away fastidiously. 'He sent for me, so he's sent for you. Though why – tell me why.'

Cord said nothing, just looking at him with his brows raised. 'God damn you, Cord,' Davriosh exploded. 'I'm not so green as I'm cabbage-looking, as my old granny used to say. And I want to know what the hell's been going on that he's sent for you. It's me what's been paying you, remember.'

'With his money, I rather think,' Cord said, and leaned forwards and picked up a newspaper. He opened it with a flourish and disappeared behind it and Davriosh leaned forwards and grabbed it and pulled it down with such violence that it tore and the girl sitting at the reception desk lost her look of boredom for the first time and actually looked across the great expanse of terrazzo floor and potted palms to stare at them.

'I'll have none of your shit, Cord,' Davriosh said loudly. 'If you've been playing silly buggers with me and trying to run with him as well as me, then you are going to find yourself in it right up to your ugly great neck. Do you understand me? I made a deal with this man, and you made a deal with me, and that's the way it has to be. I'll have none of this climbing over my shoulders to get to the big ones –'

'Shut up, Davriosh,' Cord said softly. 'Or you'll find your friend Statler will get to know a great deal more about you than you'd like. Such as what happened over the sale of the freehold of Bosquet's shop and how much that cost him compared with what L and CD got for it. Like the way you got money out for Preston too, and loaded his pay sheets. So shut up. Just shut very up. Understood?'

Davriosh stared at him and his eyes were wet with anger and frustration; his face had reddened, and he had started to sweat, and the receptionist looked at him with distaste as she said loudly, 'Mr. Statler will see you now, Mr. Davriosh, Mr. Cord,' and set down the phone.

'I've not finished with you,' he muttered at Cord as they both got to their feet. 'Not by half a bloody inch. I ain't finished with you. If you say a word in there out of place, then I'm warning you –'

'Piss off,' Cord said and turned and walked ahead of him to the door the receptionist was now holding open.

'Good morning, gentlemen,' Statler said, without looking up from the papers he had spread on the big glass topped desk behind which he looked a rather insignificant figure. 'I won't keep you too long –'

Davriosh stopped short as a secretary held chairs out for him and for Cord, staring at the man who stood behind Statler, looking over his shoulder. He was wearing a very obviously new suit and the most glittering of white collared blue striped shirts. He was sleek and benign and he smiled back at the stare and said easily, 'Good morning, Joe.'

'Malplackett?' Davriosh said and sat down hard. 'Christ! Where's the rest of the bloody army? I thought this was to be a private meeting.'

'I haven't time to waste talking to people one at a time, Davriosh,' Statler said and now he did look up and stared very directly at Davriosh. Suddenly he didn't look insignificant any more. 'Even when what I have to say is short and to the point.'

'Oh?' Davriosh leaned back, remembering too late to look

relaxed and comfortable and crossed his ankles and then uncrossed them and reached in his pocket for a cigarette.

'Not in here, if you please, Davriosh. I can't stand the smell of cheap cigarettes,' Statler murmured and reached out his hand and at once Malplackett picked up a silver box on the desk and held it open for him. Deliberately Statler lit the slim cigar he took from it and then leaned back in his own chair and looked at the two men sitting in front of him. Joe Davriosh stared back, his brows lifted in what was meant to be a supercilious regard. It looked more like an attack of nausea. Cord said nothing, sitting impassive and as genuinely relaxed as Davriosh had tried hard to be.

'Mr. Davriosh, how much of my money have you had for this little operation I asked you to carry out for me? Which you, as I recall, offered to carry out for me, assuring me that you had all the necessary expertise? How much?'

The sweat was now running in trickles down Joe Davriosh's plump body; his shirt was showing damp patches on each side of his tie.

'Now, Reggie, do me a favour –'

'I beg your pardon?' Statler said softly.

'Eh? Oh – Mr. Statler, then. Listen, don't be ridiculous. How can I reel numbers off the top of my head? We been operating together a few months now, already, a few months! Do you expect me to remember every penny of expenses, for Chrissakes?'

'Yes,' Statler said.

'Then I'll have to go and get my books,' Davriosh muttered wretchedly. He was sitting lower in his chair now, so that the shoulders of his jacket pushed up against his ears. He looked like a frightened penguin.

'No need,' Statler said. 'I can tell you.'

He hadn't even turned his head, let alone made any gesture, but Malplackett was there, reaching for a sheet of paper on the desk and coming round to put it on Davriosh's knee. He looked up at him and licked his lips and then, hands fumbling a little, reached in his breast pocket for his glasses.

He took his time putting them on the end of his nose and

then looking at the sheet of paper and the other three men waited impassively for him. They saw his face go whiter and he looked up and protested loudly. 'Are you crazy? I've had nothing like so much!'

'Oh, yes you have. You and your agents, Mr. Davriosh,' Statler said, his voice still soft. 'I have receipts, signatures, all the paper work. Do you want to examine it?'

'Yes!' Davriosh began to bluster. 'You must be crazy! I needed money to buy that freehold of course, Bosquet's freehold, and that was big numbers, very big numbers, but you said to me there was no problem, to get it no matter what. So I did. The rest I know nothing about –'

'Know or not, Mr. Davriosh, it was all disbursed in your name.' Statler shifted his gaze and looked at Cord who was still sitting looking as bored as he had ever since he sat down. 'Right, Mr. Cord?'

'Oh, indeed right,' he said readily, and smiled with great charm.

'What do you mean, right?' Davriosh turned and glared at him. 'What the hell are you talking about?'

'The money you sent me to Mr. Statler to get. As your agent. To pay the various expenses you incurred on his behalf. You arranged for me to sign, remember?'

'No!' Davriosh shouted. 'I made no arrangements –'

'No?' Cord lifted his brows. 'Oh, I understood you had. Certainly when I told Mr. Statler I was acting as your agent he seemed content to give me what you had asked for.'

'I never asked for nothing!' Davriosh howled. 'For Chrissakes, man, you know that! I made a private deal with you to work for me, sure, but I never said you should come here and give Mr. Statler a load of lies – and –'

'You told me you had people working with you,' Statler said. 'Remember? You told me they were not able to be as forthcoming as you'd like – I think those were the words – but that they would definitely deliver what we wanted. So, when this man arrives here and tells me, with chapter and verse, what he is to do under your instruction – why!' He smiled suddenly, a rictus that showed his teeth alarmingly.

'Why, I believed him. He knew all the facts, you see. Why shouldn't I believe him?'

'Because he's a bastard,' Davriosh said passionately. 'A lying, cheating bastard –'

'Much as you are yourself, Mr. Davriosh,' Statler said and again produced that rictus. 'Which means of course that any arrangement I made to employ you is null, void and dead. Except for what you owe me.'

'Owe you?' Davriosh said and had to cough, for his voice had become very hoarse. 'How can I owe you?'

'Very easily. That money there –' He pointed to the sheet of paper Davriosh was still holding in his hand. 'That's an account of what you owe me.'

'But Cord's had most of this!' Davriosh said, still hoarsely and now he turned and stared at Cord. 'You can't deny that –'

'On your behalf,' Cord said calmly. 'All of that money was spent according to your instructions.'

'You liar,' Davriosh shouted again and Statler sighed.

'I don't want recriminations, gentlemen,' he said. 'Just my money. Have your sordid arguments elsewhere. Just give me my money. I want your account of how it was spent and the return of it.'

'The freehold in Little Vinegar Yard,' Davriosh said. Now he was sweating again; his face gleamed in the rich lighting of the big office, reflecting redly the carpets and deep upholstery of the furniture. 'And people had to be softened up, paid for making efforts –' He pointed suddenly at Malplackett who had returned to stand behind Statler. '*He* had money for that –'

'I know about that,' Statler said. 'And that was earned. I have no concern about that. If you look carefully at that sheet of paper, Mr. Davriosh, you'll see that I've been more than fair. I've deducted what I regard as reasonable expenses. The money you paid to Edward here was reasonable. The money we paid to Mr. Cord was not. That you'll have to return. Mr. Cord, do you hear me?'

'I hear you,' Cord said and smiled. 'How are you going to make me?'

'There are ways, I imagine,' Malplackett said, speaking loudly for the first time. 'I'm sure we can work them out between us –'

'I wouldn't bother.' Cord got to his feet. 'I really wouldn't bother, Mr. Malplackett. There are too many problems I could make for all of you.' He turned to go, and then stopped at the door. 'You, for example, Mr. Statler. I was a colleague of David Whitehouse, you know, once. You didn't? Ah well, these things take time to come to the surface, don't they? Yes, a colleague of Mr Whitehouse. So upright a gentleman! So *concerned* for the welfare of other people, hmm? I don't think you'll worry unduly about the trifling sums I've used on your behalf, Mr. Statler, will you? You're so like him – as I recall – *so* concerned for others' welfare – it positively brings tears to the eyes. I heard about the Elderly Dependents' Fund you both ran. Hmm? So lucrative. So, as regards this money – well, you can come down on Davriosh there for it, if you like. He hasn't got it, and squeezing him will be like squeezing a lemon. So, all you'll get is sour juice no one can swallow and a dead lemon. But still, you can do it if you want to. But leave me out of it. I've done well enough so I shan't make any trouble. I could, of course. Not only Whitehouse, but the man Hersh, you see. Public servant, bribes and blackmail? Nasty, nasty stuff if it gets into the press. You wouldn't like that. But there, it was done on your behalf, wasn't it? So you see, there really isn't any more for me to talk about. I'll be on my way and leave you to Mr. Davriosh, for all the good that'll do you. Good morning, gentlemen.' And the door swished open and closed softly behind him.

There was a long silence and then Statler said, 'Hersh?'

Malplackett leaned forward and spoke softly into his ear as Joe Davriosh sat and stared blankly at the piece of paper in front of him. The figures danced on the page, making as much sense to him as rows of telephone numbers. How much had Cord got out of this man in his name? And how had he managed to persuade him to part with it? He frowned then as slowly some of his fear began to leak away and his paralysed wits began to operate, creakily, but at least a little.

Malplackett had stopped his whispering and Statler was sitting gazing with unfocussed eyes across the room, clearly thinking.

'How did you let that bastard con you this way?' Davriosh demanded. 'It's all very well to go on at me about it, but me – I was a babe unborn in this! Sure, I hired the man to work for me, but I didn't send him round here! Would I do anything so bloody daft? If I wanted to get money out of you that way, I'd have bloody done it on my own behalf, I wouldn't let a shit like Cord do it –'

'Mr. Cord will be dealt with separately.' Statler spoke with a sharp decision. 'I need time to think about him. All right, Davriosh. I believe you. It was his doing. Now I know a little more about him –'

'What do you know?'

Statler shifted his eyes and stared at him. 'That's none of your affair, since it has nothing to do with my present activities. Just leave it at that. I know more now and I'll deal with Mr. Cord in my own way and in my own time. Now, as for you, Mr. Davriosh –'

He sat back in his chair and steepled his fingers and looked over the top of them at Davriosh who tried to grin at him.

'I always thought you were a reasonable man, Reggie,' he said and even essayed a laugh. 'Now I know it. You know who can be trusted, and who can't. You can spot a villain and –'

'Yes, yes,' Statler said. 'Leave out the chat. We don't need it. Now, we deal with you, Mr. Davriosh. You told me that you had made all the necessary searches on the Little Vinegar Yard properties?'

Davriosh stared blankly. 'Eh?'

'One of the jobs you used this man Cord on was to make the searches on the properties. To see how they might be encumbered.'

'Well?'

'You told me they were freeholds. That they could be purchased by me or my agents.'

'And so they can be. I bought one for you, dammit –'

'As to who that belongs to, we'll come back to that point. I am more interested in the Hallash property.'

'I know. We got it in hand to get it for you. The man Hersh – I have to tell you I knew about that. It wasn't my idea and I didn't like it, but it seemed – well, I knew about it.' He shot a malevolent glance at Malplackett. 'He knew the most of course –'

'Yes,' Statler said. 'I know that now. That will have to be sorted out.' He turned his head. 'Perhaps you'd better see to that this morning, Edward. As soon as Mr. Davriosh here leaves us. Ten minutes, no more. See to it that the man is called off. I want none of that sort of business round me. It's not my style any more. Whatever it was once, it isn't now. Call him off, this morning.'

'Yes, Mr. Statler,' Malplackett said and, outrageously, winked at Davriosh over Statler's shoulder. 'At least there was no money involved there.'

'That's what was wrong with the whole damned affair,' Statler said with sudden violence and the other two men were at once silent, very aware of the power inside that apparently insigificant little body. 'Money's the only clean thing there is.'

They were silent for a long moment and then Malplackett moved forwards. 'See to it, then,' Statler repeated curtly and then looked again at Davriosh. 'Now, you – you told me the other property is unencumbered.'

'It is,' Davriosh said. 'I mean, its ownership is complicated, but Cord there –' He blinked. 'You may have to get him back,' he said uneasily. 'He's the key to getting that place, you see. He has his hands on a share of the property and he's the one putting the pressure on the other, especially the woman – Laura – especially on her. That's why Hersh –'

'You don't have to spell it out,' Statler said. 'I'm ahead of you. I've been ahead of you this past week. Ever since I discovered what you failed to discover about that property.'

'What?'

'It has a Grade Two listing on it,' Malplackett said and smiled sweetly at him. 'The Vinegar Trust, you know – the newsletter. I discovered it for a little article I was doing for the newsletter. There's panelling in the upper rooms and on the staircase that she had done over a while ago and the result was that they slapped a preservation order on the place. I found that out and I thought -- well, someone ought to tell Mr. Statler about it –'

'And you came straight here and told him yourself,' Davriosh said bitterly. 'Even though it was me who brought you into this, and me who was paying you.'

'Well, yes,' Malplackett said and smiled widely. 'Why talk to the monkey when you can speak to the organ grinder, hmm? I thought it might be quicker –' And he smiled down at Statler's head. 'And he thought me interesting enough to employ direct.'

'Great to be you,' Davriosh said savagely. 'So now what can we do? How do we get that bloody listing taken off so we can go ahead?'

'We don't,' Statler said and pulled a sheet of paper towards him and bent his head to look at it. 'I've got a better site. Edward has found me a better place for my building. The other end of Greek Street, near the Square. Very nice, indeed. Just a tailor to clear out. The adjoining buildings are already mine, and the Levy place is big enough to make it a prime site when I get him out. When *Malplackett* gets him out.' He glanced at the man who smiled confidently back at him. 'So this deal is off. I want my money back, Mr. Davriosh. The deal's *off.*'

Davriosh's eyes had dilated. 'You want it – how can I give it back? You said I didn't have to –'

'You don't have to deal with Cord's debts to me. I'll deal with him on my own. But your own debt, Mr. Davriosh, that I want settled.'

'What debt have I got? What sort of –' He began to bluster and Statler sighed gently.

'The other property in Little Vinegar Yard, Mr. Davriosh. *I* don't want it, do I? It's no use to me. Sell it and return me the money. You call yourself an estate agent, don't you?

So, sell the place, return my money and our dealings are at an end. That's all, thank you, Mr. Davriosh. Good morning! Malplackett, get on to that Hersh man, will you? I want that affair stopped at once. Now go away, both of you. I have work to do.'

37

'I've never done business with you, Mr. Davriosh, and I don't intend to start now,' Laura said tartly. 'I don't like being rude, but you give me no option. I've told you I have no interest in listening to anything you have to say, so I'd be grateful if you would leave me now as I have a great deal to do.' And she turned on her heel and marched into her restaurant, and closed the door with a little snap.

But that didn't stop him. He opened the door and came in right behind her and she stood very still in the middle of the floor and called loudly and urgently, 'Angie!'

There was a clatter from the kitchen and the old man came running in and glared round, alarmed.

'Whatsa matter? What happened? Did you – ' He saw Davriosh then and stopped. 'What is it, Mizz Horvy?'

'This man is making a nuisance of himself,' Laura said, still loudly, and moved away, going behind Angie. However brave her words, she was shaking inside. The man had been so urgent, when he'd come puffing into the Yard where she had been picking over the plants in the new trough that she had decided looked pleasant against the outside of the window, that he had alarmed her a great deal. She had backed away from him, but the more she had backed away the more urgent and even incoherent he had become. She had tried to understand what he wanted but his words had come tumbling out so fast and had been so hard to follow that the only thing to do was get rid of him. That he wanted to sell her something was clear; that she didn't want to buy whatever it was was equally clear.

The phone rang as Angie moved forwards threateningly and she muttered under her breath and for a moment considered ignoring it; but the lunchtime bookings had not yet all come in and business, after all, was always business.

'Hmm?' she said into the phone as Angie began talking to Davriosh in a low but very dogmatic voice and she put her other hand over her ear so that she could hear more clearly. And her face lifted into a smile as she listened.

'Yes,' she said after a moment. 'I think I can find you a table. How many? Hmm? No, of course you can come on your own. What? Well, it all depends. I can't usually sit down at lunchtime and pretend I'm a customer. But if I get the chance – what? Oh, you can hear that? It's rather odd. A bit frightening, actually. It's Joe Davriosh making a nuisance of himself. What? No, I don't suppose you know him – '

She turned her body so that her back was to the men in the middle of the restaurant. Unpleasant as Davriosh was she couldn't bring herself to say bad things about him while he could actually hear her.

'He's a nasty, greasy, little estate agent. I've never liked him and I try never to take bookings from him though he's a pushy devil and sometimes I can't help myself. What? Oh, he wants to sell me something. I don't know – I wouldn't buy a box of matches from him. But he's being very – I don't know. Unpleasant. What? Well, not really frightened. Well, perhaps I was, a bit. But Angie's here and – No! Joel – don't be silly! You don't have to! I can cope perfectly well – Joel. Joel – ' And she jiggled the telephone, and then made a face and hung up.

'Mizz Horvy – ' Angie began but she shook her head at him and turned at once to Davriosh.

'Listen, Mr. Davriosh. I've told you I don't want you here. And there is someone coming round from over the street to get you out. If you don't listen to him as well as to Angie, then I'll call the police. You hear me? I don't *want* you here.'

'Listen Mizz Horvy, I think you might want to listen to him after all,' Angie said uneasily. 'I mean he's got something important to tell you – you should hear it – '

'Nothing he says can be of the least importance to me, Angie,' she said firmly. 'I don't listen to people who push and – and well, I don't want to know. Now, are you going,

Davriosh, or are you waiting till Mr. Coplin gets here and makes you go?'

'Coplin?' Angie said and scowled. 'That man lives here these days. Ain't he got no work to do?'

Laura looked at him briefly and felt her face redden. Angie was always protective and tended to get a bit jealous when she paid any attention to people outside the restaurant and its staff. He had clearly hated Philip Cord and had made no effort to hide the fact. It was his disappearance from the scene that had made Angie so much more equable about the rape that was about to be committed on his beloved kitchen. But it was ridiculous of him to be jealous of Joel Coplin. Just a friend, dammit, she told herself; and then repeated it. Just a friend. She wasn't sure, though, that she believed it.

The door clattered and Joel came in. He was in his shirt sleeves which were rolled up his arms and his tie was hanging loose round his neck.

'Who is it you want me to – oh, this is it, is it? Out!' he said firmly and moved across the room towards Davriosh. He had been standing panting a little as Angie had turned to talk to Laura, and now he shrank back, clearly alarmed, and she grinned even in the middle of this unpleasant scene. Joel did look formidable, for his bare arms were well muscled and the open collar of his shirt showed clearly that he was no weed.

'Just a minute,' Angie growled. 'Mizz Horvy, you got to listen to me. No, leave the bugger alone, will you!' He glared at Joel who had put a hand on Davriosh's shoulder. 'Listen first! He knows about Hersh, Mizz Horvy.'

Laura frowned. 'What?'

'That's not why he came, he said. He wants to talk to you about Mucky. But he said he could be of help to us over Hersh – the Environmental man – and the kitchen. Says it's all right, that Hersh has been playing some business or other – ' He shook his head. 'You'd better talk to him, Mizz Horvy. It don't make no sense to let him go till we know why he came, eh?'

After a moment she nodded. 'I suppose you're right,

though – oh, well.' And she turned to Davriosh with a look of distaste on her face. 'Well?'

He took a deep and shaky breath. 'I need a bit of strength,' he said complainingly and reached for a chair and pulled it out from the table and sat down heavily. 'You gave me a nasty fright there, you know, Laura – you didn't have to go and – '

'Miss Horvath to you,' Angie growled at the same moment that Joel opened his mouth to say the same thing, and he shrank back in his chair, holding up both hands defensively. 'All right, all right! Miss Horvath, then. Listen, a little brandy is what I need. A mouthful'll help, believe me. I feel very strange, very strange indeed.' And it was true that his face was sweating and his skin had a waxy yellowness about it.

'He doesn't need it – ' Angie said disgustedly and Joel looked at him with approval. 'I agree,' he said. 'He's just trying it on – ' But Laura looked at the man and shook her head.

'I can spare it,' she said shortly and fetched a glass and gave it to Davriosh and they watched him drink it down in one gulp and then take a deep breath.

'Well, now, that's better,' he said with an attempt to be perky and Joel said sharply, 'Out with it, now. What's this about Hersh?'

'He came and told you you had to pull the kitchen apart?' Davriosh said. 'Eh? Because of cracks you can't see what might let in bugs and mice you don't know are there?'

'So?' Angie said pugnaciously. 'What's that got to do with you?'

'It was a put-up job,' Davriosh said and wiped the back of his hand across his mouth. 'That brandy helped a bit. I could do with a drop more and that's the truth.' But they ignored that.

'Well?' Angie said and reached out and shook the other's shoulder and again Davriosh shrank away from him. Angie might be an old man, but he was a formidable one.

'All right, all right!' he said and looked at Laura. 'The

thing is, Lau – Miss Horvath – this property has been attracting some attention.'

'I had noticed,' Laura said dryly.

'Chap called Statler, developer. A hard man. Very hard man.' He shook his head, sadly, as though grieving over the hardness of the world in general as well as Statler in particular. 'He'd screw anyone for tuppence and kill his own Mum for pleasure. Drummed out of the bloody Waffen S.S. for cruelty, that one – and got a history.' His eyes sharpened then. 'I'm going to get a bit more into that. His history. Cord can't be the only one who can play both ends against the middle – '

'What did you say?' Joel said sharply.

'Cord,' Davriosh said. 'Bloke who's been working with Statler and – well, there's been a few people involved. He came in when he found out we were after this place as well as over the Yard. Said he was family, sort of, and had a bit of clout.'

'You could say that,' Laura said dully and bent her head. She had thought she was over the worst of it, that it didn't hurt as much as it had to remember how he had used her, how little feeling there had been in him when there had been so much in her, had thought she could start over again and forget him. But it hurt as sharply now to hear his name as it had the first day she had discovered how he had abused her trust. And her love.

Joel said nothing and didn't look at her, but he moved closer to her and she seemed to find comfort in that, for after a moment she looked up and glanced at him briefly and then back at Davriosh.

'Well,' she said harshly. 'What about Cord?'

'He said he could get you out quicker if you had to spend money on work on the place. That you might be able to fight him off when he set out to buy your freehold, which he was after, for me so we could sell it to Statler – ' He stopped and then said carefully, 'I mean, what we was trying to buy for Statler. He said if the kitchen had to be pulled apart you'd have no money left for anything else.'

'He was right there,' Angie said bitterly. 'Do you know

what we've got to do out there? It'd break your heart even more. All those tiles to take out, all the fittings to be pulled apart – tomorrow they start, and I tell you, it makes me sick that – '

Davriosh shook his head. 'They don't have to start tomorrow. I don't reckon they'll ever have to start. Statler's calling him off. He don't want this place no more – '

There was a little silence as Angie tried to digest what the man had said and then Joel pulled out another chair and sat down with a bump and stared at Davriosh.

'I want this spelled out,' he said. 'Right from the beginning. Let me have it. And no messing about. I want every fact and I want it clear.'

It was, Laura decided, like the best sort of television programme, the sort that started when you were sitting with the set on, but not really watching and which drew you in until you realised you were sitting on the edge of your chair, enthralled. And it was Joel who made it that way. He questioned the man with all the skill of long experience, dragging him back to the point whenever he strayed off it, probing and pushing and nagging until it all came out, every bit of it, and she stood there, holding her arms folded against her in a sort of hug to stop them from shaking with the excitement of it all, and listened. And even when the talking stopped couldn't believe all she'd heard.

'Then we don't have to pull the kitchen down?' Angie said, and his voice was awed. 'You're sure of that? You aren't telling some bloody lie – '

'Why should I lie to you?' Davriosh said wearily. 'It wouldn't do no good. Not lying about your bloody *kitchen*, for God's sake. Forget it. There won't be no trouble.'

'Oh, my God,' Laura said and closed her eyes. 'After all that worry about the money and – oh, my God.'

Joel was on his feet then and went to put an arm across her shoulders.

'Sit down,' he said and it seemed to her that his voice had receded far away and then she realised she was sitting with her head down on her knees and his hand was hard on the back of her neck. 'Oh, my God,' she said again and tried to sit up.

'Not yet,' he said. 'Angie, brandy. A little – ' And then she was sipping it and the heat came back into her face.

'I didn't imagine it, did I?' she said and looked up at Joel. 'I didn't, did I?'

'You didn't,' he said grimly. 'Christ, when I think what you've been through because of this bastard – '

'Not me!' Davriosh protested. 'Not me. It was him, Statler. I was only acting as his agent – '

'That was what the Gestapo said about what they did. It was all Hitler's idea,' Angie said and moved closer to the man, his fists clenched. 'Christ, but I could make *aschenblatt* out of you. I could put you through my mincer, and grind you to garbage, only it'd pollute my mincer. You stinking, lousy, rotten – '

'It's all right, Angie,' Laura said and smiled shakily at him. 'The important thing is he's telling us now. He didn't have to, after all – '

'That is a point,' Joel said and perched on the edge of the table beside which Laura's chair was set, his arm still across her shoulders as though he'd forgotten it was there. 'Why are you telling us? Decided to be a born again Christian or something?'

'They wouldn't have me,' Davriosh said with a spark of his old perkiness. 'Listen, I got a problem, is why. Statler – ' He moved uneasily in his chair. 'Statler wants to get out of the deal, like I said. And I got to pay him back the money it cost him to get this far. Did I tell you why he wants out?'

Laura shook her head. 'I don't remember. It's as much as I can do to understand that I'm not going to be overrun by builders tomorrow. Oh, Angie – ' She looked round, but he had moved away and was already standing by her desk, talking softly into the phone and he looked up and made a gesture at her and she smiled. Trust Angie to know what had to be done about the builders.

'He can't develop here. There's a Grade Two listing on the buildings. Something to do with some panelling you got?'

She frowned and stared at him and then looked at Joel. 'Listing? The panelling? Good God, yes. I'd forgotten about that. When I had all that work done a while ago, afterwards they came to see it to re-rate – they never miss a chance to do that – and they told me then they'd put on a listing – but what it meant was that I had to get planning permission to do anything here in the future. And since I'd already spent so much I knew I wouldn't be likely to be interested in doing anything else till God knows when, so I never gave it another thought.'

'Laura, my dear girl, didn't you remember when that fuss about the kitchen came up? Didn't you realise then that maybe you wouldn't have to do it, that the listing meant you couldn't get builders in without permission?'

'But it was the man from the Council who said I had to do the work, Joel!' she said. 'I'm not stupid! Why should it occur to me that I had to check up on him? He's been inspecting my kitchens for years. I had no reason to doubt him!'

'I'm sorry,' he said. 'I should have realised. Forgive me.' And after a moment she nodded. But she looked ruffled all the same. It was maddening to have him, indeed to have anyone, pointing out to her facts about her own beloved restaurant that she had forgotten, and he looked at her and felt her annoyance. But he didn't take his arm from her shoulders and after a while the tension eased out of them and he smiled at her and she managed to smile back.

'All right,' she said. 'I suppose you're right. I should have thought of it – '

'The thing is, it makes the place over the Yard useless too. After all the trouble we went to get it, we're lumbered with it – ' Davriosh said and her head snapped round and she stared at him.

'That was your doing too? *You* got Mucky out?'

He looked uneasy. 'Well, you could say, in a manner of speaking – it was his nephew really. He was the one who did it. It's him you ought to get mad at – '

Joel's arm tightened across her shoulders. 'Not much point going over that,' he said quietly. 'In the end he seemed happy enough, Mucky. And he's there in Monaco – and well, let it be, Laura. Not much you can do. Too late now.'

'But the shop – ' she said. 'It's been there so long – '

'It can still be there.' Davriosh brightened. 'That's why I'm here, ain't it? I want to sell it to you. You take it, freehold and all – and you can do what you like with it.'

She stared at him. 'Me? Take over Mucky's shop?'

'Why not? Then you get the freehold for the whole patch and no one can try to cut it on you again, the way Statler did. It'd make you really safe, wouldn't it?' Davriosh said and his eyes were bright now. He looked much better, much more his old chipper self. 'It'd be the best thing you could do. I'd get my money back and could settle with that bugger Statler, you'd get the place and be safe – and you've got the money, now you don't have to spend it on the kitchen. Or some of it, I imagine – '

'Never you mind how much Mizz Horvy's got,' Angie had come back from the phone. 'None of your bloody never mind. It's all right, Mizz Horvy. He's not best pleased, seeing he fancied the job, but it's off.' He lifted his chin exultantly. 'Listen, tomorrow at the market – I'll get a suckling pig maybe as well as geese? Got it in me to cook my bleedin' head off, I have!'

'Anything you say, Angie,' Laura said absently. She hadn't taken her eyes off Davriosh. 'Anything you say.'

'Laura?' Joel said and then gently pulled her to her feet. 'Come out into the Yard. Let Angie stay here with this chap – I want to talk to you.' And after a moment she nodded and got to her feet.

'Yes,' she said. 'Yes, of course.' She was still half dazed by it all and it was easier to obey him than argue, and together they went out into Vinegar Yard to stand and look across at the boarded front of Mucky's shop, while Davriosh sat in his chair and Angie stood and glared at him like a dog watching over a bone.

'Now, Laura,' Joel said firmly. 'What I suggest is this. And hear me out before you tell me I'm mad.'

38

'But I'm a restaurateur, not a shop keeper,' she said.

'And I'm a television director, but what's that got to do with anything? It doesn't mean I can't try other things as well.'

They were sitting perched on the window ledge, their backs to the glass, and she had heard him out with ever increasing surprise and doubt and now once again shook her head firmly.

'What I want to do with my money is get the whole of the property here into my own control.' And she patted the wooden ledge beside her as though it were a living thing that could respond to her feelings for it with a matching emotion. 'It never mattered before, sharing it with Paul and Ilona and the aunts, but now – ' She shook her head. 'I don't think I've ever had so bad a time in all my life as these past few weeks.'

'I know,' he said gently. 'I know.' And they sat in companionable silence for a long time as she looked back over the fear that had so encompassed her. She had nearly lost her restaurant. Now that the danger was past and she was safe again the fear seemed even more powerful, absurd though that was, and she felt it tight in her chest and belly so that it made her breathless.

He seemed to sense what she was thinking and set one hand warmly over hers, there on the ledge of the window and she was grateful. And then frightened again, and she pulled her hand away. Allowing a man to be kind to her had started all the trouble; never again, she murmured deep inside her mind. Never again. I think –

'I could perhaps raise enough money to buy it myself,' he ventured after a while. 'I'm not rich, and these properties are clearly valuable. But Davriosh there is over the proverbial barrel and it's my guess he'll settle for the price he can get. But if I'm too tough on money obviously he'll try to sell elsewhere, and he's right, you know. You'd be safer if you owned the shop there as well as the restaurant. Then the whole of Little Vinegar Yard would be yours. And then you could do all sorts of things.'

He leaned back against the glass and looked around dreamily. It was close to noon now and the sun was filling the Yard with warmth; the broad paving stones shimmered with a heat haze, and there was even a small cabbage butterfly moving with jerky drunkenness around the plants in the trough beside them.

'Imagine it,' he said softly. 'You could have the bricks painted white, and troughs of plants over there, by Mucky's shop, as well as over there on each side of the archways, and put tables out here. Those white painted iron ones you know, like French cafés? It could be a really delightful setting for lunch. Even prettier in the evenings. Candles in those special glass holders that prevent them being blown out, you know? And maybe you could have music, too. A couple of chaps and a girl in costume playing Hungarian gypsy music – '

'Painted bricks would get shabby,' she said. 'Better to have them scrubbed so that they're a really rich red again. White tables and chairs still, of course, but definitely red bricks.'

He laughed softly. 'Then you do like the idea.'

She reddened. 'Oh, damn you. You're confusing me.'

'No, I'm not. You're confusing yourself. You've got an opportunity staring you in the face and you're scared of it. That's why you're in a state. Not because of me.'

'I can't afford it.'

'You've got expectations, remember? And if Mucky was told you wanted to take the shop over – well, maybe he'd decide to arrange his affairs so that you could buy it outright, now. I dare say there are ways it can be arranged with maximum tax efficiency. Talk to Mrs. Rose's grandson!'

'I've always run Hallash's the way it is. *Here*, and only

here. This place, the way my father had it and my grandfather and – '

'You wouldn't have to run the shop. I told you. I would.'

'But what do you know about shops? You're – '

'A television director. I know. But I grew up in a shop. My family were shopkeepers. I should have grown up in a shop here in Soho, but there it was – they went to Toronto and ran a shop there. But wherever it was done, shopkeeping's in my blood. I could run Mucky's and still be a freelance at my own trade.'

'Fiddlesticks,' she said and laughed. 'You make it sound as though people are born knowing what their parents learned. If it was as easy as that – ' She shook her head. 'What takes so much time is having to learn for yourself everything the people before you already knew.'

'Are you trying to tell me that running a restaurant isn't in your blood? That you didn't inherit an aptitude for it?'

'I never knew anything else,' she said defensively. 'That's what matters – not what you inherit but what you learn when you're growing up – '

'And that was when I learned shopkeeping,' he said triumphantly. 'So I could run that shop without making too much of a hash of it. Give me the chance? You buy the property and I'll rent it from you. Get a mortgage and I'll see to it I earn enough to pay you a rent that'll pay that mortgage. Can't say fairer than that.'

'But what about your films? Suddenly you don't care about making films any more?'

'Of course I do. It's because I care that this idea is so attractive. Listen, Laura, I came over here to work for City because I was sick of twiddling about with the sort of commercials I was doing. I was getting awards, sure, and building a reputation, sure, but it was just *commercials*. It's feature films I want to make, and decent documentaries – so what am I doing at City? I'll tell you. When I spoke to you on the phone this morning, I was in the middle of setting up my next project. No, not my Soho film. That, says bloody Brian Crowner and even bloodier Lethbridge, has to wait. I've got to get this urgent commercial done. For a baby's bubble bath, would you believe? A product called *Choochieface* – can you imagine? A baby's bubble bath called *Choochieface!* It'd really be a wrench, wouldn't it, to give up that sort of work? Such a blow to my artistic integrity, hmm?'

She laughed. 'Well, yes, I do see. *Choochieface?* Ye Gods!'

'Precisely,' he said grimly. 'Ye bloody Gods! And listening to Davriosh in there, it suddenly hit me. If I could leave City and work for you as your tenant in that shop – there's a flat over it isn't there? – I thought so. Great, then I can live there too and that'll save money. The rent I pay now is horrendous. So I'd live there, run the shop, get me an assistant who I could train properly, and once it's all running smoothly, hustle some money and make my film as a free-lance.' He gave a sudden little crow of laughter and stretched both arms up into the sunshine and grinned down at her. 'I'd feel so free! It'd be marvellous, bloody marvellous! And it all depends on you. You have to buy the shop to make it all happen.'

'It would seem so odd,' she said slowly. 'I've never done it – a tobacconist's shop – '

'We'd have to change that. Smoking is getting to be a decidedly unadmired habit. I'd make it into a sweetshop.' His smile widened. 'They're not good for you either, but I wouldn't feel so bad about selling sweets. It was what my family sold, you see, and I'm used to it. I'd make that the most beautiful candy store you ever saw.'

The excitement in him was infectious and she sat and watched him as he jumped up and went across the Yard to try to peep in between the cracks in the boards to the interior.

'You won't be able to see much,' she called and he came back, disappointed and nodding his agreement.

'Black as the pit in there. But I remember it, the time I did go in – mahogany and brass and old fittings, really beautiful old art nouveau stuff?'

'That's it – ' she said, watching him, liking the way his face was so alert and excited as he talked.

'Imagine those shelves piled high with dishes of glacé fruits and toffees and bonbons,' he said. 'And all that new health food stuff – it's about as healthy as bags of plain sugar but what the hell, people adore it. I do too! We'd sell all those and handmade chocolates as well. There must be people who still make 'em. They'd come out after their lunches with you, Laura, feeling expansive and generous and come right into my shop to buy something delicious in a pretty box with ribbons for their wives or secretaries. Damn it, for their wives *and* their secretaries! I tell you, it could be marvellous – '

'And special promotions for Christmas and Easter and Valentine's Day – ' She caught fire, too, as his excitement leapt across the gap between them to fill her.

' – And Mother's Day and Father's Day and Uncle Tom Cobleigh's Day. Oh, Laura, please do it! It really would be great fun – and profitable, too.'

'I still can't be sure,' she said and the excitement dwindled and lay low in her belly, like a banked down fire. Not quite gone, but far from the leaping thing it had been. 'Like I said, I've never done such a thing. We've always been just this – ' And again she patted the wooden ledge of the window as if it were a favourite pet.

'Listen Laura, I know how you feel about tradition.' He came and perched beside her. 'You want to keep things the way they always have been.

'That's it.' She lit up again and turned to look very directly at him. 'It sounds so corny, and daft, but I can't help it. What matters to me is knowing that my father and my grandfather and my great grandfather were here before me, running it just as I do – '

'Just as you do? Never!'

'What?' She looked startled.

'You've changed things! Of course you have. Didn't you turn the upstairs rooms from a flat where people lived into the Extras? You told me yourself you'd done that – and what about the panelling work you had done? In your father's time that was just grimy old wood, wasn't it? Now it's so beautiful and special there's a preservation order on it. The way you dress the restaurant – those blue table cloths and the glass and the china – didn't you buy all that? Of course you did! Tradition isn't – it's not the same as embalming, you know! It's letting things grow and live as well.'

'And buying a shop for you to run would be making my restaurant grow and live?'

'If you use the Yard between us for tables in the summer it would,' he said promptly. 'Absolutely! And I wouldn't object. Old Mucky – now, it's my guess he'd have objected strongly if you'd tried to do such a thing in his time.'

She made a little face. 'I rather think he might,' she said. 'He was quite a territorial little chap. He and Angie had the odd disagreement when Angie piled fruit boxes outside the side door there – '

'I'd never make a moment's fuss,' he said piously. 'Anyway, how could I if you were my landlord?'

'You think I can do it?' she said. 'Handle the money side, I mean?'

'If you want to.' He looked at her very closely and then frowned. 'Oh, hell, am I overselling this to you? I don't want to do that. It's just the best idea I've ever had. I feel it all the way through to my middle, and – '

'No one ever forces me to do anything against my will,' she said firmly. 'But I'd hate to be the rigid sort who isn't open to suggestions. And you could be right. I like the idea of summer tables out here – it's the finance that's my worry.'

'I have no right to tell you how to use your money, Laura,' he said, sober now, his excitement at his plans carefully under control. 'I don't even know how much there is, and I don't want to – ' He stopped then and looked at her and then said very deliberately, 'Yes, I do.'

'Hmm?'

'Want to know. I want to know everything about you. I – ' He swallowed. 'Do you know how much – do you know how important you are to me, Laura?'

'No!' She closed her eyes. 'I can't cope with questions like that, I really can't. I don't know and I don't want to know. I mean – ' She opened her eyes and looked appealingly at him. 'I do like you, Joel. You're a super friend. The best I could have had. But I'm – I've got a hell of a lot of bruises, one way and another. Let them fade, please. Let's just talk about money and shops. Nothing else.'

'Of course,' he said and sat there silent and after a long pause she said as brightly as she could, 'How much would you be willing to pay for a lease?'

'What?'

'The best way for me to do it is to buy the freehold, and then sell you a short lease. That way I can write into it the use of the Yard as an extension to the restaurant in the summer months – maybe put up awnings too. It gets incredibly hot out here sometimes – and I wouldn't have quite so heavy a financial burden as I would buying and renting to you – ' She shook her head. 'You can do better than a weekly or even a monthly rental. If you're going to run a shop, you need to put some real money into it. Can you afford it?'

'You watch me,' he said joyously. 'I've got dollars sitting doing damn all in Toronto which I can call in. My family left a few bob, as they say. And I've always been an abstemious sort of person. I can do it.'

'And you won't stop making films?'

'I'm not making them now,' he said. 'Am I? Only *Thrust* and *Choochieface* commercials, God help me. I've a better chance of setting up a feature of my own as a freelance than I have there, at City, that's for sure. Oh, my – ' And he smiled slowly, a broad beatific grin. 'I can just see it. Going back there, after lunch, and telling that bastard Crowner I'm walking out and he can stuff his *Choochieface*. It'll be sheer bloody bliss – total bliss.'

'That's not a good enough reason to change your life so radically,' she said and he laughed.

'Not a reason, no. But a hell of a lollipop of a reward! Come on, Laura!' And he jumped to his feet and held his hands out to her.

'What? Where are we going?'

'To tell Davriosh he's got a deal, after we've squeezed him till his pips squeak. And then to the solicitors to arrange for leases and all the rest of it – '

She was on her feet too now, and laughing, but she shook her head. 'No, my dear. No way.'

'What? You haven't changed your mind?'

She shook her head again, still laughing and jerked her chin in the direction of the Frith Street archway, over his shoulder.

'No, but I've a job to do. Here are my first lunchers. After lunch, Joel, by all means. But right now, I have work to do – '

She had turned to the door and was standing with her hand on the knob. 'By the way you've booked a table, haven't you?'

'Indeed I have,' he said happily and made to follow her, but she shook her head yet again. 'Not in shirtsleeves,' she said firmly. 'People who come here can be relaxed and comfortable of course, but I do expect jackets. Inside, that is.' She grinned then. 'It'll be different when we have our outdoors section, of course. So go and get your jacket now and I'll see you later.'

He laughed and turned to go. 'Don't be surprised if I'm gone a few minutes,' he said and looked even more pleased with himself if that were possible. 'Because if I have to go back there, now, I'm going to give myself an appetite. I'm going to talk to City and tell 'em I'm through. Save me some lecso, Laura. I'll have earned it by the time I get back!'

39

By half past one the system was running at full blast and doing it as smoothly as butter melting on a hot plate. In the kitchen Angie was roaring steadily at the top of his not inconsiderable voice as dish after dish emerged from his flashing hands to be snatched from the serving table by Dan and Janos, Miklos and Jon, and delivered to the tables in the restaurant. Leno and the rest of the kitchen staff circled and bustled, dodging and dancing to the tune of his shouting and Maxie shot in and out of his cubby hole with its wine racks beside the cold room, his corkscrew so busy it should have been red hot.

Upstairs all the Extras were full and happy, and Laura, standing at her corner desk, looked round and had a sudden and very vivid sense of déjà vu. It was as though this day had happened before, many many times, and on each of them she had been as deeply happy as she felt now. But it couldn't be the same, because there had been so many changes this past year or so. She looked across her full tables of laughing gossiping people to the window and out through the creepers at the Yard, and her mouth curved happily. There they all were, her summer tables, glittering with white paint, sparkling with glass and silver and surrounded by people, just as these tables in here were. Her new waiters Sid and Lenny hurried between them, their trays and dishes held high and she did a complex sum in her head, working out the extra takings those eight tables out there represented and her mouth curved even more contentedly.

Perhaps another four tables? Or even more? They could be set across the Yard nearer to The Sweet Shop? But that might confuse the customers, because Joel too had his uses for the paving stones of the Yard.

Outside his shop. now vivid with new paint and with

windows so crammed with piles of jellies and fruit drops, chocolates and lollipops that they looked like an illustration in a children's story book, there were three benches made of rough wood, and there sat people eating ice creams out of glass dishes with small wooden spoons. He had remembered his mother telling him of the way the old Italian ice cream sellers of Soho had provided their wares in just such glass dishes, and had done careful research into their techniques, and now, on hot days like this, could count on selling several gallons of the stuff he made in the sparkling kitchens he had created out of the small back room behind the shop which had once been Mucky's sitting room. And Laura grinned now as she remembered how excited he had been when he had managed to track down some of the old original recipes for okey pokey as well as sherberts.

'For a film director,' she had told him, 'you make a hell of an Antonio.' And he had laughed too and showed her the special gadgets he had ordered for making cassata ice cream so that it looked exactly the right shape. He had plans now for extending his operation and had an eye on a shop in Frith Street, at the Soho Square end.

'If I can get there,' he'd told Laura, full of excitement, 'I can more than double my ice cream production – and I've got the capacity. People'll be able to sit in the Square and eat it, you see. I could get boys to take a tray round perhaps. Shouldn't be too difficult to get a licence. Make a mint in a good summer –'

'And what happens to that Soho film?' she had said, mischievously, and he had made a face.

'It's still on the back burner. It won't go away. But right now, I'm having more fun than I ever did behind a camera. Why didn't anyone ever tell me how good it is to make something agreeable and watch people enjoy it and then take their money? Why didn't *you* tell me?'

'I suppose I thought everyone knew,' she had said and he had laughed and hugged her and returned to poring over the old cookery books he had tracked down. Joel Coplin was a very happy man. And not least because of the way she looked these days. Not that she understood why his face took on that particularly happy expression when she smiled at him. She had no idea of the way her smile made a triangle of her mouth and seemed to light up her whole body, and not just her face, had no awareness at all of the glow that seemed to emanate from her. She was just happy in a way she could never remember being, and certainly had not been last summer when Philip Cord had made her excited and breathless, but certainly not happy as she was now.

Happy, she thought, gazing out at the busy pretty Yard, and tentatively, as a sufferer from toothache explores an offending tooth with a pointed tongue, she explored her memories of Philip Cord.

At first, when it was all over, she had been just grateful. Her restaurant had been saved and that was all that mattered. But then she had been angry, hugely incandescently angry. She had been used shamefully, indeed abused, and had not just allowed it to happen; she had cooperated with him by falling into that stupid, ridiculous infatuation. It was almost like being raped, she had thought, being lulled into false acquiescence by promises of love. And that thought had sickened her most of all.

And then, she had been depressed, paralysed with misery as she had contemplated her own stupidity, and Joel had had to work hard and bite his tongue often as he coaxed her along from day to day. But that mood had been swept away by what happened next, and she had become joyful, wickedly maliciously joyful. For the family was suddenly set afire by the news that they all had, after all, been right. Ilona's marriage *had* collapsed.

It had been Dolly who had told her, phoning one morning just before Christmas, full of jolly chatter, and Laura, still aggrieved with her for her refusal to help when she had been in such dire need of it, had been rather sharp.

'I only want to talk to you, Dolly, if you want to talk business,' she had said firmly. 'Are you ready to sell to me yet?'

'Not quite yet,' Dolly had cooed. 'I'm still thinking of it, dear girl, really I am. Of course, if you could increase your offer –'

'No,' Laura had said flatly and Dolly had sighed gustily down the phone.

'Well, I dare say you can't at that. I dare say you'll be buying Ilona's share – such as it is. She'll need every penny she can get her hands on, poor creature, no doubt. Now she's given her husband the push. Can't say I think she's showing much sense, mind you. I know he wasn't precisely a faithful – well, dear, no need to upset *you* by going over all *that* dead ground! But as I say, to be Ilona and get haughty because a man behaves like a man – she should have the sense not to chuck away her dirty water till she's got a bucket of clean.'

Laura had caught her breath suddenly.

'Ilona's divorcing him?' She still couldn't use his name.

'My dear, yes! *And* keeping all her own money! Must have a good lawyer not to have to part with half of it, these days. Such a law! Women shouldn't have to pay husbands, for heaven's sake. What are husbands for, after all, but to provide? Still, there it is. She keeps it all, and he goes off with nothing, poor chap. Except his freedom of course. Being married to Ilona couldn't have been much fun, could it? After all, she cited no less than *three* other women in her divorce! Imagine that – three! A man doesn't wander from home like that without a very good reason, does he? But you'd know much more about that than I would, of course –'

Laura had snapped the phone down on her, not caring at all for the very real possibility that an offended Dolly could start all the fuss again, and try to force a sale of the restaurant on her. Actually she knew there was no real risk of that, not while the restaurant was doing so well and bringing her such handsome dividends for such small effort.

Ilona, divorcing Philip, she had thought, standing in the restaurant and looking out into the Yard where the men were at work in the grey afternoon, refurbishing Mucky's old shop; Philip without her money to lean on? Philip with no power ever again to hurt her through her beloved restaurant? And she had laughed aloud, and run out across the Yard to the shop to tell Joel, who was busy supervising the creation of his new domain, how good she felt about the news.

'Schadenfreude,' Joel had said, and shaken his head in mock reproof. 'Pleasure at another's downfall –'

'Don't you feel it?' she had demanded.

'Be damned sure I do!' he had said and then had made a small grimace. 'But don't enjoy it too much, Laura. If you do it will mean you're still involved with him. The only emotion you ought to feel now when you think of him is no emotion. Indifference. That's the only way to be sure you're rid of the infection. Not when you hate, but when you no longer care.'

And now, six months since that day, she knew he had been right. She could think of Philip Cord, even use his name, and not care at all. It was a wonderful way to feel, so free, so renewed, and she revelled in it.

But there was more than that to her new contentment. There was the way she was feeling about Joel. It wasn't something they talked about, or at least not yet, that comfortable feeling that had grown between them. She hadn't actually noticed it was there at first. She had just been content to go along with his plans for his new career as shopkeeper, adding her own ideas as they came up, spending more and more time with him, finding his company at first agreeable and then important and eventually indispensable to her peace of mind. He was part of her life now, the best part, as she knew she was of his. But it was still something they didn't talk about. Yet.

The phone beside her rang and she picked it up.

'Hmm?'

'Laura? Tim Wafare. Can you manage a table for four, do you think? I know I've left it late, but I've got an important client who's just come in from the States, as jetlagged as hell, but I have to make a fuss of him. I'm counting on you, Laura – I really need to bring him in to you or I swear I lose the contract and if that happens I lose the agency, so help me I do –'

She made soothing noises as her gaze travelled over the tables and then, as it reached the corner table her glance sharpened and she said into the phone, 'I think I can help, just this once, Tim. Give me half an hour or so. You don't mind waiting till two for your lunch? No? Then come then.'

She put the phone down and went across the room, stopping at some tables to talk for a moment and just smiling at others until eventually she reached the corner and then stood very straight backed and unsmiling beside the people sitting there.

'Good afternoon,' she said and her voice was very calm and cool. 'Mr. Davriosh, I see.'

He looked up at her, and grinned, very pleased with himself.

'You remember me, then! I'm honoured, Laura!'

'Miss Horvath,' she said coldly. 'May I ask who booked this table?' Her eyes moved across the three faces, and stopped for a brief moment at one of them.

'Not me, Miss Horvath,' Preston said. 'You never seem to have a table for *me*. I have to leave it to others to bring me here.'

The other man was only vaguely familiar to her and she lifted her brows at him. He was a very sleek looking person, wearing an obviously expensive white leather jacket over a silk shirt, and he smiled at her coolly and she knew she liked him as little as she liked his companions.

'My name is Malplackett, Miss Horvath,' he murmured. 'I booked the table.'

'I see. And have you ordered your lunch?'

'Indeed yes,' Malplackett said. 'A little of your excellent pink trout and cucumber salad. After we have finished our wild cherry soup, of course. Is that what you would have recommended?'

'Had I know you were here, I would have recommended you save yourselves the trouble of reading the menu,' she said and then smiled, a self satisfied little smile that was clearly not meant to please them in the least. 'Because I find I am unable to serve you.'

'Eh?' Davriosh said and Preston shook his head gloomily.

'You see Joe? I told you, if you're in my business no one

has a decent word for you. You should have stayed with your real estate instead of coming in with me –'

'I'm not sure I understand, Miss Horvath.'

'Oh, yes you do, Mr. Malplackett,' Laura said, now enjoying herself greatly. 'I don't know you, but I do know your companions. And since I regard neither of them as people I welcome in my restaurant I now ask you to leave. There will be no charge for the wine you have already had, nor for the first course I see you have started. I simply ask you to leave quietly and at once. I have other customers for whom this table is required. Had I not been occupied with my Extra rooms upstairs when you arrived I could have saved myself some expense and you and your guests the trouble of sitting down. Now, are you leaving quietly, or must I make a fuss? I can, you know.'

'Try and make me,' Malplackett said softly and the ugly note in his voice should have frightened her. But it didn't; it hardened her determination. This was the first time in all her history as a restaurateur that she had done anything like this. In the past when she had discovered that she had customers she disliked she had done all she could to get them served quickly and out, but she had never actually thrown anyone out. Now she was going to do it, even if it meant calling the police. She had never been so determined in all her life.

'I don't think I'll have any problems,' she said more loudly now and looked round. The people at the other tables had realised there was something going on, and were listening with lively interest, and as she caught the eye of the man sitting at the next table she added, 'Will I, Mr. Wilson?'

'Absolutely not, Laura!' the man said and stood up. 'I'm always glad to be of any service to you –' and the softness of his Scottish accent lent added menace to his words.

Preston was on his feet, shrugging on his coat and after a moment Davriosh stood up too. 'Thanks for lunch, Ed,' Preston said loudly. 'As much as I've had. I'll get a hamburger for the rest. Come on. Joe. Believe me – I know when I'm not wanted. It's no skin off my nose to be asked to go, but it'd hurt like hell if it got physical. Good afternoon, Miss Horvath –' And he went lumbering across the restaurant with Joe Davriosh behind him.

Someone at a table near the door produced an ironic cheer and then someone else began to clap their hands slowly and one after another took it up until the whole place was echoing and Angie appeared at the door from the kitchen, red faced and sweating under his white toque to stare in amazement.

'Out, out, out,' someone began to chant and with great promptitude everyone else joined in and then, moving with deceptive laziness the man Wilson stepped forwards and put his hands on the back of Malplackett's chair. 'Can I help you?' he murmured.

Malplackett looked at Laura and then over his shoulder at the man behind him and with a ghost of a grimace stood up. At once the restaurant burst into applause as he walked towards the door and Laura went after him.

She held the door open as Malplackett went with what dignity he could muster and stood there, pink with pleasure and grinning from ear to ear as her customers went on applauding, and then held the door invitingly open as four men appeared on the other side of it, coming from the Frith Street archway. They stood puzzled and clearly taken aback just inside the restaurant as the applause went on and the cheering and laughter increased at the sight of their faces.

'Good afternoon, Tim!' Laura said and closed the door. 'So glad you could get here. Your table will be ready in just a moment –' She looked back over her shoulder to where Janos was already stripping and relaying it. 'And there's some excellent pink salmon trout and cucumber today. I hope you and your guests enjoy it –' And calmly she led the way to the corner as at last the cheers stopped and the other lunchers returned to their meals in high good humour.

'Jesus,' said one of the men in the quartet as Janos held his chair out and settled him. His face was blank with amazement and his eyes looked dazed. 'What sort of a joint is this, for Chrissakes?'

'This?' Tim Wafare said and grinned at Laura who had brought the menu to them. 'My dear chap, this place is one of the sights of London, more important than St. Paul's or the Tower or the House of Lords. This is what it means when you tell people you're lunching at Laura's. Right, Laura?'

'Right,' she said, and handed them the menu.

FAMILY TREE

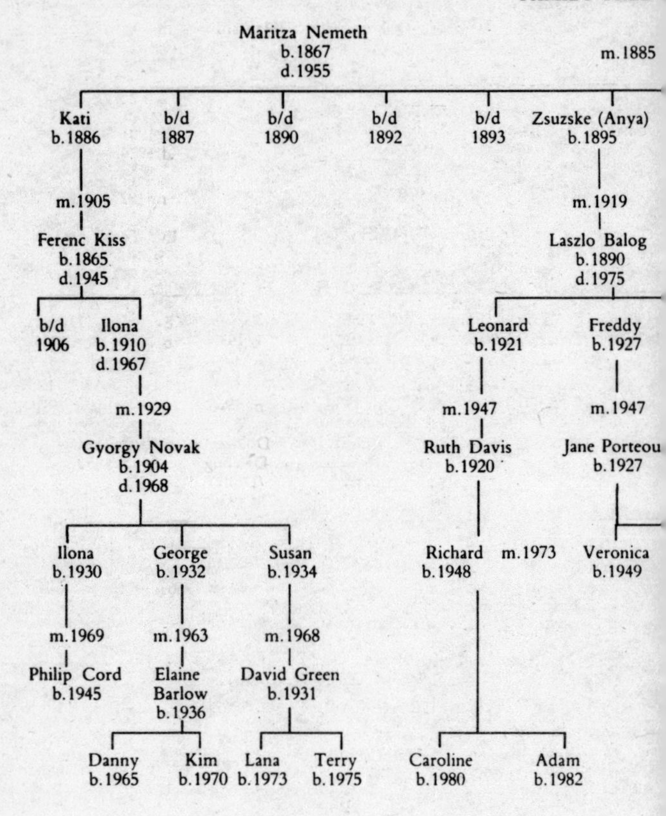
Maritza Nemeth
b.1867
d.1955
m.1885
Kati
b.1886
b/d
1887
b/d
1890
b/d
1892
b/d
1893
Zsuzske (Anya)
b.1895
m.1905
Ferenc Kiss
b.1865
d.1945
m.1919
Laszlo Balog
b.1890
d.1975
b/d
1906
Ilona
b.1910
d.1967
m.1929
Gyorgy Novak
b.1904
d.1968
Leonard
b.1921
m.1947
Ruth Davis
b.1920
Freddy
b.1927
m.1947
Jane Porteou
b.1927
Ilona
b.1930
m.1969
Philip Cord
b.1945
George
b.1932
m.1963
Elaine
Barlow
b.1936
Susan
b.1934
m.1968
David Green
b.1931
Richard
b.1948
m.1973
Veronica
b.1949
Danny
b.1965
Kim
b.1970
Lana
b.1973
Terry
b.1975
Caroline
b.1980
Adam
b.1982

LUNCHING AT LAURA'S'

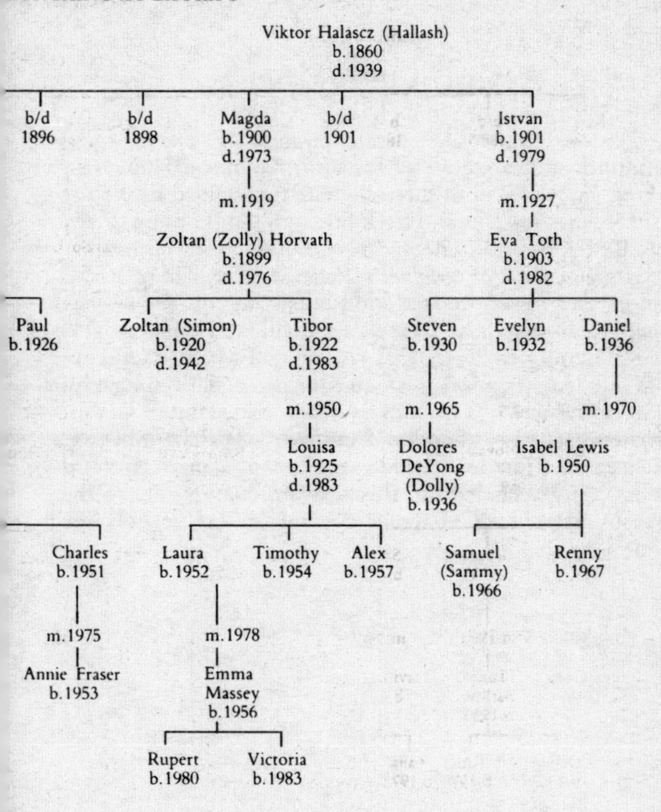

Acknowledgements

The author is most grateful for information on Hungarian cooking and the skill of the restaurateur provided by Victor Sassie of *The Gay Hussar*, Greek Street, Soho, London; Elena Salvoni of *L'Escargot*, Greek Street, London; Steven Molnár and Istvan Barna of *'Molnár's Restaurant,'* Finchley Road, London, and the entire staff (and musicians) of *The Mignon Restaurant*, Queensway, Bayswater, London. Thanks are also given gratefully to Maria Kiss (Anye) and Mariça Nemethy of Willesden, London for guidance on the Hungarian language and to Mr. Donald Cryan and Mrs. Pamela Cryan, Barristers at Law, London, and Mr. Michael Shelton, Solicitor, of Harrow, Middlesex, for guidance on legal matters. Any accuracies in this text are due entirely to the generous help of all of them. Any errors are entirely the author's.